D0276593

I2216566

HER THREE WISE MEN

The novels of Stanley Middleton

HER THREE
WISE MEN

Stanley Middleton

HUTCHINSON
London

Published by Hutchinson 2008

2 4 6 8 10 9 7 5 3 1

First published in Great Britain in 2008 by
Hutchinson
Random House, 20 Vauxhall Bridge Road,
London SW1V 2SA

www.rbooks.co.uk

Addresses for companies within The Random House Group Limited can be found
at: www.randomhouse.co.uk/offices.htm

The Random House Group Limited Reg. No. 954009

A CIP catalogue record for this book
is available from the British Library

ISBN 9780091925604

The Random House Group Limited supports The Forest Stewardship
Council (FSC), the leading international forest certification organisation.
All our titles that are printed on Greenpeace approved FSC certified paper
carry the FSC logo. Our paper procurement policy can be found at:
www.rbooks.co.uk/environment

Mixed Sources
Product group from well-managed
forests and other controlled sources
www.fsc.org Cert no. TT-COC-2139
© 1996 Forest Stewardship Council
FSC

To Tony and Martha,
with love and thanks

I

The brightness of sunshine glittered garishly into the eyes of the man and woman as they walked without haste along the road out of the village this early September evening.

'Not much traffic about,' the man said.

'No,' she answered. She was enjoying the walk and could do without his clichés.

'It's typical of him to drag us out at this time.' The man had taken no more than a dozen steps before he broached a new topic.

'Who'll be there?' he asked.

'You know as much as I do.'

'I thought perhaps he intended to do a few final auditions and had left himself with plenty of time. Or knowing him I'd guess those who turned up late wouldn't get the part they wanted. Six thirty hardly gives much leisure to those who've been at work all day.'

She smiled conspiratorially.

'I know I haven't been chosen for a part,' she confided. 'I'm assistant director.'

'Following his highness round and agreeing with his every wise word. At least he's judged you good-looking enough to add lustre to his glorious presence.'

She stopped. They were now standing under the shelter of a tall hawthorn hedge. 'Let's not go,' she said.

'Now we've got this far,' he said, 'we might just as well push on.'

They were on their way to the house of the producer of *Twelfth Night*, for an 'important meeting and try-outs and even first-time auditions' he'd told her on the telephone, 'and I want you there, Alicia, from the beginning so that you'll know what I'm aiming at. It's possible that I may not always be able to attend rehearsals and I don't want you to be left in ignorance of my intentions.'

Clarence Caldwell had thus explained his invitation in his actor's voice over her telephone.

'And make sure that man Raynor Wicks is there with you. He seems incapable of understanding even the simplest of messages. Rap it out daily on his dividing wall.' Wicks, her companion on this walk, was her next-door neighbour. She said nothing of this instruction.

'He's a wonder,' Wicks said.

'You've not been to work today?' Alicia asked.

'I have that. The school opens on Wednesday, but I have to go in early and prepare. See that next term's set books have arrived, and then I have to stamp them and put them away so that my department can lay their hands conveniently on them. And Tuesday, tomorrow, we have a staff meeting, when the head will comment on the GCSE and A Level results, and he'll explain to us what new schemes he and the Education Committee have dreamed up in the summer.'

'Is he sensible? Your headmaster?'

'I can't complain. He leaves me pretty well alone.'

'You're on speaking terms?'

'Oh, yes. We say "good morning" very affably.'

'He never asks your advice, then?'

'No, never. Nor anybody else's. Or if he does, it's just for you to confirm how good his latest scheme is.'

They walked on, uphill now. The weather wrapped them warm; it might have been an afternoon in high summer.

'I wish Caldwell had chosen somewhere a bit nearer civilisation,' Wicks groaned, wiping his brow.

'Has he lived there a long time?'

'To the best of my knowledge. I've been here ten–eleven years, and he's always lurked there, brooding over the arts, like God in his temple. At one time he was away acting in the professional theatre, films, television.'

'And the house stood empty?'

'No. His wife occupied it.'

'Had they no children?'

'Two boys. Years back. Before my time. They're grown-up now.'

'And in the theatre?' she asked.

'Not as far as I know. They rarely visit their father. Or are seen to do so.'

2

'Not to talk to their mother?'

'His wife died, oh, six years ago. Not that it made much difference to him, as far as one could tell.'

'I told Rebecca Faulks that I was walking up here this evening with you and she said you had a special name for his place. Hangman's House. Is that right?'

'No, not exactly. If Becky Faulks could only get anything half right she would do so.'

'What do you call it, then?'

'The House of the Hanged Man.'

'Why?'

'It reminds me of Cézanne's picture of that name. Don't you know it?'

'No. Should I?'

'It's a fairly early painting. *The House of the Hanged Man, Anvers-sur-Oise.*' He was proud of his French accent. 'It was done at the time when the Establishment, those who chose pictures for the exhibitions, professional critics all ridiculed such pictures of his that were shown to the public.'

'Oh.'

'Fellow painters admired and encouraged him.'

'Such as?'

'Monet, Renoir. This picture's in the Louvre now.' He coughed ironically. 'Caldwell's house isn't much like Cézanne's picture, really. From this road you come to it from above, you see it from roof level. It has three storeys and some spare trees round it.'

'You admire the picture?'

'I've a print of it at home. I'll show it to you. It's serious. There's something about it.'

'Does Mr Caldwell know what you call it?'

'Not as far as I know. And it wouldn't endear me to him.'

They climbed on in silence. Wicks clearly found the going hard, so that he pulled up to wipe the sweat from his forehead.

Alicia waited, looking away up the road.

'Unfit,' Wicks pronounced himself.

'There's no hurry.'

'No, especially as I want to arrive cool and in my right mind.'

'To impress the impresario?'

'I suppose so. I'm a bit ashamed of myself, really.'

'He always gives you a leading role. And makes a point of congratulating you in public when you've done it.'

'He's not so delighted in private.'

'Does he see you as a rival?' Alicia asked.

'If he does I don't see why. I'm a poor schoolteacher to him. He in his time has trodden the boards with Olivier and Gielgud.' Wicks's face collapsed into mirth. 'Forward, madam.'

Alicia did as she was told, but took care to step slowly so that her companion could keep up with her. He, face now set, swung his arms. Some thirty yards over the brow of the hill Alicia turned right through a wooden gate. From this point they looked down from roof level at Caldwell's house.

'No,' Wicks said. 'It isn't much like the Cézanne painting, but when I see this I can't exactly clear it out of my mind. Well, it can't matter much.' He led the way this time along the rough path that fought its way down to the rustic door. 'If I lived here I would do something about this entrance.'

'It's the back way,' she said, delicately picking her path downhill, reaching the house first.

Raynor Wicks, joining her on a huge level stone, looked at his watch and announced, '6.28. He can't complain about this.' He savagely pressed the doorbell as if he were trying to topple the wall. 'They'll hear that,' he said with some satisfaction.

'They' did and the door creakingly opened. A woman with a lace bonnet and long red Welsh witch's skirt opened the door. Neither had seen her before. 'Yes?' she enquired, glaring.

'Alicia Smallwood and Raynor Wicks to see Mr Caldwell. He's expecting us.'

'He's expecting you to use the front door.'

'We walked here.'

'Very good.' The compliment was accompanied by another stare, a screwing up of the face, perhaps to indicate thought and finally a muttered invitation to enter. The woman led them into a small room off the tiled corridor. 'Take seats,' she said. 'Make yourselves comfortable. Mr Caldwell will not keep you waiting long.' She stared at them again as if she could not believe her eyes before she backed out.

'Who's that?' Alicia asked.

'I've no idea. I've not seen her before.'

'His housekeeper?'

'Probably. You never know with him.'

They looked shiftily round the room as they occupied the two uncomfortable armchairs. A table with dining-room seats occupied

4

almost the whole of the rest of the space. Three walls were covered with shelves, brightly neat with books. Though the light outside was still high, the room, dimly illuminated by a small sash window, was in half-darkness, with irregular areas of deep shadow.

'Not exactly spacious,' Wicks tried again.

'He can't be holding the meeting in here,' Alicia agreed.

'This perhaps is the waiting room,' he said. 'Or the place where we can do the least damage to the furniture while she announces us to her lord and master.'

'I'm certain he told me there'd be auditions. I expected to see quite a few here.'

'One is never sure what Caldwell is up to. When he spoke to me and invited me to play Orsino, he said that this was his last production here. He began, he said, twenty-five years ago and the play then was *Twelfth Night*. He'd therefore chosen that to finish with.'

'It hasn't been done since then?'

'It has. I've been here for eleven years and I took part in it a month or two after my arrival.'

'Did you play Orsino?'

'No. I was Sebastian. His nibs himself played the Duke.'

'Well?'

'Oh, yes. He showed us amateurs up.' They smiled at each other. 'He was sprightlier then, looked much younger.'

'Who played Viola?'

'Some girl he'd brought in from London. Said by the knowledgeable to be his mistress. Imogen Something.'

'A professional?'

'That was the impression given.'

'Was she any good?'

'Oh, yes. She made her mark. When she was on stage all eyes were on her.'

'And did your "twin" look at all like you?'

'Not a bit. They gave us similar clothes and wigs. But Caldwell went out of his way to explain this. We did not look alike, but it was the audience's part to imagine that we were so. He gave a lecture on the play a week or two before we actually performed it. And that was one of the points he made. He really went bald-headed at the audience. It was no use watching a Shakespeare play if they were not prepared to use their imagination. Shakespeare, he

5

said, might appear to apologise for this, as in *Henry V.*' Wicks jerked his head back and began to recite.

> 'Can this cockpit hold
> The vasty fields of France? Or may we cram
> Within this wooden O the very casques
> That did affright the air at Agincourt?'

Alicia immediately recognised this imitation of Caldwell, reduced so that no one outside the room would hear it, but with something of the man's vocal power and penetration caught in the low voice. She clapped her hands in applause, laughing. 'You sound just like him.'

Outside the door they heard a rumble as if someone were moving furniture. Both listened, but nothing further attracted their attention.

'He's run a chest of drawers across the doorway, blockaded us in.'

'Why?'

'God knows with him. Perhaps it's some rearrangement of furniture he'd planned and has nothing to do with us.'

They listened again, but went unrewarded. Wicks looked at his watch. 'Twenty to seven,' he said. 'For a man so insistent on punctuality in others, he could do better.'

Outside a clock struck a quarter to the hour and the doorknob was turned.

'I do sincerely apologise for my rudeness in appearing so late. I had to help Mrs Smith complete the realignment of kitchen furniture. That is now complete.' He spoke carefully, as if to ensure that the audience in the back row of the stalls should not miss one precious word. He noticed now that both his guests had stood as he appeared in the room.

'Please, sit down.' He spoke in a slighter voice, as he juggled with the back of his seat, a wooden dining chair, and manoeuvred it into a position at the table almost equidistant between his guests. He sat, and fiddled with his thinning grey hair as if preparing his first sentence.

'I have asked you here to seek your advice.' He was back to an actor's orotundity. He breathed in deeply. 'I thank you for your coming.' He sighed and leant forward, eyes now turned up to heaven. 'It is about the Sutton Festival. This will be the twenty-

6

fifth year that I have taken some part in the event and the committee asked earlier if we could put on for them Shakespeare's *Twelfth Night* for their annual play. It was the first I produced for them twenty-five years ago. I appreciated their kind thought.' His face assumed a sadder, nobler aspect. 'I had been considering for my last connection something less well known, something demanding more thought, *Measure for Measure*, perhaps, or *Timon of Athens*. I had said nothing either to members of the committee or of the dramatic society about this. They were paying me a compliment by suggesting my first play.' He shook his head. 'I remember the suggestion came all those years ago from Alfred Vaughan, who was at the time professor of English at the University of Beechnall. He retired himself a year or two later, went right away, back to his native Wales and died not long afterwards. Did you know him?'

Both shook their heads.

'A scholarly man. He said, and he surprised me by saying, that *Twelfth Night* was the play of Shakespeare's that he most enjoyed seeing.'

'Did you know him before you came here?' Wicks asked.

'I did. I'd met him several times. I'd read his two books on Shakespeare. I'd heard him lecture.' Caldwell bent forward.

'What would you have expected him to choose?' Wicks asked.

'*King Lear*.'

'Perhaps he thought that a cast of amateurs wouldn't be capable of doing such a play justice.'

'You may be right. In my time we have not attempted it and as far as I am concerned that was the reason. A decent performance of *A Midsummer Night's Dream* or *The Merchant of Venice* is worth far more than a feeble attempt at *King Lear*, good intentions or not. Have you ever seen a successful amateur production of *Lear*?'

The guests shook their heads. Caldwell again clasped his hands between his knees. 'That was where we stood,' he said, 'until Saturday night last.'

They waited for him to continue.

'We had just finished dinner on Saturday evening and I was settling down to a cup of my housekeeper's excellent coffee when the telephone rang. It was the president of the dramatic society, Arthur Powell. Do you know him?'

Both guests indicated that they did.

7

'I can hardly claim to know him well. He's a new broom in the dramatic society. At the one recent meeting of the society I have attended he seemed quiet, unassertive, feeling his way. I believe he's a surveyor of one sort or another.' Caldwell paused again. 'This time he seemed quite different. The committee had decided at its last meeting that afternoon to replace the Shakespeare play as the main event of the festival week and perform something more up to the minute. By this it turned out he meant a kind of music-hall performance, topical sketches, songs, parodies, conjuring tricks, dancing and so forth. What did I think of this? Of course it was at present only a suggestion. They would do nothing without my express approval.'

Caldwell's face twisted with anger, but he continued in a quieter voice. 'I was furious. I hope my voice didn't show it. I asked whose idea this was.' He writhed in his chair. 'Powell said that this was passed by a large majority in the committee. I asked (and I could hardly speak with temper, with my teeth gritted together) who had proposed it in the first place. He said Alfred Arnold and he had seconded it. "You realise that I have already conducted auditions, and have selected the cast and was about to start rehearsals?" "Yes," he said, cool as you like, "I know that. Jean Ogden is a member of the committee. You had chosen her for Maria." "And she voted in favour of the new proposal?" "No, she was one of the few who was against it." "I see," I said. "I see." And I pretended to give his news some consideration. "Well," Powell asked after a time, "what do you think of the idea?" By this time, I had my feelings under control and I told him that I'd need to think carefully about it. He said they were not dispensing with my services. I was to draw up the programme. He remembered a marvellous Victorian Music Hall I had put on in Brighton a few years back. I said that was with professional actors. "You think this is beyond us?" he asked. I made him wait again and then said again that I would have to consider the proposal.'

'Had you already made up your mind?' Wicks asked.

'To all intents and purposes.'

'You didn't approve of their suggestion?' Alicia advanced the question hesitantly.

'I wouldn't altogether say that. I suppose I must always look with favour on new suggestions from the committee. They don't know what they're talking about, since they don't know the difficulties ahead, which are inherent in their spheres. But they might come up with an idea that a professional like myself could use to metamorphose into something worth trying. It's not exactly very likely, I must admit, but this should not be dismissed out of hand. No, no' – the syllables rang long – 'what annoyed me was their holding a meeting about such a radical, I might use the word ridiculous, proposal on their agenda without inviting me to attend and give them my reactions.'

'They might not have known, the majority,' Wicks argued.

'One of the reasons I asked you two to hear my story is that I could expect one of you at least to act as *advocatus diaboli*. In this case, from what I hear, this proposal has been in the air between Powell and Arnold and one or two cronies for some weeks, and by the time it was raised the committee had heard all the arguments that were in its favour so that the proposal was easily passed. When someone asked if I had been consulted, Arnold said, or Powell, that there was no intention of trying to get rid of me. And here the two of them indulged – Jean Ogden's word – in a flurry of compliments about my competence, nay, genius. It was not me they did not want, but Shakespeare.' He flung his arms wide in disgust. 'Years ago there might well have been something to be said for putting on a play set for O Levels at Sutton Grammar. Now Shakespeare is no longer studied. That is how the matter stands.'

'You've not given them an answer?' Wicks asked.

'No. I have thought long and hard about it, but I felt I owed it to the town to consult one or two people of judgement like yourselves to hear what you had to say.'

There was an awkward silence. Alicia felt the men's breathing filled the whole room. She would allow Wicks to start.

He began, rather tentatively, 'You're quite right to take seriously any suggestion that the dramatic society's committee puts forward. On this occasion their timing was badly out. The decision about *Twelfth Night* had been firmly made by the committee some time before, and you had auditioned and chosen your players. Unless there had been some extraordinary circumstances they had, in my view, no business to try to introduce this music-hall performance in its place. It was, moreover, extremely impolite and tactless not to consult you, especially as they had the nerve to ask you to script and produce the thing.' He rubbed his hands together. 'I must say they have been extremely secretive about it. I was away, in Greece, pretty well the whole of August, but when I came back I heard not a thing, not a breath of any such proposal. Did you, Alicia? You've been here most of the summer holidays.'

'No, I haven't.'

'As to the idea of a week of music hall?' Wicks to Alicia.

'They'd like it if it were well done. But it was typical of Powell, Arnold and company to come up with the idea, and then expect Mr Caldwell to conjure it from the air and to produce it for them.'

The men listened, their expressions conveyed little.

'Well, Raynor, if you were in my place, what would you do?'

'If I decided there was nothing in the music-hall malarkey for me, I'd refuse to do it.'

'And the Shakespeare?'

'I'm afraid I'd refuse to do that, too.'

Caldwell nodded, and stared fixedly at the farthest corner of the walls and ceiling. In time he breathed out, lowered his head, looked the girl in the face and asked, 'And you, Alicia? What would you do?'

'If you don't want to do the music hall, don't do it.'

'And the *Twelfth Night*?'

'If they then asked me to do it, I'd do it.'

'Even if I couldn't be certain that the committee and their friends were wholeheartedly behind me?'

She hesitated before she answered, 'I don't know the people well enough. If I were sure they'd drag their feet and put obstacles in my way, then I wouldn't do it.'

'I'm afraid they would be awkward.' He nodded, doll-like, his face void of all expression. 'I thank you for your opinions. I felt I must consult somebody who is knowledgeable and sensible. I did not wish to be accused of sulking, to let Sutton down because I couldn't have my own way.' He paused again. 'I wonder how they'll take my refusal.'

'It's a pity', Alicia said, 'that your twenty-five years of service should end like this.'

'Thank you.'

'I wonder where the idea came from in the first place,' Wicks mused. 'Powell and Arnold thought it was time they made their presence felt. Arnold's the sort of man who's looking for change. If it's above five years old in his view it's worthless.'

'Thank you, both.'

Caldwell made for the door and shouted for his housekeeper. The old lady in the red skirt appeared. He ordered her to make some of her excellent coffee. She enquired about sugar and milk for the guests before she tottered off. Caldwell returned to his chair. 'I don't know how she does it, but her coffee is nothing like mine. She uses the same ingredients in the same crockery as I do, but hers excels mine beyond all telling.' He settled on to his chair, puffing and blowing. 'I thank you both for coming. My mind is properly made up. The die is cast. I shall refuse to do either. Now that I have your approval, and your opinion that I am not acting purely out of vanity, I have no qualms.'

'We can mention your decision to anyone who enquires?'

'Certainly. I shall ring the egregious Mr Powell later this evening.'

The two did not stay long. They drank Mrs Smith's coffee, judged later by Wicks to be nothing out of the ordinary, while Caldwell gave them one or two anecdotes from his career, which seemed to him relevant to his present situation.

On the way back, as they walked, Alicia asked her companion, 'What did you make of that, then?'

'He wanted to be sure that he had a few allies?' he answered at once.

'That might be so in your case. But I'm a newcomer with no influence.'

'He's a careful old man. He wants to be sure he has supportive friends.'

'And what will Powell and Arnold do?'

'They'll put something on, fear you not. For all I know they already have a pretty little scheme in hand, with some pal hovering in the wings to produce.'

'Who'd that be?'

'I've no idea. It's just that I see Powell as an ideal conspirator.'

They enjoyed talk of this nature all the way back into Sutton.

II

In the next weeks Alicia Smallwood heard little comment or discussion of Caldwell's decision. No one consulted her; nor did she expect it. She had done two years towards a Ph.D. thesis at the University of Beechnall. Two events had contributed to this development. The first was that her tutor at Oxford, with whom she had got on extremely well, had in her last year been appointed professor and had started here as she had completed her degree. The second was that for her twenty-first birthday her father had made over the deeds of a cottage in Sutton, five miles out from Beechnall, and had promised, once she had been placed among the high Firsts in her final examinations, to redecorate the place according to her wishes and to pay her expenses for the next three years until she achieved her doctorate.

This present was unexpected.

Alicia had no idea that her father even owned this place in the North Midlands. Her mother had seemed uncertain about the gift. 'You won't want to live up there,' she opined, but once she decided on research and consulted Professor Conway, the place had seemed a godsend.

'I don't want to tie your hands too much, but I've arranged it so that you won't be able to sell the place for three years until your doctorate's over.'

They travelled up to Sutton to see it. It was larger than Alicia had imagined, with a wide kitchen, two bathrooms, four bedrooms, three rooms for recreation downstairs.

'You'll be able to take a couple of lodgers, if you don't fancy living on your own.'

'It's lovely, but the size of the garden is frightening.'

'I am making over to you some money for three years to pay your council tax, your heating bills, and to hire a gardener and a home help. I'm not short of money just at present. Your mother thinks this is a stupid present, but I want to give you something that's different, offers a challenge. She thinks I should have left the choice to you. You're my only child; you've done us proud at school and university, and as soon as I heard you were thinking of following Conway up here, to my part of the world, the notion of giving you a house burst straight into my head. And I'd no sooner thought of it than the people I rented it to let me know they were leaving. They've been there for five years, though they only took it for six months for a start, but they liked it, his firm paid the rent, it was convenient for the factory in Beechnall, so they stuck there.'

'Why are they leaving now?' Alicia wondered if her father had leant on them to move out.

'He's going to Australia. New job. They've really looked after the place.'

Alicia had enjoyed her spell in Rose Cottage, though at times she felt lonely. Her research she had done with zest seven days a week. She worked long days and frequently visited the university's excellent library. She joined the local dramatic society, took two small parts, met Clarence Caldwell, who grilled her about her thesis on eighteenth-century drama (he had for some reason a special interest in Addison's *Cato*), then quizzed her about modern Shakespearean criticism on which she had written a dissertation, which Christopher Conway had placed for her in a not too hole-and-corner literary journal. She was grateful that people like Conway and Caldwell had appeared to think highly of her literary criticism. It came, however, as a considerable surprise when the actor had invited her to be his assistant in the forthcoming production of the ill-fated *Twelfth Night*, which the dram. soc. committee had just decided against. Caldwell had said, ironically she thought, that he'd feel safer producing the play 'with the weight of critical theory' beside or behind him.

On one particular evening at the end of September, after a day's hard reading in the university library, she sat giving a first trial to her central heating system. The lorry had arrived in August to fill her tank with oil, but she had not used the boiler until this day. She had carefully worked through the instruction manual in the last two months and this evening had put the newly acquired knowledge into practice. She was surprised – she had little confidence in herself as a practical person – that the inaugural moves had brought the cold machine into warmth. She had half expected some snag, which would have meant enquiries from acquaintances for the names of local plumbers or, worse, a search in the Yellow Pages.

13

Her father had arranged the installation of the new central heating last summer. 'I don't like to think of you with that ramshackle heating you've got there. I'll get an expert to look at it.' The 'expert' had recommended a new oil-fired system and her father had agreed. Now she sat in comfortable warmth that spread through the whole house, unlike the old boiler, which gave adequate heat only in the two downstairs sitting rooms and the main bedroom. She felt proud of herself. She had set the new boiler into action. It had not been difficult, but she had managed it without snags. 'It's done,' she said out loud, walking from room to room.

She returned to her sitting room and lolled for half an hour in an armchair in the drawing room with her eyes closed, very unusual for her, before closing the curtains all round the house. She sat down, having completed the task, once more to enjoy the sensation of warmth and the thought of a good day's work done. She spent a few minutes on the newspaper she had bought that morning in Beechnall, then looked at an eighteenth-century volume of essays from *The Spectator* that she had picked up from a second-hand shop last weekend. She was too tired to read it seriously, but passed the time trying to translate the Latin poetry that headed every performance. Though each of them was accompanied by a verse translation into English, these were too free so that she decided she'd need to take down her Latin dictionary from the shelves. As she was about to do this, the bell at the front door rang strongly.

Alicia started up in alarm. No one had suggested they might call on her at eight o'clock of a darkening September evening. She opened the door, carefully leaving the chain in place. Two men stood outside, both wearing raincoats and hats.

'Miss Smallwood?' one politely asked.

'Yes.' Without encouragement.

'We're from the Sutton Dramatic Society. We shan't take more than a quarter of an hour of your evening.'

She did not answer. For the first time since she had come to Rose Cottage she felt afraid.

'Our names are Powell and Arnold. I am this year's president.'

'We would like to discuss a matter with you. We ought, I know, to have phoned, but neither of us had your number. We had been on an errand together for the dramatic society and found ourselves passing your house on our way there, and it struck us that if we were not too late on our way back, we could call in and put our proposition to you.' The second man sounded less unfriendly.

'It's about the festival,' the president said.

Alicia rasped back the chain and invited them in. Both raised and took off their hats as they entered her foyer. She recognised them now and felt less apprehensive. She signalled them forward into the second drawing room. The two stood there together.

'What a beautiful room,' Arnold said. 'And so warm. It's chilly outside.'

'Thank you.'

She sat down; they followed suit.

Arnold spoke first. 'We don't want to waste your time.' He nodded towards his companion.

Powell began immediately. 'I don't know what you know about it, but we have had something of a setback in the society over our part in the festival.' As Alicia made no reply he continued, speaking in a low voice, with his hands despondently down between his knees. 'Clarence Caldwell, who usually produces a Shakespeare play, has withdrawn his services. Did you know that?'

'Yes.'

'May I ask from whom?'

'Mr Caldwell himself.'

'You were to be his assistant producer on *Twelfth Night*. Perhaps that's why he told you.' As Alicia kept silent about this Powell spoke again, rather fiercely. 'Did he say why?'

'Yes.'

'Would you mind telling us the reasons he gave you?'

She thought it none of his business, but politely raised her eyebrows and prepared to answer him. 'He gave me the impression that you told him that your committee had decided against Shakespeare and had suggested a Victorian or Edwardian music hall.'

'That is somewhere near the truth. The *Twelfth Night* performance had been agreed some time at the end of last year because we understood that he was thinking of retiring from, severing his connection with, our festival and therefore whoever proposed the idea thought it would be a graceful tribute to him to ask him to produce the first play he had done twenty-five years before.'

Powell paused. Alicia sat still, as if deep in thought. He began again. 'One of the reasons we did Shakespeare was that we usually

15

asked Beechnall Grammar, and other schools, the name of one of the plays they were preparing for GCSE or A Level. This year none of them is doing *Twelfth Night*. Moreover, we had seen, quite independently of each other, a very successful *Evening at a Victorian Music Hall*, which Clarence Caldwell had produced in Brighton.'

'It was excellent and really popular.' The other man, Arnold, showing his enthusiasm.

'It was repeated in the West End, so we suggested that Mr Caldwell should produce this, as he had done it so brilliantly before. There was no thought of slighting him, especially in this last year. He, however, refused to do this and when we offered him the *Twelfth Night* again he turned that down just as ruthlessly.'

Alicia said nothing, but sat modestly.

Arnold took up the tale. 'We were, therefore, wondering if you would be so good as to produce *Twelfth Night* for us. Mr Caldwell saw fit to appoint you as his assistant and therefore the chain wouldn't be absolutely broken. You could continue in the same style and manner he would have pursued, and, of course, add your own ideas.'

'I thought you didn't want *Twelfth Night*?'

'Changing it was suggested at a committee meeting. People on the committee frequently come up with such ideas. It's part of their duty. It seemed a good scheme, especially as there was no practical use in the schools this year and, secondly, as both I and Alfred had seen and enjoyed this marvellous production of Caldwell's in Brighton. It was one of the most memorable evenings I have spent in the theatre. We thought he would jump at the chance in this, his last year. But he flatly refused. We were disappointed but there was nothing for us to do but drop our ideas and to tell him to carry on with his Shakespeare. He would not have that either.'

'Why was that?'

'He didn't tell you? We think he did not like our changing our minds at the last minute, as if he didn't know what he was about and needed our help.'

'We thought no such thing,' Arnold added. 'We thought he would welcome the chance to do something new, which would add to the drawing power of our festival.'

'The result was that we were left with this enormous hole in our programme. The Shakespeare was the only performance over six nights and a matinee.'

16

'We shall be in trouble with the people of Sutton now and all as a result of our trying to give them something new. We shall be in their bad books, I'm sure.' He rubbed his moustache with a strong first finger. 'We were surprised at Caldwell's attitude. He has always been, from what I hear, willing to compromise and accommodate.' Powell pulled himself upright. 'This is why we have come to ask you if you will produce *Twelfth Night*. The cast is chosen and ready. You could begin rehearsals whenever you liked.'

'We should support you to the hilt,' Alfred Arnold said. 'It would get us out of a hole, even if it is of our own making. We'd be very grateful if you'd please give it careful consideration; the whole town will be in debt to you if you feel you can undertake this. You'll find people will be most accommodating. I know you're comparatively new in these parts, but then so is Arthur.' He made a signal in the direction of his companion.

Alicia did not immediately answer. The two men sat on the edge of their chairs, upright, sympathetic half-smiles on their lips, silently urging her to comply.

'I feel flattered', she began, 'that you have invited me, but I'm afraid I must refuse.' Both men appeared ready to intervene, but she held up a hand to silence them. 'The reason is that I'm not qualified. I have never produced a play in my life and though I have taken minor, very minor, roles in plays at school and at Oxford, that is just about the extent of my practical experience. You may wonder why an experienced actor and producer like Clarence Caldwell invited me to assist him. The reason for that is he read a piece I wrote while I was still at college about modern Shakespearean criticism, which he thought interesting. He did not expect me to take over the actual direction from him, even temporarily; my job was to watch what he was about and point out if it clashed with modern ideas or was supported by them. I do not know whether that was a useful notion. We hadn't yet started. Shakespeare is not my subject of study. The eighteenth century is where my interest lies at present.'

'I think, Miss Smallwood, you are too modest about your qualifications and your gifts.' Powell, persuasively.

'You are, from what people tell me, steeped in literature and this is why we are calling on you. Everyone, even Clarence Caldwell, made a start somewhere,' Arnold argued.

'He had decided on a career in the theatre. He knew where he wanted to excel.'

17

'I'm not saying you are parallel cases. Far from it. But surely it would be worth trying. We are an amateur company, agreed, but we have some gifted men and women.'

'If that is so, why don't you use one of them to produce the play?'

'You are better qualified than they. I mentioned your name to Professor Conway at Beechnall University who had been your tutor at Oxford and is now supervising your work for a doctorate. He said he saw no reason why you couldn't or shouldn't produce the Shakespeare. "She's clever," he said, "and assiduous."'

Alicia nodded her head in thanks for this praise, but said not a word.

'Professor Conway also warned me against your manner. He told me that you were very modest, in spite of your talents.'

'And is that all?'

'No. He sang your praises at length. He made me more certain than ever that we had chosen the right person.'

'Now what do you say?' Powell asked, smiling broadly, as if he was certain she could not deny them after such recommendation.

'It's very kind of you, and of Professor Conway, but I prefer not to do it.'

'Why? Please.'

'Because I tell you that I don't think I am capable of doing it properly. Nor have I any ambitions in that field. This is not fake modesty. I know I might have to spend so much time on the play that my own work might suffer.'

'Conway said you'd manage it without turning a hair.'

'Then I disagree. Even if I were taking on a play from my own period, I would still find I hadn't the time to do it properly.'

'Have you any suggestions, then?'

'You say you have plenty of clever, knowledgeable people in your society. Use one of them. I must say I was most impressed by your *As You Like It* last year. I'd not been here long, but I immediately joined your society. And if chosen, I hoped to play one or two minor parts in future plays. I'm interested in drama, but I know my limitations.'

'There you are, then,' Powell said. 'Here's a chance to do more than play minor roles.'

'It's a challenge,' Arnold added.

'If you asked me to walk a tightrope it would be a challenge, but I shouldn't take it on, simply because I don't think I have much talent in that direction and I might do myself some serious harm.'

She looked solemnly at her visitors. 'I've not been here very long, so I can't give much help, but I'd have thought Raynor Wicks was the sort of man you want. He is, from what I hear, an excellent actor and has been in the plays Mr Caldwell has produced for you in the past ten or twelve years.'

'No,' said Powell flatly.

'I'm sorry. I made the suggestion because I know him a little and I thought he'd suit you ideally.'

'No. Wicks is hand in glove with Caldwell. He thinks that we have deliberately tried to edge Caldwell out.'

'Has he said as much to you?' she asked.

'Not in so many words.'

'You see, Miss Smallwood' – this was Alfred Arnold intervening again – 'this failure to find a producer for the Shakespeare may well be the source of trouble, of controversy. There will be those who will blame us. We're comparative newcomers to the dramatic society and when we support some proposal to bring us up to date – and it was not we, I assure you, who wished to drop Shakespeare in the first place, but we thought it was fairly strongly supported by members, both of long standing as well as new – we are blamed for this shameless brazenness, as we should not have been had we been old stagers, as it were. We are accused of trying to upset a society that has been useful and stable, and given wide satisfaction for years. We were probably wrong, or accepted too readily the view of a minority whose specious plans would not be acceptable to the large majority. I hope you see what I mean. I'm putting all this very badly, because I feel the responsibility for our dilemma lies with Arthur and myself. We should have known better, moved with more circumspection.

'Our objective was to widen the horizons of the society. And by coincidence we both had seen this wonderful show Caldwell had mounted in Brighton. I was the first to mention it, and Arthur then said he had seen it and recalled what an unforgettable experience he found it. The modernisers, if I can so call them, the younger members who are asking for the society to change, seized on this, casually mentioned by me in the course of praising Caldwell's talent, then suggested this show as a replacement of Shakespeare. Had Arthur and I been more cautious, more on the qui vive, we would have seen that with a society such as ours this was the wrong time to pursue such a course, never mind try to put it into action. We were wrong, foolish if you like; I see it now. We did

19

worse, too, by not first consulting Mr Caldwell. When we did put it to him, the day after the committee meeting, he took it that he was being faced with a fait accompli, without prior notice, and he refused. He would have nothing to do with music-hall turns.

'We returned to our committee who had sent us on this quest of something new and popular, and they were as upset as we at his attitude. Some were for carrying on with the idea, but the majority were not in favour of dropping Caldwell, who was our connection with the real theatre, a professional, one who had done wonders for us in the past. We therefore said we should return to him and plead with him to carry on as before and to produce *Twelfth Night*. Arthur and I saw him the next evening. We wasted no time. We told him the decision of the committee, and asked him to take up the production of the Shakespeare again, but he was adamant, no, he would not. We pleaded with him, but he would not change his mind. He was quite unlike himself. Arrogant, cold, even insulting, he spoke as if we had somehow mortally wounded him. In the end he cut short the interview and showed us the door. We tried appealing to his better nature, told him how much Sutton owed him, but we might have been talking to the wall. Arthur and I were shocked. His attitude was so antagonistic that we both thought he had been put up to it.' Arnold stopped, almost breathless.

'Have you any evidence of that?' Alicia asked.

'Of what? I was there.'

'That somebody had been encouraging him to deny you.'

'Not directly. But hereabouts, in a town like Beechnall, there are all sorts of rivalries, enmities and feuds. Arthur and I are newcomers to the society. We were, it is true, voted in against some few of the older members only this year, and with us a new, younger, more radical committee. Some of the more senior members did not like this. They are loyal to the older values, they'd tell you. They don't do much to help the society besides renewing their subscriptions, though God knows that's necessary these days; they don't act, do the off-stage chores, attend meetings, come up with ideas until something like this appears; then they group together, criticise anything we do, spread malicious rumours, write us critical letters, claim they are keeping standards high.'

Arnold delivered this at a gabble. Alicia thought that any minute he'd fall on his knees in front of her. Powell sat back in his chair, an expression of scorn on his face. Alicia looked at him and away from Arnold.

20

'That's about the length of it,' he growled.

'That is unfortunate for you,' Alicia said. 'I can understand that. But I can't see that I can help.' She did not believe Arnold's protestations, to be honest.

'Just produce the play for us. It will save a split in the society that might well take years to heal.'

'No. I'm sorry but the answer's "no".'

'Miss Smallwood, we beg you.' Arnold.

Alicia felt nothing but contempt for the man with his babbling sentences and his bovine eyes. She was certain that she had been low on his list of replacements, that he had tried elsewhere and failed, and was now reduced to these histrionics to save his skin.

'Would you', asked Powell, 'think it over? It must have come as a surprise to you. We should have given you notice instead of bursting in on you like this. Would you, please, at least think it over? This evening after we've gone. And then tomorrow, or perhaps the day after you could give us a reasoned answer.'

'It would be exactly the same, I'm afraid. It would still be "no".'

Powell drew himself up beside the door on his way out. 'Thanks very much for listening to us, Miss Smallwood.'

Through the window she saw them stumbling up the gravel path, heard them start the car and drive away. She looked at her clock; it showed twenty minutes past nine. She made herself a cup of chocolate and sat watching it cool. To tell the truth she would not have minded producing *Twelfth Night*. She was sure she could manage it. It would, for certain, take up some of her working time, but not to any ruinous effect. She believed one should always have a pastime that took one away from the hours spent at research. She was no good at embroidery or painting; she played no musical instrument and though she enjoyed listening to the classics at concerts, or on the radio or television, that was secondary to her thought, or her reading. She cut out the music when she came to some crisis of judgement or even something that caught her interest.

Yet, she decided, she had done well to refuse these two. If the production of Shakespeare meant that she would be caught up in civil wars in Sutton, or Beechnall, so that people refused to speak to her in the street, or talked behind her back, or criticised her every move, every flower she grew, looked with horror on her every purchase of grocery or newspapers, she was well out of it. It was possible that she had already put her foot in it with the

Powell–Arnold clique, if such a group existed. People hereabouts had been kind and welcoming; she had not asked for much help, but she had received some. In the dramatic society she had been modest. When at the end of her audition for *Twelfth Night* she had not been chosen for a speaking part she was not surprised. When Caldwell had called her over and invited her to be his assistant she was she remembered speechless, flabbergasted. He had patted her shoulder and said, 'I think you would be better employed setting me right on matters of modern criticism. I read an article of yours in *Interpretations* that gave me much to think about. "That's the sort of mind I'd like to guide my erring instincts," I said to myself.' She had been flattered, had allowed him to continue with his fatherly pawings.

She decided, almost immediately, that he had been in touch with Professor Conway, who had mentioned her article, had most probably looked it out and had it photocopied. *Interpretations* was not the sort of magazine that appeared on every library shelf. She wondered why her name had come up at all between the two men and who had first seen fit to mention it. Conway knew that she had joined the society and perhaps he had talked about her. She had auditioned for a part in *An Inspector Calls*, which Caldwell was not producing, but he had sat in at the auditions. She had not got a part of any kind, not surprising with such a small cast, but Caldwell, not the producer, had asked her to repeat the test passage. He had thanked her when she had finished, but her name had not been among those the producer had read out at the end of the auditions.

Over the cup of tea afterwards some smart young woman who had not, it appeared, been selected, said, 'You must have made an impression on Caldwell. He asked you to repeat your piece. That's his way of showing you he was pleased.' 'Not pleased enough to get me in.' 'Don't you worry yourself about that. George Cresswell, who's producing, would have the final say. And he chooses his relatives. That's not to say they are no good. They'll be very adequate, if not better, but . . .' The woman had sniffed.

Perhaps Caldwell had remembered her and her name when he was talking to Conway. There were people with such excellent recall.

Straying about the house, turning all this over in her mind, she wondered if she should give Raynor Wicks a call to tell him about the visit from Powell and Arnold. She glanced at the grandfather clock in the foyer, which showed a quarter to ten in the half-darkness. That seemed late to her for making casual phone calls, but she recalled that Wicks had confessed to her that he was never in bed before midnight. 'And what time do you get up?' she had asked. 'Seven a.m. That's long enough sleeping. Life's too interesting to spend too much of it unconscious in bed.'

She rang Wicks, who cheerfully set aside her apologies for phoning so late. 'Not at all,' he said. 'My evening doesn't begin until ten p.m.'

She gave him a brief account of the visit and invitation of Powell and Arnold.

He listened, as always, without interruption. 'Interesting, interesting,' he purred when she had finished.

'What do you think', she asked, 'about their wish that I should produce *Twelfth Night*? They must have asked quite a few before they came down to me.'

'I don't know. You mustn't be too modest. They didn't approach me.'

'I suggested you as an ideal for the job.'

'And?' He drew the monosyllable out.

'They said you wouldn't take it.'

'And about right, too.' He hummed to warn her that he'd speak further. 'They are in difficulty, there's no doubt about it. What they and their friends saw as a brilliant idea has turned out to be a catastrophe once Clarence Caldwell had refused to have any connection with it. I went to an emergency meeting a week ago and tempers flared. I can't say I felt sorry for Powell and company. They might have known what was going to happen. I thought that Powell might have resigned, so furious was the blame heaped on his shoulders. He looked bewildered when some of his supporters turned on him and accused him of handling the whole thing badly. Did he seem unduly upset tonight?'

'He played second fiddle to Arnold, who did practically all the talking.'

'And did he speak well? Persuasively?'

'He surprised me. He gabbled as if he were playing a role. As if he were demented, I thought. He overdid it.'

'But you weren't tempted?'

'No. As I say, I thought he wasn't altogether sincere. If he'd burst into tears as part of the act, I wouldn't have been surprised.' She waited. 'On the one or two occasions I've heard him speak in public he's seemed quiet, restrained, appealing to reason.'

'Yes. They are a rum pair.' He sighed. 'You did well to refuse them. You'd make a respectable job of it, because there are some decent actors there, who know the play well. You'd cut it sensibly and have some ideas that wouldn't have spoilt the play, giving it a modern twist. But by the sound of that meeting half your players would have withdrawn; you'd have to do auditions all over again and there wouldn't have been too many putting themselves forward, and they'd have made fun – and that in a malign way – of their replacements.'

'I didn't realise it was as bad as that.'

'This has really stirred them. The loss of Caldwell has annoyed everybody. Not that he was a universal favourite, but his name was a draw and his enemies had only to wait a year for him to go of his own volition. You'd be surprised how many quarrels, petty feuds, there are. I've never got used to it.'

'Why is that?'

'One reason's obvious. Twenty-five years ago they persuaded Caldwell to take over the annual Shakespeare play, a good thing on the whole. But those he didn't choose for parts hated those he did. And that's been going on for a quarter of a century, festering. And even the newcomers were somehow dragged into the conflicts.'

'Oh?'

'And they didn't always need the dram. soc. as a breeding ground for disgruntlement. Take those two visitors of yours. They're both comparative newcomers; have settled in Beechnall inside the last ten years. But when you see them shoulder to shoulder together in the dramatic society people are, I can assure you, amazed.' He heaved another of his theatrical sighs as if this gossip were being dragged out of him against his will. 'You may well be asking how the pair of them became notables, president, secretary and the like in the dramatic society, especially as neither had much knowledge of or skill at acting. Money is the answer. They contributed, both now, generously to the society. That was good. It kept the society well able to put on lavish productions with beautiful costumes, a new lighting system etc. etc. Both are comparatively rich. Powell is into property, and Arnold, a solicitor, is principal of a large and thriving firm, with offices in Beechnall, Leicester, Derby as well as Sutton where his grandfather first practised. Arnold came back to his grandparents' house about seven years ago and did it up. He'll be a very good secretary, I

24

don't doubt. One of his own secretaries will do the dull donkey work, while he sees that all arrangements, and especially finance, are in good order. But that's by the by. Once, five or six years ago, they were bitter enemies. Are you still with me?'

She nodded into the phone, murmured her interest.

'Arnold is what is called, in these parts as elsewhere, a ladies' man. And Mrs Powell was an attractive woman. Do you know her? Have you met her?'

'No, not really. I've seen her.'

'A few years ago it was the talk of the town. This was surprising because Arnold and Elizabeth Powell were rather cautious. Both were newish and I had the impression, right or wrong, that the affair had been going on before they settled here.'

'Did one or the other move so that they could be together?'

'That I don't know. Mrs Powell was madly keen on Arnold, who took every advantage of this.'

'Was there a Mrs Arnold?'

'There was, but she seemed to be prepared to put up with her husband's adultery.'

'So there was no talk of divorce?'

'It was said that Libby Powell would have left her husband at the drop of a hat, but Arnold wasn't having any. He was not prepared to leave his wife. They had a son with learning difficulties, whom he would not desert for any reason.'

'That's good,' she commented.

'Adulterers don't lose all sense of normality, you know. But the affair, for all their carefully cautious behaviour, was talked about. Powell was said to be near madness, threatening to his friends that he would kill Arnold. How serious that was I don't know. They never spoke, passed each other in the street, though again it's said that if Powell's wife was with him Arnold would raise his hat to her in a thoroughly histrionic manner, as if baiting Powell the cuckold. Then, about three years ago, they were suddenly allies, bosom friends. Nobody seemed to know why including myself. Whether Mrs Powell and Arnold lost interest in each other I can't say. Their behaviour in public together was, as always, beyond reproach. The word had got about, I guess, because Powell complained so long and so often to his cronies, and they passed the word round, couldn't keep their mouths shut.'

'So there was nothing in the rumours?' Alicia asked.

'I've no evidence one way or the other. I'd guess there was some truth in the stories. They were certainly widespread. And Powell's behaviour towards Arnold was very antagonistic.'

'Why didn't he throw her out?'

'He loved her. He felt he had a superior wife. She came from a good family, is a university graduate, was an excellent housewife.' He spoke seriously, as if instructing a child.

'They had no children?'

'Just the one. But perhaps it upset him to think she might have a child by some other man. Certainly I have it on good evidence that he was driven nearly insane by his wife's infidelities. What their life was like at home I can't say, I never heard any suggestion that he was violent with her. Close friends say that had he done so she would have left him. I don't think she was short of money. But there are other sorts of cruelties besides physical blows. I just don't know. At the height of the rumours he and his wife were out together at concerts, plays, meetings, she as serene as always. This caused comment among the wiseacres and their wives, and not always in favour of Mrs Powell. There she was, the adulterous wife, not a sign of guilt on her face, arm in arm with her husband as if there had never been a cross word or disagreement between them.'

'Perhaps', she said mischievously, 'there hadn't.'

'There is no first-hand evidence as far as I'm concerned. Maybe it's all talk and you shouldn't believe it.'

'But . . .' she mocked him.

'It has the ring of truth about it. I don't like either of them and so I'm perhaps only too ready to believe the worst.'

'Has Mrs Powell taken part in any of the Sutton productions?'

'Yes, but not successfully. It's odd to me. She's a very good-looking woman, with natural poise, but put her on the stage she becomes wooden. Even her voice changes for the worse. She must be very nervous, shy, fearful of making a fool of herself. I was quite shaken when I first saw her trying to act. It was embarrassing that a woman of such grace in ordinary life should be so awkward.'

'You sound as if you admire the lady.'

'I do, I do. She's impressive as herself. I was shaken when I saw how hamstrung she was on stage. Do you know, she seemed physically changed. I've seen that the other way round quite often when an ordinary-looking actor can become regal in a play, or a fine handsome man droop at will so that he's nothing like the impressive self he is in his everyday life. She, Libby, just looked awkward, walked across the stage as if she had risen from her deathbed, spoke like a strangled parrot. How anyone with such natural advantages could shed them so catastrophically, and so quickly, is beyond my imagination.'

'Have you never met anyone before who has had this difficulty?'

'Never. I've seen plenty of people who can't act. Why they join a dramatic society I don't know. There you are. But they are awkward in their ordinary lives. She could go on stage as she goes about the street and make an impression. It wouldn't be acting. She couldn't assume other kinds of character. I imagine her husband encouraged her to join the dramatic society, maybe forced her to, or said it would increase his chances as a notable president.'

'Would she help him out?'

'I guess so. Especially if there's anything in this Arnold story. She may think she owes him that.'

'Doesn't she realise how awful she is on stage?'

'She'll know she's not got much talent, but I doubt if she cottons on to how feeble she is compared with the effect she has on people off stage.'

'Do you not expect too much of her?'

'Maybe I do. Are you suggesting that I am very attracted to Mrs Powell?'

'I'm not suggesting anything, but it certainly seems so, now you mention it.'

Wicks spread his hands as if pacifying her. She could imagine it. His smile broadened attractively. He began to rub his knee violently as if to conjure up, like some Aladdin with a magic lamp, his next words. 'Do you know what I expect he'll do next?'

Alicia thought about this. She could not answer the question, nor understand why he had asked it.

'He, on prompting from Arnold, will send her round to see you to ask you to change your mind.'

'Why should they do that?'

'They think you are more likely to listen to her. They realise that they were ham-fisted in their attempt, calling in on a dark evening unannounced. Of course, this may not happen. I could think of one or two people outside the circle of the Sutton Players they could approach. What puzzles me is why they dropped in on you so clumsily.'

'Perhaps these people of yours are unavailable or unwilling.'

'Maybe. It's probable that they were impressed by Caldwell inviting you to be his assistant. That and your professor's recommendation.'

'I wonder how Arnold knows him.'

'Arnold's the sort who'll make it his business to introduce himself to anybody who is likely to be useful to him. But thanks for letting me know about this visit. It's intriguing. They wouldn't like to think I knew about it.'

'Why not?'

'I'm the enemy. They wouldn't like to think of me, well, poking into their mistakes, laughing at them, publishing them abroad.'

'Goodness.'

Her cliché, one word of surprise, stopped his talk. He carefully replaced the phone.

III

Mrs Powell did not attempt to get in touch with Alicia, who was not surprised. Raynor Wicks's guess was typical of the man. He made dull conversation bearable by unusual views, not . . . not *quite* outrageous, colourful suggestions that bore little connection with reality, but included to raise the flagging interest of the listener. Alicia thought badly of Wicks for using such procedures, meant to draw attention to himself. As a next-door neighbour he was unobtrusive. His house, some thirty yards away from hers, was never shaken by the heavy bass of pop, nor blasted by, say, Mahler, his favourite composer, she knew. He appeared occasionally at the dustbin, but never pottered in his garden, nor hung out washing. The ground behind his house was thick, impressively so, with shrubs, towering camellias, elaeagnus, pyrocantha, berberis, amalanchier and trees, apple, pear, old roses, a huge holly, flowering cherry; all kept pruned in their season by the old man who paid fortnightly visits to tend her flowers and lawn. Wicks had as few visitors as she did; she did not know why, for he seemed a sociable man. She had been told that he was a widower without children. He'd made her welcome to the place in a distant but cheerful way, and had offered to do any heavy bits of carrying for her.

Today, as she arrived back at about five, he had just parked his car outside his garage.

He waved a large hand. 'Back to the scene of the crime?' he asked.

'What crime is that?'

'Haven't you heard? Clarence Caldwell's housekeeper or whatever was set on last night just outside his house and left for dead. She's in hospital now, the Royal, very seriously ill.'

'Who's responsible? Do they know?'

'Not when last I heard. I had to come home this lunchtime and the road was alive with police cars.'

'Where's Mr Caldwell?'

'He's away. In London. Has been for a week or two.'

'Is she the lady who let us into his house?'

'I take it she is. I gave Mrs Gibbs a lift into Beechnall on my way back to school. She's a mine of information. The victim was, according to her, Clarence's housekeeper, who lives there all the time, even when he's away. She's an old actress from his theatre days. Her name is Megan Rhŷs-Williams. Does that name ring any bells with you? No, I suppose not. She'll be well before your time.' He pulled a rolled newspaper from his briefcase. 'Here's a picture of her, taken in her youth.' He unrolled the paper and showed her the first page. SAVAGE ATTACK ON SUTTON PENSIONER ran the headline. Alongside was a picture, rather blurred, of a personable young woman, head flirtatiously to one side, shoulders naked. 'Old age hasn't done her much good. Did you hear any screams last night? No, neither did I. The police will be coming round asking.'

'What time was this?'

'Ten o'clock or thereabouts. The old dear would go out for a walk every night about this time. She'd potter around the woods, according to Mrs Gibbs. She wouldn't see anything, especially last night, which was dark and raining a bit. I don't suppose she could. She wouldn't be seen by anybody. That's what mattered to her.'

'Were they robbers or muggers?'

'I don't know. She only got as far as the front gate, hadn't opened it even when they set about her. They must have been already inside the front garden. They robbed her, or she carried no money, it appears.'

'And the police don't know who they are?'

'Not according to the paper. I wouldn't be surprised if they were kids, from those new houses just inside Sutton.'

'Ten o'clock at night?' she asked.

'Some of them are out till all hours of the night. I don't know what their parents are up to. It's unusual that anything happens as far out as this. The occasional car burnt and that's about it. There's been nothing untoward during the short time you've been here, has there? Not that the police would want to come out here at that time for anything less than a murder.'

The houses nearby rocked with gossip during the next few days. The local papers dealt with the attack on the front page for three days, while PC Waller ponderously pursued his investigations. As Wicks cynically said, 'They'd learn more from him than ever he would from them.' It became clear that Mrs Rhŷs-Williams had set off for her late-night stroll, had dropped the catch on the door behind her, but had been knocked over before she had taken a dozen steps down the path. The old lady was badly bruised, but made a rapid recovery in hospital; she did not seem concussed, could remember her assailants, three in number, hooded, all of medium height and build. They had blacked both her eyes and spoilt her face, puffy now, with a cut on the left cheek. She had screamed and fallen, and had lain as if unconscious on the ground. The men did not speak; all wore gloves. They had made no attempt to force an entry into the house, but had moved quietly away. She had heard the clink of the iron front gate, then the starting of a car engine. It had driven off towards Sutton. No, she had no enemies. She had only lived in Mr Caldwell's house for a few months. He had been feeling unwell and had asked her to stay with him in the Hanged Man's House to see that he came to no harm. She had scrambled up to her feet, staggered back into the house, where she had rung the police.

All this information percolated to the local inhabitants from PC Waller.

Caldwell did not return. Nothing was missing from the house and Megan, a tough old bird, seemed back to normality in no time. She did not complain, nor even talk about her injuries to such neighbours as she met in the streets.

Wicks made an early-evening call each day on Alicia to enquire if all was well and to retail local gossip. He did not stay long, would not take a glass of sherry, but made his enquiries briskly, then told what he had learnt from Mrs Gibbs, PC Waller, other tattlers and the local newspaper, which she never saw. Alicia was grateful for his consideration for her, even enjoyed these visits and invited him to lunch one Saturday.

The police suspected a gang of young men from Beechnall whose living was involved with drugs. That they had driven the seven miles out from the city and then committed no theft was unusual. They would not have thought twice of manhandling an old lady, but to leave without combing the house for silverware, mobile phones, television sets and computers was unlike them. They were rogues without conscience, Wicks reported, but careful in their criminality, quick at theft and even sharper at selling the spoils.

They had been dropped on for questioning, but with one

exception seemed to have watertight alibis. The detectives had next turned their attention to the criminal element in Sutton, mostly youths with nothing to do in their spare time, all of whom seemed to have been lawfully occupied on the night of the attack. Ironically, one of these had been employed by the wife of the policeman on the night in question helping his father to do some decorating of a spare room in her house. Further than this the police had failed to make enquiries.

'Do you know,' Wicks said, pushing his plate forward having done rapid justice to an excellent beef casserole, 'it crosses my mind that this might be connected with the quarrels inside the dramatic society.'

'Powell and Arnold, d'you mean?' she said, carefully finishing her main course.

'Not in person. But I wouldn't put it past Powell and his cronies. It's said that when Arnold was conducting his affair with Mrs Powell he was twice mugged.'

'You mean he employs thugs to attack his enemies?'

'He knows some very dubious characters in the building trade.'

'Anyway, Mr Caldwell was away.'

'They wouldn't know. He's been away nearly three weeks now and I had no idea. He's not the sort to trumpet his comings and goings.'

'But why his housekeeper? I'm sure she had no part in the decisions of the dramatic society.'

'No, but they turned up in the darkness and when Megan Rhŷs-Williams stumbled out into the dark they set about her. Perhaps by mistake, or perhaps they thought it would heap trouble on Caldwell's head to have his housekeeper half killed in his front garden. I'm sure it would. You'll notice he's stayed away all this time while the investigation is going on. He doesn't like to be put out.'

'Have you mentioned this to the police?'

'Certainly not. I've no proof. I'm not daft enough to stir the waters in a case like this. I've no evidence.'

'You wouldn't put it past Powell, though.'

'I don't know. There's nothing I know at first hand connecting him to this.'

Alicia, clearing away the dishes and returning with the pudding, did not know what to make of this. She wondered if Wicks was beginning to spread a web of rumour against his enemies. Why he

32

thought she would pass on such unlikely ideas she did not know. Wicks she had regarded as a typical pillar of their community. A man in his forties, though looking younger, a widower whose wife had died soon after he came to the district, he taught at the old Grammar School in Beechnall. He attended services at the parish church in Sutton about once a month and on other high days, according to his own account, and kept the new vicar who regularly visited him for advice with his feet on the earth. He was still fit enough to referee a senior rugby game, though not regularly. He was said to be rewriting and updating the history of the school published just before the Second World War. He lived on his own and his name was untainted by scandal. Ask him to help you out, be it physically or mentally, he'd readily agree.

The vicar, on his single visit to Alicia, enquired how well she got on with her neighbour and said, after she had praised Wicks, 'He would do well to marry again. I did not know his wife, of course. She was well before my time, but he seems to me the sort of man in need of a woman's influence. He has fingers in too many pies for his own good. Such people are the salt of the earth according to some because they'll tackle any sort of voluntary job and make something of it. But I've found, in my admittedly short time as a clergyman, that such people are not as good, as rounded, personalities as they might be if they had a wife and family with all the calls that such a lifestyle demands. Raynor is prone to obsessions which, let's say, a wife's pregnancy or a child's illness would keep in proportion.'

'I don't know him well enough,' Alicia had replied coldly.

'I'm not complaining,' the vicar said. 'He's thoroughly useful in many spheres. School, church, town matters, acts of kindness to individuals.'

'I'm sure.'

Here the vicar had given her up. He had cordially invited her to join with them at St Peter's Church whenever she felt like it and made gracelessly for his car. Alicia was not impressed. The vicar, in his early thirties she guessed, let his tongue rattle too freely. She wondered what he was saying about her to the next parishioner he called on. 'I've just visited a very superior young woman, with an Oxford First and researching for a doctorate at Beechnall. She must have money because she appears to own her own house, a pricey place just outside Sutton . . . But I could get nothing out of her. She spoke as if I was intruding on her privacy.' She hoped that

33

was the impression she gave to any newcomer and sat smiling in satisfaction. She smiled ever more broadly when she considered that the vicar, in truth, might be a man of tact and discretion. He might even be falling in love with her.

Wicks, on his lunch visit, sat with her for another hour after they had washed the dishes. He had insisted that he help with this chore. After that, they finished off the wine she had opened. One glass was enough for her, but he had no trouble emptying the bottle. It made no difference to either his speech or his behaviour. He obviously enjoyed the wine and said so. She rather admired such a man. No secrets were glibly let out; he laid not one lecherous finger on her. He was the ideal guest.

A day later he called over to her from the garden. 'I've news for you,' he said. 'They've found somebody to direct *Twelfth Night*.'

'Who's that?'

'I don't suppose you'll know him. He's from Newark. John Rattenbury. He's an ex-actor. Runs a bookshop now.'

'Do you know him?'

'I've met him a time or two. He took over his father-in-law's shop when the old man died. He's said to be making quite a go of it. He's keeping Caldwell's cast, says that time's getting short, that he should be pressing on with rehearsals and not wasting it holding auditions again. So we've all been invited to attend the first rehearsal on Monday next.'

'What sort of man is he?'

'He can't claim to have been as successful as Caldwell as an actor. But he's had experience with professionals.'

'So you're going to play Orsino, then?'

'Yes. I thought about it and agreed to do it.'

'How did you learn all this?'

'Last evening Alfred Arnold honoured me with a call. He was pleased as Punch with himself that he'd discovered Rattenbury. And according to him pretty well everybody chosen by Caldwell has promised to work with him. Like me, they didn't want to let the festival down, leave it without its main cultural attraction. Arnold seemed really delighted with himself.'

'And Mr Caldwell? What will he think?' Alicia pressed him.

'I don't suppose he'll care one way or the other. I guess he'd just about had enough of the Sutton Dramatic Society and was only too pleased to find an excuse to drop out.'

'How did he come to take it up in the first place?'

34

'Oh, he was born in these parts, was an old boy of the Beechnall Grammar School. And twenty-five years ago – he'd be in his early fifties then – he found that he'd the leisure time and the money to do a bit for his native parts. It was always said that the theatre and film industry had not treated him, or regarded him, as highly as he considered they should. He'd done well for a provincial and had been careful with his money. He was appearing on the London stage when he first took up with us here. He enjoyed the fuss people made of him. He bought a house here, but his wife was not happy, and later she was taken ill and went off to one of the London hospitals, where she died. They all thought, then, that he'd sell his house and desert us. He was busy with his own career, which meant the locals had to rehearse on Sundays and at short notice at all sorts of odd times. It's been easier of late because his own career didn't make such demands on his time. He's working now, when he's nearly eighty, though he needn't. His father left him a fair amount of money and his wife, who was a really wealthy woman, saw to it that he needn't do a day's work for the rest of his life. Not that he bothered about that. He moved on. It was his ambition to do well. I guess that's why he's in London now playing some cameo part.'

'Will he be cross with you all? For joining this new man?'

'I don't think so for a minute.'

'Rattenbury's not a confrontational character, is he?'

'I've no idea what he's like to work with.' Wicks paused and rubbed his hands roughly, noisily, together. 'And while we're at it, there's one more snippet of scandal going the rounds.'

'Is there?' She tried to sound bored.

'It's said that years ago Clarence Caldwell had a torrid affair with Megan Rhŷs-Williams. And that it dragged on for years even after his wife died. Megan, it appears, thought he'd marry her, but he didn't. She never gave up hope, that's why she came up here to look after him.'

'That's recent, isn't it? A few months at the outside?'

'Yes. That's about it. The two of them don't get on, it appears. They were and are always rowing.'

'They weren't the evening when we went there.'

'No. They must have been on their best behaviour for us.' He laughed at his comment. 'But other people have heard them at it. The old girl used to shriek at him and throw things.'

'Is there evidence?'

'Their cleaning woman vouches for all this. A Miss Price from the town. She's a decent, middle-aged woman, a Methodist, not much given to tittle-tattle. She's there three times a week. And the milkman. Well, you know him. He's not the imaginative sort.'

'And?'

'The story goes that he drove back and knew exactly what time Megan went out for her nightly walk, and lay in wait for her, with some hired ruffian, who did the beating.'

'I thought there were three of them?'

'That's Meg's story. But the suddenness of the attack on a dark night may have confused her.' He rubbed his stubbly face. 'I can't say.'

'And why did he attack her? To warn her, or to make her feel unsafe?'

'Something like that.'

'Did she recognise him?'

'No. Nobody spoke.'

'Then why blame Caldwell?'

'Oh, people put two and two together. I know what you're going to say. Why come himself? Why couldn't he just send hired thugs to do it for him?'

'I don't believe any of this. People hereabouts let their tongues wag too freely.'

'You're probably right. There's no evidence at all to connect Caldwell to this attack. And there are quite a few people about who dislike him, and would harm him if they could. But I just pass the story on. Perhaps unwisely.'

He nodded slowly, as if approving the wisdom of his words, and walked away.

IV

Alicia learnt from one of Wicks's over-the-fence briefings that rehearsals for *Twelfth Night* had begun and that John Rattenbury had made favourable impressions all round. He was, it appeared, a man of ideas but by no means a bully. Clarence Caldwell had not yet returned to the village.

Back at the university Alicia found a note in her pigeonhole from Professor Conway asking her to call on him. This was unusual, as she was not due to see him for a consultation on her work for another three weeks. She gave him, and herself, time to wake up before knocking timidly at his door at eleven o'clock.

Christopher Conway sat at his desk, wild-eyed and running his fingers through his already rumpled hair. He seemed pleased to see her. 'Oh, sit down for a minute, will you, Alicia? I need to recover.'

Both sat still, neither speaking. He finally spoke. 'These bloody administrators,' he said. She smiled. In spite of his hair standing on end, he was spotless, in a three-piece suit of exemplary cut. His tie and shirt matched and were immaculate. His shoes, hidden from view behind his desk, shone polished she guessed. He drummed with his right hand. 'We've hardly been here a fortnight,' he said, 'and I've three first-year students talking about running back home or committing suicide, and the high-ups expect me to do something about it.'

'Are they homesick?' she asked.

'I guess so. I shall see them this afternoon. I'm looking at the bits and pieces we have about them. They're all clever. I don't doubt this. But they've never been away from home. They don't seem to grasp that this is a university, not an infant school. They have a freshers' week when they can get used to the place without being bothered by academic work. I think they'd be better employed copying out pages of a dictionary. They'd be bored, but at least they'd have learnt something. Were you homesick in your first week or two at Oxford?'

'Yes. Terribly. It all seemed so different from home or school.'

'At least you didn't go running with your complaints to the powers that be.'

'I was too scared. I lay on my bed and cried.'

'I'd never have guessed it. You always looked and sounded so confident. As if you owned the place.' He stroked his forehead. 'What shall I tell them?'

'That it will wear off in a week or two. Though I remember one girl in my year who never settled down.'

'Who was that?'

'Helen Savage.'

Conway shook his head to indicate he'd not heard the name before. 'Did she leave?'

'No. She stuck it. And worked hard. Took a good degree in mathematics.'

'Oh, I think I remember something about it now you give me a detail or two. She was about your year, was she? I was rather stressed – that's the term – at the time. With my divorce. Some of my colleagues were not very sympathetic. I had the impression that by divorcing my wife I was disgracing the college.' He looked up questioningly.

'I knew nothing about that.'

'No, we all live our little lives cut off from the rest of the world.'

'You godlike figures had no domestic, minor troubles. Or so it seemed to us new students.'

'Divorce didn't seem minor at the time. That I can tell you.' He laughed. It was now over and done with. 'Do you know a man called Alfred Arnold? He's a solicitor and a prime mover in the Sutton Dramatic Society. He questioned me about your qualifications to produce *Twelfth Night*. I didn't know what to say, because I didn't know whether you wanted the job or not. Later he told me you'd flatly refused. From what he said they are a contentious lot up there.'

'He's one to talk.'

'I guess he can hold his corner. The North Midlands seems a quarrelsome sort of place. I found it to some small extent among my colleagues here. They looked on me with suspicion when I arrived, expecting some fancy ideas from me, all attached to high prices that would eat into their allocations. The vice-chancellor teased them on those lines. Now that I've been here for two full years they see I'm harmless, even reasonable, so we're all good friends. Until I step out of line.'

'I didn't realise that things were so awkward.'

'You were a ministering angel to me. I could talk only to you from time to time, whether about your research – and you soon knew more about it than I did – or over a cup of tea. Then I felt at ease. You did me good.'

'Surely your colleagues were no worse than those at Oxford?'

'Probably not. But I'd grown used to their ways. Which reminds me, I've acquired a house.'

'In Beechnall?'

'Yes. Burlington Road. Far too big, but you get plenty for your money up here. I'm full of it, because I signed the contract only on Monday.' He smiled. 'As is usual with me, I did it with hesitation. That's the thing I do best. I totter on the brink. And solicitors work at a drop-dead pace that suits me.'

She could see that the professor was pleased with himself. He made two cups of instant coffee, claiming he couldn't stand the mid-morning racket in the Senior Common Room. He moved from behind his desk to drink with her, apologising that he had no biscuits, as he was, surprisingly, trying to slim.

'When will you move?' she asked.

'The solicitors say it will be about a month.'

'Can you cook?'

'In a simple way. Marian, my ex-wife, was good at the culinary art, almost theatrical. And talking about theatres, I might as well mention why I called you up here. Would you like to review a couple of little books about the eighteenth-century theatre? I know you did me an essay on it when you were an undergraduate from which I learnt a good deal. I ran across the editor of the *TLS* this last weekend and he asked me if I knew anybody capable of writing intelligently and interestingly about the topic. These are a couple of American books and I'm sure they'll add to your knowledge, since you are deep into the theatre. Or aren't you?'

'Depends how they look at it.'

'You don't want to do it?'

'I wouldn't mind.'

'Make sure, then, that I have your address before you leave, and I'll ring the editor this afternoon. He'll be in. He always is.'

'He'll include instructions, won't he? How many words and when he wants it in.'

'I'll tell him, but he'll be meticulous.'

Fifteen minutes later Alicia left the professor's room feeling pleased with herself. Conway always seemed ready to put useful work into her hands. As to the 'ministering angel, thou', she concluded that he was exaggerating to please her. Behind his sophistication, tremendously wide reading and critical acumen he was a simple soul. She set about her day's work with zest; life was worth living.

That weekend she set out for a Sunday morning walk. It had rained for two days but now the sun shone. She walked the road leading towards Clarence Cuthbert Caldwell's house. She wondered about the derivation of his Christian name. Was the 'cuth' connected with the 'couth' of uncouth? Suddenly into her head came a derivation once offered by a fellow student, a lad with a fascination for byways or unfamiliar knowledge who had suggested that it was a decisive name for a person who dodged military service, a shirker, a lead-swinger. She must look it up in a dictionary. Odd that she had not thought of it before, even when she was in Caldwell's company. As she turned this over in her head she noticed, a hundred yards ahead, Caldwell himself approaching her. His pace was by no means brisk, but he twirled his walking stick theatrically. When he was closer she wished him a bright good morning. He looked up from his contemplation of the road to stare at her, brow furrowed. He doesn't recognise me, she thought. He stopped, leaning on his stick.

'Alicia Smallwood,' she said, helping him out.

'I knew that. The expert on Shakespearean criticism.'

'Thank you,' she answered ironically.

They spoke about the beauty of the October morning. He said he could not sit indoors reading the paper at such a time.

After further chit-chat of this sort, she asked, 'Have you been working in London? That's the rumour in these parts.'

'I have. I had a small part in a film. I knew the producer years ago. He likes to hand out largesse to such as me. It replenishes my coffers. The trouble is it takes them so long. The main actors have no idea how to match body movement to speech. They can't even enunciate clearly. That means constant repeats for them and for the bit-part players like me days on end sitting about watching these young celebrities going over the same small piece of dialogue, time and time again, without one whit of improvement.'

'That must have been boring.'

'It certainly meant I was in London long enough for my small parts in two small films. I comforted myself by telling myself that I was earning money.'

'Was the shooting of the film out of doors?'

'On the whole. Three of my five snippets were under cover.'

'You'll be sorry to be back?'

'No. I'd had enough. Besides that I wanted to see how Megan was shaping after that attack.'

'Is she well?'

'Yes. Unmarked. Unmoved, as far as I can tell. She's a tough old bird.'

'Have the police made any further progress with their enquiries?'

'According to Megan, your local PC says they've a good idea of the thugs, but as they didn't go inside the house and steal anything there aren't any clues to help. And she only saw them in the dark, and as they were wearing hoods she couldn't identify them at all. Your man, I've talked to him once, said they'll be caught in the end because they'll make a mistake before too long.'

'It must have been frightening for Mrs Rhŷs-Williams.'

'Yes. But she's physically strong. She was an actress, you know, and a fine-looking girl. She's let herself go recently. She married and left the stage, but since her husband, a police inspector, died about ten–fifteen years back, she's had to struggle. She had kept herself neat in the process. I came across her and offered her a place at my house, and she jumped, though that's hardly the word, at it. She's glad to know that she has a warm bedroom at night, and square meals and somebody to talk to. She doesn't seem to want to do anything exciting. Sitting at home, keeping the place tidy satisfies her.'

'Did you act together?'

'The answer to that is "Yes". We were in several plays together but it meant little. We knew each other, but not very well. I suppose the local tattlers have her docketed as my mistress. That was not the case in any serious sense, though we were a promiscuous lot, I must confess. After she married I saw little of her. But I had reason to be grateful to her.'

He paused, as if expecting a comment. She obliged with murmurs expressing interest.

'She saved my life,' he continued. 'It was just before her marriage. We were playing in Scarborough. A Somerset Maugham play if I remember rightly. And a few of us went swimming one afternoon. The water was cold; we weren't very wise. I was suddenly seized with a most horrendous cramp, which left me pretty well paralysed and in agony. The others realised I was in trouble but only Megan did anything about it. She was a strong swimmer, and somehow she paddled me ashore and then set about reviving me. She knew the drill, had passed lifesaving exams at school. Our digs were luckily quite close and she hurried me back there.'

'You were none the worse for the accident?'

'No. I soon recovered. Or could act as if I had. I thanked her. She seemed to think little of what she had done. But I knew if she hadn't been there and taken action I should have drowned. She married and left the stage. Rhŷs-Williams was her maiden name. She now became Mrs Harris.'

'She had children?'

'I believe so. Two. I'm not sure of any of this because I lost touch with her.'

'How did you get together again?'

'I was playing in *The Tempest* at the Cambridge Theatre in London, and she came round to my dressing room. I didn't recognise her. My wife was dead, as was her husband, and her children had grown up and scattered. She was working as house-cleaner-companion to some old man, a retired diamond merchant. She did not live in, but kept her own apartment and told me how much she enjoyed having such a position. I said it was a pity that I had not known about her job seeking, for it was what I needed. I said that if she wanted a change at any time she was to write to me.'

'And she did?'

'Eight years later when I was as near retirement as I'll ever be. I asked her to come up here to Sutton and look at the place. She liked it. It was a godsend to me. My health has been dodgy. She stayed with me for a month and accepted the job. She didn't sell her flat, in case we found the arrangement didn't work out.'

'And when was this?'

'Less than a year ago. She came for the first negotiations at Christmas and it started badly. She'd only been here a month or two when she had a really bad bout of flu. I had to nurse her, look after her. I won't say I did it well but she's tough and she recovered. When she was better she never bothered any more about her appearance, and wore any old clothes and left her hair uncombed, and never used cosmetics. Hence her present reputation as an old witch. I've mentioned it to her several times, but she takes not a blind bit of notice. "I see nobody that matters," she says. "I go nowhere, so I'll dress comfortably. It takes time and effort and money for a woman of my age to make her appearance anything like acceptable in decent society." I say to her, "But I see you every day." And do you know how she answers that? "You've seen me stark naked, as I have you. You know the quality of what you've got. So what does it matter what covers me as long as I'm warm?"'

'She's healthy, is she?'

'As a butcher's dog. She keeps the house marvellously clean and cooks very tasty, plain meals. Nothing out of the way. No cordon bleu. But just what I want.' He paused frequently between each section of his commendation. 'She doesn't pay much attention to my advice. She walks out every night in the dark. I warn her, "You don't know these days who's hanging about." But I might just as well talk to myself.'

'Even after this last attack?'

'Yes. I tell her to learn from it, but she laughs and says she has. "Next time," she says, "I'll be ready for them."'

'And will she be?'

'She might well carry a long kitchen knife with her. And she'd use it.'

'Goodness.'

'Oh, she's a character. Strong as a horse. And if she stabbed some mugger and he died, she'd feel no regrets, she says. "One more person the world can well do without." She'd defend herself to her last button. She hardly troubles me at all. She shows me the next week's menu on Thursday before we go together to the supermarket in Beechnall.'

'You go together?'

'We do. She has her wits about her in the shop. While I'm trundling the trolley round, she has a sharp eye wide open for bargains or novelties. She makes my time at the meal table that bit more interesting. And orders sweeps and gardeners and window cleaners, and if they don't do the job properly or turn up late and keep her waiting, my word, she gives them the length of her tongue. And I can easily afford her wages. And she's happy. She's let off her London home at some fancy price. Of course, that's not all sweetness. Some tenants are not all they should be. She knew that and has a clause in their contract that she or the agent can inspect the place twice a year.'

'Does she go up to London?'

'She's been to town once while she's been living with me. She dressed up and oh, what a change. She had her hair permed in Beechnall the day before. Her back was as straight as a guardsman's. You should have seen her. I don't say I quite fancied her but you know what I mean. She gave the tenants notice, I believe, as their contract entitled her to do. Now their replacement is a couple of widows, elderly ladies and a nephew. An odd combination two widows and a nephew, out there, that's what people are like these days.' He patted his chest. 'So that's how we stand.'

'She's just what you needed.'

'There's not much affection between us. More convenience. We make each other's life that bit easier. What I fear is that the balance might change. As it did when she had that bout of flu. I managed, but only just. And I wondered often enough what I'd let myself in for. Now she's fit and energetic we're both suited. But if I'm ill or disabled, or she is, God knows what will happen. I must go into Beechnall and see my solicitor, and have my will changed in her favour.'

'Good,' said Alicia, so fervently that he showed surprise.

'I've enjoyed our talk. You must come up and chat to me about Shakespeare or Addison and Steele or whoever it is you're researching. I don't look forward to the winter weather when I can't get out of the house. Old invalids like me should be outside walking every day of the week; it improves, or so the experts claim, one's circulation.'

'You're looking well, I thought,' she said.

'That's what old men hate. To be told they look well, or young, or handsome when they feel like death. Flattery can't disguise the pain, the malaise.' He raised his hat. 'I'll give you a ring if I may. Is any day more convenient than the others?'

Alicia outlined when she was free, but before she had finished his hat was back on his head and he was on his way. She watched his retreat. From the back he stumbled, it appeared, at every step, but he gave the impression of a kind of rolling vigour. She wondered where he was going at this time of the morning and smiled at her own curiosity. He had made a hundred yards of progress before she turned from the place where she had stood.

44

Not fifty yards further on she glimpsed Megan Rhŷs-Williams struggling up the path from Caldwell's house. Alicia waited until the old woman had reached the road, then greeted her cheerfully. Megan stared almost resentfully at the girl, but managed a muffled reply.

'Are you looking for Mr Caldwell?' Alicia asked. 'He went that way.' She pointed.

'No, I'm not.' Ungraciously.

'I was surprised to see him out so early. Does he often take a morning stroll?'

'No.'

'He seemed quite cheerful when he spoke to me.'

'You never know with him.'

'Oh?'

'Mr Caldwell gets crooked ideas.'

'Crooked?'

'The sort nobody in his right mind would entertain.'

She was already en route, in the same direction as Caldwell.

'Have a good walk,' Alicia called, but the stiff old back, in its creased man's mackintosh, steadfastly ignored her.

Alicia, shaking her head, marched on. She puzzled over the old people and their errands. It was a beautiful morning, with the late October sun bright, but not warm and likely to tempt the old out of a comfortable house. She walked with her head down, her mind puzzled. From a considerable distance she heard sounds. A bend in the road and overhanging tree branches, still leafy, prevented her from seeing who approached. She had expected to meet no one at this time of a Sunday morning. The footsteps ceased but she pushed on.

There, at the roadside as if to meet her, stood Raynor Wicks, hands deep in his anorak pockets. 'Well, well, well,' he called out. 'Look who's here.'

'Good morning,' she replied. 'All the thespians are out this Sabbath.'

'Such as?'

'Mr Caldwell, his Megan and now you. All going along in the same direction.'

'But not to the same destination.'

'I don't know where any of you is going,' she replied.

Wicks pushed back his cuff to consult his wristwatch. 'Caldwell will be going to church.'

'In Sutton?'

'No, in Beechnall. There's an early small bus from Sutton, which picks up people round the villages. Quite a few elderly people use it. I believe some man at the church organises it.'

'I didn't know Mr Caldwell was a religious person.'

'I don't know about his beliefs, but he goes to the parish church, St Mary's, once a month, either on the first or second Sunday. And on high days and holidays, Easter, Christmas, Whitsuntide.'

'You surprise me.'

'They've a very fine choir. The music master of my school took it over a year or two ago and he's done marvels with it. He's a brilliant organist, too, they tell me. He arranges celebrity concerts on Saturdays and tempts all sorts of notables down.'

'Is Mr Caldwell a musician?'

'Not as such. But he's very interested. He has a large and very fine collection of records and CDs. I know because I helped him sort it out and catalogue it a year or two ago. It took us long enough. But he played music all the time, and on both days I was there Megan's predecessor fed us beautifully.'

'And the vicar?' she asked.

'Said to be very lively. Oddly enough, he started his working life as an actor. I often think there's not a great deal of difference between the pulpit and the stage.'

'A parson has to provide his own words.'

'To some extent, yes. Anyhow, that's where Caldwell's off to this morning.'

'It's neither the first nor the second Sunday today.'

'No, I suppose not.' Wicks looked somewhat abashed. 'I may be wrong, then. If it's otherwise I can't begin to guess where it is he'd be bound for.'

'I didn't think of Mr Caldwell as a religious man in any shape or form.'

'As I tell you I don't know either. He's never raised the matter with me. But that's like this part of the world. Sutton is a village with hardly anything to say in its favour. Beechnall will take it over before too long, if I'm to believe all I hear. Yet you'll find all sorts of people here. There's one man who's a sculptor and has made a name for himself nationally, if not internationally. And you ask yourself what he's doing in a drop-dead place like Sutton. I can't answer you.'

'Is he an old man?'

'No, not really. Perhaps fifty.' Wicks suddenly laughed. 'And here we are, the notables of the very outskirts of Sutton, all abroad together of a Sunday morning.'

'It's such a fine day.'

'I've been out since 7.30 and I must be getting back to my breakfast.'

'Aren't you hungry?'

'No. I could easily wait for my lunch.'

'Do you know what it is yet?'

'Yes. Sunday is my vegetarian day. I shall go back and scrape my potatoes and carrots, and search out a tin of cannellini beans and chop up my onions, celery and whatsoever else is knocking about in the larder, and boil them up, and make a topping of cheese and tinned tomatoes. It sounds complicated' – he looked quizzical at her bemused expression – 'but it doesn't take long.' He raised a finger to show he hadn't yet finished. 'I shall cook far too much for one man's lunch and so the rest will go into the liquidiser and make an excellent soup for my dinner tomorrow night. I don't know which I like better. I think perhaps it's the soup.'

'No wonder you're up so early in the day.'

'I wish I weren't. I'm an insomniac. I'm lucky if I manage four or five hours in the night.'

'Aren't you tired next morning?'

'All day. And if I take a sleeping tablet I feel kiboshed.'

'I don't know that word.'

'Old-fashioned slang. "To put the kibosh" on something is to stop something, to dispose of it.'

'And isn't there anything the doctor can do for you?'

'I begin to doubt it.'

'Is there a name for your disease?'

'Depression. I'm a depressive.'

'Do you know that's the last thing I'd think you suffered from. And I understand these days that medics have some pretty powerful drugs they can use to circumvent it.'

'May well be, but they haven't succeeded in my case.'

'Have they tried?'

'Yes. I don't know how hard. Perhaps they think my depression is too mild to bother with.'

'They haven't said that, have they?'

'Not to my face, at least.'

They stood in the bright October morning by the piles of pale golden leaves at the side of the road.

'Are you going much further?' he asked.

'Not really. It's time I got back home. I like to keep either Saturday or Sunday free from my university work and yesterday, Saturday, I slogged away all day. So I please myself today. I'd like to walk as far as Allsop's Farm, then I'll turn.'

'If you don't mind, I'll accompany you. Or have you some deep thinking to do?'

'No, I'll be glad to have you.'

'And I shall be delighted to get along at a good lick. When I feel down in the mouth, I go at a snail's pace. I drag my feet. Not that I notice this particularly until somebody walking at a moderate speed passes me and when I look up half a minute later she – and it usually is a she – is at least fifty yards ahead of me. That does nothing for my state of mind, I can tell you.'

They made good time down to the farmhouse and outbuildings, and there she gave the word to turn about. 'I usually finish here,' she said. 'Just a bit further down the road's filthy from the cows crossing even on fine days like this.'

They talked easily and Alicia enjoyed his company. He questioned her about her research and asked why she had chosen the eighteenth century. 'At your age,' he said, 'I'd little time for the literature of that period. Byron and Keats I admired. Even Wordsworth. But Pope and Dryden I thought nothing of, or never thought about at all.'

She explained that she had been tutored in part at Oxford by a clever young man who was working for a D.Phil. on the theatre of the late seventeenth and eighteenth centuries and she had picked up some of his enthusiasm.

'What's he doing now?'

'He got his doctorate, but there was no place for him at Oxford. I believe he teaches at one of the colleges at London University.'

'He must have been a good teacher.'

'Oh, yes. And very handsome.'

'You were in love with him, were you?'

'I ought to have been, but I don't think I was. And he made no advances to me.'

'The more fool he.'

'Thank you, kind sir, she said.' Alicia, with a simper.

They went along at a spanking pace and he showed no signs of the slow motion he claimed threatened his perambulations. He talked without shortness of breath, even accompanied what he was saying with eloquent hand movements.

'As I get older I admire Pope more and more. I see now what a master of words and metre and rhythm he is. When I was younger I thought that he had chosen a medium, the heroic couplet, that limited its users, but now I have come to realise how brilliantly he uses the limitations of his kind of poetry to show how versatile, how outstandingly fine his judgement was. Do you like eighteenth-century poems?'

'Yes. One of my favourites is Dr Johnson's "The Vanity of Human Wishes".'

'A good poem, with all the seriousness that he could muster. Did you first read it at school?'

'Yes.'

'So did I. It pleases me that schools somewhere aren't afraid of such verse. When I look at the present Eng. Lit. syllabuses I wonder why the examiners choose books, mainly modern, contemporary, that is, which the students could read for themselves.'

'It's interest,' she said.

'That's what they say. But they should be examined on something that they needed to puzzle over, that stretched them, at least for A Level.'

'Or something that's memorable.'

'Perhaps, though I'm not altogether certain of that. I can remember popular songs my father sang. He was a doctor, a serious man, yet he used to sing the popular songs of his youth. He was the last man you'd expect to do that, but these were pieces he'd sing when he was immersed at some task out in his workshop. He was very good with his hands. And I'd watch him and listen. One went something like this:

'Dancing with my shadow, feeling kind o' blue,
   I'm dancing with my shadow and making believe it's you.
Somewhere in a corner, nothing else to do,
   I'm dancing with my shadow, and making believe it's you.

'Now, neither words nor tune is especially memorable, yet he . . . and I can't think for a minute that he ever had feelings like these, or if he had would have expressed them. So what's memorable about them? Yet he remembered them and so do I.'

'You admired your father, I take it?'

'As a boy, yes, I did. Later we were at loggerheads. He thought I neither spoke nor acted seriously.' He blew out breath. 'That choosing arts subjects for sixth-form studies was a sign of foolishness or frivolity. I think he would have liked me to follow him into medicine.'

'I wouldn't mind being a medico. Being able to cure people must give one a tremendous lift.'

'But not telling them they have only a short time to live.'

'That will only apply to a small minority of cases for most doctors.'

'You're quite right. That's my depression speaking.'

Alicia quickly changed the subject: 'How's *Twelfth Night* shaping?'

'Pretty well. We'll put on a fair performance.'

'And the new producer?'

'Rattenbury is all right. He doesn't waste time in rehearsals. I don't think Shakespeare is exactly his cup of tea. He'd prefer Noël Coward or Terence Rattigan. But he knows what he's about.'

'He's not as good as Caldwell?'

'Different. Caldwell could show you what he wanted. If you made a hash of a speech, he'd do it for you, more often than not referring to the book, but from memory. You weren't supposed to copy him exactly, but I found it extremely helpful. Some didn't, but that's always the case with dramatic societies. Some of them can't or won't profit from advice.'

'Why doesn't Rattenbury seem at home with Shakespeare?'

'He hasn't done much, I guess. After drama school he went into repertory and they don't do too much Shakespeare nowadays. Too expensive. Needs too large a cast. As long as you've learnt your lines and can make yourself heard all over the theatre, he'll be satisfied. And there are one or two in the society who are really talented, and they'll carry the rest of us. The girl who plays Viola is exceptionally good.'

'Is she an ex-pro?'

'No, I don't think so. Works on computers. But she's just naturally talented.'

'Has she done a lot of acting?'

'Yes. At school and in London where she worked. She's not been here as long as you. Caldwell thought highly of her. We're lucky. In fact, all the women are pretty good. Or at least much better than us men.'

Wicks spoke with a cheerful ferocity, intent on catching her interest. When they reached his house he invited her in for a cup of coffee. She accepted, not having been further into his home than the conservatory, which covered the back door of the house hidden away from her own.

He led her into the sitting room and left her as he made the drinks.

Alicia sat, astounded by the decoration of the room. The walls were dark blue and covered, not evenly but plentifully, with golden stars. The open fireplace was also gold, as were the wide frames of the large mirror and the five pictures. The effect was theatrical, but stunning, dark, striking, strange. Even on this bright morning the place seemed night-bound, rich, sombre, brooding. She was impressed, but told herself this was the last place she'd want to rest in if she were a depressive.

When he returned with the coffee he asked if she was comfortable.

'Yes, thanks,' she said. 'I was just admiring this room.'

'You like it, do you?'

'It's very unusual.'

'I'll say. That was my wife. She had ideas.'

'Was she a trained interior designer?'

'Trained? No, except insofar as she had taught herself, mainly from books, and looking round other people's work.'

He poured the coffee and then, walking behind her, suddenly switched on the lights. A chandelier of gold in the middle of the ceiling blazed. Immediately the character of the room was changed. The dark blue became brighter and reflected the electric light of the dozen bulbs. The stars, now dimmed, seemed less menacing as they lost their grotesque shapes. She noticed, for the first time, that the carpet, which felt deep beneath her feet as she sat, was coloured green, a raw, brash, eye-splitting choice. It should have clashed with the dark-blue walls and, indeed, did so, but significantly, deliberately adding a touch of uncouth terror to this room. Her eye caught the picture nearest to her. A naked man knelt, arms imploringly forward, in front of a naked woman who occupied a throne, decorated with carved snakes. There was no name to the dark painting, only a kind of illegible square squiggle in the bottom right-hand corner, presumably the artist's name or initials.

51

'Looking at my pictures?' Wicks enquired.

'Yes. What's this one called?'

'*The Proposal.*'

'By whom?'

'A friend of my wife, James Scott-Kerr.' Almost irritably Wicks walked over to the picture and with a fingernail tapped the glass. 'Do you recognise him?' His finger poked the back of the naked man.

'No. Is it some literary figure?'

Wicks burst into a dry, throaty laugh. 'No.' He waited, then came out quietly with the answer: 'It's me.'

'And the lady?'

'That's my wife.'

'I didn't recognise you.'

'Not from my bare behind, no?'

'Did you pose for it?'

'No. He took Belle's face from a photograph. The rest he guessed or made up. He gave it to us for a wedding present.'

'Oh. Were you pleased?'

'Not really. He was something of an eccentric.'

'Was your wife's face recognisable?'

'Vaguely. She quite liked it.'

Alicia glanced round the other four pictures. All were framed in the same wide gold as *The Proposal*. They seemed to be landscapes. 'Are the others by the same man?'

'No.' Wicks backed away from *The Proposal*. Alicia noticed that in real life his hair was much shorter than that of his likeness. 'Belle picked them up from exhibitions and sales to suit the place. They had to be the right size. In fact, she cut one of them down considerably to suit her scheme. The artist would have been far from pleased, I guess.'

'But *The Proposal* was the first?'

'Yes. The rest were chosen to fit in with that and those golden frames, which she had made.' He rubbed his stubbly chin. Obviously he didn't shave at the weekend. 'My wife was a woman of parts. She decorated this room herself. Nor did she let me see it until it was completely finished. She locked the door to keep me out.'

'And were you pleased with it when she'd done?'

'Utterly surprised. I had no idea what she'd choose.'

'Does it represent anything?'

'Nothing I can put a name to from history or literature. I'd guess it was her state of mind. That's the best I can do for you.'

'Do you like it?' she asked.

'No.' That was firm enough. 'My idea of decorating a house is to paint all the ceilings and walls in various shades of white. It makes the rooms look larger, more spacious, and the other effect you get from the furniture, pictures, carpets.'

'Did she know that?'

'Oh, yes. That's the way our last house was decorated. By the time she came to alter this house she'd found out she didn't like the country and wasn't too keen on me as a husband, either. The move hadn't made things better. Then she became ill, so that I associate the place with bad luck.'

'Did she go back to London?'

'Yes. She stayed at first with a friend. Then she used the money she had from me after the divorce to buy an apartment. She wrung every penny out of me that she could.'

'Did you ever hear from her?'

'Occasionally. If she wanted anything from me.'

'Was she happy?'

'There's no mention of such things. She wrote businesslike notes, or even postcards.'

'And were her demands, well, er, reasonable?'

'No. Not always. She was the sort of woman who gets an idea stuck in her head. She was an obsessive.'

'And did you fall in with her ideas?'

'Yes, if she wanted something I didn't. Otherwise I ignored her.' He breathed deeply. 'I was glad when she cleared out. Then she became very ill. I had no idea when she left. The house was quiet and I learnt how to cook from books. I have a cleaning woman in once a week. I'm not the untidy or the dirty sort. Life is easier now. My wife had a wicked tongue and I had the length of it day in, day out.'

'Was this so from the beginning of your marriage?'

'No, not until soon after she came here and didn't like spending the day on her own.'

'Couldn't she occupy herself?'

'It appears not. She had no friends. And there was nothing either in Sutton or Beechnall that she wanted to join. It seemed to my jaundiced judgement that she spent the day piling up insults to use in the evenings or at weekends.'

'And when did she die?'

'I'm not altogether sure. I think she had a job, for a start, though I don't know what. I liked to imagine her behind a Woolworths checkout or a scent counter somewhere. You see I haven't forgiven her, die agonisingly as she did. Though when I think about it all, I see I was not altogether blameless. I put my job first. I wasn't always willing to tailor my days to suit her convenience. That didn't seem to matter quite so much in London, where she had friends and meetings to occupy her. And we were younger. And in love. Odd that two people so attracted to each other that they could hardly bear to be apart should come to such a state of hatred. It was perhaps fear at her cancer that changed her. But that's enough of my troubles. Hers are over.'

He offered her more coffee, which she refused. They talked about their neighbours, the weather, *Twelfth Night* again. Finally Alicia said she must go to prepare her lunch.

'Do you eat your main meal in the middle of the day?' he asked.

'No. I'll eat a few biscuits and drink a cup of tea at the university, and then if I'm hungry cook at night.'

'I eat school dinners on weekdays,' he confided.

'And Saturday and Sunday?' she asked.

'I cook myself something. Nothing too complicated. We're a right pair of plebs, gastronomically speaking.'

'What's the derivation, the etymology of that word?'

'Greek, *gaster*, the belly.'

She left him to his learning, both smiling.

He showed her to the door, did not touch her, slightly to her surprise.

'I'll see you again,' she called from the path. 'Thanks for the coffee.'

V

Alicia had heard nothing until her professor stopped her in the corridor outside his office to tell her that Rattenbury, the man from Newark, had resigned from the position of producer of *Twelfth Night*. 'Do you know anything about it?' he asked.

'Not a thing.'

'Oh. Your friend Arnold came round to see me on Sunday morning to ask me to take over the last fortnight.'

'And have you?'

'I have not. I advised them to persuade your neighbour Wicks to do it. He's been in the production the whole time as Orsino. He seems a man of parts. There'd be no break then. He'd know what they'd attempted so far and that would ensure continuity.'

'Why did Mr Rattenbury leave? And at such short notice?'

'According to Arnold he made too many demands on his cast. He started off well, but this last week or so he's been very demanding. They came to words at last Friday's rehearsal and he was suddenly very quiet, shrugged his shoulder and said if that's how they felt, he'd have to think seriously about going on. He finished the evening's rehearsal, rather quietly, and went out at ten o'clock without a word. Next morning he rang Arnold, or Powell, one or the other, and said he wished to resign, that the play was in a fit state to be put on, that he'd had enough.'

'Did that come as a surprise?'

'Yes, according to Arnold. All had been going well as far as he knew.'

'And?'

'No amount of argument or pleading would move him. Rattenbury said he'd had enough. So they turned to Wicks, and he immediately agreed. Why Rattenbury resigned is a mystery. Arnold couldn't understand it, he said. The man had put a real effort in and had found favour with the majority of the players. Something must have happened. Unless he's a very sensitive

55

character. I don't know, Alicia. The people in these parts seem very quarrelsome. Or don't you find it so?'

'I don't have enough to do with them.'

'Are you going to the *Twelfth Night*?'

'I hope to.'

Professor Conway leaned back, frowning shyly, screwing up his lips. 'I tell you what,' he mumbled, 'we'll go together.' He dropped his eyes as if he had spoken out of turn. She, in equal embarrassment, looked away. 'That is' – he spoke more confidently now – 'if it doesn't clash with some other arrangements you have made.'

'No,' she barely whispered.

'Have you your diary with you?' She nodded. 'Then we'll fix it now and I'll get the tickets. We'll give 'em a couple of evenings to settle to it.'

The arrangements did not take long. The most convenient for them was the performance on Friday night.

'I'll collect you and drive you back home.'

'Doesn't that take you out of your way?'

'I wouldn't suggest it if it did. It's what I'd like to do. Whatever the standard of the performance I shall have the pleasure of your company.'

'Oh, thank you. In that case I'll give you high tea.'

'What time will that be?'

'Five.'

He consulted his diary and agreed. 'That's fine. I have a meeting that afternoon, but if you don't live too far out of civilisation and I can easily find you, that will be excellent.'

Still slightly unnerved, she began to plan what she'd give him to eat.

'Do you know,' he said, 'I've been here for almost two years and I've never been out in your direction.'

'You'll have no difficulty. It's on the main road north-west out of Beechnall.'

'Doesn't Clarence Caldwell live thereabouts?'

She nodded. 'About twenty minutes' walk away. And Raynor Wicks lives next door to me.'

'But you don't see much of him?'

'No. He's busy.'

'An interesting man, our Mr Wicks,' the professor said.

'In his way.'

'And what way is that, pray?'

The professor seemed in no hurry to get rid of her. 'He doesn't seem always to be what he says he is.'

'That sounds mysterious.'

'It may be I'm a poor observer.' Conway waited for her. 'He told me that he was a depressive, but he always seems on top of his life, to know what's to be done and how to cope with it.'

'And you admire that?'

'Yes. Not that I know him well, but I expect I'd agree with the aims he sets himself. He's quite a reader.'

'Does he teach English at the grammar school?'

'No. History. But he takes an evening class in Beechnall on Victorian literature.'

'Interesting.'

'One woman in the dramatic society said he was very good. He makes them read voraciously, and he comes up with some out-of-the-way facts.'

'Such as what?'

'That Tennyson had very poor eyesight. I should have said, if I judged from his poetry, that he was a close, careful observer.'

'That may be on account of his short-sightedness. When nobody was about he would wear his spectacles and really use his eyes.'

'Spectacles have made a difference to literature?'

'That's so. People couldn't read far into their old age. That would make quite an interesting article when you've finished your doctorate and made a book out of it.'

'If.' She grinned over at him, an equal. 'If ever . . .'

'You've done enough work already to write up for the degree. And you know it. None of your modesty, miss.'

They laughed, more like two first-year students. When she came to leave he lightly grasped her elbow as he gently guided her towards the door. She liked that, wondering if she could read anything into the touch of his fingertips.

As soon as the door clicked closed behind her she moved along the corridor. Her head whirled. She had never before considered Christopher Conway as a suitor. When at eighteen she had become a student at Oxford, Conway had been her tutor. He had seemed an oldish man to her, polite, dressed in a suit, one of the best, clearest lecturers, but hardly a human being. He had a wife at that time, a tall, stately woman, who dressed strikingly, who looked on the events in the college as somewhat below her notice, devoid of interest,

57

doubtless good for twenty-year-old girls, but offering her nothing. No one among the students knew anything of her background or present pursuits. The undergraduates heard of the Conways' divorce, but nothing in detail as it was not reported in the newspapers. When she came to think about it, she guessed that the imperious Mrs Conway had decided she had had enough of her bland husband. The word in college was that he was very upset, but he showed no signs of this trouble in lecture rooms, or in seminars or tutorials. The same understanding of their difficulties, the same wise advice about useful reading, the readiness to help if some trouble occurred made him the ideal don. To her his celibacy seemed fitting; he should have chosen it from the start. Now he had rid himself of his wife he had found the mode of living to which he was best suited.

That he had spoken to her, issued this invitation to accompany him to the play, seemed right out of character. She told herself that it all probably meant nothing; he felt well, had heard some good news and in his moment of euphoria had included her. He had invited her to accompany him to an amateur performance of a Shakespeare play, that was all. He had not, she told herself, proposed marriage to her. She laughed a little wryly at herself.

She made no contact with either Conway or Wicks in the next few days. This was not surprising as she had spent them working in the university library and it was dark by the time she arrived back at home. She had glimpsed Conway from the window of the library, hurrying away to some meeting or other. Indoors he seemed quiet, almost statuesque, but once out in the fresh air he rushed about, elbows working, as if he were afraid someone was chasing him. He had been, the rumour went, a very good athlete in his youth and had gained a blue.

On the one day she worked at home, she went out to the village grocer's to make sure she had enough food in store until she did the usual large weekly shopping at Sainsbury's in Beechnall. As she came out of the place, her bag full and delicious dark chocolate bars topping the food for her evening treat, she saw Clarence Caldwell trotting along the road towards her. 'Oh, Miss Smallwood,' he called, 'what a pleasure to meet you.'

She stopped, watched his closer approach, answered his query as to what she was doing on the village street at this time of day. Satisfied, he then asked about *Twelfth Night* and she gave him a succinct account of Rattenbury's retirement and his replacement by Raynor Wicks.

58

'Oh.' He stood, nodding. 'Why did Rattenbury give them up?'

'I don't really know. Most of them, from what I hear, got along with him really well.'

'Shakespeare wasn't his cup of tea?' Caldwell mused.

'He'd do some at school, and wherever it was he did his training, wouldn't he?'

'Oh, yes. But he acted mostly in modern plays. I've never seen anything he produced, or even acted in, but he'd make them speak up so that everybody heard them.'

'Raynor Wicks used to say that you used to recite the lines you wanted them to tackle otherwise, but surprisingly you didn't want them to copy your version. But the difference it made next time they tried was remarkable.'

'That's kind of him to praise me.'

'I don't think he'd do so unless he meant it. And he has a feeling for language.'

'Yes, I'm sure. You say he's taken over?'

'Yes. But I've heard no reports of how he's shaping.'

'There're many of them quite used to speaking Shakespearean verse, or at least they think they are. No, that's unkind. They're good amateurs.'

'And you chose them?'

'They kept to my casting, did they? I wonder whose idea that was.'

'The committee, I expect. They didn't want it made more complicated.'

'Right. If you had taken over, as they asked you to, would you have kept to my choice?'

'I think so. You know more about members of the society and their abilities than anybody. And if I'd have chosen otherwise it would have stirred up trouble for no good reason.'

'You think we're a quarrelsome lot, do you?'

'It would appear so.'

Caldwell took two steps to his right, then came back with a shuffle. He dug his hands into the pockets of his stagey overcoat. 'Are you thinking of attending one of the performances?' he asked.

'I am. On Friday.'

'Are you going alone?'

'No. Professor Conway is going to pick me up.'

'Would I be out of order to ask if the professor is your usual escort at these cultural events?'

59

Alicia was taken aback by the blunt nature of the question. 'No. This is the first time.'

'Yes, um, yes. Have you known him for long?'

'Five years or thereabouts. He was my tutor at Oxford.'

'Is he married?'

'He was when I first knew him at university, but was divorced a year or two later.'

'Who was at fault?'

'That I don't know. News of that sort came out, if at all, in trickles during my time at Oxford.'

'He was a fine teacher, I believe.'

'Yes, I found him so.'

Again Caldwell stepped aside and as quickly came back to confront her. 'What does Wicks say about the production?'

'I haven't spoken to him since he started on it. It's just a few days ago.'

'Yes.'

'There'll only be a fortnight left to him, so I don't imagine that he set about any brilliant new ideas of his own even if he has them.'

'No.'

'He'd stick to my ideas, and Rattenbury's and those of the players he had acquired. He'd try to enthuse them, as if they were making a new start.'

'I've no idea,' she said, 'how he'd manage at all.'

'He'd be enthusiastic himself.'

'I never found him a man who easily let his emotions show.'

'That's so, but he's a different man off stage than on. I was always pleased if I had Wicks in the cast of a play I was producing.'

'He's as good as that, is he, as an actor?'

'Now, well, there's a puzzle. He's very competent as an actor, but not outstanding. He would learn a part in no time, and alter his performance to fit in with and improve that of his fellows. And yet there was something behind or inside the man that was powerful. When I hear myself say this, I think to myself that I'm making it up, reading a charisma in him that isn't there. Most people don't look to actors for deep thinking. Superstitious yes, some of us. But I was convinced that if I had Raynor Wicks in a play I was producing, nothing would go wrong. He'd hold it together, prop it, cover its errors.'

60

'And did things never go wrong?'

'Of course, all amateur productions have weaknesses and minor slip-ups, whether he was there or not. I've known Wicks only over the last ten or so years, since he came to the village. He's a strong man without any ostentation. I often try to think hard why I regard him so highly. I can remember once or twice when he has spoken up at rehearsal in defence of what I was trying to do. He spoke very quietly, without passion, yet put my case more powerfully than I could. And the others took his word. They were silenced. This has happened perhaps three times since he came here. And the grumblers were silenced. And that speaks for itself. They don't like interference from strangers, from Johnnies-Come-Lately.'

'Do you think he's a happy man?' she asked.

'I don't know. He's never taken me into his confidence. I would say he has had his black moments; he must have done. Like your friend Conway, he was divorced. I believe, if I'm to listen to the local tittle-tattle, that his wife upped and left him one day when he was away at an examiners' meeting. She had hired a van and two men, and they removed all her belongings, more than half the contents of the house, with never a word of warning. And do you know I met him the very next day (I knew nothing about her leaving) and we had a very interesting discussion about Shakespeare's religious beliefs, and he said not a word about his troubles. I learnt all about his wife's goings-on later from the village. They said she'd taken every bit of food from the place so that when he returned late from this meeting hungry and thirsty there was nothing to be had. Mark you, she was ill and had received that week a nasty diagnosis from her consultant.'

'What did he do?' Alicia asked. 'Wicks, I mean.'

'He did without.' He smiled his triumph, histrionically. 'It was only weeks later that, by putting two and two together, I realised we had our talk on the very next day after she'd left.'

'Did you know her?'

'Only by sight. She made no attempt to make a fool of him in public. Not that I saw them together more than a few times and, of course, Wicks never mentioned how things stood between them at home.'

'There were no signs of his distress that you missed at the time and only recognised when the pair broke up?'

'No. Wicks was exactly as he was after the divorce.'

'He told me he was a depressive.'

'You surprise me. I know I'm not good at accurately reading somebody's character from his appearance. I imagined he would be hurt, even damaged by the behaviour of this hellcat wife, but I thought that there would be something rock steady about him, that would enable him to put up with such troubles.' He shook his head. 'If ever I were in difficulty, I think the first person I'd turn to would be Raynor Wicks. Don't you agree?'

'I think highly of him,' she said hesitantly.

'But you don't find him sympathetic?'

'There's no reason why I should try him out.'

'Conway is more your style?'

'He's very helpful in academic matters. If you go to him with some puzzling question he'll sort it out for you, without making you feel small. I've come away from such a meeting with the impression in my mind that I've solved the difficulty myself.'

'He acts as some kind of catalyst?'

'I suppose so. He makes suggestions or refers to bits of knowledge I haven't heard of or have ignored.'

'That must be a gift?'

'He's a very good teacher.'

'And professor?' Caldwell pressed.

'I don't know about that. I'm not sure what professors do here. I expect he tells his department what they are to lecture on. That won't be too difficult, because they are appointed for their interests and knowledge in certain topics. He'll say who's to set and mark internal examinations, and be adviser and friend to all and sundry. Furthermore he'll have university as well as departmental duties. He'll have meetings to attend, committees to sit on and so forth.'

'And he'll manage that?'

'I expect so. He'd know all about these when he applied, and though he'll complain how these duties get in the way of his research, he'll put up with it all.'

'For the position and title, or the money?'

'For all I know. He's a human being.'

'Do you expect to become a professor in due season?'

'That's doubtful. There are more women professors about now, but it's still difficult. And my research is not very entertaining to the general public. Unless there's a change in its fortune. And the universities are all for making money. I don't see too many millionaires rushing forward to sponsor or endow chairs for my speciality.'

'Do you expect to live the rest of your life here?'

'No. I think that's unlikely. Even if I don't marry.'

'And are you sad about this?'

'No, not at all. I like this place. But my father bought me a house here and as I'm the only child he, or my mother, will leave me their London home. And if I become very ambitious and seek after promotion I shall have to leave here to achieve it.'

'Where would you choose to live?'

'London.'

'You sound confident. You've no idea of living in the country, or buying an island somewhere?' His suggestion seemed to please him.

'No.' She laughed out loud. 'Is that what you thought at my age?'

'No. I was born in Beechnall, as perhaps you know. And as a boy I used to wander around the district and for some reason my eye lighted on my present house. And I was certain that was where I'd want to live. The idea never troubled me during my working life, but when I was getting near retirement, or the age at which one retires from ordinary nine-to-five jobs, my cousin Jack drew my attention to this house, then up for sale. I had plenty of money at that time and so I bought it outright.'

'And have you regretted it?'

'No. I've sometimes thought that it was a long way from civilisation.'

'Had you ever been inside it?'

'Only with a man from the house agent's. No. It was just the outside and the position that attracted me. And it's not difficult to get to London, I've found. I'm just off again for another month's work. I'll come back for my Christmas holiday. Meg'll be out of hospital by that time, and she'll call on a cousin to come up and stay with her while I'm away.' He looked suddenly satisfied. 'I'll tell you what I would like.'

'What's that?'

'To look around your house.'

'With pleasure,' she said. 'I'll show you.'

'When I was a lad there was a curious old man lived there. He hated boys, thought we stole apples from his orchard.'

'And did you?'

'Now and again. "Scrumping" we called it. I don't know why he kicked up such a fuss if he saw us, for he never picked the apples

63

for himself, left them to rot on the ground. They weren't much good to us, either. They were cooking apples. Are they still there? Bramleys, I think they were.'

'There are two or three trees. I borrowed a ladder and picked them, and stored them in an old cupboard in one of the outhouses. I still have plenty left and they eat beautifully, cooked.'

'Isn't your house rather big for one person?'

'It's typical of my father. He was so delighted with my Finals results. He provides the oil for the central heating to keep me warm. And the money for a woman to come in to help me out with the cleaning. And he had it painted, inside and out, before I came up here.'

'Has he any connection with the district?'

'His family has. His grandfather was a solicitor in Beechnall. "Smallwoods"; the firm still exists.'

'They lived in a big house the other side of Sutton.'

'I think they still do. Some distant cousin. Great-grandpa was a great collector of property and a couple of his houses were eventually bequeathed to my father.'

'Did he live in them?'

'By that time he was married and worked in London. He had some notion of keeping a house in the country, for holidays, but my mother wasn't keen. He eventually let them out.'

'Did he never come up and see them?'

'Yes. When I was small. I remember how excited I was chasing about the place. It was empty then.'

'So the old curmudgeon with the apples didn't own the house. He had, people said, pots of money. I suppose renting houses was more common then. I wonder when he died.'

'The last tenant was called Heatherington.'

'No, that wasn't his name. Nothing so healthy. I can't remember except that it was a little unexpected, but not irrelevant. Crabbe or Burke or Skint. None of those is right. I'm getting to be hopeless with names.' He waved his hands in despair. It was delicately done. 'I shall remember it suddenly and then I'll write it down. That's essential or I shall forget again.'

'Mr Wicks said how good your memory was.'

'Not for names, I'm afraid. I'll give you a call and we'll arrange my visit.'

'In which case here's my number. I've not been in Sutton long enough to make an appearance in the phone book.'

Caldwell patted her arm and tottered off. He seemed pleased with himself.

Alicia stood to watch his progress, which became steadier and easier as he passed further along the road. He did not look back. She wondered where he was off to. He had not said.

That was the third notable who had made advances towards her in the last week. She stepped away, now, and considered this. She was not displeased, in that she no longer was regarded as a piece of the furniture or the vegetation on the edge of things and therefore likely to be ignored for most of the time. Her Three Wise Men. She laughed out loud at the title. She was not nobody, as she expected to be in these parts. All men, though all father figures. At least they would not distract her from her studies. And who was her favourite? Conway. That choice was obvious; he'd give her a hand if ever she was in difficulty with her thesis. And Wicks, was he this tremendous figure that Caldwell had described? She doubted it.

With much to occupy her mind she finished her shopping, humming to herself.

VI

Conway had made a promise that he'd be with Alicia by five o'clock on the night of their theatre trip to see *Twelfth Night*. It depended, he said, on the loquacity of his colleagues. Two of them on his committee, concerned basically about money, had been exceptionally brief, laconic, with their demands, leading the new arrival, Conway, to suspect that they had already won from the vice-chancellor what they wanted to such an extent that they kept their old habits of repetitive prolixity under control. He had had time to go home, bath and reshave, and change into a newish suit. His pink cheeks shone as he rang the doorbell. Alicia thought for one audacious moment that he looked much as he must have done as a schoolboy.

He ate, too, with a schoolboy's zest her meal, ham and tongue with salad, followed by warmed apple pie and thick cream, then a slice of fruit cake, made by a neighbour and sold for some charity. Alicia wondered how he managed to keep so slim.

He sat back and looked about him, then congratulated her on the size and beauty of her dining room.

'It's my father's doing, really. He handed over the house to me, had it decorated and then provided me with furniture, which my mother chose.'

'Your father must be a rich man, and generous.'

'He was pleased with my Finals result. And surprised, I guess.'

'Don't think you just scraped into the first class. You were well up on the list. I remember your answers on Addison and Wordsworth.'

'You chased me hard enough in my viva.'

'Oh, that was Professor Ferneyhough. He had some idea that people who were clever enough to score Firsts, seventy per cent or more, in their written answers would in all probability be poor speakers, stammering out their answers.'

'And was that so?'

'Not at all. Most were admirable speakers.'

'And if they had not been so?'

'Nothing, nothing would have happened. There was one young man, from Merton I believe, who had hardly dropped a mark on his language papers and done pretty well on his literature papers, but he spoke very little. When Ferneyhough complained about him, the language people were on to him like a ton of bricks. Grace Clower said he was the best student she had seen for years and if one could answer adequately with one word instead of six, that in her view was a rare gift and, moreover, an example that most students, and not a few of his teachers, could follow with advantage.'

'Didn't Professor Ferneyhough mind?'

'No. He doesn't think he's always in the right.'

'And Professor Clower?'

'She soon let him know what he ought to think.'

They laughed. Professor Clower had, in their time, given both of them the length of her tongue.

Conway helped her with the washing up and was shown round the house. 'You're very lucky,' he told her. 'You've been given a real jewel of a home.'

He sat quietly while she made herself fit to be seen in public, not a long task, and they set off for Beechnall at six thirty. Conway parked his car in the driveway of a colleague's house; his own place was on the far side of the city, some two miles away from the theatre. They walked to the theatre, five minutes' slow progress, with the crowded pavements and frequent traffic.

'They're not all making for the theatre?' Conway asked, jesting.

'Not they. Tonight's Friday and they're seeking out the pubs, and then the clubs.'

'Do you come here regularly?'

'Most weekends.'

'So you've been to the theatre?'

'Yes, and the Playhouse, and one very good amateur company occupying an old chapel.'

'And is tonight's place the best?'

'Architecturally. It's Victorian, but done up within the last ten years.'

'It's not large, is it?'

'No, not for a theatre. But beautiful in my view. Its stage lighting is right up to date, and the bars and foyer and the upper levels are fairly spacious.'

They reached the theatre, with its wide pillars. A notice on the wall announced the evening's programme. 'The Sutton Players present *Twelfth Night* by William Shakespeare.'

The foyer blazed with light and even though they were early, they found the ground well occupied with standing couples, or larger groups, holding glasses and talking hard.

'Would you like a drink?' Conway asked. When Alicia refused, he looked at her comically. 'What shall we do, then?'

'We'll take our seats. They'll start in under a quarter of an hour, if Raynor Wicks has any say in the matter.' At the door to the stalls, he bought two programmes and they found the way down the main aisle. Their seats were on the third row.

'I hope these aren't too near the stage for you,' he apologised. 'I'm afraid I was rather selfish in my choice, because I like to sit close so I can see something of the mechanics of the production. Will your Mr Wicks yield me anything in that direction?'

'He'll be very straightforward, very plain, all above board. "The people we want to please are those who are here to take pleasure in Shakespeare's verse."'

'Is that what he tells them?'

'I'm only guessing.' She giggled.

Conway stood up among the empty seats to look round the theatre. 'It's beautiful,' he said. 'And snug.' He breathed deeply. 'In green and gold.'

'I believe it was scarlet and gold originally, but when they did the place up, they changed to green. Perhaps for Robin Hood and Sherwood Forest, I don't know. Maybe they found that more modern and less garish. There'd be argument about it.'

'Do you think so?'

'With theatricals, if this society is anything to go by, there always is. This annual Shakespeare play is the one big cultural affair in the Beechnall Festival. Until nine or ten years ago they performed in the church hall in Sutton. That's rather large because some local bigwig left some money just before the First World War to erect the place. It's said that twenty-five years ago when Clarence Caldwell took over he wanted them to move to the Beechnall Royal. He greatly liked that theatre. He was born in Beechnall and made his first appearance on the stage there as a boy. The locals argued that this play was part of the Sutton Festival, nothing to do with Beechnall. In the end he won, but it took him twenty years. They're a stubborn lot.'

Now the theatre was beginning to fill and the ugly chatter of voices clashed with the modest décor of the place.

'They're coming in in good time,' she whispered. 'They know how prompt Wicks is.'

Exactly on the half-hour the theatre lights dimmed and the few latecomers pushed along to their seats. The curtains rose. The Duke, unrecognisable as Wicks, spoke to a lute player, then shortly stopped his performance, refused Curio's offer of hunting, listened to Valentine's unsatisfactory answer from the Lady Olivia and swept off towards his beds of flowers, frowning trouble.

'He's good,' Conway whispered.

'Regal,' she said.

'Imperious, and yet unsure of himself.'

They sat back on the edge of enjoyment, holding their breath.

Alicia, who had done the play at school for GCSE and knew it pretty well by heart, spotted no errors. At the end of Act One Conway looked at her.

'Isn't Shakespeare's verse wonderful?' she said.

'And these people don't trample it about.'

Act Two introduced Sebastian and Antonio, and Malvolio was in his most haughty, rebuking voice; Viola confessed to the audience, if not the Duke, her love for him and Maria laid her trap for Malvolio as the co-conspirators, uncle Sir Toby, bean-stick Sir Andrew, and Fabian fetched from nowhere, frolicked behind the box tree, listening with raucous joy.

As it finished, to strong applause, Conway asked Alicia where the company had found Malvolio.

'I don't know. They've had three producers and I don't know which of them chose him. Isn't he marvellous?'

'I've never seen a better.'

'I'll tell Wicks. He'll be delighted.'

'Mark you, he's not far behind him as an actor himself.'

'You're right. I never thought of him that way. He seemed a bit too concerned with himself to act as somebody else.'

'Isn't that why, at bottom, such people are so good? They have to possess all sorts of other talents, but that's the driving force.'

A large man carrying three pints of beer tottered in front of them. 'You'll excuse me,' he mumbled as he passed Alicia.

'And not a drop spilt,' she said, excited by the occasion.

They looked around the big foyer where people stood in groups, one very large, the other just two or three together. Talk hammered about the place, punctuated by shrieks of hysterical laughter. Alicia and Conway looked them over.

'They all seem happy enough,' he said. 'I wonder what they're getting out of the play.'

'It's not only the play. It's meeting all your friends decked out in their Sunday best.'

'Just so. It reminds me of the meal after a funeral. The worst of it is over; undertakers have disposed of the corpse in fire or earth; the rest are glad they're still left alive, and now can greet and talk like human beings to their friends.'

'Do you go to many funerals?'

'No, thank God. Not yet. I went about three weeks ago to Albert Thorpe's. Did you know him? He was a scientist of sorts and was the oldest ex-fellow about. He'd be well before your time, though he often called in at the college.'

The professor of physics passed them, puffing and blowing, his small wife behind him. He greeted Conway and bestowed, the only appropriate word she thought, a graceful towering of the head and a false-toothed smile on Alicia. He'd no idea who she was. 'Good, eh?' as he moved on. He paused and recited, '"Make me a willow cabin at your gate"' and followed that with 'I had to learn that at school.'

'And that qualifies him to judge,' Conway muttered once his colleague was out of earshot.

'Still, to remember more than I do of the laws of physics.'

'Oh, dear. What a confession.'

They giggled.

'Time we were back in our seats,' Alicia said. 'Wicks had it put in the programme that they'd start after fifteen minutes, audience there or not.'

'Power's gone to his . . .'

At that moment they were shaken by a huge, violent crash. The lights swung and flickered; a picture fell from the wall. Someone dropped a coffee cup. The whole building shook.

'God, what's that?' Conway muttered. 'An explosion?'

A few seconds of silence was followed by an outburst of chattering. People looked around for escape routes. Conway took Alicia's arm.

'What do you think it was?' she asked.

'I don't know. I imagine it was what a bomb would sound like. Did you have your coat, or anything, inside on your seat?'

'No.'

An alarm bell was now ringing raucously. After a few minutes' wait a voice sounded over the tannoy: 'Would you please resume your seats. You will be comparatively safe there. By the time you are all in and settled, we shall be able to tell you what has happened.'

A group of young policemen rushed in and across the foyer, and into one of the doors leading to the stalls. A second alarm bell inside the building now began to sound. The moving spectators looked around apprehensively. One of the uniformed attendants said as he took up his position by one of the doors that whatever it was it had happened outside. At the moment Alicia and Conway reached their seats the backcloth on the stage, the curtain had been opened, fell with a tearing noise, but suddenly stopped and remained in a rough diagonal across three-quarters of the back of the stage. Otherwise, with all lights ablaze, the auditorium seemed as they had left it ten minutes before. They heard the sirens of fire engines or police car.

'They wouldn't have far to come,' a lugubrious man informed the people round him. Members of the audience began to resume their seats, more clumsily than earlier in the evening, seemingly both in a hurry and yet hesitant. When they passed seats, the occupiers stood, but unwillingly as if they vacated places of safety. Even the talk seemed lower in range and power than at the interval. When they were seated a kind of reluctant silence fell as all kept glancing towards the stage expecting an announcement of some sort. For most, it was clear, the evening was ruined and the possibility of resumption of the play unlikely.

After a half-hour-long ten minutes the manager of the theatre appeared in full evening dress, donned as if for the occasion. He plucked at a sleeve and held up a hand. Silence fell abruptly. 'Ladies and gentlemen.' He paused as if for applause. 'I apologise that I have kept you here so long. We have this evening been, all of us, the victims of an unfortunate accident. A huge lorry ran out of control, mounted the pavement and crashed into the wall of the theatre. The collision destroyed part of that wall, which was less substantially built than the older main division of the theatre. Those who know the building well will realise that I am talking about the new dressing rooms built some eight years ago. The accident could not have occurred at a worse time. It happened, as you know only too well, in the interval, when the majority of the

71

cast were resting in that part of the building. There have been some casualties among them. Fortunately two ambulances in the vicinity were despatched immediately, and the paramedics began at once to treat the injured. By this time, I hope and pray, those most badly wounded will be on their way to the Royal Medical Centre. I am not in a position to give the names of those injured. I realise that as this was a local production, some of you, many of you, will know or be related to the players. You will be, I understand, very anxious to know the names of those taken to hospital or who have been treated here. I cannot give you any details of this. It would be unwise to do so, but I assure you that we are checking up to the best of our ability, and as soon as we have accurate information I shall return here and give it to you.

'For the rest, you would be better off to leave the vicinity immediately. We chose to bring you back into the theatre once we were assured that it was structurally safe. The whole theatre will be carefully examined by experts to see how soon performances can be resumed, but that examination will not be until tomorrow. One moment, ladies and gentlemen.' Again the white-gloved hand was raised. 'I ask you not to loiter about the district once you're outside. Please use the main doors and turn left. I repeat, turn left when you're out of the foyer. King William the Fourth Street is out of bounds. If any of you has any reason to go there please consult the police. The number should be small, as no one, not even theatre staff or actors, is allowed to park there. I shall be joined by a police officer in here if you have any business in King William the Fourth Street.' A young constable appeared and stood at the end of the first row. 'He will not have any information about casualties, but will take a note of your requirements and take them to a senior officer.

'For those who are staying, I shall return here as expeditiously as possible with information about the cast. Do not try to reach them, by phone or any other means. They are being cared for. Once again, ladies and gentlemen, I apologise to you for the unfortunate end of what seemed to me to be an excellent entertainment. Will those, please, who are waiting for information make their way down to the stalls and come forward as near as you can to the stage and wait there. Are there any questions?'

'How long will it be before you can tell us anything?'

'That I can't say, sir, but I assure you we understand your considerable anxiety and will be with you again as soon as we have anything like a complete list.'

72

The wait was accompanied by some restive movement, but did not last as long as they expected. The manager led a group of actors out and they lined in single file across the front of the stage, almost as if they had been rehearsed. Conway and Alicia had decided to wait to see if Wicks needed assistance. One or two of the audience were already on their feet. The manager would have none of that.

'Would you all please sit down. I shall start at this end of the line and call out names one by one. When I name that person you would like to assist, please stand for a moment so that we here can see what help is forthcoming. Then please walk to the centre aisle, then out by the doors straight ahead.' He pointed to the back of the theatre. 'If no one makes a claim' – here he smiled at his expression – 'will you members of the cast kindly stay back here and we will arrange transport for you. I'm sorry to have to issue these seemingly obstructive orders, but it is absolutely imperative to account for every single person who was backstage during the interval. You must forgive us our methods, and the delay, but we cannot afford mistakes.'

He began with the end of the line. People followed his instructions to the letter. When he came to Raynor Wicks, sixth in the order, no one stood until Alicia scrambled to her feet. She and Conway moved out to the aisle, where Wicks seemed gravely surprised to see them.

'We wondered', Conway said, 'if you were thinking of driving yourself home or if you'd like a lift.'

'That's wonderful,' Wicks replied. 'I was going to stay overnight with Hilda Clarke so that I could do some Christmas shopping in the morning, but unfortunately she was badly injured, or so it appeared, and taken to hospital. So your offer is a godsend.'

'What about the Christmas presents?'

'I'll see how I feel tomorrow.'

Conway dashed off to collect his car. The other two waited in the foyer.

'Well,' Wicks said, 'we provided you with some drama tonight.'

'Yes. Were you anywhere near it?'

'The outside wall of my room was completely destroyed.'

'You were fortunate to have escaped injury.'

'I'll say. I'd stepped out into the corridor to see if I could contact Steve Sedgwick, Hilda Clarke's nephew. There were no end of people out there and I'd just seen him in the distance when there was this tremendous crash, explosion, whatever. I thought it might be a bomb. It certainly shook the whole place.'

'We felt it out in the front foyer.'

'It really shook us. I rushed over to my door, that seemed to be somewhere near the centre of the disturbance, and this huge lorry had come right into the room. Its enormous wide front wheels were somehow lifted off the floor and were still spinning. The whole atmosphere was full of dust, brick dust, so that it was pretty near impossible to see anything at all clearly. I could, however, make out two bodies lying in a pile of bricks. A man and a woman. I'd noticed them standing against the wall chatting just before I came out to the corridor. Two of them. We dragged them out. They were both alive and conscious. Both had cuts and contusions on their faces, and they were covered thick with the muck from the wall. After a bit somebody was there with a first-aid box trying to clean them up until the paramedics arrived. The manager took names to make sure that nobody was missing. You saw how he lined us up, whether we liked it or not. I didn't expect anybody to rescue me, but he said it didn't matter. We didn't know and we must account for everybody. We were like infant-school kids and did as we were told.'

Wicks delivered this rather slowly, blurring his words as if he weren't sure how to pronounce them. Alicia spotted an empty seat, led him across and sat him meekly down. Mouth slightly open, eyes more shut than open, he blankly looked about the room. She guessed that he was more deeply affected than he knew. He did not speak, but examined his hands, which lay limply on his left thigh.

'Professor Conway won't be long now. He's parked quite close, in a friend's drive.'

Wicks did not answer, but crouched with head down, breathing noisily. Alicia sat beside him, took his right hand in her left. He did not seem to notice. Remembering old Caldwell's praise of the man, she could in no way connect it with this motionless figure. They sat in silence together.

Conway came busily towards them across the foyer.

Alicia shook Wicks's hand. 'Here's our chauffeur,' she said, 'Professor Conway.'

Wicks roused himself, but slowly, dumbly.

'Stand up,' she said and hauled at his right arm. 'Our car's here.'

He tumbled upwards, sagging. She held his arm tightly, aware that if he fell she would go with him. Conway, smiling as if his part of the rescue had gone well, came confidently in front of them and, recognising her difficulty, grabbed Wicks's other arm. This seemed to liven him and he straightened himself.

'I've parked right outside,' Conway said. 'Let's go.'

He stepped out, the others with him. Alicia was aware that Wicks no longer dragged on her arm, but walked normally forward. They crossed the foyer, negotiated the steps outside and in no time stood beside Conway's car.

The professor unlocked the doors. 'We'd better have him in the front seat,' he ordered. Between them they heaved Wicks into the car. 'You climb into the back,' he said to Alicia, 'and I'll see to his seat belt from inside.' Conway acted with decision, and precision, even slightly straightening Wicks's position in his seat. In no time he had the engine running. 'Are you all right in the back? Can you find the way with your belt? Would you like the light on?' She had already fastened it. 'Right, we're on the way.' They'd travelled only a hundred yards or so when they were halted at a red traffic light. At this Conway turned to scrutinise Wicks and to check his belt.

He drove on, very steadily, asking Alicia to be ready to advise him about the best road. 'I don't know where I am in the dark,' he said.

Once they were in the outskirts of Beechnall Alicia saw that Wicks seemed to be asleep, but was surprised to hear him say, in a normal voice, 'This car of yours is very warm and comfortable.'

'We do our best,' Conway said.

Conway drove with such quiet skill that it seemed no time before they reached the road outside Wicks's house.

'We're here,' Conway said rather loudly.

Wicks struggled upright, grappled with, then undid his seat belt; after a pause his left hand groped for a handle to open the door.

He was still unsuccessfully touching and fumbling when Conway came round the car, pulled the door open and helped Wicks to his feet on the rural pavement. 'How's that?' he asked jovially.

'Professor Conway will give you a hand down your steps,' Alicia said. 'They're like mine, rather awkward, especially in the dark.'

Wicks shook his arms and hands as if to restore himself. 'I would like you both to come in, if you have a few minutes. Just to make sure I'm myself again. Is that possible?'

The other two reassured him and the two men hesitantly took to the steps, one foot joining the other on each step. Alicia followed this slow descent from well behind and was glad when they all reached the path. At the front door Wicks clumsily searched his pocket, took out a small bunch of keys, selected one and handed it to Alicia, who did her duty and unlocked the doors. Wicks entered first to find the light switch, which he did after some small time sweeping the wall with his gloved hand. His hall suddenly was flooded with light.

'It's quite warm in here.'

'When I'm away I arrange for an hour or two of low heat at night. I've had trouble with frozen pipes.' He opened the door of a room, asked Conway, once the lights were on, if he would draw the curtains.

'I'll go to the kitchen with Alicia and turn the heating up, and ask her then to make us a drink. What would you like? Tea, coffee, cocoa, Options, chocolate, Ovaltine? I have the lot.' Conway chose cocoa, Alicia chocolate and then enquired about the amounts of milk and sugar they preferred.

'There's plenty of milk. Have it all milk.'

They did not argue, relieved to see Wicks recovering.

When Alicia returned with the steaming drinks and a biscuit barrel the two men sat either side of an electric fire. Neither was speaking. She distributed hospitable cups and biscuits.

'Would you like plates?' Wicks asked.

'No thanks; that is if you don't mind a few crumbs.'

Alicia chose a chair and sat, admiring the room, which she had not seen before, seriously appealing in a heavy red wallpaper with golden Gothic crosses climbing solidly up to the picture rail. Above that the border and ceiling in decorated plaster stretched in the purest white, even under the subdued lamps they had switched on. The heavy, highly wrought chandelier, with golden stems and branches, remained unlighted. She guessed its effect would be spectacular. A few pictures, largish, full-length oil portraits, were hung on the long wall facing the fire. Three small round-topped Georgian tables stood about the room, each carrying three big framed photographs. The one that Alicia could see mostly clearly from her position was of a young lady, in academic dress, hood and mortar board, who stared out at the camera, as if daring it to record her as anything but proud. She wondered if that was Wicks's ex-wife. She sipped the delightful hot chocolate, wondering why she never stored such a delicious beverage at home.

Now Wicks was sitting straight-backed in his chair. He was speaking quietly across to Conway. 'I was convinced it was a bomb,' he said. 'The noise was so great that the floor and the walls of the corridor shuddered. I know that sounds unreasonable, as if I'm paranoid, and it never crossed my mind in those first horrific moments. I ran to the door of the first dressing room, which I'd just quitted and which was pouring with smoke, or dust. I was shaking like a leaf, and my arms and legs were trembling. Somebody spoke to me and I could not tell what he was saying for the dreadful ringing noise, tinnitus, in my ears. I leaned back against the wall and closed my eyes. I thought for the moment I was going to faint, but I pulled myself together and looked about me. I staggered a few steps towards the door, which was clearer now. I've already told Alicia about the lorry and the two bodies. A young man rushed in at the same time that I did, and bumped into me, knocking me sideways to my knees. "Let's get these two out," he said, "before the ceiling crashes down on us." My body was that of a boy, eyes tight shut. The young man was dragging a young woman. We somehow forced them through the open door and out into the corridor. We pulled them to safety and set about bringing them back to consciousness. A man took over from me. "I'm a doctor," he said. "Is he alive?" I asked and staggered off to lean against the wall, the same one I started with.'

'And how were you feeling?' Conway asked.

'That bit of action, useless as it probably was, had done the trick for me. I did not feel steady. The dreadful bang had precluded that, but I could carry on with my bit of help, settling people as comfortably as I could in a bare corridor, wiping blood and muck away.'

'There's no chance of giving your final performance, is there?'

'I've been thinking about it since I sat here. They took the sea captain, Viola's friend, a small part, two officers, a priest and a lord to hospital. If they are not too badly injured or affected we might manage it. People might feel it wouldn't be right. There's a school performance, a matinee, beginning at two, and the final evening performance. Somebody will have to make up his mind pretty sharp first thing in the morning. What I don't know is whether the theatre will be in a fit state to use by tomorrow. The stage itself and the auditorium are pretty well untouched as far as I could see in my dazed state, but the lighting, I don't know about that, I think it was affected. I expect they could set up some temporary system, but of course they'll be looking towards next Monday and the professionals.'

'What's on?'

'The pantomime. *Aladdin and his Wonderful Lamp*. They're starting early by a week. They usually open on Boxing Day, but this year it's all changed. They'll need to get that right because it runs on right until spring.'

Wicks outlined his plan of campaign for the next morning. He seemed in every way normal, pointing out snags and how he'd deal with them. He sounded lively, a man on top of his job. He thanked them for 'rescuing' him. 'I could have done nothing from the place I was staying.'

'I hope you can manage something. The piece you gave this evening was as good as any performance of the play that I've seen, amateur or professional.'

They finished their drinks and took their leave.

Tramping up the steps to the road Conway said, over his shoulder, 'He's soon recovered.'

Back on the main road Alicia answered him. 'Clarence Caldwell praises him to the skies. He said that if he had Mr Wicks in his cast he knew nothing could go awry.'

'Tonight's events show how wrong he could be.'

'Yes.' Glumly.

'Is Wicks a modest character by nature?'

'With me he is, always. Sensible, soon sorts it all out. And I think he was almost perfect as Orsino.'

'He was so.' Conway smiled, braced himself. 'Time I was on my way. I have to go to York first thing in the morning to viva a Ph.D. I don't like working on Saturdays, but it seemed the only day. I suggested Christmas morning to Oliver Stirling there, but I daren't pull his leg too much. He's the man I have in mind as the external examiner for your thesis. And we don't want my childish sense of humour ruining your career for you, do we?'

He wished her goodnight and leaned forward to kiss her on the cheek. It was the first time he had done this. She was unsure whether it meant anything, but tripped down her steps delightedly, warning herself not to read too much into it.

Professor Conway stood at the gate of her house until she had let herself in. Still smiling, she saw his headlights as he turned to drive off.

VII

As it happened the last two performances of *Twelfth Night* were cancelled.

The electricians found that their system had been badly damaged, situated, as some of the controls were, in the new wing of the theatre. The announcement was made on local radio by ten o'clock on Saturday morning. Alicia felt disappointed by this for Wicks's sake. She kept an eye open on his doors but she saw nothing of him. By nine o'clock that morning his garage was empty; he must have been up and away before she was awake. Nobody in the village post office made any mention of the truncated Shakespearean performances. The weather stretched dully across the way, but at least it felt warmer in the streets. Alicia spent the day reviewing her thesis and, on Conway's advice, considered rewriting the introduction and thinking about the final chapter. Thoroughly immersed in her work, she found the days too short.

On Sunday morning she went out for her usual walk. Wicks's house, she noticed from the road at the top of her steps, seemed thoroughly shuttered. The garage doors were shut tight and she took this to mean that Wicks was at home and probably in bed, sleeping off his troubles. She walked along the road. As she passed Caldwell's house she saw the old man sweeping leaves outside his door in overcoat and a woollen scarf wrapped round his neck, the two ends flapping as he moved. She shouted her greeting down to him, so that he looked up with a start.

'Oh, good morning,' he said. 'Have you five minutes? Would you come down? It will save my legs.'

She carefully picked her way down the steps to where he stood leaning on his besom. He wore some kind of woolly Russian hat.

'I heard about the trouble with *Twelfth Night* on Friday.' He grinned widely at this, then fell into a bout of coughing.

'Yes,' she said, when his paroxysm had subsided.

'Was anybody hurt?'

'Two or three of the cast were taken to the hospital for treatment. And the driver. No one was badly injured.'

'They couldn't give either of the Saturday performances?'

'No. It was decided to try to get the rooms and the lights ready for the next week's rehearsals and performances. That's the story from local radio.'

'Who took that decision? Wicks?'

'I shouldn't think so. It would be somebody in the theatre.'

Caldwell dabbed at his boots with his besom. 'Were the two acts you saw done well?'

'Yes. They were excellent. Mr Wicks was very good as Orsino and the girl who played Viola was outstanding. She seemed very young, but lively. We all loved her. And Malvolio was very accomplished.'

'So you were sorry you didn't see it all?'

'As you say. So was Mr Wicks. We brought him back home.'

'We?'

'I went with Professor Conway.'

'And how did Raynor seem?'

'I think he was shocked for a start, as anybody would have been. It was the dressing room he was in that was so badly damaged. Luckily he was out in the corridor. He hardly spoke a word as Professor Conway drove us home. But he recovered and before we left he was beginning to plan ways of getting the last two performances on the boards.'

'Good for him. That's Raynor all over.'

'He obviously couldn't persuade the management to allow him to have his two final performances.'

'No, I see that. Reason doesn't go far with theatre administrators. Their mind would be on their workmen and what they say could be done.' He sighed as he straightened his broom. 'He'd be very disappointed.'

She left him fiddling with the fallen leaves.

That afternoon she saw Wicks come to his door, stand hesitating there before taking two or three strides into the garden. She guessed that he had not been up long, for the garage had been closed and the curtains in the house pulled across. She grabbed one or two packets as an excuse for going outside. As she dropped them into her new wheelie bin she called out to him. He turned towards her, obviously, from the expression on his face, pleased to

80

see her. He crossed towards the low wall between the two properties.

'How are you?' she asked.

'Well. I've just about got over my disappointment over not being able to finish off the last two performances. They were about as unhelpful as they could have been.'

'Who? The management?'

'Yes. They were even hinting that we amateurs were the cause of the whole trouble.'

'That wouldn't please you.'

'It did not. I asked if they thought I'd bribed the driver to run into their wall.'

She easily imagined Wicks's reddening face and hectoring voice as he stood there straight-backed and with his fists clenched. 'It's ridiculous,' she said.

'I don't expect reason from them. They don't think we deserve to perform in their theatre. We're amateurs. They or their financial masters let us have our week at a cheap rate. Clarence Caldwell negotiated that in the first place, when he had convinced the society that they should take the theatre for a week.'

'Where were they before that?'

'Sutton village hall. That's a big place, for what it is. There was considerable ill feeling about the transfer. Some ten years or so before that Steadman gave the Sutton people a considerable sum, or even sums, he kept coughing up, to enlarge and improve the hall.'

'It's not so large as the Royal.'

'No. It has only the ground floor, no galleries. As I expect you guess we'd make more money at the village hall, which doesn't cost us nearly as much as the real theatre, and there are some in the society who resent this. They want us to make more and more money.'

'Where do you get your cash from, apart from sale of seats?'

'Oh, the usual events. Raffles. Garden parties. Two minor entertainments in Sutton. Gifts, donations, that sort of thing. There are quite a few of our patrons who are very generous. The society is financially very sound.'

'What's the advantage of taking the Theatre Royal?'

'It attracts people who wouldn't turn out for a performance in Sutton. It also attracts more publicity. And it boosts our players to be performing on a stage where film stars and celebrities appear

81

from time to time. I'm sure that's what made Irene Wagstaffe, the girl who played Viola, so good. In three years she's come on by leaps and bounds.'

'Is she going to make a profession of it?'

'She's doing A Levels this next summer. Then she'll have to choose between university and drama school.'

'And which will it be?'

'I don't know.'

'Which would you advise?'

'I don't like to say this, but it would be RADA. She has such a wonderful talent that it would be a shame not to concentrate on it.'

'She was certainly very good. But then so was the whole production. Christopher Conway said just before the explosion that it was the best *Twelfth Night* he'd ever seen.'

'Good. Kind of him to say so. We have some talented people.'

'Yes, for sure. And you made good use of your last three weeks.'

'It's kind of *you* to say so. I certainly was delighted with the performances. What I'm trying to do now is to fix up two or three more fairly soon after the schools go back. The two matinees were intended for schools, which studied it for examinations. It would be a pity if they missed so good a performance.'

'Where will you do them?'

'It won't be the theatre. It will either be in Beechnall High School, or failing that, Sutton village hall. I can't get hold of our headmaster. He's been inveigled into a conference and then dragged off to Italy for Christmas by his wife, and he won't make any arrangements until he's back and knows what else is happening. I shall also have to see the cast. I think that will be all right, unless we're very unlucky. They knew how well it was going and were as disappointed as I was that we couldn't finish the week.'

'It certainly was very good.'

Raynor Wicks rubbed his chin. 'I've been thinking about this. Everything went wrong. Caldwell chose *Twelfth Night* because he was about to retire and this was the first play he did up here. That seemed admirable to most of the society until Powell and Arnold began to interfere. They demanded something new, different.'

'Why?'

'They were newcomers to their positions in the society, president and secretary, and they wanted to make their presence felt. When Caldwell refused to fall in with their plans, they were shocked and had to give in. Then the old man would not come back. That landed them in a quandary and they approached Conway, who didn't want the job and suggested you. In the end they scratched about and found Rattenbury. That wasn't a bad choice; he hadn't nearly the knowledge of Shakespeare Caldwell had, for all his years on the stage, but he was a worker and wanted to impress the yokels up here. He nearly overdid it with his extra rehearsals and, in fact, resigned three weeks before the opening night as you know. At that point Powell and Arnold banished their pride and came crawling to me, a well-known Caldwell fan and Shakespeare lover. It worked out pretty well. Rattenbury had over-rehearsed them. I took it easy with them and polished bits that weren't quite up to standard, with the results you saw. Powell and Arnold were delighted and when the *Guardian* sent a man to review it, an old friend of mind, may I say, and he praised it so highly, they claimed their interference, and their choice of new men in adversity, had made the society a success, talked of all over the country. And I found a superb Malvolio.'

'You were pleased, though, weren't you?'

'Of course. I'm human. And there had been trouble in the society. Some of Powell's opponents would have been pleased to see us fail. And bringing in Rattenbury wasn't to everybody's taste. But it worked out well until that Friday, when I heard this great noise and the whole place seemed to shudder, I must confess the thought that first came into my mind was that somebody in the society had placed a bomb.'

'You didn't really believe that, did you?'

'It seems silly now, but, yes, I did.' He looked despairingly upwards.

'For a disagreement about a Shakespeare play?'

'Yes. It seems ridiculous. But it could become an obsession. And if we're to believe the media, bombs are not expensive. They say you can learn it all spelt out for you on the Internet. I don't know. For the moment, with the shock, and seeing people who were laughing and talking just a minute before lying stretched out in blood on the floor, nothing seemed impossible.'

'It sounded like a bomb to you? We were several walls away from it.'

'I've no idea what a bomb sounds like. I imagine, imagined, that it was something like a very large firework. And, remember, I had the original, thick, outside of the theatre between me in the corridor and the explosion or whatever it was. It wasn't until I walked back to the door of the dressing room that I saw the bonnet of the lorry inside the place and knew the true cause. It wasn't too long before the police, and then the firemen and ambulance men – paramedics they call them now – were all there and sorting us out. I've no idea of the time this took. But they divided us into groups to lead out to the theatre to see if anyone would claim us. I allowed them to direct me though I hadn't a hope that anyone would take me, so that it came as a shock that you and Conway laid hands on me.'

'Did you get any sleep that night?'

'As soon as you'd gone I sat in my chair and drifted off. When I woke I rang Geoffrey Butler, my host, to let him know where I was, and then began to think how we could arrange more performances. I went to bed and slept fitfully, worrying myself about the future rather than what had just happened. It's amazing to me now how much I had been knocked about by the explosion, not physically but mentally; it was as if I was another man.'

'Has that cured itself?' she asked.

'Yes. From the next day onwards. Not counting small intermissions of loss of control, I'm almost normal now. I don't like it, I can tell you. What the effect on me would have been if I'd been inside the room at the time I don't know. I've often thought of those poor men in the trenches in the First World War. Enormous shell bursts, deafening you if they went off near you after screaming over your head; your friends' bodies lying about dead and rotting, and any day the order to go over the top to almost certain death. And living in filth, eating hot rubbish, with your skin caked in the mud and rashes and unhealed scratches. God knows how those men survived to live normal lives, to marry, father children, hold down a steady job in civvy street.'

She thought he was about to cry. She had never seen him so disturbed. Where was Clarence Caldwell's unmoved man now? The one who would see any performance through to its end, however many the obstacles?

He thrust his hands down into his trouser pockets and was himself again. 'The lorry driver had been drinking,' he said. 'What he was doing with that great load on Friday night I don't know. He'll be charged.'

'When you've organised these extra performances, let me know, will you please? I'd like to see the whole.'

'I will,' he said. 'It's a marvellous play, but I think those first two acts are the best part.'

She looked him quizzically over. He was better-looking, with more manly features than Conway. Even in his weekend gardening clothes he looked well dressed. She wished him good afternoon and set out for her favourite short walk in the woods. The sun gamely struggled out low down among the clouds.

VIII

Alicia Smallwood left for London and her parents' home the day before Christmas Eve. She felt pleased to go but knew she would be thoroughly bored before a week was out. She'd be glad to help her mother with last-minute shopping and preparation for festival meals. Her father would be working until the Eve, and would be back at his desk the day after Boxing Day. On the days her father was at work, her mother would talk her to death, mainly with complaints about her father and his ignorance of what was required of a married man.

'What we shall do when he retires God only knows. We've bought this lovely cottage down on the coast in Dorset, and we spent all his summer holiday down there, painting and decorating, or instructing plumbers and joiners. It looks very well and is very comfortable.'

'Are you going down there this Christmas?'

'No. We can't. We've let it out until the end of May, to a couple who have a house in Scotland. The husband is in the RAF and is instructing some long-term course.'

Alicia did not exactly enjoy more than a few days' stay with her parents. The first forty-eight hours passed pleasantly enough; they were a change from a time of looking after herself and labouring hard at her thesis. She helped her mother at this time of the year with her preparations for Christmas. Her mother threw herself into these activities for weeks. Nothing was too good for her guests, or even casual callers. She'd buy a couple of boxes of Christmas crackers at her nearest superstore, but she would put in it presents and mottoes suited to the person at whose place at the table the crackers would be laid. Her Christmas cake would be decorated beyond belief, with Santa Claus and his reindeer progressing along a winding path towards a house where the family waited outside the door for the welcome visitor. Trees, ponds, fences, were staggered across the snowy surface of the icing sugar. Her father complained about this. A process of demolition had to take place before slices of cake were cut.

'We only see the thing for five minutes while we eat a ham sandwich, and then have to watch you destroy hours of artistic endeavour on your part before we can eat our cake. Don't you think you could spend your time better? That's so, isn't it, Alicia?'

'Not if my mother enjoys it.'

'Oh, hello. You're ganging up on me now, are you?'

Her father, who made a great deal of money in the investment bank where he worked, treated her like a thirteen-year-old. He did it politely, but she was never sure whether that was how he seriously saw her. He invariably asked about young men and said he couldn't think that the University of Beechnall had no handsome suitably qualified males there. 'You're twenty-four now, y'know,' he'd mock. 'Just the age your mother was when she married me.'

'I'd probably have done better to wait. And to make you wait,' her mother said.

He pulled comical faces, one struck to the heart.

When she was telling them the story of her ill-fated visit to the theatre to see *Twelfth Night* he listened carefully to the account of the explosion, but soon began his banter, as she expected. 'Do you go to the theatre on your own?' he asked, face innocent.

'Sometimes.'

'On this particular occasion?'

'No.' She was thoroughly aware of the purpose of his question as always.

'With a girlfriend?'

'No.'

'Oh, a man, was it?'

'Yes.'

'And aren't you going to tell us about him?'

Her parents stared at her. A long minute's silence extended itself. Both, she knew, would be keen to hear her answer. She made them wait. 'It was my professor.'

'Professor Conway?' Her mother this time.

'When are you bringing him home for us to have a look at him?' Brashly, from her father.

'This is the only time we have been out together. I told him I was going and he said it might be pleasant to attend together.'

'And was it?'

'Apart from the accident with the lorry.'

'There was a silence.

'What's his first name?' Her mother innocently joined the questioning.

'Christopher, and he's forty-three.'

'Is he not married?' Father back in the lead.

'Divorced.'

'Is it serious?'

'No. Not on my part.'

'And on his?'

'I've no idea. I keep in with him as he's supervising my thesis.'

They asked a few more questions and then the conversation petered out. She knew her mother would question her again once her father was no longer with them. He was now in the kitchen preparing drinks, orange for her mother, whisky for himself and gin and tonic for her. As he clashed about with the bottles, she heard him singing in his light, bland baritone:

'A thousand times o'er I've repeated my suit,
But still the tormentor affects to be mute;
Oh, tell me, ye swains who have conquered the fair
How to win the dear lass with the delicate air.'

There was no doubt whom he meant. She was his lass with the delicate air. He was fond of her. He meant well. He'd won a grammar-school scholarship and gone on to his local university, where he'd easily won a first in maths. He'd enjoyed his time there, had played chess for the university and had sung with the chorus of the Gilbert and Sullivan Society, but apart from solving some puzzles in mathematical journals, he had concentrated on his course work. In term time he had written once a week to his girlfriend who was training to be a teacher. She had been at school with him, in his class, was two months older than he and the match was approved by their middle-class families who lived within a few tree-lined avenues of each other. His professor, a comparatively young man, had told him that he would have liked to offer him a teaching job at the university, but there was, it appeared, no possibility of such an opportunity. The prof had, therefore, introduced him to a friend in London, a banker. 'He's a hard man to please, a stickler for making big profits. There's a lot of money to be made, I'll tell you, but you'll have to work for it.

He'd give you three, six months' probation, and if you're not up to standard you'll be out on your ear.' There had been two interviews and he was offered the job. He soon grew to like it, but not living on his own in London and after a year proposed to his girlfriend. 'There are plenty of teaching jobs going,' he'd told her, and she, to his surprise, seemed glad to leave home. They bought a house and by that time he was earning well. After two years' teaching in an excellent school, his wife became pregnant and she had in due time resigned to look after Alicia, so named after Mrs Smallwood's grandmother.

Her father loved her, of that she had no doubt. But his humour, treating her as a child, grated on her. He was a clever man; his employers thought highly of him. For these last three years his bonuses had been astronomical. Yet neither his school, nor university, nor his working life had altered him from the boy in Newark, with his rough near-insults and innuendos. Indeed, his success had merely made him more certain that he had the right to pull her leg, lord it over her, in this uncouth way. He had no feeling that his words might hurt her. He spoke to his wife in this rudely jovial way and she had put up with it. She imagined his boyhood home, where they'd blast a question at each other, never mind people who'd annoyed them, and he'd grown into the habit, and his adult life had only confirmed him in his ways. She wondered what he'd think or say if she objected: tell her, perhaps, not to be so thin-skinned, or even be hurt himself and build a wall of reticence between them. How would he treat Professor Conway or Raynor Wicks if she introduced them into her parents' household?

Her mother, now, was a different case. Selina Smallwood had never gone back to teaching, though she had hinted that she had missed it. By the time Alicia was ready to start school Tony, her father, was beginning to earn really well and had made it clear to his wife that there was no longer any need for her to go out to work. He had bought a fine house in Finchley and had told his wife, in his usual voice of bravado, that she would have her work cut out looking after him and Alicia, and the house and garden.

'But what if anything happened to you? I should have to work then?' she had asked.

'Such as what?'

'Well, if you lost your job.'

'That's not very likely. I make a great deal of money for them. Why should they sack me?'

'If you were ill and weren't capable of going to work.'

'Look here, my good woman, I'm thirty-one years of age. Both my parents are alive, as well as two grandmothers and a grandfather, all fit and thriving.'

'You never know.'

His face darkened; he smiled arrogantly. 'We don't,' he conceded. He loved her, too. She was a good-looking woman. 'But what do you mean? A stroke? A heart attack? Or falling under a bus?'

Selina gave up and spent her time on the garden, and his money on seeds and plants and garden architecture. He seemed very satisfied. He took her and their child abroad for holidays at least twice a year, though Alicia guessed he would have preferred to be at his desk in the bank, making money for his clients.

This year they celebrated a Christmas lunch. Both sets of grandparents were there, two elderly aunts and a married couple of about their generation, and a thin man, aged around forty, who wore granny glasses, which he kept shifting up and down his nose. Who he was Alicia had no idea, but was surprised to learn from her mother that he was a well-known journalist, with a regular column in *The Times*. He sat next to Alicia at table and proved an interesting talker. When she explained the nature of her research, he spoke knowledgeably about music in the eighteenth-century theatres and suggested a man who was a great expert on the subject at Durham University. 'If you're interested, write to him and mention my name. He won't mind; he's energetic and will think that he can learn as much from you as you from him. That's not very likely. I'm only guessing as I don't know the extent of your studies. But he's a very learned man and you'll find him an admirable ally, that is if you need such a thing.'

They all ate heartily after their characteristic fashions, and wore their paper caps. The *Times* man and Mr Smallwood were the only ones who did not drink the excellent red wine. The old aunts, who lived not too far away, not distantly in fact from each other, but who had arrived in two separate taxis, described some eccentric old gentleman they knew who had donned a Santa Claus outfit and called in with presents on two or three aged lady friends. One of these had not shown gratitude, but had complained that his reindeer were nowhere in sight and ordered him off her premises.

The more laconic old lady ate steadily from the small portions, a look of satisfaction about her whole posture. She, actually a great-aunt, had spent the half-hour before the meal questioning her great-nephew about her investments. Tony Smallwood answered her enquiries with a slow clarity as if he liked nothing better than explaining to his relative how she stood financially. Every so often she broke in, her squeaky voice aggressive, with 'My broker says . . .' Smallwood listened. Sometimes he dismissed the broker's advice with 'nonsense', 'twaddle', 'tosh'. When he might on other occasions explain why the broker was likely to be right, and even from time to time approved, he did it with a brief 'good' or 'exactly'. His face showed interest; his brow screwed permanently in earnest concentration. Alicia knew all this was hypocritical for when the old ladies were out of the way, in bed or in a taxi, he'd take his daughter to one side and whisper, 'Aunt Grace was on form today.'

'She's not ruined, then?'

'No. She doesn't understand a word I say.'

'She can't understand well enough to reinvest her money?'

'Very little. Tiny gambles round the edges. She's pretty well-to-do, but she likes to demonstrate that she has money to spare. She talks to me for reassurance. Her husband was in my line so she won't die in poverty.'

'But she listens carefully enough to you and asks questions by the dozen.'

'And I look forward to the inquisition. It's a kind of thrice-yearly Finals examination. To see how much I can remember.'

'If you can't answer?'

'I tell her so. But I've a very good memory.' He smiled. 'And I prepare myself.'

'Does she question you every time she sees you?'

'She does. But she doesn't pay a blind bit of attention to what I say.'

'That's not surprising, is it,' Alicia asked, 'if she doesn't understand what you're saying?'

'No, but she'll remember bits here and there, which she'll throw at her broker to make him think she's au fait with all the changes that need to be made.'

'And he?'

'He'll give her a list of things she must do.'

'And does she?'

'I think so. He's good at his job. The alterations and suggestions are cautious and, as I tell you, small, making no great difference.

She'll squeeze out a little profit each year, I'm sure, but whether it's much more than she pays him I greatly doubt.'

'Doesn't she realise that?'

'I expect so. But it leaves her with the feeling that she's in charge of her money. Her old man made a great deal and she likes to think she's confidently following in his footsteps.'

After lunch the guests retired to armchairs, sofas and the log fire in the drawing room. Alicia helped to pack away the dishes into the two dishwashers. In the ordinary way Mrs Smallwood had a girl, perhaps two, in to help with the preparation and serving; she produced, at her husband's bidding, special meals for visitors, but she would not ask the girls to come in on Christmas Day.

'They'd be pleased to,' her husband argued. 'They'd be glad of the money at this time of year. As long as you don't order them to appear before eleven o'clock. If you're afraid to ask them, I will.'

'You won't,' she said. 'Alicia and I will manage. You can get the vacuum cleaner out and use it.'

'Ay, ay, sir.' He slung up a mock naval salute.

The guests fell asleep, even the *Times* man. Their heavy breathing and short, well-mannered snores sounded comforting, against the crackling of the fire.

'It will be our turn to rest tomorrow at Aunt Grace's.'

'Surely she isn't capable to providing for all of us?'

'No. It'll just be you, your father and I, and Aunt Amy. We've done them well, you can see. If they hadn't enjoyed the meal they'd have been wide awake complaining and quarrelling.'

'Who'll prepare the meal tomorrow?'

'Mrs Pilkington. Grace's lady. She's in every day with the exception of Sunday. And if Grace has visitors, Mrs P. will bring her daughters over. And Mr Pilkington will drop in to open the bottles. They like to come to the big house, as they call it. And Great-Aunt Grace will have given instructions that they are to order enough for their meals as well as ours. Oh, it's all well arranged, goes like a bomb. And Grace, mistress of the feast, loves it, is never wider awake, bless her.'

When the visitors emerged from their naps the aunts dominated the conversation with the talk of deaths. At least three of their friends, apparently in the best of health, had dropped dead in the last month as they pursued the most humdrum of domestic chores.

'And they were no age,' Grace said.

'How old was Arthur Carter, then?'

'Seventy-three. He was overweight. His widow will miss him. She tried long enough to get him to diet, but not he. He loved his food too much.'

'Are you ladies dieting?' The *Times* man asked.

'Our first rule is not to eat too much. And then only foods that don't fatten or poison.'

'You watch the Glycaemic Index?'

'You give it whatever fancy name you like. It's common sense, really.'

'And', the younger aunt said, 'we take regular exercise each day. We walk out in the afternoon.'

'Together?' he asked.

'No. We live quite close to each other it's true, but we're into the habit of taking our walks separately. Then we don't stand about talking.'

'Have you always taken an afternoon walk?' he asked.

'For years,' Grace said. 'I started after my husband died. He went suddenly. We had just arrived on holiday at Monte Carlo and put our things down on the beach when he sat, sighed, dropped down flat and was dead. There was a doctor there, a friend of ours, and he examined him and said he had died. He rang the hotel and they had an ambulance there in no time. They were quick and efficient and very kind.'

'Did you come straight back?' The *Times* man continued.

'Yes, I did. I gave some authority the name of our funeral director, who agreed to collect the coffin from the plane. They were very good.'

'Were you there?' he asked the younger lady.

'No. We might, from time to time, spend up to five days away together, but not in the main summer holiday. Aubrey invariably went with Grace on that and always to the South of France. He enjoyed that. Grace tried to talk him out of it, but he wouldn't have it.'

'A man of habit,' Grace said, as if praising him. This led her to describe another couple who had died within days of their return from Spain. 'Neither had been ill.'

'But neither very well in themselves,' Aunt Amy corrected.

'What do you expect at their age?'

'And what was that?'

'Early seventies.'

'No sort of age to die these days.' She did not notice her change of mind.

Mr Smallwood, who had listened to this in a post-prandial stupor, suddenly intervened. 'You're a cheerful lot,' he almost shouted, his face beaming. 'This is a season of good cheer and here you are groaning on about people dying.'

'Anthony,' Grace rebuked him, 'we talk about a matter that's constantly in our minds. You will find it will impinge more and more on your thoughts as you reach my age. Pretty well all of my contemporaries are dead and a good part of the following generation. I can't myself have too much time left. I'm eighty-nine next.'

'You've plenty of oil in your lamp yet.'

'What do you do in your spare time besides walking?' asked the *Times* man pacifically.

'I used to play golf, but not now. My husband used to enjoy a game.'

'Was he a good player?'

'A handicap of seven.'

'Better than most of us.'

'He would have given his eye-teeth to be better, to be playing off scratch. He never managed it. He used to say that he took up the game too late. He encouraged our son to play when he was quite small, six years of age. But the child never got anywhere with it. I think he rather despised the game.'

'He doesn't play now, I take it?' The journalist.

'He's dead.'

Great-Aunt Grace seemed to have perfected her technique for bringing a topic to a sudden end, but the *Times* man proved more than a match for her. He talked with ease about an interview he had conducted with Tiger Woods. The man who should have conducted it was suddenly taken ill and so he was sent in his lace. 'My knowledge of the game was limited, and I had to admit it at once and throw myself on his mercy. But he was charming, he came up with all sorts of anecdotes about his parents, his coaches, his opponents, the courses, the weather, skill and luck. It was interesting and I wrote it with some zest. The sports editor was pleased; he wouldn't believe I knew nothing about golf. And to crown it all, the paper had a note from the player thanking us for the article.'

'Aren't these professionals dedicated?' asked the little man who with his wife had slept longest. 'I mean they don't allow anything to stand in their way.'

'One must be at this level. But he showed no sign of it. He'd just won, was happy and had plenty of time to spend on me. But he never seemed to boast. The interview wrote itself.'

The journalist caught their interest. The day outside was bitingly cold and dark, but he held his audience and charged the atmosphere in the house. Grace, no easy conquest, was won over and listened, questioned with zest. By the time the Christmas tea was prepared, they all talked as friends.

'Who's that?' Alicia asked her father out in the corridor.

'The best journalist in England. And you can see why.'

'Will he end up as the editor of one of the big papers?'

'I doubt it. He's not that sort of man. His ambition is to be the best writer, not to organise the rest of his colleagues.'

'How did you come to meet him?'

'He spoke at one of the bank's dinners a couple of years ago. He seemed a quiet, inoffensive sort the owner had chosen until he got to his feet. Then he surprised us all. He's the best speaker I've ever heard.'

Her mother showed equal enthusiasm. 'He's been your dad's best friend this last year or two. They met at one of the social functions at the bank. Your father isn't keen on the like, but this man made a wonderful speech.'

'What's his name?' Alicia asked.

'William Wolfe. We found out that he lives a few hundred yards away and he and Tony meet at least once a week in one another's houses. He's not married and he seems not to have any close family. He comes from the North, Durham I think, but he has a house in London and one in Oxford. Your dad says it's a real education just to listen to him. He reminds him of you when you talk about your research. You know so much and can put it over so well, that those who know nothing are attracted. But he knows an enormous amount about a good many subjects, not just one or two.'

'Why hasn't he married?'

'That's what I asked your dad. He says it's because he hasn't the time. He likes women, but none is so attractive as to drag him away from his studies.'

'He certainly talked very sensibly and attractively and knowledgeably about eighteenth-century opera to me.'

'Did he know anything about it?'

'Yes, he did. He surprised me.'

'And occasionally your father can explain some mathematical stuff to him. Mr Wolfe knows quite a lot about mathematics, but he's caught out sometimes and then your father piles in. If he doesn't know either, he likes to learn from some mathematical publication he takes. And I also guess that he gives him a tip or two on investments, though your father says he's not really interested in making a lot of money. Wolfe says his journalistic work is pretty handsomely rewarded, allows him to live quite well, since he's no wife and family to support. He lives very sparsely, I should say. He's satisfied with his books and computers. Their friendship's done your father a power of good, I must say.'

'How's that?'

'Your father hadn't much of a social life outside banking circles. He had no real friends. I don't think he had as a young man at the university. He wasn't shy or rude. He quite liked people, but he preferred his studies.'

'How did he come to marry you, then?'

'Oh, we were at school together and when he thought marriage would suit the purposes of his life, he proposed.'

'And did you have to think twice before you accepted him?'

'Not really. It meant a change. I could continue with my teaching in London. And I suppose living in the capital meant something to me in those days. Actually, being a wife had its attractions. When you were born I left teaching. I had my hands full with you. It was a disappointment to us that we had no more children. I lost two, both boys, and the doctors said I'd be better off if I gave up the idea. And you did us so well, at school and everywhere else you went. Your father adored you.'

'That's good to hear.'

'I think he was sorry that you didn't follow him and study mathematics.'

'He never as much as hinted at it.'

'No. He doesn't broadcast it to all the world, even when things don't go his way.'

'Has he been dissatisfied lately? About what?'

'A couple of years ago he began to mutter about retirement. He was only fifty-one at the time and it surprised me. I thought he had the sort of job that suited him and he enjoyed. He had quite recently been promoted to the board of the bank and he earned a lot of money. That had always been one of his ambitions, to become a rich man. Not that he knew what to do with it when he earned it. He used to talk about a larger house, but I told him that this was plenty big enough for a family of our size. We did buy that house in Spain, but when we used it I could see he was bursting for the day when we set off back home.'

'Even though he seemed dissatisfied with his work?'

'Yes. I didn't understand it.'

'Is he prepared to spend money on you?'

'Oh, yes. Always has been. If I wanted new clothes, he coughed up straight away. And it was the same with the house. New furniture, decorating, carpets, I'd only to ask. Not that I'm unreasonable. I'm typical of my class and upbringing when it's a case of spending money. I'm careful. And you'll remember that if we wanted to go abroad in your school holidays, just you and I, and leave him at home to look after himself, he never complained. No. And yet he began to talk about retirement. I used to ask him straight out what he'd do. He hadn't any plans. He'd be lost. He was just a bit bored at work and since he's met William Wolfe he's been different altogether. He'll go off there to Wolfe's house – it's a different day of the week each time, on account of Wolfe's duties – as pleased as punch after dinner and it's often past midnight when he comes home.'

'Is he sober?'

'Yes. I'm not saying they don't have a drink, but next morning he's up with the lark as usual. I'm pleased about it. That's why I kept asking him to invite his friend round for dinner. This was the first time he's done so. At Christmas. I don't know whether he enjoyed it. The old aunts aren't exactly marvellous company and the Comptons, well, you've met them before. He's an ex-employee of your father's bank, nothing like as high in position or status as your dad. But he'd been in the bank a long time and he was very kind to Tony when he first started there.'

'He doesn't throw his weight about, Mr Wolfe, that is, does he?'

'No. Your dad says he'll sit through a whole meal hardly speaking a word, but then somebody will ask him a question and he'll hold the whole talk with his brilliance. That's one thing Daddy likes him for.'

'Does he talk to you?'

'I've hardly met him. But on one of the two occasions I met him, he talked to me about Italian cookery and my word he knows what he's talking about. Half of it was in Italian. Yet Daddy says he's not interested in eating.'

'How does he know so much?'

'He lived in Italy for three years. Our Rome correspondent.'

'Dad doesn't mind his knowing so much?'

'No. It's surprising really, because your dad's always enjoyed being one up on everybody.'

'It keeps him happy, you say?'

'It seems to. Wolfe's not only a polymath, but he's very interesting about his life as a journalist. He interviews all sorts of famous people and some of them are strange, very strange indeed. He tells Tony all about them, but he'll never pass the information on to me, although I'm bursting to know. He thinks I'll spill it all round the neighbourhood.'

'And would you?'

'It's quite likely.'

Alicia enjoyed these talks with her mother, who spoke freely to her now as to a close friend or contemporary. This had only begun since the daughter had left Oxford. Before that she had sometimes let slip some snippet of scandal or family history, but had almost at once appeared embarrassed. Now she had no compunction about the confidences she came out with. It was clear that her husband's friendship with the learned Mr Wolfe had pleased her, had set her mind at rest about his imminent retirement, that she had been relieved he'd given up that idea. Alicia smiled. And where had her mother picked up the term 'polymath'?

Immediately after Boxing Day Alicia had gone over to Brighton to stay two or three days with a friend. This had been arranged when Mary had spent a week in the Midlands with her last summer. They phoned, once a month or thereabouts, but just before her Christmas card arrived Mary had rung to announce that she and her fiancé had broken off their engagement. The wedding to Adrian Seagrave was to have taken place in July at the end of the school term where Mary was teaching. She had been matter of fact in her breaking of the news, did not seem concerned, but Alicia found herself worried. She had known Mary for three years; they had met in Oxford, where she was a year ahead of her friend, but even then Mary was already engaged to Adrian. Their compact had seemed almost like an eleventh commandment, utterly serious and not to be broken.

Adrian, whom Alicia had met two or three times, had been at

school with Mary in the sixth form when she was in the fourth. He had studied chemistry at Birmingham and now worked in one of the new factories just outside Cambridge, where he was reported by Mary to be doing well. They seemed an old-fashioned pair, dedicated to each other, standing shyly hand in hand in photographs, immersed in their love for one another, the ideal pair. Why they had not married before Alicia could not make out, but they had waited until she had done her four years and successfully completed her probationary year's teaching in a large girls' public school in Sussex. It had all seemed so inevitable and right. They appeared to consult each other's interest and plan the minutiae of the wedding day down to the last exact detail. Alicia was to be a bridesmaid. There would be children after a decent, short interval, then the long life together that they deserved.

Now this was all over.

Alicia was curious, but unnerved. Here a couple, devoted to, meant for each other, in a marriage made in heaven, had decided otherwise. Mary's flat appeared, as always, neatly furnished, the furniture bright, the walls hung with small pictures, mainly watercolours done by her clergyman father of the Derbyshire landscape near his home in the Peak District. The photographs of Adrian were missing and that seemed to Alicia best described by the Shakespearean phrase 'a gap in nature'. The man himself went unmentioned for the first few hours, when they chatted about their work. Mary's teaching duties had their satisfactions and ennui.

'Are your pupils co-operative?' Alicia asked.

'On the whole. Their parents spend a lot of money to keep them there, and only the girls who need physics, or think they do, opt for the subject. I teach only examination candidates, A and one GCSE; otherwise the rest is taught by amateurs, people who haven't taken honours degrees in physics, but seem to me good, all-round teachers. I'm drawing up syllabuses, syllabi, for the whole subject. They seem grateful. I often wonder how often this happens. I'm only in my second year, am head of department and laying down the law as to what's to be taught and how. I got some good physics results last summer, but I think that's nothing to boast about. I teach clever girls who aren't afraid of work.'

'Will you move from here?'

'I haven't even thought about it. I like living by the seaside even when it's crowded in the season. And the headmistress and governors say that they are pleased with me. Physics teachers are

99

like maths teachers, thin on the ground. If we can get a reputation for good physics results, it means we'll have more applications for places. And that's what we're after.'

'And so you're pleased with life?'

'With that part of it. I have to work hard, but it seems appreciated by the powers that be.'

'You recommend teaching, then?'

'I've dropped on my feet and I'm learning quickly. I sometimes think I'd have done better if I'd begun with an experienced senior teacher to show me the wrinkles and tips. But I didn't have the advantages of that, so I have sorted it out for myself. I went on a course and I can also ask my old physics teacher, Alice Ratcliffe, for advice. She's retired and hates it. I sometimes think she'd like to be invited in to do a bit of part time. We'll see.'

'Does she live hereabouts?'

'Oh, yes. And I mark papers for the Board.'

Mary seemed so settled and content with herself that Alicia was immediately suspicious. How she could have broken with Adrian, yet draw an equal satisfaction from her work might seem an ideal solution, but one not often found. Later on their first evening they took a walk in the dark down to the cold threatening sea, then returned to lounge with a glass of sherry in the ravishingly warm flat.

'It's comfortable here,' the guest complimented her hostess.

'That's one of the things that Adrian complained about.'

'The comfort? What did he want? A monk's cell?'

'He thought that I wouldn't leave it too easily. Especially as I'd taken a mortgage on it.'

'Doesn't seem altogether reasonable on his part.'

'He liked to instigate new ideas. He wasn't averse to large change as long as he had thought up the scheme and set it in motion.'

'And that was enough to make you decide against marriage?'

'Not entirely. If you'd have asked me three or four months ago, I'd have claimed all was well. We'd had a good holiday together, we'd fixed the date of the wedding, we both had jobs we liked, we knew each other inside out. Or so we thought. He came over the first weekend of my new term and said I'd changed. I asked him in what way. He said I was more interested in my job than in him.'

Mary paused, rubbing her chin, as if trying to recall exactly what was said.

'Was there anything in it?' Alicia asked.

'Well, I'd started teaching a year before and found I liked it. Meanwhile in August I'd had these excellent A and GCSE results. That gave me confidence. The headmistress said how pleased she and the governors were, and that I was now acting head of physics. It meant no more pay, but if I continued to do well I'd get an extra allowance. It went to my head a bit. And when she asked me to prepare syllabuses, perhaps I did talk a lot more about it than I should have to Adrian.'

'Was he jealous?'

'That didn't strike me at the time, but when I came to think about it later perhaps it was so. Anyway we had a row about this.'

'Was this your first quarrel?'

'No. We'd often had words. But this was quite bad and got worse. In the end he said if that was how I thought of him, he'd better go. And he put on his jacket and left.'

'Slamming the doors?'

'Not that I noticed. While we were arguing I felt excited, putting my case. But when he went out like that I felt empty and I cried. After all, we'd spent the night before in bed together.'

'Have you seen him since?'

'Yes. He stayed out of sight for a week or two. Then he came back and I returned his engagement ring. He seemed surprised at that. I guess he thought I couldn't do without him. It upset me again when he'd gone, but I'd made up my mind to do this.'

'Were you sure?'

'Not perfectly, no. But I thought that it would show us where we stood.'

'And did it?'

'Yes, in a way it did. Now when I'm going about the house part of me, a large part, seems to belong to him still. And I have to stop myself and make it clear that there'll be no wedding next July. I feel a pang, I must admit, but I fight it down, if that's the expression.'

'You wouldn't marry him now, then?'

'No. I wouldn't. I'd like to be married, a bit of me, even to him, no, especially to him. It would be marvellous if I could be married to him for a part, a small part, of each holiday, and for the rest to live on my own as I do now.'

'Adrian wouldn't wear that, would he?'

'No, he wouldn't. And he'd argue, reasonably enough I suppose, that we should spend time with each other and learn, gradually, to adapt to each other's ways. The snag with that is I know he means I should give in to him and do as he orders.'

'That wouldn't do?'

'No. And yet I'm not sure. Sometimes I think I'd like him back but at bottom I am tired of him, I know how he'd react to any situation, even in bed' – she gave an apologetic giggle – 'and I'd be bored, and that there'd be no relief for me from him. When I put it plainly like that, it seems wrong and ridiculous. It must happen to all married people, that they grow bored with their partner. But they don't break up the marriage on this account.'

'A large number of them do.'

'But I'm bored with him before the marriage has even started.'

'You've been living as a married couple to all intents and purposes. And almost under your ideal conditions.'

'I suppose we have. In the old days people didn't have sexual intercourse before they were married, so that was a great change of life. They had to learn about it, practise it until they were good at it. Though in our case I don't, I mean I'm not sure that that was it. There was something not quite right between us, in our ordinary everyday dealings. In some ways I was glad that Adrian was there, in the background of my life, but after we had had this quarrel I was certain I didn't want him in the foreground, there all the time. I made this clear to him when we were quarrelling. I told him that he couldn't rule my life for me, make all the decisions, and that even when we were married I'd need some space of my own. He said he couldn't understand that and I don't think he did. He seemed to think that when we were in tandem, that was his daft phrase, that he did as he wanted and I just followed his instructions. I made it clear that his ideas weren't so brilliant that they couldn't be bettered. He didn't like that. All he could say was that he liked doing things for me. I said he never consulted me as to what I wanted. He said he did. I answered that just telling me what we were going to do wasn't consultation. He said I'd changed. I said he ought to expect that; I was no longer in the fourth form while he lorded it in the sixth. We really went for each other.'

'And he?'

'He grew hot round the collar. His face was red and when he spoke he was pretty well spitting at me. In the end he just went off. Oh, he said Oxford had spoilt me.'

102

'And that was that?'

'Yes. He never apologised or said he'd try to do better or he had realised what he was doing wrong.'

'I see.'

They sat together in silence. In the end Alicia breathed noisily and asked, 'How much older is Adrian than you?'

'Two years. I suppose that seemed a lot at school. But not now.'

Mary looked up, smiling beatifically. 'You all right?' she asked.

'Yes. Very busy. Not much life outside my thesis.'

'And will that do?'

'It will have to. Next term I shall start writing it up.'

'Are you looking forward to that?'

'Yes, though there are all sorts of bits and pieces I keep coming across, and things people draw my attention to.'

'And they make you change your mind about what you're writing?'

'No, but they all add to the picture.'

'Is Christopher Conway guiding you?'

'He's tutoring me; I don't know about guiding. He tells me if the research is up to standard.'

'Don't you fancy him, Alicia?'

'He did take me to the theatre to see the local Shakespeareans do *Twelfth Night*. But before we were halfway through a great lorry ran off the road and into the new dressing rooms.'

'In that moment of chaos did he throw his arms protectively round you and confess he'd always loved you?'

'As a matter of fact, no.'

They laughed, crowing like college girls, pleased with each other.

Mary invited Alicia to stay an extra day and she agreed. When she rang to tell her father he sounded neither surprised nor disappointed. That afternoon Miss Ratcliffe, Mary's old physics teacher, appeared by prior appointment to look over the syllabuses her ex-pupil was preparing. Alice Ratcliffe was an unmarried lady in her early seventies, stiffly built, with blue lenses in her spectacles and her hair drawn savagely back into an immaculate bun. Her mouth cut a thin line sternly across her face as if she had already judged you as worthy of very little of her time. She moved vigorously, swinging her arms and almost breastless torso whenever she made a point. There was little chance that the listener failed to mark what to her was important. Her appearance was in no way friendly, yet when she talked to Mary about her preparation her voice was rich with interest; her judgements were rigorous, but her suggestions seemed, as far as Alicia could see, both sensible and comprehensive.

Miss Ratcliffe listened to Mary's suggestions but answered at once and with certainty. 'When I was seventy a year ago, the Board put an end to my marking. Their rules lay that down. Oddly, those same rules say nothing about setting the papers and so I continue with that. And also,' here she grimaced as at the foolishness of mankind, 'I act as ombudsman if there is a complaint from a school about unfair marking of their candidates.' So she explained herself to Alicia at teatime.

'Are there many?'

'There are some every year. Not a large proportion by any means considering the number of candidates.'

'And what happens?'

'If they have been unfairly assessed my marks are accepted.'

'Why have they been so badly treated?'

'I don't know. There must be many reasons, illness, domestic or other trouble. When you look at the markers' qualifications they are eminently satisfactory. On paper. We take endless trouble explaining our schemes to the markers.' She shook her head. 'I think of one case this last summer. It was, I regret to say, a clergyman with a Ph.D. in the subject. He had some bee in his bonnet about falling standards. He'd been a university lecturer in physics and had retired at sixty to take holy orders.'

'And what happens to him?'

'Oh, we shan't employ him again.'

'He'd be short of money, would he?'

'I've no idea about his private circumstances. He'd obviously no intention of following our carefully thought-out schemes of allotting marks. We'll probably see letters from him in the papers about the poor methods of teaching or how one can pass GCSE physics with hardly any knowledge of the subject.'

'And there's no truth in that?'

'No. Knowledge is necessary, believe you me.'

When after tea Miss Ratcliffe had left, Mary questioned her guest. 'What do you think of her, then?'

'She seemed certain about her ideas.'

'So she is. Though she confesses that quantum mechanics or astrophysics are getting beyond her.'

104

'You didn't talk about very modern physics at school, then?'

'No. We didn't. But we had a firm foundation to build on. That was her position. She's sharp. Oh, yes, you went into her classes to work. If you were genuinely in trouble she'd help you out. She'd got me well into first year degree physics by the time I reached university.'

'How does she spend her time now she's retired?'

'You heard about her position with the Exam Board, but what she does over and above that is vague. She doesn't talk about it. She goes to church most Sunday mornings. She'll have few friends. She'll take a walk on fine days, do crosswords and Su Doku and the like. She'll write a few letters. She has a brother she visits once or twice a year. He's a master at Repton.'

'What does he teach? Physics?'

'No. English and divinity. And he has five children, making up for her, he says.'

'She's never been married?'

'No. And I don't think she's missed it.'

'Does she not like children?'

'Between the age of eleven and eighteen and doing well at physics. I've wondered this past week or two if I shall end up like her. Do you think so?'

'No, I don't. You like men, to be in the company of men. The fact that you're making a success of teaching and organising physics seems important to you just now, but in a few years you'll not be satisfied with it. It's great that you're doing well at it, but I don't think that will last a lifetime. I was asking myself what your Miss Ratcliffe as a young woman would have made of Adrian.'

'What did you make of him, never mind old Ratty?' The schoolgirl nickname revealed her uncertainty.

'He wouldn't have suited me altogether. He liked his own way, but that wouldn't have suited me because his ideas were nothing to shout about. I thought he was lucky because he'd found a girl like you and you'd have knocked a few ideas into his thick head before long, especially if you had children.'

'You talk to me like the big sister I never had.'

'I'll tell you this. You underrate yourself. You've sorted out this physics business in your first year. Not many would manage that. And I have no doubt that if you married Adrian you'd soon set him right.'

'It's too late for that.'

'There'll be somebody else.'

Mary smiled broadly. 'Will you marry, do you think?' she asked.

'I expect so. I'm only twenty-five. But I like to finish one job off before I start another. Give me the chance to get this thesis out of the way.'

'This year?'

'Yes. I keep finding new things. Only a month ago I heard from a man I didn't know. Professor Conway had given my name to him. He had found some interesting letters written in the eighteenth century by some ancestor of his and she was a great playgoer. And he allowed me to use her letters. She wrote home to her family and gave great detail of one or two of her visits to the theatre. She was a lively writer, so I'm lucky that these accounts of hers have been put at my disposal.'

'What was her name?'

'Emma Steventon. Her descendant, he's an old man in his eighties, had these letters photocopied for me. I visited him and spent a whole day reading the letters.'

'Does he live in Nottinghamshire?'

'No, Leicestershire. When I've finished my thesis, I might bang out a little book. She wrote very well about other matters than the theatre.'

'When you've done looking for a job, you'll have to move, won't you?'

'It depends where it is.'

'Will you find one easily?'

'Again it depends what they want. For instance, neither university in Beechnall has an eighteenth-century specialist.'

'There might be an opening for you, then?'

'Maybe. They may find someone who is so good that they can't miss the chance of such a paragon and take him or her on.'

'And you don't count yourself such a marvel?'

'No. I'm known as a worker. Christopher Conway will write me a good testimonial. And the principal of my college at Oxford will do me proud. And though she's a scientist she's very well known. Her name and photograph are always in the broadsheets. It can't do me any harm.'

'Won't Conway offer you a job at Beechnall?'

'I doubt it. It's always a matter of money these days.'

'You might have to sell your house, then?'

'I keep it in good order on that account.'

'Wouldn't you like to stay there?'

'If I could find a job that interested me nearby then I would.'

'And have you got your next piece of research lined up?'

'Once I've finished the Ph.D., I shall try to make a book out of it.'

'Is that difficult?'

'I shouldn't think so. I'll do my best to make it as interesting to the ordinary reader as I can. But publishers are a tricky lot. They can always claim that there's little call for such a topic.'

'Even if it's extremely well written, which it will be.'

'That's a matter of personal taste.'

They talked discursively of their futures, neither being sure. That night as they were drinking Horlicks before going up to bed at midnight, Mary said, 'I really have enjoyed having you here, Alicia. You make me see things straight.'

'I've enjoyed it, too. It does me good to be taken out of myself and my concerns. Living on one's own has its drawbacks.'

'You've made me see myself so much more clearly. I've begun to wonder about myself again. I thought that when Adrian and I quarrelled I'd finished with men for life. Getting my teaching off to a good start has been a blessing for me, in a way, but it's not enough. Even Miss Ratcliffe, who's been an enormous help to me, seems to have stopped her development too early. She's mastered the art of teaching, and that would be in her twenties, as she was a determined figure. She refined it as she grew older, and altered it, and made it into a real art, and she seems to have been satisfied with that. She hasn't widened her experience outside her schoolwork.'

'What ought she to have done?'

'Had a husband and children. Or a satisfying lesbian relationship. Or taken to looking after others outside her work. Or become interested in literature, theatre and music.'

'Has she tried these?'

'I don't know about falling in love. As to the others, she'd as soon read this morning's *Times* as a great novel or poem. And she doesn't seem to have friends, mere acquaintances with whom she occasionally does things, a trip to the cinema or theatre or a concert. But not very often. And it seems not to have any great effect. And music is something she plays while she's cleaning the house or washing the dishes or changing the bedlinen. It's pleasant but no more.'

107

'To do just one good thing superlatively well is not to be sneezed at.'

'But she's not allowed to teach or mark more than a few exam papers, so what's left to her? You see how excited she is to have the opportunity to lay down the law to me.'

'Even if she had other strings to her bow, old age would put a stop to them.'

'Not of necessity. There's no law to stop people over seventy from doing the crossword from the morning papers or running through a Mozart sonata or a Bach fugue on the piano.'

'But won't you find you are worse at these things as you grow older?'

'Yes, and that is a tragedy. If I lose my memory or dementia of one sort or another sets in, I don't know what I'll do.'

'That's no case for not trying a range of intellectual or emotional tasks or pleasures in your youth. If people stopped having babies in their earlier life because they know they'll be incapable of this in their seventies, what sort of mess would the human race be in?'

'Well argued.' Alicia clapped her hands and her eyes shone.

'I love talking with you,' Mary said. 'It makes me think life's worth living.'

'Don't you have good conversations in your Common Room?'

'Not really. They talk about holidays and what they ate at a dinner party or their children's ailments.'

'You must mention educational matters sometimes?'

'Yes, but never very seriously. They tell each other how stupid some girl is and how she never pays attention to any instruction. I think we are an exam-passing factory.'

'Aren't all schools?'

'To some extent. But the good schools try to introduce their pupils to culture, mental, moral and physical.'

'Didn't you find that when you left school for Oxford the university offered you a whole raft, as they say, of cultural opportunities. There was a musical performance pretty well every lunchtime. And lectures and talks. I remember going to a lecture one of the new dons at our college gave. He was a nice-looking young man and he tried to give us some notion of what he'd done for his D.Phil.'

'Could you understand it?'

'Not a word. He might have been talking Sanskrit. I did my best to follow him, but it was useless. And yet I found it in a way uplifting, that somebody who looked no longer than us students, should be following such abstruse studies. I did A Level maths.'

They went up to bed, pleased with themselves.

Next morning Alicia set out for a quick walk before breakfast. Her idea was to buy a newspaper. She bought *The Times*, thinking that was the newspaper Mary would read. She opened it outside the shop. A sharp wind made the opening of the paper difficult. With a few shakes she rigorously disciplined it. On the front page was the photograph she recognised. Inside the house she laid the paper beside Mary's plate. Mary, returning from the kitchen with a rackful of toast, looked at the paper with pleasure. 'Anything interesting in it this morning?'

'The Queen's New Year's Honours List.'

'Oh. Are you in it?'

'No, but I know someone who is.' Alicia tapped the photograph with a fingernail.

Mary peered down, then picked up the paper. 'Sir Clarence Caldwell,' she read aloud. 'He's wearing a funny hat.'

'It must have been part of the costume he was wearing in one of his plays.'

'For services to the theatre,' Mary read slowly. 'How do you come to know him?'

'He lives in the same village as me.'

'Very close?'

'No. Some few minutes' walk. I live on the outskirts of the village proper and he lives even further on.'

'Do you know him?'

'Yes. He invited me to be his second in command of the play he was producing. It all came to nothing.'

'Is he . . . will he be pleased with his knighthood?'

'I expect he will, or otherwise he wouldn't have taken it.'

'Is he married?'

'No. He's a widower. There is an old theatrical living with him. She looks after him.'

'He must have friends in high places to put his name forward.'

'He's done some big roles in his time. And he's still acting. Just recently he's managed some cameo parts in films. And he's produced the festival play, almost always Shakespeare, in Sutton for the past twenty-odd years. He deserves it, late though it is. I must send him a card of congratulations.'

'Well, don't for heaven's sake buy one. I've a drawerful here.'

109

She pulled it out and Alicia marvelled at the uneven, sliding piles of cards.

'Where did you get this lot from?' Alicia asked.

'An old friend of my mother's had a shop and when she retired she left a sackful of these ancient cards. I mean to do something with them one of these days.'

'Do what?'

'Make a picture or fill an album with the best of them.'

They sorted through a hundred or two of the cards, and left the choice between a drawing of Buckingham Palace, a photograph of the Pavilion at Brighton and an ugly painting of Sir Henry Irving in armour. They argued and laughed, and Alicia finally chose the Pavilion.

'I'll post it at once. I know he made a good many appearances there.'

She wrote her congratulations in her best handwriting and added Mary Winters's name to hers. She always carried stamps in her purse and thus was able to post the card immediately in the box outside Mary's flat.

'It will remind him of his triumphs,' she said. That sounded stilted to her, if not daft, but she excused herself by saying this was the first time she had ever had the opportunity to congratulate an acquaintance on his knighthood.

Soon after lunch she kissed her friend goodbye, and set off to chase and overtake the card on its way to the Midlands.

IX

Back in the village Alicia found herself at a loose end. Nobody was about; if people celebrated the New Year they did it at home, the best place, for the weather was not only dark but cold, with harsh frost night after night. She had called in at her parents' home on the way back from Brighton, and they had invited her to stay over the New Year. Her father, she knew, would be glad to potter in the garden, if the weather allowed it, or stare vacantly at their huge new television set, and thus had no wish to play host to anybody, not even his only child. Mrs Smallwood spent the mornings cooking and did not wish to share the pleasurable chore even with her daughter who would offer to join her in the kitchen. Her father criticised himself and his wife. 'You'd think we were in our eighties not fifties. We like the place to ourselves without anyone to interrupt. Even your mother, who's a social soul, doesn't want to go out to classes, or to see friends at this time of year. I don't know what we shall be like by the time I come to retire. We'll be a couple of eremites. Is there such a word?'

'Yes, it's a poetic form of hermit. As in Keats's "Like nature's patient, sleepless Eremite".'

'I wonder where I picked it up from.'

'Me, I expect.'

He looked at her in surprise. 'I'm glad my head's not full of poetry,' he said. 'And you'll be, too, when you find out how much I leave you in my will.'

She kissed him and he rubbed his scalp gently in surprise. 'Say us a bit more of that poem,' he said, almost reluctantly.

She carefully, almost whispering, repeated the first six lines of the sonnet.

'Very good,' he said. 'You really make something of it. As if it's important.'

'Don't you like it, then?'

111

'I'm impressed by the way you recite it and that you've taken the trouble to learn it by heart.'

'That's no trouble.'

'No, not to you. And I can see it's memorable. But he seems to be using the language to sound fine. "Of pure ablution." Why "pure"? If the sea is washing earth's human sores they'd be clean, surely. And why human shores? Does he mean people who live by the sea? I think he'd be after fine overblown phrases, never mind if they don't mean much.'

'Using language is a very tricky business,' she said.

'I suppose it is if you think about it. I just put words together to get things done.'

'I remember one of our lecturers telling us about a boy standing looking into a shop window. Down the hill, a very long way off, another boy is approaching. The first boy looks and says to himself, though out loud, strongly enough to catch my attention, "Here comes the great Majóoba-lóola." He's made that word up. He was glad to see his friend, or even his enemy, and to mark the occasion, and to show his pleasure or otherwise he'd made up this title, on the spur of the moment. It was nothing like English. It might have been an African word, but the repeated "oo" sound gave it some magic, even authenticity.'

'Good grief, Alicia. You and your lecturers think up some odd explanations.'

'But it's marvellous that that boy, nine or ten years old, had conjured up these sounds, just to impress himself. To say something worthy of the occasion.'

Her father laughed and turned away. Clearly his view was that if he thought of such rubbish it wouldn't be long before he was in prison or the bankruptcy court. Yet he was proud of her; she knew it.

Back in her own garden she swept up leaves, noticed snowdrops, aconites and one or two rogue primulas showing colour. This week she'd arranged with her gardener to confer about what she'd want for the summer. That pleased her; he seemed a reasonable man who, seeing that she knew little about it, suggested plants that would keep the garden bright with flowers. He showed her pictures, brought along catalogues for her, grew enthusiastic.

'You and I will get on, I see. In this village there's hardly a soul who's interested in what's worth growing in their gardens. They fetch me in to keep the places tidy. Look at that actor fellow, Sir

Something Caldwell now. "Keep my lawns trimmed and my paths clear," he says. I know his garden is not altogether flat but that presents me with a challenge. And that professor you recommended me to, Conway. He knows names, but he shows no real interest. I guess he's lived with gardens before, but he's had no responsibility. Where did he come from?'

'Oxford.'

'I thought it would be somewhere like that. You could tell he'd been round the horticultural department's greenhouses; he had all sorts of snippets of knowledge, but nothing solid, basic.'

'I'm sorry we're all such a disappointment to you.'

'Oh, no, miss, not you. You've a real interest. It won't be long before you're telling me what to do.'

Like her father, this man approved of her. She did not deserve it, but enjoyed his moderate praise.

On Sunday morning she took her small walk. The little shop that sold newspapers was open; she bought a *Sunday Times* and a large bar of dark chocolate. The woman behind the counter, neat as always, seemed glad to talk.

'It's a lovely morning, isn't it? They delivered the papers from Beechnall very early today. Before six o'clock. I ask you. Who's up and about then? Sid and I got up and sorted them out, and that's not at all easy these days, and then he goes back for an hour or two. I got his breakfast and took it upstairs, and when he's eaten it he'll drop off again until I'm ready for church.'

'Where do you go?'

'St John's, Beechnall.'

'You don't walk, do you?'

'No. I go on my bike.'

'Even when the weather's bad?'

'No. Give me credit for a bit of common sense. There is a church bus. But I shall enjoy it this morning. The vicar there doesn't hang about with it and I'm back well before noon. I help in the shop as I cook the lunch. We close at one o'clock and the rest of the day's our own.'

'Do you go out?'

'Not usually. Not at this time of the year. It's dark by four thirty. It's our time for lounging about. This is a seven-days-a-week job. Up early every morning. This is our only real half-day of the week. We just waste it.'

'I don't think I'd waste that length of a day's work.'

113

'Well, we knew what we were in for when we took it. The people who read the news on the wireless and telly have to get up earlier than we do.'

'They don't have to go out into the cold streets.'

'No. We don't deliver too many. I know this is a village to which people retire, but they mostly are still active. Like our knight.'

'Night?'

'Sir Clarence. Not that he's going out much. He's said to be quite ill.'

'What's wrong with him?'

'Pneumonia or something of the sort. Doctors don't seem so keen these days to send people to hospital, because they can catch all sorts of diseases in the place.'

'He must have been taken ill at Christmas? I spoke to him just before I went off on holiday.'

'Anywhere interesting?'

'To my parents in London. And then Brighton.'

'What's it like at the seaside at this time of year?'

'I enjoyed it. We walked by the sea at night, when there was something of a wind, and one could hear the whoosh and swish of the waves washing in.'

'Beautiful. Mr Caldwell – I beg his pardon, Sir Clarence – was down there a lot at that time.'

'Had he still got the house here?'

'Yes, though it was empty most of the year. He'd come back when he wasn't working. And sometimes he'd have a lady with him and she might stay on. That's after his wife had died. She was his second wife, I believe. He was unlucky; both of them died. He was always something of a ladies' man.'

'Is Mrs Rhŷs-Williams with him now?'

'Yes. She's there for good. Celebrating his knighthood. Not that they'll be doing much if he's so ill. The doctor calls in here when he's driving about on his rounds. He won't come in today, Sunday. I don't blame him. He won't come at all. He told me how bad the old man was. And only the old crosspatch to look after him. I don't know how he puts up with her. I don't see ever so much of her, but the bit I do see I don't like.'

On her way back Alicia stood for a few moments at the gate of her grounds because she had noticed shuffling up the road Mrs Rhŷs-Williams. It looked for a moment as if the old woman would ignore her, pass without a word.

'Good morning,' Alicia called out clearly and cheerfully. Mrs Rhŷs-Williams started, almost like a horse, then stopping turned and stared. There seemed a hint of recognition in her eyes which were, Alicia noticed, of a washed-out blue.

'How is Sir Clarence?' Alicia spoke too loudly, she thought herself. 'Is he any better today?'

The old woman growled in her throat.

'Is he better?'

Again the insolent stare, a pause while she dug into the road with her stick. 'Yes. He is. And so he ought to be, the amount of tablets he's taking.'

As Alicia was about to speak again, the old woman raised her stick and pointed at the house. 'Do you live there?' she asked, furiously jabbing the air, as if she resented needing to enquire.

'Yes.'

'Do you own it?'

'Yes.'

The old woman was clearly puzzled by the two answers. 'I've never been inside,' she said.

'Would you like to look around?' Alicia asked. Megan Rhŷs-Williams glanced up suspiciously. She was unused to having her bait snapped up so readily. She accepted with another throaty rumble and shuffled forward. Alicia opened her gate and, pointing to the steep steps down asked, 'Will you be all right on those?'

Megan angrily indicated she'd manage.

'There's room for me to lend you an arm.'

The old woman was already stumbling her way down. Alicia, expecting an accident at every step, cautiously followed, eyes half shut against disaster. Both arrived at garden level, the guest less disturbed than her hostess, who now seemed unable to turn the Yale lock. She opened the door of the small conservatory at last and signalled Megan to follow her. The door to the home swung open easily and Megan stepped into the hall with a huge intake of breath. 'Very nice,' she approved. 'Very nice indeed.' She was in no hurry to move, but turned on her heel to look about her. Satisfied, she now walked to the wall and began to examine the pictures. 'Did you do them?' she asked.

'No. They're by the father of a man I met at university.'

'Which university was that?'

'Oxford.'

115

'My eldest boy was there. At Christ Church. These pictures are very good. They're watercolours.'

'Yes.' She was not provoked into rudeness. When Megan had concluded her scrutiny of the rest of the paintings they moved together into the front drawing room. Megan stood in the doorway keeping Alicia out.

'My word,' Megan said. 'This is something. What they call on those televised programmes about preparing houses for sale "The Wow Factor".'

Alicia noticed that her voice was different. Megan spoke very quietly, but clearly, her pronunciation received standard. She pointed out the furniture she liked, commented on the balance of the place.

'You haven't packed it out. You've some beautiful objects here and you've placed them to advantage. It's a gift.'

'You should see the furnishing next door, Mr Wicks's home. His rooms are really stunning.'

'Are they? Clarence is hopeless. As long as his chair's comfortable and the room's warm you could run a circus or an infant school in the rest of the place.'

'Wouldn't he object to the noise?'

'I suppose he would. But you know what I mean. He's no taste when it comes to decorating a house. Words, yes. He's a genius there. We're odd. But this room pleases me. And I'd like to see it when the sun's going down. In the gloaming. Is that a Scottish word?'

'Old English, I think.'

Megan's eyes widened at the correction.

'Now, let's look at the dining room and my study.'

Megan walked around murmuring approval. She no longer appeared as an eccentric old creature. 'You've some beautiful furniture in the rooms,' she said. 'My word, young lady, you can't be short of money.'

'It's my mother,' Alicia said, smiling. 'Daddy bought me the house and pays for its upkeep, but my mother chose the furniture. She likes nothing better. As they've got richer they've moved into larger houses. And each time they've moved she's changed the furniture. She spends quite a bit of her leisure around antique shops and auctions. I guess I've got some of the furniture she considered suitable for this house, while she went off and bought pieces to fill the gaps in her house.'

116

'And doesn't your father mind?'

'Oh, no. He doesn't know how to spend the money he earns. They go off for a two- or three-week cruise in the summer, and a spring week or two in Scandinavian waters. They don't live luxuriously, nor dress expensively. So my mother is allowed to spend her time and money with antiques. She's quite an expert, I believe, and is always reading up the subject, and she's invited to the big auction shows.'

'She has very good taste. Don't you have any say?'

'Not really. She holds the purse strings. I'm only a poor student.'

'You're a lucky young woman.'

They moved on to her study where the books for the morrow's work lay in piles by the computer.

'All ready for tomorrow?' Megan asked.

'Yes. I start tomorrow to write up my thesis.'

'Is that for a degree?'

'Yes, a D.Phil. or Ph.D., as they call it here.'

'And then we'll have to call you Dr Smallwood. I must be going or Clarence will be complaining.' This all came out at speed. As they moved towards the door Mrs Rhŷs-Williams seemed to transform herself back into the crouching, hunched figure she presented in the street. She thanked Alicia, who invited her to come again.

'Could I come to see Sir Clarence or is he too ill?' Alicia.

'I'll ask him. I'm sure he'll be pleased. You're one of his favourites.'

The old woman mounted the steps up to the road with surprising agility. There she straightened herself, waved, bent over and hobbled away.

Alicia hummed to herself, spent an hour with the Sunday paper, then set about preparing her lunch. The house was warm; she felt happy. An hour later Megan Rhŷs-Williams telephoned to say Sir Clarence would be pleased to see her. The visit was arranged for five the next day. Monday, the day she was determined to start writing her thesis.

She ordered flowers to be brought to her house from Beechnall on that morning. She had started writing by nine o'clock, breakfast being dispatched and the table cleared. She began with a chapter from which she expected little difficulty or need to reorganise her ideas: a history of the English theatre up to the eighteenth century. She had sorted her thoughts and had written a rough draft, and knew where she was going. Even so, although she wrote steadily, she had to alter the order of the chapter twice. She broke off twice, once to take the flowers and write the florist a cheque, the second time to eat her lunch, cheese sandwiches and fruit salad with ice cream. She idled after she had eaten with a cup of coffee for perhaps fifteen minutes before she washed her few dishes and went back to her desk and began to write. She glanced at her clock as she started: a quarter to two.

She wrote on steadily until 4.30. Although her introductory notes were plain and properly directed, she had not progressed quite as far as she had expected. She was not disappointed, sure that what she had done was sensibly solid, even interesting. She left matters on her desk ready for the next morning's start. Sighing with satisfaction, she made for the bathroom where she briefly, to use her father's expression, beautified herself, returned the roses from the bucket of water where she had left them straight from the florist's hands, made them fit to carry, donned long scarf, fur hat and topcoat, and set off for the 'House of the Hanged Man' as she always now thought of it since her visit there with Raynor Wicks and walked swiftly, knowing it would be a few minutes after five when she got there.

It was almost dark as she climbed down to Caldwell's house and rang the bell.

Mrs Rhŷs-Williams duly arrived, but she had clearly made no great hurry to reach the door. 'Miss Smallwood,' she said.

Inside it seemed to Alicia nothing like as warm as her house.

'Roses,' Mrs Rhŷs-Williams said. 'Singularly beautiful. I must find a suitable vase.' She laid the flowers on a small, empty table and led the way upstairs. 'Clarence, Clarence. Your visitor's here.' She backed out, closing the door.

The room was dimly lit, but a fire burnt in the grate. As Alicia approached the invalid she saw that he lay flat and well down the bed, his covers drawn up high to his mouth and nose. His head, in spite of a kind of knitted cap he wore, seemed small, like a child's.

'Hello,' she said and timidly approached. 'Are you feeling any better today?'

He gave some kind of muttered answer, which she made nothing of.

'I beg your pardon?' Alicia spoke as clearly as she could. He answered again; she caught the words 'not well' and 'rotten'.

'Is it some kind of flu?' she asked.

He turned slightly towards her, the movement something like a shudder of the whole body which, completed, left him where he was before. 'Sit down,' he ordered, looking towards a single kitchen chair, which stood some feet away from her. She obeyed. They sat in awkward silence.

'I ought' – her voice was hesitant – 'to congratulate you on the honour you have received.'

'Oh, thank you, thank you.' The voice coming from the blankets seemed stronger, warmer. 'I doubt, though, that I'll get to Buckingham Palace to receive it.'

'I think you will when the spring comes and the weather's better.'

'I doubt it. It won't take much to shake this old crow off his perch.'

'Your knighthood was well deserved.'

He did not answer that and again they sat silently dumb. She heard his breath, which seemed curiously noisy, yet weak.

'Are you beginning to feel better?'

'I thought so this morning. But now I'm just as ill.' The last words of the sentence groaned.

'Are they looking after you well?'

'Megan does her best. The doctor's been and issued his antibiotics, and I have a nurse in twice a day. They keep me clean. The doctor spoke about sending me to hospital, but I told him that was no place for anyone as sick as I am. We have a woman in to help Megan.'

'That's good.'

'She's a worker, but stupid. I dislike lying here flat out on my back while she's there clearing out the fireplace, knocking and banging, then laying and lighting the fire. She tells me over her shoulder what she's doing. She means well. It's boring lying in bed. I ought to be grateful to her. The day seems to drag. I tried to read this morning.'

'What was it you read?'

'Some of Kipling's verse. I don't suppose you know much about that.'

'No. Is it good?'

'I used to think he never gets the praise he deserves these days.'

'But you don't think so now.'

'It doesn't seem to matter.' He breathed deeply. 'Can you move your chair round to your right so I can see you without twisting my neck?' She made tentative movements. 'A little more. Nearer to me. Then to the right.' She stood, lifting her chair. He did not move. His eyes were closed half the time. 'That's it. Thank you, thank you. Can you repeat a line or two of Kipling's poetry?'

She giggled.

> 'Far-called our navies melt away;
> On dune and headland sinks the fire;'

'He threw that into the waste-paper basket.' Caldwell chuckled weakly. 'Have you any more?'

> 'If you can meet with Triumph and Disaster
> And treat those two impostors just the same.'

'Well done. That's up on the wall or over a door at Wimbledon for the tennis players to read. Is that where you found it?'

'No. I don't know why I remember that. The other, from "Recessional", I remember because we used to sing it in school once or twice a term. It was one of the headmistress's favourites. I liked it, too.'

'Do you know what "Recessional", the title, means?'

He's like an old-fashioned schoolmarm, Alicia thought, finding out what you know, or what you don't. 'I'm no expert on Anglican services,' she said, 'but I think it is the hymn that's sung during "Recession", the retirement of the clergy or choir to their vestries after a service.'

'I see you're a scholar.'

'As Sir Toby said to Sir Andrew, "Thou art a scholar."'

'Oh, dear, I'd forgotten that.'

There was some sort of mild commotion on the stairs outside the bedroom. Megan Rhŷs-Williams appeared, followed by a stout woman. Both were breathless. Megan turned, swooped and snatched a vase of red roses from the other woman and made for the bed, where she stood and held the flowers for him to see. 'Look at these,' she called. 'Miss Smallwood brought them for you.'

'Roses at this time of year,' Caldwell said and heaved himself upright. As he sat at a curious angle propping himself up with his stick-like arms, one of the buttons of his pyjama jacket came undone, so that an untidy bunch of white chest hair burst through. Alicia noticed how thin he was, more like a skeleton. He smiled.

He was not wearing his false teeth and this altered the shape of his wasted face. 'Thank you, thank you,' he gasped towards Alicia.

'Aren't you lucky?' Megan cackled. 'Young ladies bringing you roses.' She stamped her way over to an ancient dressing table where she put down the vase. 'Can you see that?' she asked the invalid. 'It has the mirror behind it, so I guess that from some angles you can see two. How's that?'

'Thank you. Superb.'

'That's the Latin for "proud". Now it's time for Miss Smallwood to leave. Wish her goodbye and thank you.'

Alicia stepped forward and shook his claw-like hand. He thanked her and attempted to lie flat again. Megan put both hands underneath him at the waist, dragging him further and straighter down the bed. Then, with infinite care, she arranged the bedclothes tidily over him, before finally lifting his head and placing it in the centre of his pillow.

'Say goodbye, Miss Smallwood.'

'Goodbye, Sir Clarence.'

'That sounds well, now, doesn't it? We'll be back in ten minutes with your tea. He'd like you to kiss him. On the forehead.' All this was delivered with the same power.

Alicia bent and kissed the old man's brow. As she straightened she happened to glance at the other woman's hand. The nails were clean, the flesh slightly puffy, the colour odd in the poor electric light. She guessed they'd be bright red in sunshine, the hands of someone who dabbled them all day in water.

Once they were downstairs Megan thanked Alicia for her visit. 'He looked that bit better, didn't he, Betty?'

'I think he did.' The other woman. No introductions were made.

'He always appreciated good-looking young women. Did he talk to you?'

'Yes. We talked about Kipling's poetry. His voice seemed very feeble.'

'Yes,' the other woman said, 'he had such a beautiful voice, so deep and resonant. I remember him saying that "If" poem by Kipling:

'If you can fill the unforgiving minute
With sixty seconds' worth of distance run
Yours is the Earth and everything that's in it
And – which is more – you'll be a Man, my son!

'I was in bed at the time.' She turned to Alicia. 'I'm a poor sleeper. And there was a poetry programme on the wireless. He recited that "If". I don't remember anything else he read, but I shan't ever forget the way he put that across with such power and grace. We had to learn it when I was in the third form of the grammar school. It made me smile a bit then, because it didn't seem suitable for girls. I didn't want to be a man, or anybody's son. Not that I said anything to my teachers. They'd have called it impudence.'

'We could do with a few more like that, nowadays, from what I hear,' Megan said. 'You're not a schoolteacher, are you, miss?'

She shook her head as she was led to the door. Both women accompanied her, thanking her or discoursing on the beauty of the roses. Outside it was now both dark and cold.

'Come again,' Megan shouted from the lighted doorway. 'You've done him good.'

The next morning after she'd finished breakfast Alicia took a turn round the garden before she started work on her thesis. She kept to the paths for the ground looked sodden and uninviting in the dull morning light. She stood for a moment by the wall at the bottom of her land looking over at an empty meadow. She shuddered. There was no advantage to living in the country on a morning like this. As she turned and made for the house, she was hailed by a masculine voice shouting 'Ahoy, there' and then 'Alicia'.

It was Raynor Wicks coming alongside the wall between the two plots. 'Good morning, madam,' he said in his best butler's voice.

His appearance did not match the gentlemanly suavity. He looked as though he had just got out of bed, having slept the night in his clothes; nor had he shaved or brushed his hair.

'Have you been away?' he asked.

'Yes. To London and Brighton.' That cut the questioning down.

'I thought you must have been. Your professor called twice, on two separate days, and stood there ringing the bell. I went out the second time and said you must have gone elsewhere for the holiday.'

'Hasn't he heard of the telephone?'

'He tried that, apparently. But he thought you might have turned the phone off so your work wouldn't be interrupted.'

'Did he say what he wanted?'

'No. He said it wasn't important.'

'I hope so. I wonder if he's come across some useful piece of information that might be crucial for my thesis.'

'Is that likely?'

'I shouldn't think so, but you never know with him. He loves keeping up his reading and comes across some unusual knowledge.'

'And then unloads it on you?'

'That's just it. He's very conscientious. But I wouldn't think he'd come out here for some trivial snippet he'd picked up.'

'Not unless it was important enough to change the entire direction of your research.'

'I hope not. I don't think such a bombshell exists.'

'No. You heard in your foreign parts that Clarence Caldwell has been knighted? But the locals tell me he's ill now, with pneumonia.'

'Yes. I went to see him yesterday. I had met Mrs Rhŷs-Williams and she said he'd be glad to see me.'

'And how was he?'

'They said he was much better than he has been, but he looked ill enough to me. He was lying right down in his bed, the sheets pulled up to his mouth. His face looked so thin I don't know whether I'd have recognised him. His talk was just a faint echo. You know how rich and full of harmonics his voice was, but now it was more like a squeak. You had to listen most carefully to make out what he was saying.'

'And was what he said interesting?'

'After a bit. He'd been reading Kipling and he asked me what I knew about him.'

'And did you know anything?'

'Not much. He asked me for a quotation or two from the poems. I could manage that.'

'You never studied him? At school or university?'

'We read *Kim* at school. I enjoyed it, but it hardly seemed a girls' book. And at Oxford I cannot remember anyone even mentioning his name. Perhaps that was my own fault.'

'Did he regard Kipling highly?'

'He said he was neglected these days.'

'True. Don't you find it so? People are highly regarded and then twenty years later they are never mentioned.'

'Do you read Kipling, then?' she asked.

'I hardly read poetry at all, shame on me. And poetry keeps a very low profile on television or radio.'

'The other woman there said she'd heard Mr Caldwell – I beg

his pardon, Sir Clarence – read "If" on the BBC Foreign Service in the small hours.'

'That would be Mrs Berresford. They say she's helping Megan Rhŷs-Williams out. Rumour has it that when he used to come back to this part of the world he made a great fuss of Betty Berresford, who was a schoolgirl then. Nothing scandalous. No hint of paedophilia. He greatly encouraged the child, predicted a bright future for her. She went to grammar school in Beechnall, did well. Kept her head above water, but left at sixteen to work in an office. This is all local talk; I can't say how true it is. She then married Eric Berresford. He worked for the Beechnall Transport Company as a clerk. He was another with a great future behind him. He was said to be a wizard with figures. He rose to some sort of responsible position with the buses, but no further. He wouldn't leave the place for a higher salary in some other part of the country. He did well enough, they say, to buy a house out here in Sutton. He died just a year or two ago, not long before you arrived. Betty used to visit Caldwell and, I believe, he her, and she'd always give Megan Rhŷs-Williams a helping hand if the old girl was not feeling up to it.'

'She doesn't look particularly beautiful now.'

'No. She'll be in her sixties.'

'I'd never seen her before, to the best of my knowledge.'

'No, she lives the other end of Sutton and isn't very sociable.'

'Where do you get all this information from?'

'Until a year ago I had a cleaning woman and she never stopped talking. She was a good worker, but, my word, her tongue would rattle.'

'Do you not still employ her?'

'She died and the present one, the one you now share with me, is laconic. I seem always to land myself with employees who boast extremities of psychology or habit.'

'Do you miss the first one?'

'Yes, I do. She got on my nerves from time to time, but I enjoyed her gossip.'

'Was it accurate?'

'Yes, as far as I could find out. She might have exaggerated from time to time, but not by much.'

He moved away, waving a hand and a white bag of bread, seeds, fat balls from which he fed the birds each morning. He had not taken five steps when he turned to look back over his broad shoulder. She had not moved. 'I say. If I were you, Alicia, I'd give your Professor Conway a bell.'

'I thought he said it was not important.'

'He did. But he may have been up here to invite you to a concert or a film, you never know.'

'It's unlikely.'

'You never know.' He laughed. 'He went with you to *Twelfth Night*. And rescued me.'

'Perhaps I will.'

'Are you busy now?'

'Yes. I've started writing up my Ph.D.'

'And how's it going?'

'I've only done one day at it and it went pretty well. This isn't surprising because I've known for some weeks where I was going to start and how.'

'The exact words?'

'Yes. It's not the real beginning of my thesis, but a chapter on the theatre of the time. I may have, I even hope that I've found my way to one or two insights, but on the whole it's background material, that everyone who knows anything about the period will have heard.'

'Why are you starting on this elementary stuff?'

'To take my mind back to the period, so that the reader who's never looked at either period or topic will be kept interested. And when it's completed, I'd like to make a book of it, and a book that can be read with both pleasure and understanding.'

'Not all academics will approve of that. There are quite a few I can name in my own subject who like to baffle or bamboozle their readers.'

'Perhaps they're puzzled themselves,' Alicia said.

'I don't think so. If they can put it down in some exotic form so that the reader's not quite sure what he's just been told but feels that it's very intelligent, or deeply thought out, and so is impressed, they think they'll acquire some sort of reputation. So they do with me. I think they're charlatans.'

'I can't understand', Alicia said, 'what some of the astronomers are saying about the universe. And I mean when they're speaking or writing English. Their mathematics is just Greek to me.'

'Didn't you learn Greek at school?'

'No. Though I wish sometimes I had.'

Wicks thought about this with pursed lips and nodding head. 'If I were you I'd give your professor a ring.'

'You've said so already.'

'He might think I hadn't mentioned his visits to you.'

'Is that important?'

'No. But I don't want to get a reputation for untrustworthiness or uncertainty or even eccentricity. Having a lorry burst into my *Twelfth Night* has been bad enough.' That, she could tell from his expression, was meant as a little joke. When she made no answer, he thought up another question. 'When you've finished your thesis, what will you research next?' A pause. 'Kipling?'

'It depends.'

'On what?'

'First, if it is judged successful. Then, what sort of job I have. I shall have to look for work. I can't afford to sit about and write all day for the rest of my life, an amateur of criticism of literature.'

'So you aren't sure what will come next?'

'Something on Pope.'

'Haven't all the good, the necessary things about Pope been said?'

'That's never the case with any great writer. Each new generation finds new things.'

He looked startled at her certainty. 'Off you go, then. I'll feed the birds as you widen our understanding of literature.'

Back at her computer she glanced at her notes, knew what came next. She lifted her head to read the time from the one really accurate clock in the house. Five minutes to nine. Conway would be up and about.

He answered almost as soon as his phone rang.

'Professor Conway? This is Alicia Smallwood. My neighbour, Raynor Wicks, told me that you called at my house twice while I was away this holiday.'

'Yes, I did.' He seemed unwilling to go further. 'Could you call in to see me some evening? I've visitors now.'

The arrangement was soon concluded. She went to the thesis.

'I stayed a few days with my parents in London, and with a school friend in Brighton,' she explained two evenings later.

'And you enjoyed them?'

'Yes. They were different. And I've started writing my thesis.'

'Ah,' he said with satisfaction, as if some penny had dropped. 'Has it gone well?'

'I started, if you remember, at your suggestion on the theatre.'

'And it went swimmingly?'

'Yes.'

'No snags?'

'No, not really.'

'Yes. Well, I thought you would have started writing before Christmas. And it crossed my mind (I don't really like to mention this, because all the evidence pointed the other way) that you were having difficulties in making a start.'

'No. I did a good day's writing.'

'You weren't overburdened with the amount of knowledge you'd acquired?'

'No. I can see that might be the case, but it didn't seem to hinder me. So far.'

'I feel ashamed to have worried about you on this account. I ought to have known better. You're not only very hard-working, you're also clever and have common sense. You've demonstrated it to me clearly over the past four years. And yet I had this feeling, this intuition so strongly that however long I argued with myself I could not convince myself that you were not having difficulty. And I therefore, against my reasonable judgement, came up to see you, to find out what the difficulty was. I feel rather foolish. It was probably with me.'

'Oh, no. I'm glad you came to help me out.'

'You didn't need it.'

'I might before too long.' She changed her tone. 'Have you ever met this sort of difficulty with any of your students?'

'Yes. One of the brightest students I've ever had. She easily out-topped the other girls of her year. And the males. She did out-standingly well in her Final Schools. I had no difficulty in encouraging her to set about a D.Phil. but we soon found she couldn't cope with her research. In her undergraduate days I'd have thought she was coping with similar problems in a smaller way and her results looked at more frequently by her tutors.'

'And what happened?'

'She left in her third term. I've puzzled myself silly over her case, how someone so clever could find herself unable to handle not terribly difficult work. I argued with her, and pleaded, but in the end she just threw in the towel. I felt utterly beaten. I wondered if she'd lost interest in the subject, or come to the conclusion that three years was as long as she was prepared to waste on English literature. When she looked at some specific piece of work she was just as good as she ever was, but putting a lot of these small insights together seemed beyond her. I would have said it was impossible. Perhaps she thought that for a doctorate one needed more complex answers than she could give. I don't know. She'd convinced herself that she could not manage the work and that was that.'

'And what's she doing now?'

'She married a very well-to-do young man. I don't know if she works now. They had a long honeymoon abroad. She sent me a card from Sri Lanka. I've heard nothing since. But she took away my confidence. How anyone could do as well as she did and then almost immediately lose all her gifts is beyond me.'

'It wasn't that she wanted to leave Oxford and get married, was it?'

'I suppose that's a possibility. As I tell you, it took my trust in my own judgement completely away.'

'And has it returned?' Alicia enquired, interested.

'I imagine you ask that because I had this feeling that you were struggling. You're nothing like her in character. But I failed her because I didn't step in early enough. Her first postgraduate term she wasted utterly. And yet she'd been a worker. At least I thought so.'

'As soon as I've finished this chapter I'll let you see it. It shouldn't be too long.'

Conway sat staring at the wall, as if his confession of failure had knocked all the energy out of him. His suit hung loosely on him; his eyes were pale. His attitude – she dared not stare too closely – was that of an embarrassed schoolboy.

The silence between them stretched longer. His house in Beechnall, which he had bought recently, seemed only half furnished. Presumably he had not moved his furniture from his place in Oxford. The bareness of the room, with no pictures, ill-matched carpets, bare light bulbs, ancient curtains, suited their unease.

In the end he shook himself, sighed deeply and spoke. 'There is one other favour I'd like to ask of you.'

'Yes?'

'I don't want to interfere with your studies . . .' He broke off again and sat wringing his hands. 'The week after next my mother is coming to visit me. She wants to talk to me about decorating this house and furnishing it. She has a whole lot of very good furniture, which she says I can have. She's selling one of her houses and I can have as much or as little as I like. She wants a hand in all this. She has been over a time or two to look at this place and she'll suggest where this piece or that will go. She's said this all along, ever since I bought this place about fifteen weeks ago. As she seemed so intent on it I've done little about either furnishing or decorating, and that's why I'm living in such a bare barn. Now, at last, as soon as she has seen the house once again, she'll see the house agents. I shall go down and stay over night, and look at the furniture. She will have it all listed, if I know her, although she might listen to one or two of my suggestions.'

'Is she an expert, then?'

'She's been interested in auctions and car-boot sales for long enough. And she visits shops. My guess is that she has every room in this house on a plan and she'll have every stick of her furniture assigned to a place. There'll be minor changes, surely, but she likes nothing better than sorting things out for other people. And as some of her stuff is valuable, she'll want to place it, or hang it, to advantage. Now while she's here I wonder' – his voice faltered – 'if you would come and have dinner with us?'

'With pleasure.'

They consulted their diaries and chose a suitable date, a Thursday.

'I tell you what,' Alicia said. 'Why not bring your mother to see me?'

'It will interfere with your work.'

'I don't think so. I shall have finished that chapter by then and I'll run off a copy and give it to you. I don't like driving in the dark.'

'You've come tonight.'

'It'll be a change of scene for your mother and save you cooking. Either lunch or dinner. Take your choice. Moreover, I shall have started my next chapter. I've been thinking about it and am keen to get on with it. So' – she drew the adverb out comically long – 'I shall deserve and enjoy a day off. If I've earned it.'

'And if not?'

'None of your pessimism,' she warned.

'No, ma'am.'

'Moreover, your mother can look over my furnishings and give me her opinion.'

'She'll do that.'

'There we are, then. All happy and content.'

She left, with her mind whirling. At Oxford it was rumoured that Conway could take no domestic decision without consulting his mother. It was said that when he was first appointed to a fellowship his mother would appear and look over suitable female pupils in whom he showed interest. The scrutiny all came to nothing. He married a girl from outside Oxford, an Honourable. Whether his mother had any say in the choice no one seemed to know. And the marriage, childless and wife-dominated, had come to nothing. Alicia drew her lips into a thin and bitter line. Perhaps, she thought smilingly, she was now under scrutiny.

She drove without difficulty along the dark country roads. She recited aloud some lines from Hardy:

'Who feels that delight is a delicate growth cramped by
    crookedness, custom and fear,
Get him up and be gone as one shaped awry; he disturbs the
    order here.'

X

Alicia made great progress with the writing of her thesis, to such an extent that she wondered if she was doing it properly. By the time Professor Conway and his mother came to dinner she had completed the chapter on the theatre (a copy lay on the large sitting-room table ready for her tutor's perusal). She had begun chapter one, her real introduction outlining the scope of her whole work. She was afraid that Conway, or Christopher as she was now encouraged to call him, might tell her she should have written this last, because she'd find, having finished, that she'd need to alter so much she might as well not write it now. This did not discourage her. Like Hardy, the blot might be in herself, but she carried on. She reread what she had written with pleasure. She feared sometimes that this might be early enthusiasm that would fade after some weeks or months of writing, but she had decided she might disturb the order here, the manner of presenting a doctoral thesis, but she'd exact her long look at the Worst to find a way to the Better, whether this drew disappointment or even failure in the end. That she'd have to trust to Christopher. Now she was concerned to write down accurately the enormous factual evidence she'd collected and her conclusions therefrom. It was best that she wrote with verve, with gusto, though she had found most of the theses she had read were dull indeed unless you were particularly interested in the subject matter. She wondered if this was the reason for Conway's gifted student, who in the end threw over her research and left Oxford, that she refused to write dully, that accuracy of learning had every advantage over attraction of writing.

The weather for the visit was sunny, if cold, with a sharp wind from the north-east. Christopher had rung the evening before to confirm the final arrangements. His mother had already been five days with him and would leave Beechnall on Saturday morning. She had spent one critical day at the university and had been

131

impressed. The vice-chancellor had come from the same part of Yorkshire that she did and had used all his much-vaunted charm on her. She had appreciated her welcome, but had pronounced his manner acquired, if not hypocritical. 'You should hear him when he's crossed,' her son said, only to be warned that she could not bear it if he opted to be all style and no sincerity. He laughed, and replied that he had been too well – no, too strictly – brought up for that. He had freed himself this Thursday and they'd arrive between 2.30 and 3.00, so that she could stroll round the village. His mother, he said, was looking forward to meeting Alicia.

Five minutes behind time the professor rang her doorbell.

Mrs Conway was quite unlike the figure Alicia had imagined. There was nothing either aggressive or brawny about her. She had the thin pale face of her son, his long violinist's fingers, his nervous stance. She was dressed in a tweed two-piece of impeccable cut, and she carried a light-coloured mackintosh over her arm.

'Mother,' Conway brayed, 'this is Alicia, Miss Smallwood.'

They shook hands. Mrs Conway's strong clasp gave the girl confidence, rather than otherwise. 'I'm glad to meet you. I've heard a great deal about you.'

Alicia lowered her head.

'Christopher thinks highly of you. He'd told me, as he won't have told you, that if you get your doctorate out of the way this summer, he hopes to take you on to his staff at the beginning of next year.'

At this Conway blushed deeply and shuffled a yard sideways.

His mother looked at him with displeasure, then turned. 'A nice place you've chosen to live,' she said to Alicia.

'I take no credit for it. When my family heard I was coming up here, my father found this house for me. I was very lucky.'

'Does your father know all about property?'

'To some extent. They've changed houses three times since I was born. My mother overlooks the interior decoration.'

'Is she a professional?'

'No. But she learns quickly and knows her mind.'

'Like her daughter,' Conway said, having recovered.

'If this foyer is anything to go by, she has very good taste.'

'I think that's so,' Alicia answered.

'Are you the only child?' Mrs Conway, before her son could beat her to a question.

'Yes.'

'You must forgive all these questions of mine. I'm curious and I save a lot of time.'

'How do you know truth from fiction?'

'That doesn't matter. I like to hear people telling me what they think.' Again her gaze swept up and across the foyer.

'Would you like to look around the house while it is still daylight, or would you prefer to see the garden first?'

'I'll leave that to you.'

'Then we'll have ten minutes outside. It's too cold to stay out long.' Alicia walked across to a stand to retrieve a coat and scarf. 'Would either of you like to borrow a scarf?' she asked.

'How thoughtful of you. I would, please.' Mrs Conway was handed a long woollen scarf, which she wrapped round her throat with a hockey mistress's enthusiasm.

Alicia led them outside. The sun shone, but a north-easterly wind cut coldly into their shoulders. Mrs Conway walked quickly, leading the party. She called plants and shrubs by their Latin names, and commented on their state of health, and now and then handed out a piece of advice.

'You should have brought a notebook out,' Professor Conway said, somewhat tartly.

'I think I shall remember,' Alicia modestly claimed.

At the bottom of her piece of land, behind a wooden fence and a tall, ill-kempt hawthorn hedge, was a field bordered on one side with a wood. The field was empty, but bright in the sunshine. Mrs Conway enquired about its owner, what he did with the ground, what sort of farmer he was. Suddenly she stopped and asked, 'Doesn't Sir Clarence Caldwell live somewhere near you?'

'That way,' Alicia replied, pointing. 'You can't see it from here, but it's in easy walking distance. Fifteen minutes. It's a curious house, actually partly built on a hillside. He told me that when he was a boy in Beechnall he used to walk out here, and he always admired the house because of its unusual shape and position. My next-door neighbour, Raynor Wicks, calls it "The House of the Hanged Man", after Cézanne's place.'

'I know his painting of it.'

'Are you getting cold?' Alicia asked.

'Yes. It is chilly.'

Alicia rushed them inside, ushered them into the large drawing room for a cup of tea. Again Mrs Conway made complimentary remarks about the room. She particularly admired a snow scene in oils done by an uncle, Alicia's mother's brother, an art teacher.

'Is your mother artistic?'

'Yes. In her way. She could always sketch well for me when I was small. And she was clever with her fingers: embroidery and sewing. I'll show you some cushions she made and decorated. When she puts flowers in a vase, their placing and shape are really extraordinarily surprising and beautiful. My father, who really does admire her, says "You give your mother an egg cup and a few daisies and she'll make a picture of it".'

'Your father's artistic, is he?'

'Not particularly. He says the only thing he understands is money.'

'Not a bad thing these days,' Christopher said.

The rest of the visit passed pleasantly. At dinner the casserole was praised to the sky and the spotted dick with white sauce that followed tempted both visitors to second small helpings. They drank water, because Christopher had said his mother would not endure it if he drove her when he'd imbibed alcohol, however little. Mrs Conway said she loved wine in moderation, but would drink none as her son denied himself as her chauffeur. He asked to see the bottle she had brought out and praised her choice. They left, congratulating her on her hospitality.

Alicia judged that she had played hostess with some success.

Mrs Conway had continued her cross-examination throughout the meal. The questions came more slowly, because the guest was a slow eater and was obviously enjoying every mouthful of the fare. Alicia had been ready for questions about her family, her schooldays, her hobbies, her holidays but was more than surprised when she was questioned, of all things, about her knowledge of English literature. Christopher looked embarrassed at this stage, put in a question to his mother and indeed provided some learned addition to give Alicia the opportunity to display further the breadth of her knowledge.

That evening an acquaintance from her Oxford days rang out of the blue to try to arrange a weekend reunion for a group from college. When she heard that Alicia had played hostess to Professor Conway and his mother she buzzed with excitement. 'What's she like?' she asked. When she had heard a rather subdued account of Mrs Conway's behaviour she said, 'You should be careful, child.' Bettina often spoke like this to her friend, as she was two or three years older. 'You must stand high on her matrimonial list.'

'Has she told you so?' Alicia asked sarcastically.

'It was always said in my time' (one year ahead, Alicia thought) 'that she cross-questioned Christopher's lady friends to judge how worthy they were to marry her one and only son.'

'But he was married at that time.'

'Yes, and his mother considered she had fallen short in her duty. Nobody liked Mrs Conway junior, not even Christopher. But this was such a talking point years before: the meetings with large numbers of suitable girls, reduced to two or three, then one or two finally put on the rack.'

'Then how did he come to choose for himself?'

'Oh, he's a man of parts, is our Christopher; he can make his own mind up. If he didn't agree with his mama he followed his own preference, but I bet she didn't half put him through the mill when he discovered he'd chosen a nasty shrew.'

'He seemed genuinely fond of her.'

'His wife? He was not after a year or so. She wouldn't live in Oxford in the end.'

'No, I meant his mother.'

'Yes. I think he is, but I don't suppose he'll follow his mother's advice if ever he decides to marry again. But, if the tales I heard were true, she won't give up. To tell you the truth, he always seemed to me to be a typical bachelor, content with his scholarship and his college life.'

'Doesn't his mother know that?'

'I expect he's made it explicitly clear to her, but she wouldn't believe him. She thinks she knows what's good for him and she would like grandchildren. That's why I tell you that you should be careful.'

'Oh, thank you.'

'A friend of my husband teaches at Beechnall and is fairly friendly with him, but his view is that Christopher is not satisfied with his present chair and won't be pleased until he gets appointed back at Oxford.'

'And is that possible?'

'He's well thought of there. His last two books are really highly regarded. Or so Jack thinks. He's a historian, not in your line, but he's serious, wants to know everything. And you know how they talk up there at high table. There are no secrets.'

Alicia remembered from time to time what her friend had said. A few days later she received a letter from Mrs Conway thanking her for the delicious meal and the opportunity to walk round her beautiful house. She and Christopher had enjoyed every minute; it had been the high point of her visit to Beechnall and she could, at last, begin to consider life in the Midlands as not without advantages. Her letter ended with the sending of love from hers, Mildred. There was not a word about marriage, or her son's future but, Alicia concluded, unless the woman was a complete hypocrite her verdict was favourable. Alicia could not make up her mind about that. She could remember her first meetings with Christopher at Oxford, when he went carefully over her essays, pointing out weaknesses or omissions, or cautiously adding expressions of praise. He had seemed a godlike figure and that image of him had hardly changed in her three years at university. Certainly, he had praised her more lavishly, or dropped more heavily on her few errors, had encouraged her to work for a first and had, after consultation, approved her choice of subject for her doctorate. She had followed him, it was true, to Beechnall, but not out of personal affection. He'd had enough of marriage she had heard and, as to wedding her, she had not considered it, even as a pipe dream.

XI

Alicia worked hard at her thesis in the next few weeks and found the writing of it came easily to her. Twice Professor Conway asked her to rewrite sections, because she had not been sufficiently rigorous in drawing conclusions from her wide reading. Otherwise he was full of praise for her work and at her last meeting said it was the most enjoyable thesis he had ever read. 'You combine a beautiful, readable fluency with an unusual thoroughness of research. And you're not afraid to add small illustrations from other periods that appear utterly unlike yours. That's not advisable to most students; they lack the gift of judgement and so overdo it. You don't. You demonstrate your learning and yet never lead us slower readers off the subject. You enlighten us. In my case I sometimes wish for more. And I guess your external examiner, if I know him, will feel the same. Do you enjoy writing this?'

'Yes, though I sometimes go at such a pace I miss out something essential.'

'You do well. Don't you sometimes wish you were writing on a more important topic?'

'No, or not insofar as I'm not bored with this. If it were somebody like Pope I'd have to think harder. Eighteenth-century tragedy, even comedy, is not great. Interesting, so that I'm glad I've read it, but I can't say that these are superb pieces of literature.'

'This' – Conway tapped the pile before him – 'is so well written that it won't take much sweat to turn it into a book. And somebody in the theatre might read it, and put one or two of the plays on stage. You'd like that, wouldn't you?'

'Yes,' she said, 'but I don't think it likely.'

'Why do you say that?'

'Fashion. We've lost the feel for their language. Even with Dryden, Pope and Swift, unless we are thoroughly immersed in their diction and realise how flexible it is in the hands of these

137

masters, it seems too stiff, bowed over to convention to be very great. I'm glad we did Pope at school so that his couplets seem natural, a marvellous way to use our language. But for the ordinary playgoer to visit a theatre and tangle with this verse is not easy. Addison's *Cato* didn't last long with contemporaries and Dr Johnson's *Irene* had an even shorter life.'

'Is that likely today?'

'Yes. I was talking to an old man in the university library only yesterday and he made quite a lament over Christopher Fry. He said that when *The Lady's Not For Burning* appeared first in 1948 the young playgoers, after the war when the lights were dim and half the theatres shut or barely working, thought that spring had come again, that a new burst of English had exploded in the theatre, so witty and light and colourful. I quoted,

> 'Something
> Terrible to somebody is always happening
> In a garden. Nature never seems to have heard
> Of the ten commandments.

'The old man was delighted that I knew a line or two of Fry. I don't know why he asked me questions about somebody he knew something about.'

'Did he wear a bow tie? And have very white hair?'

'Yes. And highly polished shoes.'

'That would have been old Samson, emeritus professor of classics. Somebody would have pointed you out as an English scholar researching into drama and he therefore had to establish some sort of superiority over you in your subject. It's as common in universities as in the world. They have to examine you for ignorance in your own subject.'

'He seemed quite pleased that I knew something of Fry and could quote him.'

'Yes. Josh Samson is pleasant enough. And the fact that he was on the right lines with a drama scholar would please him. He'd found for himself somebody who was worth remembering and his taste had now been certified as fine by a respectable scholar. Some of us can never forget we've been examiners.'

'Is that good?'

'We're still using our brains even at an advanced age.'

Professor Conway thanked and praised her, said that if she ever felt she had come to a stop in her work she wasn't to waste time over it, but was to get in touch with him at once. 'You know a deuce of a lot more about your topic than I do, but I stand away from it and can suggest possible moves. Not that there should be any; you're doing very well and should be ready to submit your thesis well before the end of the summer term. I'm impressed.'

This was good, but not a declaration of love. Perhaps his mother had decided against her, or he had not followed her advice. Or he had decided not to interrupt her academic progress with proposals of early intimacy, if not of marriage. He was a marvellous teacher, who encouraged her careful but still headlong speed with her writing. She went away pleased, but found, when she became honest with herself, that she had expected more.

Back in the village she had one burst of excitement, a fire at Caldwell's house. He had recovered rather rapidly from his illness and had gone off to stay with friends in Surrey. One evening Raynor Wicks, out for fresh air after a hard day enclosed at his school, was taking a short walk before settling down to an evening of marking and reading. Passing above Sir Clarence's house, he noticed first a strong smell, then a swirl of smoke from one of the back windows.

He rushed down the path, rattled the door, found it open and bundled himself indoors, scarf round his mouth. He banged open the kitchen door, which still had a hundred-watt bulb steady among the shifting fumes, staggered across towards a black shape on the floor, Megan Rhŷs-Williams, Caldwell's housekeeper. He turned her over; she groaned slightly; he easily picked her up and rushed her into the fresh air, where he laid her safely away from the house in the unlocked outside shed. He called her name and she opened her eyes and stared at him. He reached for a pile of blankets, which he saw by the light of a single dust-caked bulb swinging at about face height. He covered the woman, who was now whimpering and moaning.

'Are you all right?' he asked.

'My head,' she groaned and lifted her hands.

Peering in the dim light, he noticed a small scratch or cut. He dabbed at it with a clean handkerchief and found the wound almost dry, the blood congealed. 'Lie still,' he said. 'Breathe the clean air.'

'Mr Wicks,' she said. 'Mr Wicks.'

He was surprised she knew his name. 'Don't you worry,' he

said, 'just lie there. I'm going back to see if I can do anything about the fire.'

'Be careful,' she warned.

He pushed his way from the shed, crossed a lumpy grass plot. The smoke from the kitchen window appeared to be thicker. Inside the house he eased open the kitchen door; the knob seemed hot under his hand. As soon as he had achieved nine inches of gap a blast of black smoke and heat struck him like a blow to his face. He flung the door wide. Smoke was so thick he could see nothing. A sudden crackle at the other side of the room became a low flower of flame in the pitch-darkness. He pulled the door slam-shut, coughing and choking as he found his way out to the garden.

Once outside, he dialled 999 for the fire brigade. The girl seemed to have difficulty following his instructions how to reach the house. He tried again. 'It's Sir Clarence Caldwell's house. The actor.'

'Are you Sir Clarence?'

'No. My name is Wicks. I live in the village.'

'Do you need an ambulance?'

'I don't think so. I'm not sure. The housekeeper was in, but I got her out and she's in the garden shed.'

'And Sir Clarence?'

'He's away on holiday. Somewhere in Surrey.'

'Go back to give directions when the firemen come.'

Once the phone call was finished, he gulped in cold air through his wide-gaping mouth. He saw another figure, a dark shape holding a torch. The kitchen window now seemed red with flame.

'Is it just the kitchen on fire?' Wicks recognised the voice, that of one Jack Morris, a market gardener, who lived not two hundred yards away.

'As far as I know. I've kept the door shut so it wouldn't spread. I pulled the housekeeper out and laid her in the shed.'

'The old lady?' The situation seemed to encourage daft irrelevancies like this.

'And I've rung the fire brigade. They'll have to come from Beechnall, which will take 'em time.'

'Oh, I don't know. The station's this side of the city, or one of them is. And there won't be much traffic about. They'll be able to get water from the mains up on the road. I've a point as well just outside my house.'

140

They went over to the shed where they found Megan lying with her eyes closed. On the entry of the two men she sat up slowly and said she was all right.

'Tell you what, I'll get my wife to bring the car over and take you back with her. I'll wait until the firemen have arrived before I send for her. She's sure to park just where they want to be.'

'I haven't any nightclothes.'

'Don't you bother your head about that. My Elsie's got enough clothes for the whole village. She'll fit you up. How we shall get you up all those steps I don't know.'

'I'll carry you,' Wicks said. 'I've done it once tonight.'

'You rescued me. I was knocked out.'

'Just you lie still until Mrs Morris comes. Are you warm enough? Are you sure? Are you in any pain? We can get an ambulance.'

She groaned, almost comically loud.

'Was that the fire engine?' Wicks asked.

'I didn't hear it.'

They listened together in vain.

'It won't be long now. I'll get up to the road to show 'em where the water main is.' Morris trotted off, as one justified.

The fire engine arrived almost without noise. Wicks moved outside to watch. The firemen talked, but casually, did not appear to hurry, but had a hosepipe down the path and indoors. Their drill seemed perfect; they worked at high speed. No sooner were they inside the kitchen than the fire blazed up and then retreated, sank. Even when there was no vestige of a flame they worked.

Morris trotted down to say his wife had arrived with her car. The announcement seemed to revitalise Megan who, once helped on to her feet, said she could walk. Wicks draped her with a respectable blanket. She fiddled in her pockets and handed him her keys. 'Could you, would you . . .?' she stammered.

'I'll see to it that the house is safely locked up once the firemen have finished.'

One either side, they helped her up the steps. Mrs Morris, a motherly woman, took charge of Megan, who began again her complaint that she had no nightclothes with her. Quietened and comforted, she was half lifted into the front seat of the car and driven off. By this time the fire was out, to the casual onlooker.

'That's done it,' a fireman told the two men, who had now

descended again to door level. 'Wasn't much, really. Could have been worse. Would have if we'd been ten minutes slower.'

'What was the cause?' Wicks asked.

'Usual. Something left too long in the frying pan. You'd be surprised how many combustible objects there are in a modern kitchen. I don't think it's done any structural damage. Wasn't on long enough. But it'll be one hell of a mess. The whole place will need decorating. And some of the cupboards you might have to replace. I don't know. They looked pretty substantial. And I wouldn't like to guess at the state of the stuff inside. China all cracked. Jars of food ruined. We're checking as far as we can. And we'll clear up a bit, though it won't seem like it, so you can assess the damage for yourself tomorrow in the light of day.'

The fire officer then stood back, stroking his upper lip. 'We'll make sure that the fire's completely out. They are seeing to that now. And if one, or both of you gentlemen will walk round the rest of the house with me now, we'll just check that there's no damage. We're dealing with two very destructive agents, fire and water. If tomorrow the fire broke out or half the house fell down we'd be in for trouble.'

The two men accompanied the officer up the stairs and round the interior. The electricity was cut off only in the kitchen and passageway. 'That's lucky,' the officer said. 'The fuse box's often in the kitchen.' The civilians were surprised at his care and his scientific zeal. What he was searching for, he knew before he entered a room. As they finished at the bottom of the stairs he said, 'Some valuable old furniture about this house. If that had gone up in flames, the insurance would never cover it.' His final search of the wrecked kitchen was even more thorough. 'I don't suppose we can get anybody out here at this time of the night to the windows. My lads'll make them safe. Burglars are on the lookout even as far out of the city as this.'

When the fire engine left, Morris left with it. Wicks went back to the kitchen with a torch and poked about, but felt he would waste his time trying to clear up. He checked the windows, returned the keys to Mrs Morris at her front door, where she said she would hand them over to Megan Rhŷs-Williams.

Alicia heard nothing of all this until the weekend when she called in at the newspaper shop. There, Wicks was already, it appeared, regarded as a hero. She heard from the proprietor of his dash into the burning house and his rescue of Megan.

'He's a real man,' said Mrs Routledge from behind the counter. 'And he's so modest with it. To hear him talk he saw the fire, strolled in, took the unconscious woman into his arms and marched out to safety. If he hadn't been passing she would have died.'

The local paper printed some heroic version of this story, which was stretched wider by some of its retailers. Wicks seemed embarrassed by these epic bursts, cut them politely short and gained even more in reputation.

'I pushed the kitchen door and there she lay. She's no flesh on her bones. Any teenager could have picked her up and carried her out as I did.'

'Poor Megan – her second major accident. But she's so strong. What does Sir Clarence think of it all?' Alicia asked from her garden boundary.

'That I don't know. He's ordered cleaners and decorators in already. They've made a start. Mrs Rhŷs-Williams moved back the next day and directs operations.'

'I suppose it's all covered by insurance.'

'I expect so. You never know. You never can tell with these gypsies, fairground people and vagabonds.'

'You mean actors,' she corrected him. 'Sir Clarence wouldn't thank you to be called a gypsy.'

'I exaggerate. But Caldwell has some strange ideas and not insuring his house may well be among them. It's a beautifully furnished place for certain.'

'As good as yours?' she asked.

'In its fashion.'

When she set out next Sunday morning for her usual walk he emerged from his garden gate to join her. She suspected he had been waiting. He then said as much.

'I always come out on a Sunday morning,' she said, 'at much the same time.'

'I know. I've watched you,' he admitted.

'I must get some exercise. I'm trying like mad to get my thesis out of the way. Though I'm enjoying writing it.'

'It's going well?'

'Yes. I think so. And so does Christopher.'

'Is he a good supervisor?'

'Excellent. He has such a wide knowledge that he can easily point out omissions. What he's trying to do is to keep it all within the set limits.'

'I didn't know one had to do that.'

'Oh, yes. He tells me I can spread myself when I make it into a book.'

'Will that be your next job?'

'I guess so. It depends what I'm doing. As daily work.'

'Won't your university extend your time if they think the thesis is good?'

'That's a possibility. I suppose that'll depend on Christopher Conway.'

'Will he recommend you?'

'I hope so. So much depends on money these days.'

'You've not been on any more visits to the theatre with him?' His question seemed crude.

'No. He and his mother came and had dinner with me.'

'And was she impressed?'

'She admired some of the things in the house. And the general effect.'

'I should think she did. Yours is one of the most attractive homes I know.'

'It's nowhere near the standard of your house.'

'Oh, I won't argue, though I disagree. My place depended on my wife's taste. She would not buy any addition, however small, unless she was sure it fitted in with the rest. She was very good at it. She wrote a book about house decoration.'

'And you haven't changed it?'

'No. I daren't now. Taste in furniture and decoration alters, so I suppose it may seem a bit out of date. But it's extremely good of its kind. When we first split up I was so angry with her that I thought of throwing it all out, but then I found I couldn't afford to. I wanted to keep the building so I had to buy her out. I'm pleased I did. And when my temper finally simmered down, I realised I could quite easily live with a house as well planned and looked after as this was.'

He strode on, nose in the air. She could easily imagine him in front of 800 boys issuing orders and expecting them immediately to be obeyed. His complexion, with its light-brown tan, matched the high points of red in his cheeks; his hair was short, springy and slightly touched with grey, like a general's, she thought. It was no wonder that old Clarence Caldwell thought so highly of the man, felt certain of the success of any enterprise he undertook.

Alicia enjoyed the smart pace at which they moved. In this cold

144

weather she kept warm without becoming breathless. They turned into a small piece of woodland, which ran by both sides of the road.

'I always go this way,' Wicks said. 'At least I shan't be run over.'

'This would have been a larger piece of forest, would it?' she asked. 'At one time?'

'Yes. The road went through it and the farmer thought he'd make more profit with an open field. I'd guess he'd have other copses about where he could gather wood for building or to keep his home fires burning.'

'You don't know to whom it belongs?'

'A family called Tindall. They've been squires hereabouts since the Middle Ages.'

'I've not heard of them.'

'No, they've not taken a large part in public life. They've kept themselves to themselves and gradually acquired a fair amount of acreage.'

'But no title?'

'I'll introduce you to Geoffrey Tindall one of these days if you like. He descends on me from time to time. He's an old boy of the school.'

'He just looks after his broad acres, does he?'

'Oh, no. He's an accountant in quite a big way. Not only in Beechnall. He has branches in Derby, Leicester and Mansfield, and, I think, London unless he's spread himself even further. Most of his land is let out to farmers. Geoffrey knows what he's about. He'll be glad to meet you. They have a very nice house. His mother's still alive and lives with them.'

The sun splashed among the branches and trunks of the trees.

'Not very high yet,' she said.

'No. It's early in the year.'

A few energetic steps further on he laid a hand on her arm. They came to a halt. 'I wonder', he began, 'if you'd come to a concert with me, or a play, or the cinema.'

'Yes,' she said. 'That would be good. But not this week.'

'What's wrong with this week, then?'

'I'm at a stage, a chapter in my thesis where I need to do quite a bit of alteration. I shall try to cram in twice as much as I take out and make the whole a lot shorter.'

'And do you find that difficult?'

'Slightly frustrating. I think I've covered a topic, then the prof thinks it should be organised otherwise.'

'He's a terror, is he?'

'Not exactly. He thinks that the theatre from the Restoration to the beginning of the nineteenth century is not one of the great periods of literature. And he is sorry that he edged me towards the subject. I'd done a bit on it as a student and he'd liked that, and before we knew where we were I was launched on the theme. He sometimes says now that he wishes I had chosen one of the big figures of the period and blames himself.'

'And it, the work on the thesis, has not changed your mind about the value of the works you study?'

'No. But it's made Christopher all the more careful. He wants my thesis to be a kind of model, so that when people read it they'll know a great deal about the period, and what people did and so forth. And then, when I've finished, I can look at the poets: Dryden, Pope, Swift.'

'What about people like Thomas Gray?'

'He wrote one of the great poems of the language. Johnson, who didn't much like him said, "I rejoice to concur with the common reader", about the Elegy.'

His hand still rested on her arm. 'On the Tuesday of next week I'm going to a concert. A string quartet. The Kodály Quartet. I don't know what they're doing, but they're certain to play something Hungarian, Bartók, Dohnányi, Kodály. They don't come to England, or the Midlands, very often these days, but a friend told me some months ago to make a point of hearing them when they do appear here because they are so good. They're like players from another world, he said. Will you have cleared your decks by then?'

'Thank you, yes. I'd love to come.'

'In the theatre I don't mind going on my own. But with music it's different. I like a companion I can talk to, to exchange views with. Not that I'm any sort of musician.'

'That will be two of us.'

He squeezed her arm, then let her go. 'I'll call for you between half-six and quarter to seven. Unless you'd like to go a little earlier and have a drink before the concert.'

'No, thank you.'

'No need to gild the lily, eh?'

'"To paint the lily",' she corrected him, '"gild refinèd gold".'

'I beg your pardon. How does it go on?'

'"To throw a perfume on the violet".'

146

'Thank you. *King John*, is it not?'

They marched on smartly, both smiling. He seemed delighted at her pedantry. There was no sense of triumphalism about him. He had invited her out with him and she had accepted, he wondered whether on account of the accomplishment of the Kodály Quartet or his own attraction. She had never heard of the quartet before this morning.

They emerged out of the wood and on to the road where a red sports car hurled itself past them.

'I wonder who that idiot is.' She spoke out of her fright.

'I guess it's Megan Rhŷs-Williams's grandson. He comes up quite regularly to see her.'

'Is he a theatrical?'

'No. I think he's a medical student. I've only met him once. They seemed genuinely fond of each other.'

Wicks talked easily to her as he questioned her about her work. 'Professor Conway says you're the best research student he's ever had. You not only read hard, but have something to show for it fairly quickly. That's not always the case. And he said that like all really talented hard workers you're lucky, and all sorts of new material seems to fall into your hands.'

'He's not so flattering to my face.'

'He must praise you, though. He knows the value of encouragement, even to his best students.'

'Yes.'

'He seems rather sparing with praise. Not that I know him well. Does he go overboard when he's lecturing on some important figure?'

'Yes. But delivers his idolatry in the same tone as when he buys potatoes.'

'Oh. Have you been shopping with him, then?'

'Of course I haven't.'

Wicks laughed out loud and clapped his hands together. Soon he was cajoled into talking about the school where he taught. She asked him if he thought the place was any good. He looked down at her with cynical respect. 'Of its kind, yes. You'll find our name in the national newspapers very high in the list of examination passes. You'd expect that. We have some clever boys there when they're not distracted by girls.'

'Don't you get disciplinary problems, like other schools? Drugs, bullying, antisocial behaviour?'

'Yes, but the head won't put up with that. They're out on their neck. Drugs, first time. Others, after one warning.'

'If there were large numbers, wouldn't that leave holes in your ranks?'

'Yes, but they are very few.'

'What do they do? Smoke cannabis?'

'No, not these days. Cocaine is the choice. I was talking to one of the policemen in the drug squad we had up at the school and he told me it was sold under all sorts of fancy names, "zip" or "tickets". It's more sociably acceptable than cannabis among adults, he said.'

'Isn't it expensive?'

'Again I quote: £25 for a half-gramme packet. That'll be no trouble to some of our students. You'd be surprised what pocket money they get, or what they earn on weekend jobs or at work at home that Dad doesn't want to do.'

'How many of your pupils take cocaine?'

'They say that on average one in fifty children between the ages of eleven to fifteen has tried the stuff. It'll be higher among university students, I guess. Don't you find it so?'

'I don't see much of the undergraduates here. At Oxford there were people who had a reputation. I wasn't ever troubled by dealers. A boy once offered me some drug or other, but he seemed to think none the worse of me when I said, "No".'

'Did their parents use it?' he asked.

'I've no idea.'

'We expelled quite a small boy for actually selling drugs.'

'Where had he got them in the first place?'

'Again, I've no notion. I don't imagine his parents were in the trade. I suppose some dealer gave him a cut on what he sold.'

'It seems a pity.'

'The head makes no exceptions in drug cases. And these days parents don't seem to have much idea what their children are up to. It was different in my day. My father seemed to know within a couple of days when I had a quick cigarette behind the bike sheds.'

'How did he find out?'

'Some blabbermouth passed the news on to his father who told my dad.'

'Were there drugs in your school?'

'Yes. Possibly. It's less than thirty years ago. I'm not Methuselah, you know.'

They laughed together, still walking strongly.

'Don't you ever wish to be a headmaster?' she suddenly asked, bold in their new intimacy.

'No. Not really.'

'You don't think you'd be better than your present head?'

'No. I sometimes disagree with his decisions. But I see how his hands are tied. As mine would be if I were in his position. I'd try to be a bit freer than he is, but that would bring its troubles. He'll tell you that when he punishes some boy over-harshly, he's saving half a dozen more from breaking the rules.'

'When he retires the governors won't elect to appoint you?'

'No. Not even if I applied, which I shan't. The present man is ten years older than I am and if his health allows it he'll serve on to sixty. I shall then be fifty-four, far too old for a first head-mastership. They'll appoint a young man in his late thirties. And they think it enlarges the horizon of the school if they call in someone from outside. They might well make me acting head if there's a gap between James's retirement and the arrival of the new man. They'll know I'm a steady, conservative sort of teacher, that I shan't be introducing new and daft ideas in my few months' tenure, that I'll keep the school steady and working hard until the new man arrives with his brilliant ideas and innovations.'

'And will they recognise such a paragon?'

'God knows. They'll have the interests of the school at heart. At least they say so. And we have a good reputation throughout the country. There'll be plenty of excellently qualified candidates in for the job. How they set about choosing the best I don't know. I often think they're influenced on the day by somebody on the selection committee.'

'Are they mainly old boys?'

'Yes. Solicitors and businessmen. They know what's going on in the school, on the whole. They might be influenced unduly by what they've read in the newspapers that morning, or something they've seen on television. The secretary and the president are both lawyers, and both sensible men. I believe the present headmaster was appointed because he'd taught mathematics at Manchester and Bradford Grammar Schools, and had some impressive schemes for IT, computers, you know.'

'We had them at school,' Alicia said.

'Do you have a computer at home? Are you writing your thesis on a computer?'

'Yes.'

'You make me feel old-fashioned. I have one at home, and at school, and use them. But they're not second nature to me yet.'

She laughed with him. He was good company and, once you had broken through his reserve and encouraged him to talk, he seemed younger, less distant, livelier. When they reached the gate of his house, he invited her in for what he called a pre-prandial drink. She refused, telling him that the rest of her day was planned and that she mustn't lose time. He did not seem disappointed and made no attempt to dissuade her or closely enquire into the nature of her timetable. 'I'll watch out for your computer,' he said.

Alicia felt pleased at this new, less formidable Raynor Wicks.

He came close, lowered his head to kiss her, not on the mouth but on the cheek. He stood, arms round her, one hand lightly on her buttocks, his lips immobile on her face. It seemed some time before he drew back and they did not move, still a yard or more apart. He looked exactly the same to Alicia; the kiss had changed nothing. He was the same broad-shouldered, upright man in a tweed overcoat, his face square, bright and well shaven, his hair blowing in the north-east wind. She wanted to say 'Now kiss me properly', but prevented herself, smiling shyly up at him.

Finally it was he who took the first step away. 'I'll see you.'

XII

Alicia expected to see something of Raynor Wicks in the days before the Kodály concert, but he kept out of the way. Only once did she catch sight of him, at 7.30 in the morning as he piled neatly packed parcels of rubbish into his wheelie bin. He had switched on his outside light and there he moved from darkness to bright clarity on his shirtsleeved way from back door to bin, twice, before all became silently black again; and a few minutes later she heard him drive off, headlights sweeping as he turned the car.

On the night of the concert they had arranged to meet by the bottom gate of her garden where the garages of the two houses had been built. Exactly on time she emerged into the unlighted lane. Neither Wicks nor his car was there. This surprised her; she had imagined, without any evidence, that he was a punctual man, on parade, as her grandfather used to say, five minutes before time. The wind buffeted twigs on the bare branches of the sycamores nearby. There was no sound from Wicks's house. She looked at her watch by the light of the small torch she always carried in her handbag. He was four minutes late. No sooner had she returned the torch than she heard the doors of his garage flung creakingly open. His headlights blazed as he drove the car out.

He shouted towards her and she shuffled along to where it stood. He was back at the garage doors, busy locking up. 'I'm sorry,' he said, as he joined her. 'I hope I'm not too late.'

'About five minutes.' She had not enjoyed standing alone in the cold darkness.

'As much as that. I'm so sorry. That's a bad start to the evening.' He opened the car door and held it so, like a servant. 'Please get in. We shall have plenty of time. I must apologise. I'd lost the small key to my pocket watch. I hadn't put it back where it should be. I'm always doing that these days. I must be getting old.' He closed the car door on her. She fought round for the seat belt, which lay conveniently to hand in this huge automobile.

151

He let himself in purposefully, buckled his belt and turned his attention to her. 'I must apologise again,' he said, turning on the engine.

'Oh, that's all right,' she answered impatiently.

'It isn't. To leave you standing alone in the darkness is no joke these days. One never knows.'

'I didn't see or hear anybody.'

'I misjudged the time. I thought I had plenty.'

'Did you expect me to be late?' she asked.

'It would have been your privilege.' She said nothing. 'Are you comfortable?'

'Perfectly, thank you.'

'We'll make a start, then.'

They moved sedately down the lane.

'We'll soon warm up,' he said, 'once we're on the road.' As she made no comment he began again. 'In the last school I was at they used to call me "Punctuality Pete".'

'Why Pete?'

'It's my first initial. It's Paul, really.' He eased them into the main Beechnall Road. 'In those days pupils did not know the Christian names of their masters.'

'Was that good or bad?'

'Fashion. Nowadays at some universities the students call their lecturers, and even professors, by their first names.'

The car was warm, the seat comfortable, legroom plentiful. Wicks drove well, without hurry or awkward jerks. Within a few minutes of their objective Alicia was thoroughly relaxed, and by the time they had reached the private car park and her companion had said this was where they had to walk the rest, she had forgotten her ill temper at being left to wait in the dark.

'It's no more than five minutes' walk away,' he told her. 'According to the BBC there's no chance of rain tonight so I won't take my umbrella. We're in excellent time,' he added as they reached the doors of the concert hall. 'We'll go straight in and sit down. I dislike the last-minute rush for the seats.' Certainly the foyer was crowded with well-dressed people clearly, from their overloud voices, pleased with themselves. 'We can sit and study the programme.'

Their seats were in the gallery and as they pushed up at speed the noise from below sounded powerful, discordant, punctuated by odd wild laughter or the calling out of names. At the door of the gallery Wicks bought two programmes and received instructions about how to reach his seat.

Once inside, and there was hardly a seat occupied, they proceeded to the aisle where they saw a man approaching them making for the door. With something of a shock Alicia recognised him: Christopher Conway, who lifted his head. He stared at her as if he had never seen her before in his life, stopped in his tracks and stared again. This time he knew her and smiled without pleasure. 'Alicia,' he said and glanced towards her companion. 'Wicks.'

'Professor Conway,' Wicks said. 'How good to meet you.' He pushed out his right hand.

Conway shook it limply. 'I didn't expect to see you here,' he said.

'All my friends who know anything about music', Wicks said calmly, 'have been impressing on me for the last three months how good these Hungarians are and warning me not to miss them.'

'So everybody says,' Conway agreed. 'Are you an expert on chamber music?'

'No, not at all. Especially not Hungarian music.'

'And Alicia?'

'No. But Mr Wicks told me what a reputation these four have.'

'What are they playing?' Conway asked. 'I came in so early that there was no one on the doors selling programmes. I thought we started at seven.'

Wicks opened one of his programmes. 'Mozart,' he announced. 'Dohnányi, Quartet No. 2 and Kodály Quartet No. 1.'

'Do you know any of them?'

'No. The Mozart is one of the latish works. I've heard the so-called Haydn Quartets more often.'

'And they're supposed to be better?'

'That seems to be the accepted opinion. It appears that he was in trouble at this time. His wife was ill. The King of Prussia asked him to compose a set of six, but he managed only three.'

Alicia was impressed with this information. Clearly he had prepared himself for this concert. Conway smiled and thanked him for the answers to his questions. Alicia said nothing, but pressed back against the wall to allow others to pass. She watched the two men carefully. Conway was perhaps an inch taller, but less robustly built than Wicks. Both wore suits, newish, grey. Conway's decorated with thin blue lines, Wicks's with red.

Conway's shirt was yellow, with a sober blue tie. Wicks wore what looked to her like a rugby club design on a white, starched shirt. Both had made an effort, both wore highly polished brown shoes. Now she concentrated on their hands. Conway's were delicately thin with long fingers, Wicks's powerful.

'I'd better get off and buy a programme to mug up what's going on.'

'You'll find one or two grammatical errors,' Wicks warned.

'As long as they make me understand what's happening it'll do.' He pushed forward and spoke to Alicia. 'Lovely to see you,' Conway whispered to her. 'Now I'd better get myself a programme before they sell out.'

Alicia modestly inclined her head.

'He's an odd fellow,' Wicks said. 'You'd think he'd buy a programme at the desk downstairs. They're open at least an hour before the concert starts.'

'Perhaps he likes to stretch his legs.'

'Why does he want that?'

'He knows he'll meet someone he knows,' she said. 'Like us.'

'Hasn't he got many friends, then?'

'That's my impression.' She wondered if Wicks was trying to run him down.

'He's shy?'

'He likes to go his own way. He's a loner. He had that reputation at Oxford.'

'Do you approve?'

'Approve? He's very useful to me. He makes my work that much more straightforward. Some of the tutors give you the impression that they've glanced at your thesis just an hour or so before they arranged to see you. He looks and thinks about it for the three or four weeks before he interviews you again. And you feel you're learning something.'

'He concentrates on his work?'

'As I do.'

'Isn't literature supposed to tell you about life?' Wicks asked.

'You can learn a great deal about life. That's for certain. But it's the way that it's presented.'

'And which is more important?'

'I wouldn't like to guess. The second if I'm forced to answer.'

'Is your research teaching you more about life?'

'People thought as we do. I notice that, even though standards of

154

behaviour sometimes seem radically different. And fashion plays its part.'

This conversation was interrupted several times as they stood up to allow people to pass them on the way to their seats. The auditorium had been empty when they arrived; now, ten minutes later, it was full with garrulous men and women, not sitting still, but indulging in a writhing dance of settling comfortably or removing outer garments. The young woman seated alone next to Alicia played with her gloves, her hat, her bag and sniffed the air. She caught Alicia's curious eye and said, 'It's very exciting this,' then mined her handbag for a programme and a tiny, lace-edged handkerchief. She spoke in a whisper. 'I used to live in Hungary,' she said.

'Was it much different from Beechnall?'

'I suppose it was, if I think about it.'

A rising spatter of applause greeted the appearance on the platform of the players, who moved their chairs the expected inch or two, sat down, examined the music they had laid on their stands. Silence fell. The quartet looked to their leader. He nodded and the top three instruments were away. They surprised Alicia by the quietness of their playing. Usually the string quartets she had heard had felt it their duty to demonstrate how much sound they could generate. These played with intense care, variety and mastership, but in a kind of low voice achieved a summit of beauty, of balance, of poignancy that held their listeners breathless.

Alicia sat stunned with pleasure. She liked music, as did her parents, had been well taught at school, had attended a few of the very many concerts at Oxford, but this seemed as if she heard the piece for the first time, as in one sense she did. She sat still, hardly daring to breathe. At the end she clapped with delight.

'Superb,' Wicks said. 'Out of this world.'

She was grateful to him. During the performance she had forgotten him on one side and the lady who lived in Hungary on the other. She was a different being and only in the short pause between the first two items did she become something like herself. She judged the players: the first violin had about him a sort of elfin energy. The second fiddle, a lady, played with a vigour that belied the friendly expression she had assumed as she had stood before the audience. The viola player looked older than the rest, baldish and superior, as if he had been part of the group longer than his juniors. She imagined that at rehearsals his word would carry

155

weight, and the size of his instrument was his badge of rank. When the others bowed to the audience, he inclined his head, though he stood back to usher the lady from the stage. The cellist stood, almost ashamed at the bulk of his instrument.

With the Dohnányi, and the Kodály to come after the interval, she felt less at ease. The music she had played as a child, in the concerts she had heard, had made the language of Mozart familiar to her. The two Hungarians used a different dialect, not quite unknown but odd enough to make her unsure quite what was happening. When, in the second movement of the Dohnányi, the quartet suddenly played a kind of hymn tune in straightforward, old-fashioned harmony, she at once felt at home, as though the composer spoke in her vernacular. She determined that when she had more time she would go to more concerts, buy the right compact discs, become familiar with all the messages a string quartet could offer. Afterwards, she reflected with some regret that she had no such thoughts during the Mozart; there she had concentrated on the music. True, she had much to learn there, but she had been to some large extent well prepared.

During the interval they moved out of the hall and she had the opportunity to thank Wicks again for his invitation to this concert.

'You're enjoying it?' he asked, obviously pleased.

'Every minute.'

'Even the Dohnányi?'

'Well, that showed me how little I know.'

'You didn't think it was because he wasn't in Mozart's class?'

'I didn't know enough to make that judgement.'

At that moment some acquaintance of Wicks's came along and began to praise the playing they had heard. 'They're wonderful,' he averred. 'Magnificent. And they suited their playing to the place. I feared when I heard they were to play here that this hall would be far too large for them. But no, not they. They sounded just as delicate as always, just as masterful as needs be. That's an art one has to acquire when one's learnt the right notes. I've not reached stage one yet.'

'But you haven't given up?'

'Not likely. But I know I shall never be in their class.'

The man, middle-aged with a short-clipped military moustache, embarked on a story of how he was once asked to play a rehearsal with a professional quartet. 'A friend had recommended me to them. They were to play some Mozart and Beethoven they had not done in public for some time. I was surprised about this. They'd have no difficulty with the notes; it's the approach, the nuances, the agreement between the four, that's what mattered. The cello couldn't be there the day before so that they'd only have the morning or afternoon of the concert. They told me, in a bluff manner, that if three of them came to some agreement that would be an advantage when the whole four played together. I was dragged in one Thursday and the concert was on Saturday. Could I give them the Friday? I said I could but I wasn't sure I'd be any use to them, as I was only an amateur. I told them that to their faces on the Friday morning. I knew all three works, or at least had played them moderately recently, and I spent the whole of what remained of that Thursday practising them, getting them up to standard. They weren't particularly difficult, I suppose, but I was terrified.

'The other three were most polite, said how grateful they were, looked at my cello with interest but when we started to play they were different men altogether. They were so confident, had such magnificent variety of tone that they left me staggering. I gained in positiveness as we went on, joined their bits of rubato and felt quite proud. They thanked me and only once did they ask for something different. The leader said, "Can you play that louder, please? When we get Felix back he'll blast the ears off us and we give him tit for tat." We repeated the cello solo twice, and they accompanied my feeble efforts with real power. It was something, I can tell you. I was pretty well on my knees when we'd worked through all three pieces. They thanked me, said they liked my cello though its sound was quite unlike Felix's. I asked what he had and they said a Stradivarius. The real owners of it wanted it played regularly.' He rubbed his hands, poked at his moustache. 'It was some experience; I shan't forget it. I often think about it. Of course, they'd be more talented to start with than I was, and then look at the amount of practice they get. They live in another world.'

Alicia smiled and Wicks offered a few words of interest. The man left them, shoulders back.

'One always meets somebody interesting at these concerts,' Wicks said, leading her back to her seat.

The Kodály puzzled her. It seemed overlong and from minute to minute she lost interest. The players concentrated hard, finding it worth their while, but losing her. She determined to expand her knowledge once her thesis was out of the way. She had not thought

157

like that before; her thesis had seemed exactly the right occupation to fill her life. Now it was like a small hill in a country towering with mountains. The audience applauded with enthusiasm, bringing the quartet back three times to the stage. Finally they sat down again and once they had sorted out their music the leader made some sort of announcement. Alicia could not hear him properly; the only word she caught was 'Schubert', but that comforted, helped to ease her fears.

There followed what Wicks called on their way home 'five minutes of heaven'. Their instruments soared, but without effort, it seemed. Once they had finished the four stood smiling in their different ways, confident that they had expounded a rare beauty.

Wicks laid a hand on her arm, steadying her from hurry. 'There's no rush,' he said, then with a breathy gruffness added, 'You'd think they were being let out of prison.'

Downstairs they saw Professor Conway, standing in the thinning crowd as if waiting for them. He signalled with his hands. Wicks guided Alicia towards him. 'There's one thing I forgot to ask you,' he said. 'Have you seen anything of Clarence Caldwell? I've heard he's been quite ill and has gone off to relatives in London to recuperate.'

'That's so,' Wicks said. 'But I've heard nothing of him for a week or so. I've not seen Mrs Rhŷs-Williams. I ought to have contacted her. Have you heard anything of them, Alicia?'

'Not a word. But I never go out.'

'I was also told that there was a fire in his house, and that you went in and saved her life.'

'How the news gets around,' Wicks said sarcastically.

Conway made an ironical little obeisance in Wicks's direction, wished them goodnight and walked briskly away.

Wicks cleared his throat and said, 'Hardly the answer he wanted.'

'Don't you like him?' Alicia was surprised.

'He's like all academics. Knows the answers to all his questions and yours before you've asked them.'

'Oh, dear.'

'Otherwise he's all right.'

He drove her home in a subdued manner without speaking much. Back in the village, she thanked him for the outing, said what a treat it had been. He invited her in for a drink, but she refused, claiming to be tired. He kissed her warmly and saw her

158

through her garden gate. She thanked him again: 'You don't know how much good you've done me.'

He acknowledged her thanks with a gentlemanly inclination of the head. She locked and bolted the garden gate, rushed up the path, banged her way indoors to switch on her electric blanket, then spent ten minutes in her cooling house making a mug of hot chocolate, fondling it then drinking. She saw with satisfaction her work laid out for an early start next morning. She gave it no more than a cursory glance, but it added the final touch to an outstanding day.

XIII

A few days later Alicia to her surprise received a letter from Sir Clarence Caldwell. It was not long and there was no obvious reason why he should have written. His handwriting was large and reminded her of a biggish bird, a magpie, say, rising from the ground.

He said he was now in good health, but he had been thinking of his future and had decided that it was unlikely that he'd come back to live in the village again. 'I have a small apartment that will contain me in my last days here. Not, dear Alicia' (he had apologised already for beginning the letter with her Christian name, but had thought her generosity and his age sufficient excuse) 'that I am thinking of dying. Far from it. In fact, since I have been here I have made two cameo appearances in films and enjoyed both in spite of the drawbacks, of which the very early rising was the worst.' He went on to say that he was doing nothing for the present about his house in Sutton because Megan was still living there and he did not know if she could easily make alternative arrangements for herself. She had been kind to him when he needed help and he would not rush her out now that he had decided to live in London.

In any case, she was recovering from the shock of the fire. Perhaps Alicia would be sweet enough to talk about this to her. Megan was the sort who profited from discussion about her problems with someone she liked and trusted. Alicia was to pay no attention to her complaints that she was short of money. She had her husband's pension, or part of it, and two decent terrace houses her husband had owned as well as her own savings. She was frugal, didn't throw her money away. The financial side was not a worry at all in his view. What he feared was that, when she heard his plans, she'd lose her head, rush away from Sutton and do something she'd regret. She was a decent old stick, but had some crazy ideas when provoked, so that he'd feel much more at ease with himself if Alicia could talk Megan's future over with her.

The letter ended with a short paragraph saying that she was, doubtless, surprised at receiving this letter from him. He thought very highly of her. On the two or three occasions they had held anything like conversations together he had been impressed. Perhaps, he concluded, his old age would give him the privilege to say that had he been fifty years younger he would be madly in love with her. He was hers, Clarence Caldwell.

She reflected that Megan Rhŷs-Williams was not the only one with odd ideas in her head. Whenever she had met Caldwell he had seemed pleased to see her, but in a distant way, an old man to his granddaughter perhaps, a person of experience and consequence to a girl barely out of her teens. She had seen no outward signs of this mad love, and she wondered if he wasn't, pen in hand, acting a part. It did not seem proper, but she did as she was bid, rang Megan and invited her over for a cup of coffee. She begrudged the time, but felt she could do no other.

When Megan appeared she had made an effort to smarten herself up and Alicia thought she had succeeded. The drama of the fire seemed to have left her untouched. One could see that she had once been attractive, even pretty in her youth. Her eyes were dull now, bloodshot, the veins in her cheeks broken and her wrinkles cut deep into bloodless skin. The voice was, as ever, without power, but as they talked it grew stronger, with variation, almost melodious. Her hands, claw-like as they were, drew fetching patterns in the air to match her speech.

Alicia was surprised to learn that Megan already knew that Caldwell had no intention of returning to the Midlands and that, moreover, she was not put out by the news.

'What will you do?' Alicia asked.

'I don't know yet. He's told me I needn't hurry. I'll give him time to settle. He's gone into one of his London flats. It's an attic, a poky little place. You couldn't swing a cat round, even if you wanted to. He'll soon tire of that and will move. He owns the whole house. And he won't like looking after himself. He thinks he can do it well, but he's hopeless and at bottom he knows it.'

'So you'll go back to him?'

'That's my plan so far. Did he tell you to talk to me about what I wanted?'

'He did. Will he expect me to tell him what you said?'

'He might. If he thinks highly of you and would like a letter back from you.' Megan laughed, with no witch's cackle this time but on a high, clear note. 'Did he tell you he loved you?'

'Yes. Or rather he would if he were fifty years younger.'

'Um. That means he's lonely and sorry for himself. Well, you'd please me if you'd write back and tell him you think I'd come back to London as his housekeeper without too much argument if he asked nicely. Of course, you must do as you think best.'

'I think I could manage that without overburdening my conscience.'

'Conscience, eh? Good word, that.'

The subject was dropped and Megan began an amusing account of how she spent her day. She 'wasted' half her time reading. 'I'm not using up all my energy vacuuming his house and cleaning his windows, that I can tell you. I don't make his house dirty. And I like to spend my evenings lolling in front of the television.'

'What time do you go to bed?'

'Never much after eleven.'

'And what are you reading just now?'

'*Abinger Harvest*. A book of essays by E. M. Forster.'

'Are they good?'

'I used to think they were marvellous, but now they seem in some way old-fashioned to me. It's how he writes that gets on my nerves. I mean he's clever and he tries to be honest. I guess he'd be more brutal if he were writing today.'

'Yes, but would he be any better?'

That set Megan back. She put a hand over her mouth as if to stem too easy a flow of words. 'I don't know. It depends on the reader. I'd like it better if he were a bit more ferocious, less gentlemanly.'

'So you don't recommend me to read it?'

'Yes, I do. I'd like to know what you make of it. Both Clarence and your neighbour Wicks say you're clever, that you've read a lot, so I'd like to know how you judge him.'

Alicia was delighted at both the old woman's fluency and her subject matter. Before, she had written her off as an old witch, chuntering unintelligently to herself as she shuffled hump-backed along the street. Now she was a reader who made sensible pronouncements on what she read. 'Do you and Sir Clarence talk together?'

'Sometimes. It depends on how we feel. Sir Clarence, as you call him, can sit for hours on end not saying a word. At other times he never stops talking.'

'Is he a well-read man?'

'No. I wouldn't say so. And when he does read it's *The Times*.'

'He told me to read Kipling.'

'You surprise me.'

'So you don't have literary arguments?'

'No. If we have words it's about the meals.'

'He complains, does he?'

'Not really. He makes daft suggestions. That, for instance, some dish would be improved by a touch of cinnamon or garlic or something. He'll have heard it on the television. He has a good appetite for a man of his age.'

'Do you, did you, ever go to see him act?'

'As often as possible. When we met again later in life. He was a wonderful actor in that you never thought of Clarence Caldwell when you saw him on stage, only the person he was portraying. In real life I found him rather bland, even when he took to the high horse, as he sometimes did. But on stage he was a marvel. He played all sorts of rubbish, but he added something to the most insignificant play. He was never out of work. Offer him any part when he was within sight of resting and he'd snap it up. I sometimes wonder if that was the reason why his knighthood came so late.'

'I don't quite understand you.'

'He appeared in such feeble plays instead of the classics of the language. But he did them so well.'

'*Nullum quod tetigit non ornavit.*'

'I don't know Latin.'

'He touched nothing that he did not adorn. I think Dr Johnson said something like that about Goldsmith as a writer.'

'I see. Well, when you write to him tell him that and that I shall be glad to join him again as long as it's not in that shoebox of a flat he's in now. He's more likely to take it from you than from me. He's a silly old man in some ways.' She laughed. 'At our age we're none of us exactly in our right mind.'

Megan left in high spirits, climbed sprightly up Alicia's steep path, but once on the main road resumed the old, ugly, public shuffle. Alicia watched her, then wrote a note to Sir Clarence, passing on the old woman's message. She made no mention of love, except formally at the end. Nor did she post it that day, but waited until she had to go out. He'd attribute the tardiness of its arrival to the post office's inefficiency. She remarked on Megan's account of her reading and wondered what he'd make of that. Nothing, she supposed; it wouldn't interest him.

Twice in the next few days Raynor Wicks asked her if she'd go out with him one evening for a drink. Both times she declined. She was on a rather lengthy piece of her thesis and wanted to be sure that she had completed it before she presented it to Professor Conway. That was accurate enough, but she wondered when she turned her thoughts to men, male escorts, possible husbands, whether she liked Wicks sufficiently to accompany him on his pleasure trips. She did not actively dislike him; he behaved in a proper and accommodating way when they were out together, but she feared that if she became more intimate he would bully her, politely enough, to be sure. She had no real evidence for this. She recalled how highly Sir Clarence Caldwell had spoken of him as a person one could utterly depend on, who would see you through some trickily awkward passage. She also remembered that it was Wicks who had rushed into Caldwell's burning kitchen, snatched up the unconscious Megan Rhŷs-Williams and saved her life. Alicia could never see herself snatching someone from the jaws of death. All this worried her to a certain extent, on the rare occasions she thought carefully about it. Wicks was a next-door neighbour and she did not want to annoy him. He would be an implacable enemy.

When on the last day of the term she handed in the large section of her thesis to Professor Conway's office she expected that he'd see her at the beginning of the summer term. Thus she was surprised when she received a note a week later, to say he was back from some conference in America and would have read the work in two days' time, and would she perhaps be willing to see him then? She replied that this seemed excellent and set about the two final short concluding chapters. The date and time and venue were fixed by e-mail.

She knew Conway's address but had never been near the place. Kirk White Avenue was a short street of detached houses, built in the twenties or thirties, yet still preserving the appearance of newness, shining white paint on the windows and doors, the front gardens neat behind their low stone walls and, beneath its three cherry trees, primulas. His bell, when she rang it, sounded extraordinarily loud, as if the house were empty.

No one answered her summons, so she tried again, violently and at length. That should have woken the street, she thought. Someone appeared at last; she heard the withdrawing of bolts, rattling of keys in locks.

'Have you been waiting long?' he asked. 'I've been out in the garden.' He held out his dirtily gloved hands in evidence, then showed her awkwardly into the front room and what proved to be against appearances a comfortable chair. 'Just give me a minute to clean up.'

She saw the pile of her thesis on the table and beside it his notes, presumably comments on her work. Glancing uncomfortably about the room she wondered why Conway had chosen such modern furniture. The chair she occupied had metal arms and, though fine to sit in, displayed in its softer parts a highly strikingly orange with jet-black lines. No flowers disturbed the starkness of the rest of the room. The floor, in some sort of light, polished wood, was bare except for a grey carpet in front of a modernistic fireplace and hearth. There were two pictures, one each on the naked walls, in thin frames matching the colour of the floors: watercolours of a grey rolling sea under threatening clouds. The fourth wall behind her stood packed with shelved books, from floor to ceiling. The whole effect was of haphazard neatness.

Conway appeared to be in no hurry and she cast her eye about the room. Nothing seemed to match. True, the two easy chairs were similar, but the table looked cheap, as if bought in some backstreet second-hand furniture dealer's. Her thesis, and his notes, toppled as if he had hoiked them out of his case and dropped them on the table. The thesis kept its squareness as a packet, but had been placed, dunked at an angle to the edge of the table, and his notes askew to both. It looked untidy, as if he didn't much care. The whole room seemed randomly assembled. The curtains drawn back from the curved bay window were heavy and darkly green, and would have suited a crowded Victorian parlour with hardly room to move. Perhaps they had been left by a previous owner. She drew in her breath sharply. She had expected something better from Christopher Conway. She remembered his room in Oxford where she had been regularly for tutorials. That had been larger than this, and darker, with ivy trespassing round the window frames outside so that one needed the electric light to read by on all but the brightest of summer days. There the walls were thick with his books and a small, ticking electric fire in the hearth half-heartedly heated the place. In this respect this room was superior; the low radiators under the windows kept it hot.

Alicia, on the *qui vive*, heard Conway's footsteps on the stairs. He rushed in, stuttering excuses. He had changed out of his gardening clothes, and now wore a shirt and tie, a smart sports jacket and flannels, and polished brogues. His hands were scrupulously clean, showing no signs of his toil in the garden.

'How are you?' he asked. 'You're not working yourself to death?'

'I'm well, thank you.'

'How far on are you with your thesis?'

'I'm working on those last two chapters.'

He placed his right forefinger on the thesis. 'I've left it in case you wanted some alterations on account of this lot.' The nails were exquisite. She liked that. 'There won't be much need for change here. It's very good. You've excelled yourself. I've made one or two donnish suggestions, but you needn't take them too seriously. The thing about you, Alicia' – he leaned back so that his chair stood on two legs only – 'is that you write so well. Most theses are to be praised on the amount of information the researcher has dug out and the conclusions the writer has drawn. Yours is admirable on those grounds. You really have amassed a great deal of knowledge of your subject, but you've made it interesting. You draw your reader in. This is unusual. Many tutors would regard it as dangerous. Your intention should be to collect relevant material and then demonstrate a thorough grasp of your topic. You go further. You make your reader prick up his ears.'

'Oh, thank you.'

'It's no thanks to me. You're the best D.Phil. student I've ever had.'

'That's because you won't let me stray. You tell me where I'm going off course.'

'You sound quite pleasant with me, Alicia. But I'm even more delighted with you. The eighteenth-century theatre is not something I'm desperately interested in. Well, with a few exceptions. Human beings always turn up something of interest, but this is not a period that grips me particularly.'

He went on, in this quiet voice from between beautifully even teeth, to praise her, and gave his instructions that as soon as she had finished her last two short chapters she was to show the work to him. If he was satisfied with it, she was to get it bound, and he'd

166

send a copy to the external examiner so that it could all be over in good time for the summer degree-awarding ceremony.

Then began an hour on his 'donnish suggestions'. This was where he was at his best. He made clear points and explained why he thought as he did. Alicia more than held her own and he admitted it. 'You know so much more than I do about the subject,' he said at least twice.

Alicia thoroughly enjoyed the argument. His initial praise had given her confidence to answer in the give-and-take, to hold her own against his doubts.

'Good,' he said. 'You'll be able to defend yourself against Oliver Stirling.'

'He's a tartar, is he?' That was one of her father's expressions.

'A tartar? Well, he knows a great deal and lets you see that this is so. You see, Alicia, you give the impression that you've done a large amount of reading and profited from it. That's why Caldwell and his Megan Rhŷs-Williams try you out on your knowledge of their favourite authors. It's to some extent envy on their part, but mainly, mostly, admiration. They do their best to catch you out with their Christopher Fry and Kipling. I expect Stirling will do much the same. Hasn't your friend Wicks tried you on his reading?'

'No. Not that I remember.'

'You surprise me. Do you see much of him?'

'We went to that concert together. A Hungarian string quartet. You were there. And he's invited me out for a drink a time or two, but I said I was too busy.'

'I was going to offer you a drink when we're finished this morning.'

'No, thank you.' Her answer was immediate.

'Do you not drink, then?' His mouth drooped like that of a disappointed schoolboy.

'Not when I'm driving. My father bought me this car and made me promise that I wouldn't take it out on to the roads, even after one drink.'

'And you never go back on your word?'

'Not in this case. The lines were so clearly drawn. I don't drive if I've tasted alcohol.'

'I like you, Alicia. You let me know exactly how you stand. Will you look at my garden? In lieu of sherry. If you have no questions of me.'

They walked together round his garden.

'This must seem small compared with yours?' he asked.

'Yes, it is. But it's very well planned. And full of flowers.'

'Nothing out of the ordinary. I'm what my ex-wife used to call a "parks and gardens" man. I buy bulbs and seeds and sow them. I can cut the grass. I can make a compost heap.'

'Your wife was an expert, then?'

He nodded. 'She was a plants woman. That's an awkward phrase, but it exactly describes her.'

'I have to keep ringing my parents for advice.'

'They're knowledgeable, are they?'

'My mother would spend all her spare time in her garden.'

'Have they got a greenhouse?'

'Yes. Quite a large one. They keep me well supplied with tomatoes and grapes in season. And seedlings.'

'Where do they live?'

'London. Finchley. They're usually at least a fortnight ahead of me here.'

'Spring has been very slow this year. It's lovely to see the blossom on the cherry trees now. The primulas don't seem to have suffered. They're appearing in all sorts of places all over the garden. I blame the birds.'

'What's that beautiful large bush with red flowers?'

'That's a camellia. It's usually more forward than this. That's one thing I like: the exotic flowers out so early in the year and the polished leaves. It's a plant, or so the books say, which is akin to tea. It comes originally from East Asia.'

'You've not tried to make the tea from it?' she enquired skittishly.

'No. You'd brew it from the leaves, would you? They're tough. You'd have to boil them long enough.'

Alicia enjoyed this. Neither of them knew much about the topic but just to talk to each other out in the garden on this changeable spring morning seemed admirable. His remarks to her about her research had lifted her spirits; she would have been pleased to stand with him in a filthy coal cellar and been more than satisfied. They stood in front of a tall pieris; she did not know its name, which he gave her. He seemed particularly proud of this bush, which he had pruned, on the advice of a colleague, rather severely and had not expected it to recover. It stood in pride, with its white blossoms, which he invited her to sniff. 'It's delicate,' he said.

'And bears me no malice for my butchery.' They moved away, laughing, and sat together in a shelter at the end of the main path. The sky had darkened and they noticed spots of rain on the stones on the floor of the shelter that projected into a small patio.

'I don't like the shape of this house,' he said, looking out.

'Why?'

'It's like a shoebox, and the bricks at the back here are pale and second-rate compared with the front.'

'Do they keep the rain out?' she asked.

'Perfectly,' he said. 'I'll give the builder credit for that.'

They sat contentedly, swinging their legs. There seemed no need for conversation. In the end it was he who broke the happy silence: 'When this thesis is out of the way, what will you do next?'

She hesitated. It was a topic she often contemplated, but felt that Conway might have some influence on her decision. 'I thought I'd take a thorough look at Pope. I did quite a bit on him at Oxford. If you remember, you sent me to Dr Edith Speirs and I wrote one or two essays for her.'

'She died, you know, only a week or two ago.'

'I didn't know. I hadn't seen anything in the newspapers.'

'There was a good obituary in *The Times*. How did you get on with her?'

'She didn't seem very well organised. She knew a great deal and could point out some interesting aspects of the topic, but she wasn't very good at preparing you for an exam. She'd no idea what the examiners were likely to ask you to write about.'

'No. She was old. I only sent my very bright students to her. Those who needed an elementary grounding went elsewhere. Those who didn't really need teaching I sent to Edith, because they'd be given some insights, which they could use to advantage.'

'She didn't seem that wonderful at arguing a point.'

'No, her mind was made up and she didn't see the sense in changing it. Even in my day she wasn't much good at arguing the toss. But she knew a great deal. And there were plenty of useful books and at least two lecturers who would make the basic points about Pope's ideas on verse that any good examinee would need for his or her Finals.'

'I never felt sorry for her. I don't know why.'

'I should think not. She had been a real scholar in the early part of her career. She began to lose her touch rather soon, so that she was never elected to a chair. George Caunt thought highly of her.'

Caunt had been Conway's tutor, a man you crossed at your peril in a literary debate. Conway stroked his already smooth chin. 'Pope. I think that's right. It's always sensible to tackle big subjects when you're young.'

'Not when you're experienced?'

'If you're any good you will have done a great deal of reading in the years after your degree. And you'll have the energy to look at it properly and draw useful conclusions. It doesn't always work out that way, I will admit. Some people need longer. Another man who taught me, Fred Gent, seemed to get better as he grew older. He was sixty-three when he died and had just brought out his book on the Metaphysicals, a marvellous piece of work.'

'I'm not quite sixty-three yet,' Alicia said, smiling.

'No.' Conway drew out the vowel. 'There is another thing. If your doctorate goes through all right, and I don't see any difficulty there, you'll be able to apply for a lectureship here, mainly on the seventeenth and eighteenth centuries. That will fit in nicely with your study of Pope. I expect we shall have to advertise the job. If it were left to me I'd just appoint you. You seem ideal for it. But you know what the vice-chancellor's like.' Conway stood to demonstrate. 'It costs only a few pounds, and a few extra hours of work, and that mainly for the secretaries.' It was not a close imitation of the V-C, but was quite unmistakable. As he came to the crux of his argument, he thrust his belly backwards and forwards at the salient points. He lacked his superior's embonpoint but again the movement was perfectly recognisable. 'We may in return for our small expenditure of time and money make perfectly sure that we do not overlook some outstanding candidate.'

'Thank you,' she said, both for the guying of the vice-chancellor and his stated wish to have her as a member of his department.

'We'll see.' The professor rubbed his hands together as if he would enjoy dismissing the other hopefuls. 'I shall be grossly disappointed if I can't welcome you as a colleague.' His lips seemed stiff as if to match or emphasise the formality of his words. He breathed in deeply. 'And when your doctorate's done and dusted I'd like to ask you out for a meal or a play or a concert.'

She noted the relaxation of the language. 'That would be lovely,' she said. 'I'd enjoy that. And perhaps you'd come up to my house for a meal. I haven't had much time for culinary experiences while I've been writing my thesis and I'll be glad to get my hand in again.'

'Perfection,' he said.

When they had walked all the small paths of the garden he allowed her to gather her bits and pieces and leave without making any serious attempt to delay her with interesting talk. That disappointed her slightly, but she contented herself with the few minutes he had given her sitting on the garden seat and making casual conversation. He was like her in that he had priorities; if he had work to complete of whatever kind, hoeing his garden or preparing some article for a learned journal, and if he had allotted time to that then other matters were put aside, even if it meant postponing his first confessions of love. She stopped the train of thought there. She had no reason to think that he had any temptations in that direction. She was attracted to him, for sure, but that did not mean he felt anything for her. She must not be carried away. He liked her work and said so. But he said no more; his invitations were mere signs that he thought she would make a good literary critic. She smiled grimly to herself: cast her doubts in the form of an examination question. Talent at literary criticism is not an indication of successful wife-and-motherhood. Discuss. She drew up at a huge traffic island, grimacing.

By the time she reached home her mind was back to those last few pages of her thesis. She'd have it ready by the beginning of next week. Then, when she had made sure that Conway approved and she was satisfied, and the printers had properly bound it, she'd have a week or two off. That did not mean doing nothing. She'd do some reading of Pope, but for pure enjoyment, she hoped. She'd glance at the work of modern scholars on the eighteenth century, picking up ideas casually, in readiness for the months of solid reading, note-taking, the forging of her own ideas about the poet, the comparisons of good and evil between her chosen poet and the other giants of the language. That's what she enjoyed doing or did best; making up her mind.

She remembered a topic she had been set. If you were to compare and contrast a poem by Pope and one by Gerard Manley Hopkins, what elements would you find common to each? What differences are important? How would you decide who was the greater poet? She'd spent a fortnight on the topic and, she remembered, had chosen Pope as the superior. She did not feel sure that she'd come to the same conclusion today. When she'd rid herself of her thesis she'd look out her old essay and find out how sensibly she'd written. She'd done the work for a youngish don

171

called Trevor Jones, who now and again set subjects that weren't likely to appear in Finals papers. He said to her, and she remembered the flash of sunlight on his spectacles as he nodded, 'We don't want you clever girls to be trained as mere exam passers. I'd like to imagine that you had thought about the subject for yourself. It's good to know what your Professor Caunt or Miss Speirs have written about it. In fact, it's essential. But you should make up your own mind. And it might so happen that you find the conclusions of these experts so exhaustive and brilliant that your own views seem feeble or indefensible and you are ready to drop them. That's not as important as it appears. You haven't spent the years on the topic that the scholars have. But fashions change and when you reach my age (he was at most ten years older than she) you'll find the next lot of acceptable critics are chasing after different fashions, new writers, more modern gods and commandments.'

She wondered where Jones was now. He'd left for America in her last year at Oxford. She'd admired him greatly as a scholar, but felt nothing towards him as a human being. She did not care whether he drank tea or coffee, liked cricket better than rugger or soccer. It's true he was no Adonis, but one girl she knew, a really clever girl with a mind like a razor, had once or twice given her to believe that she had set her cap at Jones, unsuccessfully it appeared. As a teacher Christopher Conway was as good as anyone else in Oxford, but she felt even as he lectured brilliantly that she would have liked to hold his hand or hear him defer to her views on the making of Christmas pudding. She did not deceive herself, she instructed herself, in deciding that Conway felt more for her than admiration for a clever pupil. That would be good, but in the background lurked her intuition that a better conclusion existed, that she was regarded by him as one with whom he'd be prepared to share his life, bear his children. It was true that his first marriage had been a failure and perhaps had fallen so far short of what he wanted that he would never risk it again, or at least until he was quite certain that his choice was sensible enough that he wouldn't be humiliated as he was at his first attempt. Perhaps the initial move would have to come from her. That seemed against nature and her ideas of status.

Without difficulty she completed the thesis and decided that her first draft would do. She felt that she ought to rewrite these last line sections because, short as they were, they brought the whole

172

structure to completion. But she could not see how any major alteration would make even the slightest improvement. Hardly believing this, she dispatched her typescript to Professor Conway and waited.

He took a week to speak to her about the matter, as he was away. When he finally rang, and she had been on tenterhooks for the week, he expressed satisfaction with her work, told her to get it typed up, then to take it to Derry's, the printers, who knew exactly how to bind it. It was as well done as the rest of the work and this was not always the case. He said he was pleased and moreover, while he was away he had met Professor Stirling and had told him to expect a fine thesis to read inside the next month. Stirling had said he'd be glad to examine a really readable piece of work since turgidity seemed to be the order of the day among doctoral students, so she was to be prepared for her external examiner to be on his high horse. 'If he seems awkward, then he's impressed. He's clever, but you'll manage him, Alicia. He doesn't know everything.' Conway gave her his advice about such mundane matters as the number of copies she should have made. He seemed cheerful, told her that the eighteenth-century lectureship would be advertised in a week's time and she was to apply. She felt apprehensive about this, shivered at the thought.

She was pleased to be occupied in preparation for her viva.

'Keep up your reading,' Conway advised her. The thing she remembered most of this period was the skill of the man at the printer's who took the thick pile of each copy and, still talking to her, tapped it gently between his hand on the counter until every angle was a right angle and the whole thesis was straight, as if sculpted from stone.

'I wish I could do that,' she said admiringly.

'Everyone to his own job,' the man said. 'I couldn't write a thesis if I lived to be a hundred. They don't judge it on the straight edges, so I'm told. It's what you've said. I read a page or two as you were waiting, and do you know I could understand what you were saying. You should see some of the maths and science efforts. It might as well be in Greek.'

She left the place cheered, but a day or two later, when she handed in the copies to Professor Conway's office, she was unsure of herself and her work. Conway was not at the university to cheer her with a word or two.

Alicia was on her own and did not like it.

XIV

The next few weeks Alicia passed in limbo. Christopher Conway had immediately rung her to say he had received the copies of the thesis and that he had packed off one at once to Professor Stirling in York. This had not in any way helped to set in motion her viva so far. Winter and spring had disappeared in a heavy trench warfare of work. She could easily wait another week or two.

'He's very well known, you know. If he passes you he'll be prepared to write a favourable account of your research when you start job seeking. He's made a considerable name for himself. In your case he's trying to fit in your interview with one in Leicester, you in the morning, the other, a man, in the afternoon. The trouble is this man has not yet completed his thesis and so hasn't yet submitted it.' Conway seemed embarrassed as he stumbled through these excuses. 'I've told him I want your work to be assessed in time for the interview for this post here. He tells me all will be well, but I don't know whether I believe him or not. But I'll keep nagging him. I'll be like the importunate widow on your behalf.'

This delay troubled her more than she would admit. 'Keep abreast of your thesis,' Conway advised, 'because Stirling, being what he is, might suddenly descend on us, giving us one or two days' notice only. It will be worth it if he thinks highly of it, as he will, if I'm any judge, especially with publishers. If he recommends it they'll be prepared to look seriously at your project of turning it into a book. You'd be surprised if you knew how keen even large publishers can be with a manuscript that has a big name recommending it.'

'Has he read it yet?' she asked.

'I don't know. I doubt it. But it won't take him long.'

'Will it be over by the time the lectureship interview comes up?'

Conway seemed to hesitate. 'I'll do my best for you.'

She felt she might burst into tears, but kept a steady voice over the phone.

That Conway seemed not very successful over these arrangements dashed her optimism and she decided it would be sensible to set about the spring-cleaning she had vaguely promised herself. If Stirling turned her down, demanded another year's work on the theatre in the late seventeenth and eighteenth centuries she would still be living here, and a spick-and-span refurbished house would be a comfort. She planned the new task as carefully as she had set about her thesis. She'd start on the kitchen and then the dining room, and when she'd found out how long this part of the operation took, and how well she was suited to such work, she would decide where to move next.

The kitchen was the only room that needed repainting. Why her father's decorators had done it so carelessly she could not guess. She consulted wall charts, decided on light blue and white, then changed her mind. With those colours the room would be too cold in winter, when she came back after a day's slog at the university. She couldn't imagine what additions Stirling might suggest. One day she had finished her day's work painting the kitchen, she sat down in her living room before starting to prepare the evening meal and burst into tears. The bout, rising to a crescendo of sobbing, left her eventually hunched across her chair-arm. Trying to account to herself for this breakdown, she felt she could not altogether blame it on her physical exhaustion. She had worked all day, made good progress, clambering up and down her ladders she had worn herself out, and this must have accounted to some extent for her lack of emotional stability, but she realised that her disappointment with the slowness of Professor Conway's effort on her behalf and her own, a week or so after completing the thesis, lack of confidence in her achievement must have played a larger part.

She remembered her father recounting an episode at work. He had seemed to have made some gross mistake, which had left him, he feared, blameworthy in the eyes of his seniors on whom he was dependent at the time for his next promotion.

'Is there nothing you can do about it?' his wife had asked. She was of a much sunnier temperament than her husband. 'Look on the bright side, man.'

'I have gone over the whole business in my mind time after time these last few days.' He wiped a trace of sweat from his brow, glancing apprehensively round.

'And?' His wife, with sweet sarcasm.

'I can see nothing I have done that could have caused this trouble. If the same circumstances arose again I should act in precisely the same way.'

'Then what are you worrying about?'

'My own lack of confidence. I fear there may be some important aspect I have overlooked, some minor action which, had I taken it earlier and with more rigour, would have cleared the whole business up.'

'But you can't think what the action was?'

'No.'

'Are you sure?'

'Yes.'

'Listen to me. If you can't think what you should have done that would have altered the whole situation then such action doesn't, could not, exist. Tony, you know more than all these inspectors looking at this case. More than all three added together. Now, isn't that so?'

'I suppose so.' He spoke in a miserable whisper, still dabbing with his handkerchief. 'But with this, I may have stood too close and missed some simple, salient point.'

'I don't believe it. Whenever I talk to your workmates, be they equals, subordinates or superiors, they all praise your knowledge, your grasp. You know the rules and what the rules mean. One man said to me that he doubted whether more than half a dozen in the whole country knew more than you. He's come up, grown up with our rules, not like some of the others learning fancy sequences while you have learnt the basics. These clever dicks with their MAs and their B.Sc. Econs have to sidle along to him to ask what they should do next.'

'But I seem to have no control over what's happening.'

'When these inspectors come to question you, stand up for yourself. You see what they have to say and find out how much they know, if anything. You're just as expert as they are, so I don't want you creeping back here with some cock-and-bull story that you neglected something that was the cause of the trouble.'

Alicia remembered this exchange into old age. She had no idea what the initial trouble was. Her parents must have discussed this before the day where they spoke so freely in front of their daughter. On the day of the inspectors' visit, her father came home smiling and bearing gifts, a box of Black Magic for her mother, a half-pound of fruit pastilles for Alicia and a large carton of chocolate

176

ice cream for tea. Obviously the inquisition had gone well and shortly afterwards he received the long-desired promotion.

'I told you so,' his wife bragged. 'Speaking up for yourself can do you no harm if in the first place you have made no mistakes.'

'Yes, I'm as pleased as Punch. This Saturday we'll all go to the pictures. You consult with Alicia here about what to see.'

Alicia had been only eight or nine at the time. That her father should be accused of making errors seemed wrong. He had seemed to her then, and afterwards, so confident about mathematical matters. She remembered when she was in her GCSE year that if she brought to him some arithmetical or algebraic problem she couldn't manage, she'd wait while he made sure he understood the nature of her difficulty, then he'd smile and in no time work it out in his head. Then he'd sit down with her and explain the problem; once you had grasped it, it was as good as done. 'Can you do it like that every time?' she used to ask. 'By and large,' he'd say, 'yes. The arithmetic sometimes takes some working out. They deliberately used to do that to try to tempt you into error. You'd make such slips in long boring computations.'

But this exception, when he could not understand what he was supposed to have done wrong, left him shaken and frightened, the sweat standing on his forehead and his lips in a thin line of imminent defeat. She must have inherited or acquired the same trait from him. Usually she saw the problem clearly, thought about it, solved it. But not today. She had suddenly burst into tears and unless she was continually praised by her seniors she saw herself as likely to wreck her work. She knew this was nowhere near the truth, yet she could not dismiss her weakness. She despised herself, as she despised her tears.

Three days later Professor Conway rang to say that her viva was on the following Tuesday and he thought her best plan was to read carefully through the thesis to make sure she was ready for all the questions Stirling would sling at her. 'Don't be afraid to argue with him, especially when you know you're on safe ground,' he repeated. She answered that she'd complete her decorating of the kitchen and use the following nine days in revision. He then said that he'd be willing to talk to her a day or two before the ordeal and outline the sort of questions he'd put to her if he were the 'external'. 'It will all be very informal,' he said. 'It will take place in my study and I shall have to take care that we are not interrupted by importunate students or phone calls.'

'How long will it last?' she asked.

'Not less than an hour, probably longer. But Stirling is down for an early lunch, that's twelve o'clock, as he has another engagement later in the day.'

'Has he read it yet?'

'I don't know. He didn't mention the content of your thesis at all. That's usual. He's a very experienced examiner. He knows what he's on about. He's done it often enough. Don't you worry yourself. I think you'll enjoy hearing a clever man questioning you on your work.'

She was grateful to Conway. At least he had warned her of the date as soon as he could. And his offer of giving her a rehearsal must be unusual. She wasn't sure whether this demonstrated unease on his part about the quality of her work, or a kindly effort to set her mind at rest.

On the same day she decided on an afternoon walk, although the weather was unwelcoming, with grey, threatening skies and a wind that seemed to penetrate the heaviest coat. She rattled along at a good pace, her footsteps matching the racing of her mind. Just above Clarence Caldwell's house she came across the owner himself staggering up the steep path leading from his back door to the main road. His hat, a battered version in khaki of the headgear known in the army as 'hats, ridiculous', was pulled down to his ears and a huge grey woollen scarf was wrapped round his neck with two long ends flapping over his tweed topcoat. She watched his unsteady progress. He had obviously not seen her. Should she press on or delay to exchange a word or two with the old man at the expense of further flaying by the north-east wind? She decided on kindness.

'Sir Clarence,' she called out. 'Hello. How are you?'

He stopped, tottered forward a step, then raised his stick tremblingly towards her. He had difficulty with his breathing, but continued his ascent. ' "Labour up the heavenly hill / With weary feet and slow",' he gasped out as he reached her. 'Thank you for talking to Megan. I've thought of you every day since I left this place.'

'Oh, thank you. You haven't changed your mind about returning here?'

'No. But I had a few days to spare, so I decided to see how Megan was progressing. As you know, I'm thinking of selling this place.'

'Are you quite better now?'

'Yes. I've been working. I had a note from an old friend who invited me to take a small part in a film he was making.'

'You said you would.'

'Oh, yes. I never thought I'd work again and when I'd done it he offered me two other cameo parts. Ted's offer was a lifesaver. I had to get up early to be there and dressed and made up in good time. And I could get a decent meal in the canteen. It brought me back to life. I felt more like myself.'

'Good. That is good. I'll look forward to seeing you on the big screen.'

'Don't close your eyes for too long or you'll miss me.'

They laughed, weakly, the pair of them.

'And how are you doing, young lady? I rang Raynor Wicks a time or two to hear what was happening in the village and he told me you were nowhere to be seen, that you had hidden yourself away to finish your doctoral thesis. He said it was on the eighteenth-century theatre. Is that right?'

'On all counts.'

'Have you finished it?'

'I have.'

'And has it been examined yet? Do I call you Dr Alicia?'

'No. That depends on my viva voce in three days' time.'

'Who's in on that? Is it in public?'

'No. Professor Conway, my tutor, will be there. And the external examiner is a Professor Stirling from York.'

'Stirling? Stirling? I've never heard of him.'

'Oliver Stirling. He's a big noise in the academic world.'

'Does he know anything about the theatre?'

'Presumably. Conway wouldn't choose him otherwise.'

'He should also know whether your thesis is up to standard.'

'Yes, but these academics will never say anything exactly. He tells me as I go along whether what I've written is good or bad, but he won't now say whether I shall pass. That's up to the outsider, the external man.'

'And if he dislikes it and Conway doesn't?'

'They'll have to argue it out between themselves.'

'Will this happen?'

'I don't know. I don't think so. If Stirling thinks I've omitted some important topic or even misinterpreted something, he might ask for a rewrite, or if he considers it's nowhere near his standard, he'll just throw it out.'

'Does this happen often?' Caldwell asked.

'I don't know. I suppose it depends on the subject matter, or the examiner.'

'In the theatre you find all sorts of conflicting opinions from the critics.'

'That's different, isn't it? They see the play once, rush to the office or dictate their reviews over the phone. It's all in a desperate hurry. Academic judges have at least days or weeks to mull over what they're reading. And they are looking for their examinees to tell them something new. This can be something they've found out about in their reading, or some new slant on old stuff that nobody has put forward before.'

'And if you go against his opinion?'

'He might not like it. That's not unusual. But taste and knowledge will always count, and will be seen as the proper way of judging.' She watched him, still trying to replenish his lungs. 'In other subjects it may well be different. I have heard that in some prestigious mathematics departments doctoral theses have been thrown out, yet when experts reread them years later they were found to be making real advances in the subject.'

'What happens then?'

'I don't know. I don't have names or evidence. Perhaps it's only one of these daft stories that float about universities.'

'And you don't think it will happen to you?'

'No. If Professor Stirling doesn't like it he'll question me on what he considers its weaknesses and ask me to correct them.'

'And are there such weaknesses?' He seemed to have recovered both breath and spirit.

'Nothing's perfect.'

'Professor Conway once told me how hard you worked. He said you were the perfect research student because you got on with it really fast, but were careful at the same time.'

'Let's hope Professor Stirling thinks so.'

'He will, he will.'

'I work fast because I'm lucky. People have recommended me to all sorts of experts in odd holes and corners of my subject. You know that. The librarian Julian Heron you introduced me to was very useful indeed and could show me all sorts of things that were still extant after all these years. I would never have reached him without you.'

'But then you had to worm information out of him and that's not easy, as I know only too well.'

'Oh, he wasn't too reluctant to share his knowledge.'

'I obviously hadn't a pair of beautiful blue eyes to match yours. You just turn them on to your Professor Stirling and he'll be clay in your hands. If he isn't, he's not fit to write about theatres.'

Caldwell was intending to visit the village shop not far from Alicia's front gate and invited her to accompany him down the road. She, meaning to walk on further, changed her mind and strolled back with him. Progress was slow, but conversation was lively. The old man talked fluently; he spoke about the difference between acting on stage and on the screen. 'You learn to work on a theatre audience as the play gives opportunity. The film has no time for "one chance only"; the director repeats a scene until it's right. Or so he says, but only when you see what he chooses from the numerous takes does his idea become clear. He must make the leading lady beautiful at all times.'

'Aren't they all that?' she asked.

'Some are, but some aren't. You're a long way off on stage. You have to interpret the face, or the body from a distance. On the screen the camera can bring you within inches, wrinkles, faults and all.'

He turned his head away, as if the subject bored him, before he spoke again. 'Will it be any use calling in to see Raynor now?'

'No. He'll still be in school.'

'Of course. I'm getting to the stage where I don't know what day of the week it is. It's not important. I'll pay for last week's newspapers and collect this morning's.'

'Would you like to come in for a cup of tea or coffee?'

'No, thank you. Most kind of you. I've taken long enough over this so far. In any case Megan will pass the shop this afternoon. I thought I'd be clever and do two things at once. Men, they say, are notoriously bad at doing this. I know I am.'

He took a step towards her and threw his skinny arms round her. He kissed her awkwardly on both sides of her face. His cheeks were rough.

'All the very best to you. Not that I have any doubts. Raynor here' – he nodded towards the next house – 'thinks the world of you. As a scholar and a woman. I give away no secrets when I say he is in love with you. Has he declared himself yet?' She shook her head, shocked. 'No? That's like him. He thinks he's not good

181

enough for you.' He clapped a hand over his mouth. 'I shouldn't say such things. You must forgive me. I'm a garrulous old man. And you have turned my head to such an extent that what should be confidences bubble out of me.' He hung his head like a reprimanded child. She leaned over and dabbed a kiss intended for his left cheek, but missed. Her lips fell on his reddened, wide-pored nose. He, almost overbalancing, fell backwards towards the stone wall at the top of her grounds. Like lightning she grabbed his coat, pulled him upright.

'There,' she said. 'There.' She held him. He breathed heavily. His mouth opened wide, as if he had lost his wits. He straightened himself, still with his gloved hands on the top stones of the wall. As soon as she was certain that he was safely on his feet, she backed away. From two yards' distance she enquired if he'd manage. The word seemed to liven him.

'Manage. Yes, that's about right.'

Now she was certain he was unlikely to harm himself, she opened her gate and positioned herself beside it. 'Are you sure you won't come in? Just to sit down, even if you won't have something to drink.'

'No, thank you, madam. I'll move on. I've been too long in this place.' He spoke like a drunk, consonants blurred.

'You're very welcome.'

'I'm sure of that. I'm in control now. Or very nearly so.'

He straightened himself. She came out to the pavement to rescue his walking stick, which had toppled some feet away. He took it from her, pressed it hard into the ground, blew out his breath and took a step forward.

'Thank you,' he snapped. The drunk had now become a scarlet major. He shuffled forward as she skipped through her open gate. He made a small obeisance in her direction. She kept her eyes down to his faltering footsteps, watched him as he swayed forward. She followed him until he reached the shop doorway and she heard the vulgar clang of the bell.

Alicia skipped down the steps, but paused with keys in hand before she unlocked her house door. What Caldwell had said had surprised, no, shocked her. If it were true then Raynor Wicks ought to have declared his love for her himself. It was possible that Wicks had no say in the matter, that Caldwell in his usual crafty manner had decided to advance his friend's cause, under the appearance of casual chatter from an old man without judgement.

182

He admired Wicks, had said so with some force to her, but had then decided that his praise did nothing in her eyes for his friend and had therefore let slip these words, these confidences of love, to her. He was an orator, who had often convinced members of his audience of decisions, emotions, extraordinary actions by his delivery. Even when he spoke in short sentences, in a weakened voice – 'I'm in control now. Or very nearly so' – he carried his listeners with him. They were convinced. As she was, or almost.

But she could not help watching for, searching out the art behind the speaking of these small, trivial bits of prose. At the age of sixteen she had seen him on stage, as Lear. 'I pray you undo this button.' She'd heard him say this when she was in the Lower Sixth and studying *Lear* for A Level. 'Why should a dog, a horse, a rat have life / And thou no breath at all? Thou'lt come no more, / Never, never, never, never, never.' Miss Squires, the senior English teacher, said no actor in her experience had managed to make sense of the line, and thus clever Alicia had been on watch for it. Caldwell had not laboured the repetitions. She tried to imitate the way he spoke the five words. The whole pentameter sounded more like a sobbing, though the first word was clear enough. All in a low key, sometimes in the back of his throat in a kind of strangled falsetto. Then he had paused as if he partially recovered his senses, and very quietly, but heard even at back of the gallery, humbly asked, 'Pray you, undo this button.' Now he remembered, recovered his manners with that 'Pray you' and his 'Thank you, sir'. Lear the King had reached the nadir of his pride. Alicia felt the tears flush her eyes in the theatre with that 'Pray you', and when the old dying man invited the survivors of that bitter war to gaze at Cordelia's dead face, Alicia was openly crying. 'Do you see this? Look on her, look, her lips / Look there, look there.'

She could not forget that afternoon nearly ten years ago and how she had walked out into the bright street, warm with sunshine, amazed that people made their way along the pavements, the roads, where ordinary buses and newer trams were caught, and used to carry smiling, grim, chattering, laconic passengers to their homes, to their meals, to the letters that had arrived after they'd left that morning. It did not seem possible. Shakespeare had changed the world for that schoolgirl that summer afternoon, and had altered it, through the voice of Clarence Caldwell. By the time she had reached her home and high tea she had, to some extent, calmed herself, could describe without a tremor in her voice how 'good' the play had been, how much she had 'enjoyed' herself. She never forgot those simplicities of words at the end of the violence of language that had battered the listeners all afternoon: 'Pray you, undo this button.'

And that same voice had been directed at her. She opened the door, stepped in, closed it behind her and stood in the wholesome warmth of the kitchen passage, thinking not of herself and her imminent test, martyrdom, call it what she will, but of a voice that remained with her still, even when it repeated its trivialities and broken confidences.

Standing inside her house, cut off from the rest of the world, she tried to fathom her own ideas. It was only in the last few minutes, as she stood, keys in hand, at the door, he had completed her pattern of thought. Such were Caldwell's vocal skills that he could, had he so chosen, have convinced her of the opposite of what he was now saying. But he was not speaking the words of some gifted writer, he spoke here for himself. She made herself a cup of black coffee. At least for the past ten minutes she had forgotten the forthcoming viva. That seemed odd; she must this week concentrate on what was important. The whole of her future life, she tried to convince herself, depended on her success and Professor Stirling.

Suppose she was successful with the research and after she had come home pleased with herself, and Raynor Wicks had called in to congratulate her and, that over, had proposed marriage or declared his love. How would she answer? She would put him off. Her next step forward was her application for the lectureship in Conway's department. She knew what she would decide, at Wicks's expense, but it seemed shabby. She decided against preparing herself a proper lunch; a cheese sandwich or Welsh rarebit would do for the present. With a thump of derision she plumped down in a chair and wondered how she had come to that decision. Do without a cooked meal? That was ridiculous. It carried no weight either way. She must be losing her power of making rational choices. If old Sir Clarence with his chatter could so lead her away from rational decision, how would she fare when arguing in favour of her ideas against the egregious Oliver Stirling's cunning interrogation? She was not pleased with herself. Of that she was certain. She was going to pieces.

At first the rehearsal for her viva with Christopher Conway did nothing to reassure her.

'How do you feel about this viva?' he asked.

'Shaky.'

'That's better than overconfidence.'

He sat behind his desk, opening his morning mail, rapidly reading it as if their confrontational practice meant little. Alicia blushed angrily, but said nothing. He began by asking if she thought her subject and period worth the time she had spent on it. She said it had profited her personally by teaching her how to do research.

'Were the facts and answers you found worth the trouble?'

She had no difficulty with that. The background helped her to understand how a certain class of people thought, entertained themselves, spent their leisure time and money. He then questioned her more closely on various points, many of them very minor. He concluded this line of questioning by asking if she thought the theatre played a more important part in their lives then than the modern theatre in ours. She said it raised more crucial points about living than the modern performances. 'Remember,' she said, 'they had no cinema, no television, no computers, no DVDs or compact discs.'

'That meant', he said, 'they had to perform plays for themselves when they were away from London or Bath or other centres of culture.'

'Yes.'

'As in *Mansfield Park*?' he enquired.

'That's very late in my period, but yes.'

'And what was the advantage?'

'At least they knew what it was like to appear on stage, to play the part of some person not much like themselves.'

This led to a long ten minutes as to whether this really was advantageous. Alicia thought that it had little relevance to her research. When she had answered him, she complained that that had not much concern with her work.

'Oh, but we must be prepared for Oliver Stirling. He'll be certain to have half a dozen points ready that he'll claim to be just as important as those you raise. And if you make a satisfactory riposte to him, he'll be round to psychological questions: how are you affected: what effect on actors or audience these plays had; were these plays of any importance to the lives of these eighteenth-century men and women? And if you shape cleverly on that he might well ask if plays in any period, ancient Greek or the

Shakespearean era, had any effect on listeners. And he might well then quiz you if you thought literature itself, of any sort, had any sort of effect on the people of its time and their behaviour and thus on human history, then or now.'

She sat back at this, tapping with her fingernails on the side of her chair. 'They're not much read,' she said, 'these days, never mind seen. But I suppose that applies to Shakespeare.'

'And yet you are prepared to spend your working life teaching literature, which will have no effect?'

'It will have an effect on me.'

'Good. That's a beginning.'

He smiled broadly, and poked a finger towards her. 'You're doing well, Alicia,' he said. 'You'll know more than Stirling and me together. I'm trying to think what I'd ask you, if I were an external who didn't know anything about you except what I could deduce from the thesis. He will sling all sorts of little factual questions at you: dates, names of characters or actors, just to see how detailed your knowledge is. And he might ask which half-dozen plays you would put into an anthology for twenty-first-century readers. Or even if you could make an anthology of tragedies, six plays, say, from your period. It will depend entirely on his interests. Stirling's lively and he'll be prepared to learn from you if he thinks you're good enough.'

'Have you learnt anything that you didn't know before?' she asked.

'A great deal. I look forward to the book you'll make from your thesis. He might well ask you about that, what you'd have in, or leave out.'

'I'd sooner be examined on what I've written than what I shall write.'

'Oh, Alicia. You mustn't take umbrage so easily. If I asked you that it would be a sign I thought highly of you and your work. Listen to this:

> 'Wheresoe'er I turn my View,
> All is strange but nothing new;
> Endless Labour all along
> Endless Labour to be wrong;
> Phrase that time has flung away
> Uncouth Words in Disarray . . .

186

'Do you know that?'

'It's Johnson, isn't it?'

'Good. Yes. It wasn't written about dramatic poetry.

'Trickt in Antique Ruff and Bonnet,
Ode and Elegy and Sonnet.

'But do you think it could be justly applied to any of the plays you've considered?'

'It would apply at any period. "All is strange but nothing new" applies today, I'd think.'

'Stirling might argue that.' They laughed nervously. 'Poor Johnson didn't do very well with his play, *Irene*. Why was that, I wonder?'

'The audience didn't find it entertaining enough. Or even, they went not expecting to be and so weren't disappointed. However gifted a playwright, he has been sometimes brought down to the level of his listeners.'

'Like Shakespeare?'

'Yes. We don't give Shakespeare his outstanding place in literature for his comedies.'

'No. Though, though . . .' Conway threw back his head to contemplate the ceiling. ' "A play read" ', he quoted, ' "affects the mind like a play acted." Discuss. My word, this thesis of yours gives us plenty to think about.'

' "The style of Shakespeare was in itself ungrammatical, perplexed and obscure." Is that right? The players according to Johnson didn't understand what they were reciting. Discuss.'

'Well done,' Conway said. 'Don't be afraid, if Stirling stirs it, of giving him a mouthful of learned polemics in return.' They talked in this way for another quarter of an hour, perhaps, when he said, 'You're well prepared, I see, Alicia. You show yourself as learned . . .'

'On this topic.'

He stood, then began silently to pack his scattered letters into their envelopes. When he'd finished this chore he said, 'May I take you down to the students' restaurant for a cup of coffee?' He glanced at his watch. 'We've just time before they start setting tables for lunch.'

Alicia wondered why he'd not invited her to stay in his room where he'd have the means to provide her with a decent cup of coffee.

The restaurant was almost empty and the waitresses were dashing around laying the tables for the next meal in an hour's time.

'Am I too late?' he enquired of the woman behind the counter.

'Depends what you want,' came the slovenly reply.

'Two cups of coffee.'

'I think we could manage that for you, sir. If you could drink it at the table down there. That's the last one they'll set.'

Professors rarely patronised this part of the university and the woman obviously did not recognise him, but his voice, his suit, perhaps even his companion's appearance and his air of utter politeness won the servant over to compliance. As he was paying her she said, 'I haven't seen you in here before, sir.'

'I've come in once or twice.'

'You're not a visitor here?'

At that moment the vice-chancellor appeared, strolling steadily, hands clasped behind his back. What he was enquiring about in this spot at this hour was anybody's guess. He was said to turn up in all manner of places in the university unexpectedly. He wasn't expected to ask awkward questions, merely to suggest that his knowledge of the working of the departments, large or small, academic or administrative, manual or mental was in no way second hand.

'Good morning, Christopher,' he said. 'A bit out of your way.'

Conway glanced at Alicia as he replied; the V-C's eyes followed his and brightened. 'Good morning,' he said politely to Alicia. He then raised his eyebrows in questioning to Conway.

'Miss Smallwood is a postgraduate student. She has the viva for a doctorate in three days' time. She was my student at Oxford.'

'Are you checking up on her? Is that so?' he asked Alicia.

'He's trying out possible questions on me.'

'Is that useful?'

'Professor Conway has much more experience of these matters than ever I have. He raised some interesting points.'

'That's invariably the case with bright students,' the V-C said.

'Miss Smallwood will be applying for a lectureship in the English department.'

'An eighteenth-century expert?'

'Yes.' Conway nodded solemnly. The V-C didn't forget much. 'Exactly.'

The V-C joined his colleague in nodding. He looked comical and very young for his post. No older than Christopher. 'I wish you luck,' he said. 'They might even allow me to sit on the appointments committee. You never know.' He turned to the woman behind the counter. 'Look after Professor Conway for us,' he said. 'He's a very distinguished man.'

The woman beamed. The V-C knew how to lay it on. 'Can I get you a drink, sir?' she asked.

'No, thank you. I mustn't spoil my lunch.' He turned to Alicia. 'Goodbye, Miss Smallwood.' He'd remembered her name. 'We'll possibly meet again.' Then to Conway, 'Christopher' and was instantly gliding away.

'Wasn't that the head-sirrah?' the woman said in an awed voice, as soon as he was out of earshot.

'The vice-chancellor,' Conway replied. 'Sir Charles Farnell.'

'I've never spoken to a sir before.' She shook her head. 'And I didn't recognise you as a professor, sir.'

Conway nodded his forgiveness. He and Alicia sat down at the free table.

'When this degree is over and done with we must have something more elaborate than a cup of coffee.'

'Thank you. Won't you be busy? With marking and so forth?'

'Yes, but I shan't lose all sense of proportion. I'll get my priorities right.'

As they sipped their coffee, he suddenly asked, 'What, no, how are you going to spend these last three days?'

'Going through the thesis again. And when I'm tired of that, reading Pope, or cooking.'

'You'll be perfectly all right, you know. You might even enjoy your little tourney with Stirling. He'll be pleased with you. If you could see some of the theses that are submitted. You have to plough your way through them.'

'But do they pass?'

'If the work they've done is sufficient, yes. Old Colin Mawby at Oxford used to say he wished he were able to throw some candidates out until they'd learnt to write English properly. But his fellow examiners wouldn't have it. He'd lead off for hours about scholars with doctorates in English literature who had no idea how to put two or three sentences interestingly together.'

'Could he?'

'Yes. But not very often.'

'Has Stirling any of these King Charles's Heads?'

'I expect so. We all have. His will all be under control. The one I'd be ready for in his case is this: "Is this topic worth researching in such detail?"'

'Johnson thought as much. I mean, his contemporaries couldn't handle tragedy.

> 'Then crushed by Rules, and weaken'd as refin'd,
> For years the Power of Tragedy declin'd;
> From Bard to Bard, the frigid Caution crept,
> Till Declamation roar'd, while Passion slept.'

'Good. You've a splendid memory, Alicia. That'll impress Stirling.'

'I hope so. Dr Johnson blamed the audience, not the writers.

> 'The drama's laws the drama's patrons give
> For we that live to please, must please to live.'

They parted cheerfully enough at the entrance to the car park, where Alicia had managed to find a place. He wished her well, shook hands and bent to dart a small kiss on her right cheek. This pleased her. He stood, toes turned inward like a shy schoolboy, head dipped. She noticed he'd not cleaned his shoes that morning. That endeared him to her; she did not know why.

XV

The last three days before her viva passed quickly.

Alicia felt she was wasting her time in that she seemed to acquire nothing by way of knowledge that did her any good. She read Stirling's book on T. S. Eliot, or part of it, to see if it gave her insight into his mind or method. She enjoyed the hour or two she spent on the book, finding the author very knowledgeable and a clever teacher. A good student would go immediately back to Eliot to read him with real understanding. Stirling made points that seemed obvious to her once he'd drawn her attention to them, but she had never enunciated them so clearly. Poetry, he instructed her, had to leave some lines fast in the memory, as a novel did not. A novel could do this, but its strengths lay elsewhere. She wasn't certain whether he considered poetry the greater art on this account. He never clearly said so. She had no doubts in her mind; poetry held the highest position. She was glad she had decided this and looked about for other reasons, but not for long. It would do her no good on the witness stand before her examiner. She chided herself for this conclusion. The study of literature should raise such questions in the reader's, the listener's, mind. It would make her think more profoundly about life, about what we were doing here, and whether our relationships with family, neighbours, newspapers, or television notables had any importance when we considered the course of our existence and its meaning. Was grief more powerful, influential, than, say, happiness? She allowed these thoughts to flutter about her head like bats in a darkened cave. The answer did not matter greatly, it was the question itself that counted for most.

She took a walk each morning soon after eleven. By this time she had cleared away and washed her breakfast pots, done two hours' solid reading and prepared the vegetables for her lunch.

The mornings at this time of year seemed dark, though there were signs of spring in front gardens and hedge bottoms. There were few people out on the roads, and fewer who were willing to stop and talk. One old man with a barrow made out of an orange box and a child's toy pram-wheels stopped to tell her that winter seemed loth to finish this year. 'Mark you, it's easier to put up with than in my day.'

'Why's that?'

'Central heating. In my day there was only one fire in the house, in the living room, and that provided the heating, the cooking, the hot water. If you stepped out into the kitchen, by God it was cold.' He breathed in deeply. 'Young people these days don't know they're born.' He pushed on with his orange box, having established his right to comment on life to this young woman.

On her second morning two housewives, swabbing the front doorstep from inside the house, called out to her. One asked if the rain was ever going to stop; the second said it wasn't fit to turn a dog out. Both seemed cheerful. Alicia wondered what their equivalents to her final viva were, if they had them. One woman in the village had lost a child, an eight-year-old boy, a few weeks ago. The local papers had been full of it. That put her troubles into focus, but did not help her.

She ate a substantial meal at midday and was in bed by ten o'clock. She ate her five pieces of fruit and took no alcohol. She would be fit, and sober, for her ordeal.

On the day itself, after a restless night, she rose and showered at 7.30, and ate her bowl of cereal, her slice of toast spread with blue cheese. She dressed in a dark two-piece suit over a snowy white blouse. She looked impressive as she pinned a jewelled circle to her collar. She had asked Conway about academicals, but he'd said they were unnecessary. 'At least our outward and visible signs will be measured, temperate, unassuming.'

She arrived in good time and reported to the English department office with a quarter of an hour to spare. Everything there went on as usual; people walked smartly about, keyboards clacked, the computer was frequently consulted. Alicia stood, rather at a loss, by the enquiries desk until the secretary spotted her and made her way across. 'Miss Smallwood. Professor Conway left a message. He'll ring down when they're ready for you. That'll be about 10.30. You can sit and wait here for him. Or you can use our loo next door, just to make sure you look and feel all right.' She smiled. 'You look very smart. It must cost all of 50p to speak to you this morning.'

Alicia thanked her and went out to the lavatory. She stared into the large mirror; her face showed no trace of anxiety, was even serene. She tried a smile, showing her teeth. That seemed rather fierce, unsuited to the clothes she wore. She washed her hands again, dried them suspiciously on a towel that was not too clean, picked up her thesis from the single chair and marched back to the office. Mrs Grainger was on the phone, saw Alicia and shook her head. This meant no message had arrived from Professor Conway. She sat down on her chair and, with her copy of the thesis on her knee, straightened herself. She glanced at her wristwatch. She compared that with the office clock and it was one minute slow. Her breathing seemed difficult. Everyday work continued in the office, slightly more noisy than was usual.

At twenty to eleven the phone rang again. Mrs Grainger lifted it, listened, replaced it, turned towards Alicia. She walked across. 'That was Professor Conway. They'll see you now.'

'Where?'

'Oh, Room 13, Professor Conway's study.' She smiled. 'Good luck.'

'Thank you.'

Alicia left, preventing herself from running up the stairs to the next floor. She tapped on the door, was invited – Conway's voice – to come in.

The room was as usual with one exception: the table, which on ordinary days was pushed up to the wall next to his desk, had now been turned through a right angle and placed in the centre of the room, and cleared of all the piles of books and heaps of paper that had cluttered it inches thick every time she had been here. On her side of the table, perhaps six feet back from it, someone had placed a chair. On the other side sat, presumably, Professor Stirling, with the windows behind him.

Conway stood at ease behind his seat, alongside Stirling. 'This is Miss Smallwood,' he said.

'Good,' Stirling said. 'Good morning. I'm pleased to meet you. Do sit down.'

She liked deep voices and his seemed rich. Now her eyes had grown accustomed to the light from the windows behind him she allowed herself to stare hard. He was slim, with a good head of hair, streaked with grey; and his face was thin, his eyes dark, thick-browed and his nose prominent.

Professor Conway sat himself down with what sounded like a

sigh and signalled to his colleague that the examinee was now his.

Stirling's initial questions were almost a reflection of those that had opened Conway's rehearsal. She answered fluently enough, but not until they were ten minutes into the viva did he comment on her answers, or use them as a basis for more questions. She couldn't have made much of an impression on him. Conway had implied that if Stirling asked difficult questions or tried to tear her replies to ragged incoherence only then did he regard her as an outstanding candidate. This was run-of-the-mill stuff. She glanced up at Conway at a pause in the proceedings and he smiled encouragingly as if all went well.

Now Stirling was shuffling his papers. 'You spend quite a bit of time on eighteenth-century theatre audiences. In fact, I don't recall the topic dealt with in anything like the detail elsewhere. It was very well done, but is it important?'

He was after her now, she thought. 'Very good critics of the time thought the subject matter and the treatment depended on the expectations of the audience.' She solemnly gave chapter and verse.

'Was it so in Shakespeare's day?'

'Yes. To some extent in any period.'

'As we rarely see eighteenth-century plays on our stages today and Shakespeare pretty often, I take it you'd conclude that our modern theatre audiences have tastes more similar to those of the Elizabethans than of, say, Johnson's time?'

'Yes. But of course the influences are different.'

'Influences?'

'Our modern audiences rarely see tragedies by Corneille or Racine.'

'We don't know enough French.'

'True. In the same way that eighteenth-century diction is nearly as foreign to us as a foreign language.'

'Is that the only reason?'

'No.'

Now they went hard at it for at least five, maybe ten, minutes about the effect of an audience's demands on playwrights. What about originality, he wanted to know. Were we more inclined to experiment than our predecessors? Stirling never raised his voice as he questioned her conclusions. He sometimes tried personal reminiscence as when he recalled his father's excitement at *Murder in the Cathedral* and Eliot's later plays. 'I don't think my father yearned after verse drama, yet his sixth-form masters in grammar school made them read *Murder in the Cathedral*, so he and his contemporaries felt they were up to date with it, on the front line of the battle for modernity. And' – here Stirling shook his finger at her – 'the local theatres and dramatic clubs produced it.'

'But it petered out,' she said, as if she were the examiner. 'Do you teach or read the play today?'

'I'm no teacher of drama. But it's on our syllabuses at York.' He looked heavenwards. 'Syllabuses, syllabi. Have you any idea of the etymology of the word?'

'No. I'm sorry.'

'It's a misreading, they say, of a word in an early printed work of Cicero. The word was sittybas, Greek *sittubas*, accusative plural of sittyba, *sittuba*, the parchment label or title slip of a book. Later scholars derived it to their own satisfaction from Greek *syllambanein*, to put together, to bring together. Or at least that was the story the last time I looked at it. Same or similar word as syllable, originally.'

'Very interesting,' Conway said sarcastically.

Alicia felt relief. Stirling had put one over her and would now be satisfied that he'd shown his credentials.

They then began to talk about Johnson's *Irene* and why, after the author had spent so much time in the preparation and writing of the play, it found so little favour with the audiences.

'Did you find it undramatic?' he asked.

She explained that she found it no more difficult than other tragedies of the period.

'Do you think Johnson hadn't much idea what being dramatic entailed?'

Again she said that Johnson admired other matters; that those we should consider dramatic were not always the virtues Johnson looked for. Dialogue needed to show 'quickness of reciprocation that characterises the English drama' and to be 'fervid and animated'.

He asked where Johnson had said this and she told him that the Earl of Carlisle had written a tragedy called *The Father's Revenge*. Some of the nobleman's friends had prevailed on a Mrs Chapone to ask Johnson for his views of the play. At first when the tragedy reached him Johnson refused as he was very ill, but later gave a generally favourable verdict on the merits of the piece: 'The catastrophe is affecting. The Father and Daughter both culpable, both wretched, and both penitent, divide between them our pity and sorrow.'

'Presumably Johnson thought his *Irene* to be fervid and animated?'

'Did you not agree?'

'I greatly admire Johnson as a writer, but the eighteenth-century diction does seem to hang a veil to some extent between me and the intended effect. But that is my fault.' She quoted from the play to good effect and at some length.

'My word,' he congratulated her, 'you know the work well.'

'Yes. I blame myself that I cannot do the play justice. Johnson is an excellent poet. "The Vanity of Human Wishes" is in my opinion one of the great poems of the language.'

'Oh,' he said, his eyebrows rising skywards.

'When I was at school,' she said, 'some girls in my class used to complain that Shakespeare's verse got between the action and their feelings. I remember their arguing with the teacher that when Hotspur is mortally wounded he wouldn't be making speeches about the honour he has lost by being defeated by Prince Hal at the Battle of Shrewsbury.

> 'But thought's the slave of life, and life time's fool;
> And time, that takes survey of all the world
> Must have a stop.

'The teacher used to argue with them that it wasn't meant to be realistic.'

'And you didn't agree with them? Or with the teacher?'

'I thought Shakespeare was affecting the audiences, making them feel how much the earth would be missing by the death of this brave man.'

'A brave man. Shakespeare is critical of him elsewhere.'

'But the prince completes his last words for him and praises him. And it's all prepared for by the speech the dying Hotspur makes. I had no difficulty with it, because I went prepared to admire. I always thought Johnson was hard on Addison. He dismissed *Cato* in the way we might, as "rather a poem in dialogue than a drama".'

'Was he right?'

Again she came into her own, quoting from Addison,

196

commenting on the beauty of his diction, his control of rhythm, yet failing to be dramatic as we'd demand.

Stirling congratulated her: 'You're a very learned young woman.'

'I've a good memory.'

'And modest with it.' Conway, smiling. One of very few interruptions.

'I must say your introductory chapter on Restoration theatre was one of the best short accounts I've read. Perhaps it was rather long for the thesis.'

'I wanted to make sure that my readers knew how theatre audiences had changed since the time of Shakespeare or Ben Jonson.'

'Why was that so important?'

'Because the audience in quite a large measure determines the nature of the play and the playwright's concern.'

'Yes, you've said as much before.'

'Don't you agree?'

'To some extent. But here we might look at the effect of closing the theatres during Cromwell's period of power. I sometimes used to think it hadn't recovered by the time I was a boy. My parents, decent Methodists of the working class, regarded the theatre as one of the devil's traps for the unwary. They'd have claimed that even if the subject matter was salubrious, the whole thing was a waste of time, like hours spent at the pub or the fair or playing card games or bowls.'

'Couldn't they say the same of a symphony concert?'

'Don't ask me to defend their views. They certainly never went to a classical concert apart from an amateur performance of Handel's *Messiah*.'

He then questioned her sharply, but rather inconsequentially, about the subject matter of the tragedies in her period. She had no difficulty here, demonstrated that she knew more about it than he did. He seemed, as question after question tumbled from him, to bear no resentment to her superior knowledge. In the end he scribbled a note on his papers and closed the copy of her thesis on the table before him. 'I think that'll do,' he said to Conway, 'unless you have some questions.'

'No, thanks. Miss Smallwood and I had some discussions as she was writing.'

'I must congratulate you. This is one of the liveliest theses I've

197

read in the last few years. Professor Conway will tell you I showed no great enthusiasm when he asked me to examine a thesis on your subject. Well, now I can say, "Almost thou persuadest me."'

'Agrippa to Paul,' she said. 'Thank you.'

'I meant to question you rather more than I did about the effect of these eighteenth-century plays and those of our modern theatre on contemporary audiences. I don't know what we'd have decided or whether we'd mainly have agreed or argued. That's really interesting. Anyhow, I hope we meet again. I'll write to you shortly about using your chapter on eighteenth-century drama in my history of English literature. You did brilliantly there. It will need to be slightly shortened, but I'll explain what I want.'

Stirling walked round the desk with his right hand extended. He gripped her hand hard and muttered further congratulations.

Conway ushered her to the door, whispered 'Well done' and came back into the room. She looked about her. She had stood in this exact spot many times outside the door in the corridor, but now she felt lost. Breathless and lost. She shuffled away; the professors would soon be emerging. She glanced at her wristwatch: ten minutes past twelve. Stirling was already late for his lunch.

She forced herself to walk on towards the far end of the long corridor. Her mind seemed elsewhere, or blank. Once she swerved as if she were drunk, but managed to right herself and press on. Twenty steps later she was jolted, hurt, alarmed as she banged into a wall, perhaps after another quite violent swerve. She felt hands round her, holding her steady, and opened her eyes. She was being supported by a middle-aged man, who was himself breathing heavily as if he had been shocked or left breathless by the collision. 'I'm sorry,' she said, trying to excuse herself. 'I didn't notice you.'

That seemed even in her unbalanced state to be ridiculous. He was a tallish, broad, middle-aged man with a paunch. His face, close to hers, glowed red as if he'd just come in from sunbathing. He loosened his leaden-handed grip on her and she straightened herself. She recognised him although she did not know his name. He was a lecturer in the mathematics department.

'Are you sure you're all right now?' he asked. From a yard away he held his arms forward as if to catch her.

'Thank you. I must have lost my balance.'

'You were walking along at a safe distance when you suddenly swerved straight across at me, almost, it seemed, deliberately.'

'You must have thought I was drunk.'

'I was baffled by the possibilities. It is not often that beautiful young women stagger into me these days. More's the pity.'

'I've just come out from an examination room. That must have upset my sense of propriety.'

'On balance, had you completed your examination?'

She nodded, felt another surge of dizziness, supported herself on the wall. He seemed not to have noticed.

'May I ask what sort of examination it was that you had been taking?'

'An oral exam on a Ph.D. thesis. English literature.'

'I see. Who was the examiner?'

'A Professor Stirling from York. And my tutor, Professor Conway.'

'I know him by sight.' The man drew in a huge lungful of breath, blew out and asked, 'Do they usually have this sort of effect on their pupils?'

'They weren't to blame. I suppose I must have been concentrating too hard. When I came out of the room I suddenly felt at a loss, out of touch with the world. It's never happened before. I must go. Thank you for your help. I hope I didn't hurt you.'

She walked steadily this time, straight ahead. The man did not move, cleared his throat, wished her goodbye, warned her again to be careful.

Out in her car she sat, staring ahead. She remembered she had placed a post-exam bar of chocolate in the dashboard pocket. She did not immediately eat it, wondering if it would make her sick. She ate the piece she had broken off, a small square at a time.

She drove home normally, without untoward incident.

XVI

Back in the village in the days after her oral examination time seemed to stop.

For three days Alicia had no mail. She didn't bother to collect a newspaper, nor prepare very carefully for her meals. She reread her chapter on eighteenth-century drama, wondering how she could shorten it, what she could erase. She had twice cut it down in the thesis, questioning whether this, to her quite drastic, revision wasn't making the whole thing useless. Obviously Stirling didn't think so, or he wouldn't want to use it in the history he was editing.

She had no word from the university, officially or otherwise. She had expected a message from Conway telling her that all was well. They were friendly and he'd trust her to be discreet about any news he passed on. She thought hard about his silence. Her university teachers had always been utterly silent about examination matters that concerned her. Otherwise they'd chatter about the private life of a colleague, or some error a department had made. Conway had been something of an exception. She tried to explain away the silence. On the day of the interview both Stirling and Conway had praised her to her face. She recalled his murmured 'Well done' to her as he held the door open for her to leave the room. The words of praise had been loud enough for Stirling to hear. But doubts gnawed. Perhaps they had disagreed and could come to no moderate conclusion. Conway would speak his mind, so perhaps it was Stirling who held the thesis not worth the doctorate she aimed for. But Stirling had as good as invited her to contribute a chapter to his history of English literature. That must surely mean he thought highly of her work. Or some of it. Dons were odd people. He thought little of her topic, would have dismissed it on a casual paragraph or two, but saw in her apprentice chapter a way to block the tiny gap he was leaving and thus to show that her work was not invariably without merit, if not on the whole up to the standard he required for a doctoral thesis. Why should he want to encourage her if he thought her efforts below standard? That was mere foolishness on her part. Perhaps he had a soft spot for pretty women and let them down lightly. She decided that such trivial explanations bore no connection with what was happening in the real world, but were the results of her bout of depression. That comforted her not at all; both conclusions were equally unacceptable. She must grit her teeth and wait.

Next door, Raynor Wicks seemed occupied to such an extent that she wondered if he was away. That seemed unlikely at this time of the year. She saw him on Saturday morning beating the dust out of a carpet he had hung on the clothes line. He struck with a violence that matched his breadth of shoulder.

'Hello,' she said. 'Practising?'

'For what?'

'Caning the boys.'

'You're behind the times. Corporal punishment is banished these days.'

'Even from the private sector? Is that good?'

'I never hit anyone in the days when it was legal.'

'Your word was enough.'

'Exactly.' He twirled the beater between his hands. 'When's the big day?' he asked.

'What big day is that?' She knew quite well what he meant.

'Your oral examination. It must be soon. For your doctorate.'

'That was last week.'

'Oh, I thought . . . How did it go? Well, I hope?'

'I hope so, too. They don't tell you the result.'

'Did they seem pleased? As far as you could tell?'

'As far as I could judge, yes.'

'They didn't catch you out, then?'

'Not enough to upset me.'

She felt disappointment heavily again. Although she had told him the date often enough, he'd forgotten it. What to her was a matter of constant worry was something he only vaguely recalled. She could not fault him for this. If their positions were reversed she would have acted as he did. Yet in her present state she felt a grave lowering of spirits. He had not shown her and her concerns the attention she expected. This was ridiculous and she knew it, but it did nothing to reduce the hurt.

'I've had a visitor most of the week; that's kept me occupied in the evenings. Did you not see her during the day?'

'Not at all. You should have told me. I could have asked her over. I've had my first free time for weeks.'

'I thought you'd be thoroughly occupied with your thesis. Anyway, you could meet her now.' He turned towards his house and bawled out, 'Diane, Diane.' A figure appeared in answer at his back door. 'Come and meet Alicia, Miss Smallwood.' The lady crossed the garden. She was wearing pyjamas still and a heavy dressing gown against the cold weather. They shook hands. Diane was strikingly handsome and, in spite of the informal nature of her dress, seemed not at all put out to greet her cousin's neighbour. Her face was made up with care as if she were about to attend some grand ceremony. She said she was glad to meet Alicia; cousin Ray often spoke of her. After a polite sentence or two she excused herself, claiming that she was not dressed to meet with the rigours of this northern place. Seeing the slight twist on Alicia's face, Wicks said, 'She's like all Londoners. Anywhere beyond Watford is the icy North.' Diane snatched the beater from his hand and dealt him an elegant but harmless swish across the buttocks before handing the weapon back to him and hurrying towards the door.

Wicks watched her with something like intensity before turning back to face Alicia. 'Interesting,' he said.

Alicia did not understand him.

'My cousin Diane,' he said in explanation. 'She's not exactly a first cousin. My father and her mother were cousins. Still are, come to that. We're much of an age. I'm forty-one; she's thirty-eight. We've known each other since we were toddlers. We lived next door to each other for a few years when I was in the sixth form. Now what I'm going to say to you may surprise you. Our parents seem to have decided among themselves that Diane and I should marry.'

'Did they tell you that?'

'Yes. As her parents made it clear to her.'

'But you didn't want it?'

'I wouldn't say that. She was, as you see now, a very good-looking girl. We went to the cinema or pop concerts together. When I went off to Oxford we wrote to each other. She went to London University to read medicine. She did well, passed her Membership first time and is a consultant now.'

'In what?'

'She looks after old people. I don't know what her subject's called exactly. Gerontotherapeutics. Is there such a word? I believe she's making quite a name for herself. It's said she'll be a professor before too long.'

'And?'

'Here am I, a provincial schoolmaster.' He pulled a wry face. 'If I'm to tell you at least half my tale, do you mind if we went indoors, into your house. It's freezing out here.'

'A pleasure.' She felt no pleasure; this was all too paltry. He seemed determined to joke all seriousness away. He scrambled over the wall and she led him into her kitchen.

'My word. This is warmth indeed.'

She sat him down by the table and offered him coffee, which he refused. She parked herself opposite him. 'Continue,' she said. 'I take it you did not marry her.'

'No. I've been a roving bachelor. But she? She married a fellow medico. It came as a surprise to me. We had been writing in a casual way as usual and occasionally meeting after she had qualified. Then in one letter she began by saying she had news for me. She was about to marry another doctor, Bernard Baine.' He paused as if the name should have meant something to her. 'He appears sometimes in the newspapers, giving his opinion of this or that treatment or drug. I thought you might remember his name. I attended the wedding. Large affair. Her parents did her proud. They had the means. One thing spoilt it for me. Her father, an engineer, said to me, "I thought you'd be the bridegroom on this day." I told him she'd done better. He'd had a drink or two. He said, "If you believe that, you'll believe anything." That rattled me. I hadn't minded her not marrying me until that moment.'

'And?'

'Her father was right in a way. Baine was not a suitable husband. He could not stand opposition. Diane was as clever as he was and could hold her own arguing a case with any man. He didn't like it. His wife was there to play second fiddle to him, and if she didn't she was useless and he said so. They divorced after they'd been married nearly three years. She'd continued writing to me during that time. Neither said anything about it to me on the rare occasions we met, but I don't suppose it went down too well with him. But let me cut a long story short. About four months ago we met and she suggested that we contemplate marriage.' He laughed lightly at his expression. 'I was surprised but I suppose I'm inexperienced in these matters. I thought it was the man who proposed marriage. I had in my case. But she's strong-minded and says what she thinks. Her view was that we should seriously consider it over a period. During that time we should spend some time together. "I don't want to make any more mistakes."'

'And have you done so?'

'Twice, and this is the third and last trial. I said I should be at school and she said that was all to the good; she'd like to see what I was like when I was busy at work.'

'When was this?'

'Three weeks ago. She suddenly found she'd this period she could take off between jobs. She goes back to London on Tuesday next and before that we should make up our minds.'

'Do you love her?' Alicia interrupted him.

'That's not easy. I'm not bowled over as sometimes I was in my youth. I'm forty-one. I admire her and I'd support her in her plans for herself. She'd earn considerably more than ever I could.'

'Does that concern you?'

'No, not theoretically. But if we had children, it would be sensible for me to stay at home and look after the family. I'm not sure about this. I like my job, although I'm not very ambitious. As I see it now I'd willingly serve my time out here at Beechnall High. I'm old-fashioned. I think it's the mother's place to stay at home. There's nothing logical about that. I haven't spent years teasing it out. It's mere male prejudice.'

'Have you told her this?'

'Of course.'

'And what does she say?'

'She says we may not be able to have children, though she would like a family. And there are, moreover, plenty of competent young women, men even, who are willing to spend their time looking after other people's children. That was not a major objection and would only last in any case for a mere five or six years. She knew I liked my work as much as she enjoyed hers, but she also would take time off from her duties to look after children if it were possible. She thought, too, I would make a good father. A historian knows much about human motivation and culture, and my temperament seemed almost perfect.'

'You'd be flattered.'

'Now, now. None of your cynicism. I was flattered because I thought she meant what she said. She emphasised how much it would please her parents and she'd like to do something for them. So far she'd been utterly selfish. When once she'd married Baine and discovered what sort of man he was, she just went flat out to advance herself, in her clinical work, in her research, in her contacts with those in her profession who had influence. 'I got on faster than Bernard did and he neither liked nor understood that.'

'And what about you? How do you feel?'

'What do you mean?'

'Would you object to playing second fiddle to her, talented as she is? Or giving up work you think you're good at and which is worth doing, to look after small children, to which you may not be very suited.'

'It worries me. But I think I am willing to try. We're very compatible sexually, good at it. We know that from experience. We have plenty of interests in common. I have convinced myself that her work is superior to mine and is not very likely to be carried out by others as successfully as it is by Diane, and I'd therefore be willing to give up my job at the drop of a hat and follow her about. I expect I'd grumble, but . . .'

'I expect you would.'

They stood without a word, until he spoke. 'Well?' He drawled the word upwards.

'It depends on you. Only you can decide on what you'll think will be advantageous, and that's too weak a word, for the pair of you.'

'But what do you think I should do?'

'Why should my opinion be of any value?'

He drew in a deep breath. 'I thought' – he spoke with long breaks between the words – 'a month or two ago that you felt something for me. Call it love, if you will. I was certainly greatly attracted to you. I can't begin to say how serious it was, but it was, I was sure, the start of something. If I married Diane, I wonder if I'd be reproaching myself for marrying her and not you. For letting you down in some way. That's if you would have accepted me.'

'Isn't that the case with most people who decide to marry, that there are others who are as good, or nearly so, as the chosen spouse?'

'That's a possibility. One must make the most of the one you've chosen. In Diane's case she found she couldn't, though I'm sure she tried, or at least at the start, and so, failing, she pressed for divorce.'

'Didn't he want it?'

'They were both unhappy. He didn't put up much by way of

objection. May I ask you now, before we wander more deeply into this fascinating topic, if you ever considered me as a prospective husband?'

Another silence followed. He sat still as a stone; she shifted uneasily in her chair. She spoke first, in a very small voice, as if she was unsure of what she was saying. 'I found you a very attractive man. There's no doubt about that. You were clever and attractive and considerate. You didn't bother me while I was busy with my thesis. But marriage. I was quite a long way from thinking about marriage. I should have needed to know you better. Besides, I'd my thesis to prepare. If that's successful, the next thing I'd concentrate on would be finding a job. I think this will always be so. When I got a First in my Finals at Oxford I thought in my elation that there I was, set up for life. Instead, I'm always immediately up against a new obstacle. Probably that's the way all ambitious people are. So I can't, you see' – she tried to keep her voice steady – 'claim to have seriously thought of marriage, to you or anybody else.'

'Were there others, then?'

'Yes.'

'I wasn't the only competitor?'

'Yes.' Single words, not complicated excuses, seemed most honest, though 'No' would have done as well.

He stood up and, as he did so, she admired the energy of the man, the muscle. 'Have you any advice for me, then? In my present predicament?'

'Nothing that I'd trust, or be certain about.'

'Give me your uncertain advice, then.' He spoke with strength as if drawing a correct answer he knew to be there from one of his sixth-formers.

'You should marry her. You know, like, admire each other. Your parents wanted it years ago. It all seems pretty obvious.'

'If that's so why didn't I marry her years ago?'

'You wanted to come to your own conclusions, not your parents'. Now you're older, wiser, more experienced and the opportunity presents itself again you should thank your lucky stars. In plain words you should propose marriage at once.'

He took a half-step backwards and stood staring at her. 'Thank you, Alicia. You're a marvel.'

'Only because I've told you to do something you already want to do.'

'Then why the blazes do I have to ask you?' There was no malice about his question.

'Because you wanted to be a hundred per cent certain about anything or everything you want to do. You're a typical middle-aged schoolmaster.'

He smiled, stepped forward, threw his arms round her and kissed her violently. He smelt beautiful, she thought, manly. He kissed her again, squeezed her until her own breath was cut off and then released her. He took her arm, led her from the room, down the corridor masterly to the closed back door. 'Thank you,' he said. 'Thank you. I'll go and do as you tell me.'

He bent swiftly, lifted the heavy latch and, pulling the door ajar, slipped outside. There he waved, made for the wall and his own premises.

She stood bemused.

It puzzled her why she had given such forthright answers. She had been uncertain whether to speak to him in such a way that he'd remain on her list of suitors. But no. She had told him to marry elsewhere. Without doubt she admired the way he had put it to her that he had at this time or before considered her as a bride. And she had spoken back to him like an unskilled agony aunt confidently answering what she knew little about. Alicia stood at the kitchen door off the corridor from where she had observed Wicks's firm, gentlemanly exit. There was none of that other worldliness she had felt after she had closed the door on her examiners after her viva. She was aware of everything about her, colours, designs, the two sea pictures on the walls, of the small sounds of the house, the smaller, indeterminate swish of the wind in the leaves outside.

She began to cry.

After her viva she had kept a straight face. Now, on this less important matter (or so it seemed for she had not considered Raynor Wicks a serious candidate for her hand) her spirit seemed broken so that she cried, noiselessly, unable to stop, vulnerable, without a friend, leaning on a wall, ashamed of herself and her weakness. She walked steadily upstairs to the bathroom, washed her hands and face with vigour. As she dried herself with a huge bath towel she heard the sound of her front-door letter box. The postman. She walked out to see what had come. One letter.

Was this the note giving her the examiners' decision on her thesis? Returning to the bathroom, she replaced the towel squarely on its rail as if that were important. She looked at herself in the mirror. The tears had gone. Her winter pallor suitably remained. She took the stairs one by one, forcing herself not to hurry. The envelope had the name of the university printed on it. Again she made herself pause and think, before walking into the kitchen to pick up a knife to open the envelope neatly. She slit it open, gently, and removed the contents. First she read a printed advertisement for the post of lecturer in the English department: speciality 1660–1790; official forms from Professor C. H. R. Conway. Then she unfolded the note. Typed, it was from the department secretary, 'Professor Conway asked me to send you this notice. He is away examining at Oxford. Yours sincerely, Elsie Grainger.'

Again Alicia swallowed her disappointment.

These people had no idea of the effect of these printed advertisements on such as her. One needed to be without hope. She had waited for GCSE results, then A Level, the yea or nay of her application to Oxford and more recently her degree. She could not recall feeling so fearful except in the week before the last. She remembered she had met the headmistress of her old school while waiting. Miss Gurney had looked smilingly at her and said, 'I know it feels like life or death to you, Alicia, but in ten years' time it will mean nothing.' She had shuddered. All that intense work, all those decisions taken, the hours of thinking and writing had been wasted, or so it appeared. When the college had telephoned the news of her First, by prior arrangement, she had tried to hide her savage delight. She had shown them. She could not resist telephoning Miss Gurney, and learnt later, at third hand but from four sources, how it had been announced in Hall at senior morning assembly, and how the headmistress had dwelt at length on the honour brought to the school by this girl who had reached the heights of academic prowess, and who would be remembered as a fellow pupil by a good number of them only three years ago. She received an invitation to attend the end of term ceremony and had sat, much at ease, on the platform with the staff and governors. But now, here she was, frightened again, awaiting another verdict from the academics.

An hour after he had left her, Raynor Wicks and his cousin Diane had come over the wall and invited her to join them in Beechnall that evening at a concert by the local male-voice choir. The choice had surprised her. Wicks had announced to her his official engagement to his cousin, then whispered that after an early lunch they would be off to search for a suitable ring. 'There are some very good jewellers in this town,' he said. 'I've been keeping my eyes open for the past few months in case Diane yielded to my supplications.' He pulled faces at his choice of words and his fiancée put on a comically stern expression as if he'd been out of order with his taste. 'Not that we shall be certain of finding a suitable ring, but we can, or Diane can, scour the London shops. Then we did not think it proper at our age to sit at home drinking our healths until we were silly. So I searched the papers for some suitable place to celebrate. Now do you know, Alicia, that on this evening Beechnall seemed devoid of cultural activity until I remembered that John Barnes, an up-and-coming young man in charge of music at my school, was conducting the local male-voice choir in a concert at the Co-operative Hall? It is said that he has knocked them into marvellous shape over the last two years since he became conductor. Just before Christmas they won a national competition at the Albert Hall in London.'

He looked at Diane for support. She made a wide gesture with her arms implying agreement. 'And then Diane thought of you and wondered if you'd care to accompany us. I rang Barnes and he will guarantee us three seats. Diane was doubtful. She has, or her ex-husband had, some Welsh relatives and she remembered male-voice choirs there. "Bugeifio's Gwenyth Gwyn", "Comrades in Arms", "Ar Hyd y Nos". And pompous old men, vice-presidents, filling in with speeches of praise, boring encomia, and the members' wives and families sitting there clapping their hands off and all standing at the end to sing "Land of My Fathers". I told her I didn't think Barnes would put up with such behaviour and do you know what she said? "But will there be enthusiasm?" Why, she even learnt the Welsh words of "Mae hen wlad fy nhadau" so she could stand, eyes popping out of her head, to bawl away with the rest of the audience. Now, will you go with us on this our blessed day?'

'I couldn't refuse.'

The concert was a great success.

Alicia went into Beechnall by bus, and was met at the terminus by Wicks and Diane. She saw them as the bus drew in standing together, not touching, faces Sunday-solemn. They livened up as they led her off towards the Co-operative Hall and their seats in the middle of the auditorium. The place was almost full, but the audience was to Alicia's eyes and ears remarkably subdued. They had come to enjoy a prize-winning choir and were preparing themselves.

The choir filed on, black bow ties on dazzlingly white shirts and in the breast pocket of each black suit a neatly ironed triangle of white. They entered with impressive speed and were immediately followed by their conductor, John Barnes, dressed exactly like the rest of his choir members. He bowed first to the audience, then to his choir. Alicia glanced at the open programme and recognised none of the first half-dozen items, all of which were by contemporary, and foreign, composers, none of whom were known to her. Their first song was called 'Sunrise' by some Czech. The piece began just this side of audibility, but the quality of the singers was startling. Something like forty men sang with confident discords so quietly that a whisper in the audience would have been heard above their efforts. The song moved slowly, but cogently, convincingly with only one peak of climax, to its conclusion, which was almost as silent as the beginning.

There was no doubt that they were listening to a beautifully balanced choir, each voice blending with the rest; be the work loud or soft, its timbre rang unique. Something like forty men sang as one. The second song was fast-moving, contrapuntal, riddled with stretto, part tumbling over part at breakneck speed. It seemed young man's music, yet the choir had perhaps three or four singers under forty. The grey-heads, in three cases grey-beards, sang with consummate ease, not stretching themselves. It was impressive. Diane whispered to Alicia, 'I'm no musician, but I've no idea whether they're singing the right notes or not.' Wicks, overhearing her, beamed at his two escorts.

The last two items of the first half of the concert were different from the other songs in that John Barnes introduced them together in a short speech. 'Two songs, now,' he said, 'quite different. The first is a request from Mrs Ethel Thomas, the widow of Emlyn Thomas, a founder member of this choir, who retired from it some eight years ago when he had completed forty years' service and who died only last year. He wished us to sing that old favourite of male-voice choirs, a song not in our usual repertoire. It is "Myfanwy", and you'll be able to judge whether entering all these competitions and singing ultra-modern compositions has ruined us as purveyors of the old-fashioned fare. And the second item is one of these modern works, written especially for us by Thomas Troy, who is composer in residence at the university and which we shall sing later in the year at Zürich in a worldwide competition. It is an outstanding work, in my opinion, difficult but worth every minute one spends learning it. So.' He turned and raised his arms.

'Myfanwy' was superb. The magnificent voices of the choir, the musicality of the singers and the taste and direction of the conductor were demonstrated beyond all criticism.

'That's something like it,' Diane said in a whisper. 'That's perfect.'

The silence at the end of the song showed the breath-held delight of the audience. When once they did applaud it was with shouts, foot stamping and the rising to their feet of several men. Even the choir members allowed themselves to smile. Barnes stood relaxed, as Wicks said afterwards, exactly like a circus performer who had thrown knives round the body of a half-naked woman.

The choir stood still, solemn for the Thomas Troy, a setting of Lord Byron's 'So we'll go no more a-roving'. This was complicated, difficult, yet in the voices of these men seemed melodious. The lament for the need to be human and take it easy from the pleasures of loving by the light of the bright moon was made with a tender roughness like love itself resting, all passion not spent, but put aside as if this night's ungallant temperance was accepted, yet without understanding or hope of profit.

'They say he's a genius,' Wicks said during the clapping. 'What do you think?' he asked his fiancée.

'It was quite beyond me,' she answered.

'I'm glad I knew the poem. It seemed to help,' Alicia said.

They went outside during the interval, but both women stopped Wicks who offered to get them coffee or ices. The floor was crowded. Each group encroached on the next. From the noise from the packed foyer the audience seemed to be trying to match the powerful fortissimo of the choir. Suddenly to Alicia, who had been enjoying the crowded place, it seemed not unlike hell, as she noticed Wicks mouthing 'Excuse me' and then shouldering his path away from them.

Surprised she asked Diane, 'Where's he gone?'

Diane, unmoved by his unexpected desertion, grinned impishly. 'He's just seen somebody who's said or written something he wants to correct or from whom he thinks he'll learn something.'

'You don't mind?'

'No. I'm much the same myself. He'll come back full of apologies, but his problem will have been solved. That's one thing I like about him. He's on the prowl intellectually all the time. This

211

concert tonight has baffled him and he wants to restore his mental equilibrium by telling somebody something, or grilling some information out of him. I rather like it.'

'Has he always been like that?'

'Yes, but nowadays he's more direct about it. You won't believe me, but when he was a boy he was rather shy. I don't say he wouldn't say boo to a goose, but it would only be in a whisper. I'm glad you could come with us tonight, Alicia. Now we've made our minds up at last, we didn't want to spend the evening together. You'd think the opposite was the case, but neither of us wanted it. We're a pair of funniosities, or you might think so. For the last two or three months – you won't believe this – I've regarded you as a serious rival. We'd never met, but he often talked about you in an enthusiastic way. If I know him, you'd never have heard my name. That would be like him. And when I saw you for the first time this morning I wasn't surprised. And when he clambered over your wall, I grew so uncertain. He seemed so long in your company, so that I told myself, "It's all over between us." I cleaned my teeth for ten minutes. I'd already done them once, and had a shower. I made him wait. I dressed as slowly as I could and came down. The thought in my head all this time was, "She's twice as pretty as you are, and from what he says just as clever."'

'That's not true.'

'I'm like you. I've no confidence in myself. He told me that you were fairly dreading your viva. I was the same with my MD. When I got near the examiners I found that I knew as much as they did, and that I'd used my knowledge to advantage in the writing. I thought I hadn't made too much headway, that I'd just told them, however neatly or even eloquently, what everybody knew. They didn't think so. They praised me for the advances I had made in an out-of-the-way subject.' She spread her arms as far as she could in this crowd. 'And there I was. It's a long time ago since all this happened. And now I know I was wrong. I'd opened the subject up as no one had before.'

'Why didn't you recognise it at the time?'

'I was too modest. To myself I just felt I was stating the obvious, but I see now it wasn't so.' Somewhere quite near to them an electric bell snarled and people began to move back to their seats. Diane looked about her for Wicks. 'We'll go back in. I can't see him anywhere.'

They jostled their way into the hall and were comfortably seated

212

when he backed his way along the row, causing people to stand, or to rearrange the programmes, handkerchiefs, handbags on their knees. Wicks smiled, quietly thanking those whom he had disturbed. He passed Diane and sat down heavily on his chair. She thrust the programme on to his lap, and by this time the choir had reassembled on the platform and were applauding, along with the audience, their conductor, who now stood bowing at the front of the stage.

The second half was more popular than the first. This was explained to Alicia later by one of the singers, a young lecturer in the physics department at the university. 'He begins a concert with these difficult pieces, so that we have to start from cold, as we do in these national and international festivals that he puts us in for. It doesn't suit everybody. One or two have left, but most of us are competitive creatures and know that we're on to a good thing. We're as near a professional set of singers as amateurs can get. And we're prepared to put up with extra practices and trips abroad, which cost us all money, to make a name for ourselves. We're recording a concert for Radio Three next Saturday. I don't know how long all this high-flight stuff will go on, but I guess John Barnes will disappear to some fancy post somewhere else before too long. He's been in Beechnall five years now and he's very ambitious. He's not married and can do as he likes. And he knows quite a lot of influential people, so I don't give him more than two more years here. So we'll have that short time at the top of the tree, then he'll vamoose and the choir will break up or wither away. Still, we're enjoying it while we're doing so well.'

In the second half they sang to please Wicks, it seemed. They did folk songs, pieces by Dowland that Barnes had arranged, some Vaughan Williams, Britten and his teachers Frank Bridge and John Ireland, and to cap all two comic songs by some modern composer, a friend of John Barnes apparently. These were difficult enough on paper, but were sung with such elan that the audience laughed out loud.

'That's something like singing,' Wicks enthused on their way back to the car.

'What sort of man is John Barnes?' Diane asked. 'Does he fit in with you at school?'

'A perfectionist. And ambitious. He's quiet and polite, but there's temper lying underneath it all. He had a hell of a row with the head last term, because the old man accused him of using the

213

school as a jumping-off point for his personal ambitions. If we're to believe the head's secretary, Barnes said that was better than wasting his ambition on a mediocre school in a provincial town.'

'How did the headmaster take that?'

'He's a wily bird, but he can shout and bawl with the best. I think he realises that he's found a man of unusual talents on his staff and will let him have his own way.' Wicks laughed. 'Pausing only to give Barnes a good kick up the arse from time to time, to keep his talents on the boil. I'm surprised that the governors appointed Barnes in the first place as they're a pretty hidebound, ancient, conservative lot.'

'Is he good with the pupils?'

'As far as he's allowed. Each form below GCSE has one music period a week, and they spend that on learning songs for public occasions, Speech Day, Founder's Day and so forth. And the head will grant Barnes two or three periods before these concerts or whatever for whole-school practices. He's a good disciplinarian, so he makes the most of these extra periods, but I guess he feels it a waste of time drumming tunes or harmonies into the heads of unmusical louts. And these Prize Distributions and so on make very successful occasions mostly because of the musical items; and that gives him a good name with both the students and their parents. The school choir's good, and the few he teaches for public examinations, GCSE and A Level do exceptionally well.'

'So he's popular in his everyday job?'

'As far as he's allowed. Employers and university tutors don't see much advantage to their place of work or to themselves. But it's another A, A* to the few who do it. Nowadays they think forward to their working years as adults. And so modern languages, sciences, economics are pre-eminent on our syllabuses.'

'And your history?'

'It's held its own so far. But Latin's sinking, as Greek did, and I think that's a pity.'

'Do your medical schools indulge themselves with cultural subjects?' Alicia asked.

'Not they. There are choirs and orchestras in the college, and as long as these don't get in the way of medical studies the teachers say nothing. But they think medicine has enough tough learning to occupy all but the very brightest without their chasing off after symphonies and plays.'

'That's a pity.'

214

'I suppose it is. But there are not many students who want these other subjects. What free time they have they can fill with beer, or rugby football, or fornication.'

'You're so cynical,' said Alicia.

The drive to Sutton was uneventful. Conversation had petered out, Wicks at the driving wheel hummed loudly. Alicia could not name the tune he attempted. Diane, who sat alongside her fiancé, stared hard through the windscreen, back straight, head unmoving. They arrived by the unlit lane to Wicks's garage. Once he had locked away the car, he came towards the women standing together trying to find shelter against the wind and invited Alicia in for a celebratory drink.

'You don't need me,' she said.

'We may not need you, but we'd enjoy your company. Isn't that so, Diane?'

'Yes, please.'

'I've a bottle of champagne cooling off.' He locked his back gate and walked them towards the house. 'This is a big day. I don't want it to end just yet.'

Indoors he relieved them of their coats, then led them to two large armchairs in one of his sitting rooms. The room was beautifully warm and the subdued lighting enhanced the impression of spacious comfort.

'My word,' Diane said. 'Ray certainly knows how to look after himself.'

'He's had to, these last few years, all on his own.'

'Yes. This is one of the most striking as well as comfortable houses I've been into. I think Belle, his first wife, saw to that.'

'I didn't know her. She disappeared before my time here.'

'She was an interior designer and very well known. I guess she became better known once she was back in London. Then she died. I don't think she relished spending the rest of her life up here, but she chose the house once he'd found a job in Nottinghamshire. She then set about making it beautiful. It was she who paid for it; you don't get a house decorated and altered like this on a schoolmaster's pay. She was often away, for she kept her London office and often slept there. In the end it all proved too much for her and she left.'

'Did she marry again?'

'I didn't hear anything. But that's not surprising. She died suddenly. I've seen references to her in the fancy magazines, and

215

in the architectural journals. I would guess – I don't know – they weren't suited. Ray would have been prepared to hang on and she lasted longer than anybody imagined. He's a strong character. Much to be said for him.'

'And you meantime had married?'

'At much the same time. We hadn't had a great deal to do with each other. I don't know why. We were getting ahead with our jobs.'

At this point Wicks burst back into the room, with the champagne bucket and three gorgeous glasses. He managed his burden with skill, his red face wrinkled into smiles. 'I had to wash the glasses,' he said excusing his long absence.

'I should think so.' Diane tartly.

'See how she treats me,' he said to Alicia, 'already.'

Wicks neatly had the stopper out of the champagne and filled their glasses. 'To this happy day,' he said, sipping. They drank the toast. The champagne was delightful. Alicia tried to read the label on the bottle, but failed. She did not ask for information.

'Let's all sit down and take the weight off our feet. We know now why we're here.'

They did as they were ordered. Wicks, rather breathless, lolled in his chair to ask Diane, 'What are you thinking, madam?'

'How lucky we are.' No hesitation about this. 'We've made the right decision at last. After false starts. We've wasted each other's time.' This last was addressed to Alicia. 'But we've had enough sense and good luck to come together again. We might quite easily not have done so.'

Wicks raised his glass to his fiancée, who nodded a sober agreement. He turned to Alicia. 'Is there anything you'd like to add?'

'Not really.' Alicia's voice was unemphatic. 'Except to say how glad I am to see the pair of you so happy.'

'Do you think we deserve it?'

'I do.' Said with strength. 'I think this marriage is marvellous in itself, but I can't help thinking that something remarkable will come of it.'

'Children, do you mean?'

'If you had a family they'd be above the ordinary. But even if you don't you'll go on to do something big.' She smiled at the smallness of the adjective, three letters only, she had chosen.

'Diane will, make no bones about it,' Wicks said.

216

'I'm sure of that. And it will be because you're there.' Wicks blew out his lips. 'You should have heard Sir Clarence Caldwell talking about your husband-to-be. There he is, famous, still acting in films, laying down the law in the magazines, has a face that's instantly recognisable, yet he says he feels safe, sure that he can outdo himself only when he has Raynor by his side. I was surprised that he spoke so highly of a man so much younger than himself. He'd only one criticism of him, he said. He was sorry that this paragon wasn't married. His first wife, Belle, must have been a fool to leave him. She was a talented girl, but she seemed to have no idea how much she owed to him.'

'He always exaggerates, does Clarence.'

'I see I'm going to marry a saint. And it's taken me all this time to recognise it.'

Wicks blew her a facetious kiss.

They talked on about the marriage. They were, Alicia thought, like children with a new toy. Alicia basked in their happiness. They smiled at her as if she were the sole cause of their delight. Now she felt tiredness gradually, overwhelmingly, capturing her, as if the evening, the concert, the champagne had proved beyond her strength. She was not unhappy. The reciprocal pleasure of the other two she shared disinterestedly, altruistically, yet it seemed to remove her doubts, her fears. The examiners and their decisions about her work lacked importance this evening. Perhaps that was the champagne.

'I shall fall asleep if I stay much longer.'

Wicks swigged – she could think of no other word – his glass empty and said he would accompany her back home. She said there was no need in that she'd follow his usual route, over the wall. All three moved into the hall, where Wicks helped her with her coat. Buttoning up she noticed Diane had put on her outdoor clothes. 'Don't come out. It'll only take me two minutes at most. And it will be cold,' Alicia said.

'On this night I'd go with you to the North Pole.'

Alicia walked over and kissed her. They stood hugging as Wicks watched. Finally when they emerged from the back door Diane warned Wicks, 'I won't lock you out.'

At the garden wall Wicks scrambled over first. Alicia, who was quite capable of mastering the obstacle for herself, he helped down. The cold bit into their faces but above the stars seemed larger, brighter.

'Another frost tonight,' Wicks said and took Alicia in his arms. He kissed her. His face was rough, his arms strong. 'Goodnight and thanks,' he added.

'Thank you, you mean.' Before she had finished this short sentence he was back and standing by Diane, his arm about her waist. Diane waved excitedly as Alicia turned away. She looked again at the stars, fumbled at the lock but finally stood indoors in the corridor. Her house seemed cooler than Wicks's, but comfortable. She bolted her back door, sighed and made for bed.

XVII

As she prepared her Sunday breakfast, cereal, toast and marmalade with a mug of black coffee, Alicia heard the voices of Wicks and Diane outside. They were walking towards the bottom gate and garage. Slightly disappointed that they had not called in on her after their intimate evening together, she chided herself for such feelings, however ephemeral. They were off to see their parents to announce their engagement. Already they would have phoned the news through and had been invited, she guessed, to drive up to London for lunch and celebration. For which family house they had set off Alicia did not know. She had gained the impression that the parents were no longer close neighbours, nor was she sure whether the old folks still lived in London.

She heard the car drive off, the engine roaring, as Wicks signalled his triumph on the accelerator. That was more silliness on her part, she decided as she took her first spoonful of muesli. Wicks would certainly be pleased with himself, but he would not show it with wild and dangerous speed in his car. He was carrying a precious cargo and he would drive fast, but within the legal limits, talking to his beloved, pointing out matters of interest, be they architectural, agricultural or foolishness in the signs. He would be relaxed, a master of the job he'd undertaken; he'd drive Diane, his fiancée, as quickly as safety allowed to their destination, wherever that was, and at the same time talk to her, catching her interest over and over. Alicia remembered his loud humming on their way back the night before from the concert and wondered if he'd burst into some song on this bright morning. She thought not. Wicks, husband to be, would opt for sanity as he demonstrated to his prospective bride what a sensible man she had chosen.

They had made no mention of the engagement ring that they were to have sought out and bought yesterday afternoon. Presumably the jewellers had not come up to scratch, had produced nothing to match the expectations of the lovers.

219

Eating slowly and poking about in the *Sunday Times*, she guessed that the pair of them would deliberately pursue, occupy themselves with, their second thoughts this morning. That people aged just above and below forty should have reached this decision after nearly twenty years would seem ridiculous. Both were firm-minded, quick-witted people. On her clinical judgement lives had depended and had been preserved; on his considered advice careers for bright young people had been settled. Now they had sorted out their own lives but, always self-critical, they would blame their judgement that they had taken so long about so simple and obvious a task. Was it that at rock bottom they were simpletons, did not know what was good for them? And how would they face their parents who had proposed this solution all those years ago, only to be rebuffed by these two clever children who were just beginning to make a name in the world. Would there be repercussions or would the old people be so delighted that their earlier disappointments were forgotten?

She finished her breakfast at leisure, cleared the table. Next she set about preparing her lunch. By the time she had finished she had made up her mind how she'd spend the next three days. She'd walk out today, Sunday, in the cold. In the afternoon she'd listen to a Mahler symphony on Radio Three, idle an hour or two reading and end the evening with two hours of a murder mystery on television. That was a calm end to the day; she knew the faces of the detective inspector and his underlings, and as long as they worked and talked that was sufficient. She felt herself among friends. It was true that she only paid half-attention to the plot and could never deduce from the half-dozen suspects who was guilty, nor quite why he or she had chosen to murder that person lying by the shingle near the river bridge or the other one hanging bloodily over the arm of a chair. She made fun of herself; she treated the programme as some of her less able contemporaries had read the classics of the language. But they had turned before exams to pamphlets or the computer, hoping to give the impression of careful reading or thought to the innocent examiners. Alicia smiled to herself. Her academic self would regard the evening's entertainment as two hours of time wasting. Her ordinary self, waiting in apprehension for her examiners' decision, saw it as a sensible method of resting both body and brain. She did not feel so afraid of their criticisms now. She had done her work well, or at least she had come round to thinking so.

As she set off for her walk she decided that she would spell out to herself how she would spend Monday. It was useless going to the university, although she needed to collect the forms to fill in to apply for the lecturer's post. That could be put back by a day. She wanted to contact Conway to see if he would tell her when her result would be officially announced and what it would be. He'd tell her, for sure, if she had qualified for a doctorate. Universities were half dead on Mondays: there'd be no information to hand. Very well, she would go there on Tuesday. How then would she spend this bare, spare Monday?

She would decide the shape of her chapter for Professor Stirling's history of literature. That might be a waste of time, because she needed his decision on how many words he'd allow her. That would alter the shape and size of the subject matter. Immediately, doubt arose. Perhaps the excitement of the moment had caused him to make his suggestion. Further thought, academic common sense had now intervened and he had decided against her chapter, instructed some other underling to tack a short page or two on the drama of the period on to his or her lengthier chapter on the poets of the time. She kicked at a large stone on her path through Winter's Wood with a muttered repetition of Johnson's rough judgement on Bishop Berkeley. 'Thus I refute him.' The pain in her toes burst agonisingly. Any thought of Professor Stirling lowered her spirits, but she was determined now. She would spend her Monday deciding on the content of her chapter. She passed another large stone laid out on the path and wondered how it had arrived there. She did not kick this, but gently manoeuvred it into the long grass, where it would cause no trouble. She thought of the word 'manoeuvre' as she slowly got rid of the stone, and asked herself whether she could manoeuvre (Latin *manu* – with the hand) something out of her way with a foot. By the time she had dismissed pedoeuvre, *pede*, and admitted, to her own surprise, 'manure', she was out of the wood and making haste, exhilarated by the stiff movements of her limbs, and had made up her mind about this day of her life and the next two.

On Tuesday she would drive up to the university, call in at the English department office to collect the application form and then, if a suitable moment presented itself, enquire from the secretary, Christopher Conway's right-hand woman, whether the professor was about and available to see her or, failing this, whether there was anything known about her result.

Monday like Sunday was bright, but she did not venture out. She set off early working through her chapters on the eighteenth-century theatre, its plays, playwrights and audiences. The postman brought nothing of interest, neither that slip of paper with the names of successful Ph.D. candidates, nor a note from Stirling setting out what he wanted from her and in how many words. By the end of the day she had decided what she wished to write and had a fair idea how long it would be.

On Tuesday the weather had changed. The grey skies lowered curtains of fine, cold drizzle. It was warmer than the last week, but dull, heart-sinkingly so. Cars used their headlights; coat collars were turned up, umbrellas unfurled, and faces were uniformly grey and miserable. She waited for the postman who, half an hour late, poked a single card through the door, from the South of France, from an older sister of her father, complaining that the weather was dreadful. Nice, Antibes (her aunt's handwriting went spare here, chiefly, Alicia guessed, because the old girl in her misery had forgotten how to spell the place) and Cannes were cold and windy as Siberia, and the Mediterranean, to use her grandfather's expression, 'the colour of Old Ma Cotton's gravy'. The card, bright colours contradicting the other side, she perched on the nearest shelf in the kitchen. Alicia pushed out in topcoat and down the garden to collect her car and make for the university. She stepped out lively enough, reminding herself to ask her father who Old Ma Cotton was.

She sat for at least ten minutes in the lane, at her steering wheel, engine turned off. She had heard Raynor Wicks drive away for school at eight o'clock. There had been no hesitation or loitering about his departure. He knew what awaited him at the other end. She feared she would return carrying a pile of application forms and nothing else, without a word from Mrs Grainger or Professor Conway. With a sigh that was almost a groan she drove off. Traffic was thin on the roads, but she made no attempt to hurry. At the university the car park she used seemed unreasonably full, but by dint of driving slowly, steering carefully round she found a place at the furthest distance from the most convenient one she would have chosen. That was typical of the day. She put on a mackintosh, raised her umbrella, snatched up a thin, shabby valise to keep the rain, heavier now, away from her application forms when she had them and set off for the English department office. The briefcase was too narrow to carry easily under her arm, especially as the

222

umbrella seemed unusually lively and needed the whole attention of her right hand and arm. She stepped twice into puddles, the water slopping upwards over the feet of her tights. No one else seemed about. Every window in the building was lighted, but added nothing to the cheerless grey outside. She entered by the main door with its spacious stairs. 'Pretentious,' she thought in her misery.

Once through the door she immediately relished the warmth.

On a large mat she clipped her wet umbrella shut. She hung it on a radiator and removed her shoes. They were not seriously damaged, nor were her tights. Still shoeless, she took off and shook the rain from her waterproof. The action spread drops of water on the terrazzo beyond the mat. Thank goodness there was nobody about. She slipped back into her shoes, rescued her umbrella from the radiator, vigorously cleared the water from it, rearranged umbrella, raincoat, valise and stepped out. She felt better for spreading something of the open-air nastiness about the complacent warmth of the administrative block.

In the department office the usual rush of business was in full spate so that she had to wait at the enquiries counter for someone to attend to her. In the end an eastern young girl, a Chinese or Malayan, politely but unsmilingly asked what she could do for her. Her request for application forms seemed to puzzle the girl, but in the end she slipped away, presumably to search. Alicia looked round for Mrs Grainger, the head of the office, but she was nowhere to be seen. When the girl returned with the forms, which Alicia checked, and asked if there was more she could do, Alicia asked if it were possible to see Mrs Grainger.

'What name shall I give?' the girl asked.

'Smallwood. Alicia Smallwood.'

Another pause ensued as the girl crossed the room and pushed her way out through a door Alicia had never noticed before. The others in the office worked on as if their lives depended on it. Alicia at the counter felt deserted and grew angry.

The girl returned. 'Mrs Grainger will see you if you don't mind waiting a few minutes.' She politely pointed out a chair for the visitor to sit on. Alicia took it rather ungratefully. The Chinese girl now occupied herself at a desk with a computer.

After six or seven minutes Mrs Grainger entered with a young man who carried a briefcase efficiently under his arm. As he left the room Alicia noted that he wore brown shoes, nicely polished, which nevertheless seemed more suitable for a golf course than a university office. He must have been occupied with the chief clerk behind the door Alicia had not noticed.

'Ah. Miss Smallwood.' The voice sounded from the far side of the room, so all could hear it. 'You wanted to see me?'

'Yes, please. I wanted to ask when I need to get these in.' She tapped her bag hoping this was clear enough. 'And the second thing was when the Ph.D. results are published.'

'Yes. The applications for the English department are due in three weeks next Saturday.' She came closer and lowered her voice. 'And there was one matter I could enlighten you about.' She led Alicia towards the mysterious door, saw her safely inside shut off from the world and invited her to sit down. There were two chairs, one on each side of the desk. The room seemed very crowded, narrow with shelves, but light from the large window, which occupied almost the whole of the outside wall. 'You were talking about the application for the lectureship in the department. Professor Conway said you might well call in to collect the forms. He's away again now. He does more work in other universities than he does in his own, what with all the examination stuff and other business. He must be very popular. I said as much to him, but you know what he's like. "I do as I'm told," he said. I don't know when the interviews will take place. I suppose that depends on how many applications we receive. Professor Conway will go through them, and show them to the vice-chancellor, and they will call up five or six. There'll be a week or two past the closing date. So you've plenty of time.' She breathed deeply, as though these arrangements had thoroughly satisfied her.

'And the Ph.D. results? When will they be made public?'

'Ah, now. That I don't know. The professor sent in the results last week. But you never know how long the V-C's office will be. They issue a list, and that is printed and posted at various public places in the university, and sent on to the press. It's all very secretive.'

They stood silent for some little time. Then Mrs Grainger took her arm, squeezed it. 'Miss Smallwood, what I am going to say now is strictly confidential. Not a word must be heard outside this room. Before he left for Cambridge yesterday morning he took me to one side. "You know Miss Smallwood? I expect she'll call in this week for the application forms. I know you'll help her with those. And while she's here she might very well ask you about her

Ph.D. result. She is a young woman of great tact and judgement, and therefore I want you, if she asks about her thesis, I want you to swear her to secrecy and then show her the office copy of the result which we sent to the Administrative Office. I see no reason why she shouldn't know what it is, nor for that matter why other people shouldn't know, but we'll respect the culture of the university, unwritten as it is." All you have to do, Miss Smallwood, is read the result but say nothing to anyone else. Is that clear?'

'Yes.' She spoke breathlessly, but she suspected that the Grainger woman, decent as she was, was making something of a celebration of this moment.

Mrs Grainger picked up a foolscap envelope already lying on the desk. Slowly she eased out a smallish sheet of paper and handed it over. 'University of Beechnall' across the top. Under it, 'Department of English' and the address. Below this, typed, was a date. Now holding the paper, she took all this in. Then, after four lines of space, typed:

Degree of Doctor of Philosophy in English Literature,

and two lines below in block capitals:

ALICIA MARY GUEST SMALLWOOD, BA

then in brackets

(WITH DISTINCTION)

Underneath were two sets of initials, O.S.S. and C.R.P.C. and under each the names in full Oliver Stanton Stirling and Christopher Robert Peterson Conway. Her hand trembled.

'Congratulations,' Mrs Grainger whispered and, quite unlike herself, kissed the new doctor. She took the sheet and replaced it uncreased in its envelope. Having secreted the envelope on her desk, she turned again and said, 'That's something, now, isn't it? With distinction? You can really be pleased with yourself. I said to Professor Conway that they didn't often give doctorates with distinction.'

'I didn't know that they did.'

'Neither did I. But Professor Conway said Professor Stirling insisted on it. And he has something of a name. People here seemed a bit frightened of him. And I said to Professor Conway, "This will be an advantage to her when she applies for the lectureship." He agreed. He said he'd be glad to have you in the department straight away without any interviews, but he said he was not allowed to do that, because people might think it unfair. I'm so glad for you, Miss Smallwood. I mustn't call you Dr Smallwood yet until the degree ceremonies. I know it's nothing to do with niceness but with your cleverness that you've done so well, but it couldn't have happened to a nicer person. Not a word, remember, to anybody.'

'I'll not breathe a syllable.' She laughed at her expression. 'When will Professor Conway be back, do you know?'

'I've a list here. He'll be back tomorrow.' She passed the paper over. 'You can see he's in and out like a dog in a fair.'

They chatted for a few minutes longer, Mrs Grainger expressing her satisfaction at the result while Alicia hid her delight with a smiling modesty. When she had collected her belongings, coat, valise and umbrella, Mrs Grainger guided her through the main office. 'Don't forget,' she said. 'Three weeks on Saturday. Either send it or bring your application back here.'

A few yards from the door Alicia slipped on her raincoat and took a firmer grip on her other accoutrements. Now her joy was beginning to make itself felt so that she could easily have skipped along the corridors.

Outside it was no longer raining, but gloomed as inimical as before. She legged it towards her car, where she sat gently slapping the steering wheel. Here she considered her life, a doctor of philosophy with distinction. She was no different from the girl who had arrived just about twenty-five minutes ago. She had now done something well and been recognised for it. As she looked out of the car window she saw an old lady taking her dog, a wire-haired terrier, for a walk on a short lead. They made good progress, the old lady keeping up with the almost ridiculously sharp steps of her pet. Quite a few old women from the town walked their animals or fed the fish in the two large ponds each morning as they chatted, chattered with their well-wrapped-up contemporaries. Alicia compared their lives with hers. As an excuse to walk and talk with their friends they brought their paper bags full of bread, torn into small pieces for birds or goldfish. Alicia had a faint notion that bread was not good for fish, but doubtless the old ladies would argue that it was better than nothing. What did she think? Her doctorate gave her no ideas; she did not know. Sometimes notices appeared: 'Do not feed the fish', but these were ignored.

She drove leisurely home, parked her car, walked the length of her garden to the village street, where she collected her newspaper. She did not loiter in her garden, the weather was not conducive to outdoor work. Inside the house it seemed cold and damp. She concluded that she must have turned off the central heating before she left. She wondered if she had intended to spend the day at the university. She must have been more troubled in her mind before she set off than she realised. With an exclamation of disgust at herself she turned on the heating, which she knew was efficient and would soon have the house warmed through. She removed her rainproof and donned an outdoor topcoat. Looking into the first mirror in the corridor, she grimaced at herself and her solemn face. Smiles, skipping steps, snatches of song were arguably the order of the day, so why was she now so down in the mouth?

The trouble was she could not share her academic triumph. If only she could ring her parents. She could easily imagine her father's comment and question. 'With distinction, eh? How many get that?' Or her mother's joy. Her mother would not, could not, refrain from touching her. This laying on of hands spoke more eloquently than any grandiloquence of words. Her friends from Oxford would be surprised. They had expressed doubt about drama in the Augustan period. Apart from Sheridan and Goldsmith, who was worth writing about? She had not, she thought, altered this judgement, but she had dug up enough about theatres, actors, audiences, critics as well as plays to catch the interest of two of the leading academics. In Conway's case the fact that he knew her from some time back, and liked her, would, given his character, make him all the more cautious about praising her work above its deserving.

And Stirling? The man they all feared? It was he who had insisted on the phrase 'with distinction'. Her thesis must have had something about it that most dissertations at this level had not. Perhaps Stirling had been so delighted not to have been bored by some novice's searching the byways of English literature that he had surprised himself by admitting that this woman could make something out of the ordinary from this rather unimportant study. True, she had showed up the weakness of the drama, made it clear she had read plays with care as well as criticism. The melodramas of Lillo, *London Merchant*, and Edward Moore's *The Gamester* had both outlived in their time the plays of Addison or Dr Johnson and she had tried to make a case for these now forgotten plays, as well as for those few of Gay or Colman that enthusiasts had produced, not without interest, for modern audiences. She had shortly rehearsed the virtues of the operas, but made no great claim for them as works of literature Italian or English. Handel's music had been responsible for their revival and Handel, as Christopher Conway had said in an offhand way, had been like Mozart, capable of taking, had they existed, the jokes off the backs of matchboxes and setting them to memorable, even immortal, music.

Alicia stared out into the garden. Spring had been late this year, but now signs of new growth were everywhere evident. Slightly cheered, she decided she would ring Professor Conway who'd be back and talk to him. He'd surely be able to say why she'd so impressed him and Stirling. She had already written to one of her teachers at Oxford, an Augustan Age man, for a testimonial. She hoped he'd show some enthusiasm, buttoned up as he was. She'd mentioned that she was waiting for the result of her Ph.D. research. He, Alfred Leggatt-Holmes, would ring Conway about that, and if his former colleague praised her he'd tend to follow suit. And if he didn't, Conway would give the rest of the board an analysis of Leggy's methods of miserly praise.

She remembered writing an essay for him, which he had awarded the mark A (pronounced alpha) plus, and the word 'scholarly'. Conway, who by this time was taking notice of her, had asked how she had done with her essay and when she gave him the thin evidence of mark and one-word comment had said, 'It must have been outstandingly good to get into the A category at all' and the one-word comment meant she had said all the right things and illustrated them with well-chosen quotations. Then he had grinned and said, 'His recent marriage must have aroused his generosity.' Leggatt-Holmes must have been well over fifty at the time. He had never been given a chair, nor expected one, because harsh as his judgements on others were, he made no attempt to shout them at street corners. He would plainly tell a colleague where he had gone wrong or come short of sense, but quietly using the language of reason.

She rang Professor Conway at 9.30 on the next morning. He was already in his office as she had expected. 'I've been here since eight o'clock marking, so I'll be glad of a break talking to you: 10.30. I'll have a coffee break up here.'

Very carefully she hung about the building until she was within time. As she knocked at his door the university clock chimed the half-hour. He called her to enter; his voice sounded weary. As soon as she opened the door, he stood and welcomed her in with a handshake. 'I'm glad to see you. You don't know how boring I find these dissertations. They're done by my own students, so I suppose I'm to blame.'

Shyly – she felt awkward about her approach – she spoke to him. 'I want to thank you for your generous marking of my thesis.'

'Generous? I don't think so. Your work was outstanding.'

'Mrs Grainger allowed me to see the result. She said you had given permission. That was very thoughtful of you.'

'You were pleased?'

He jumped forward and made for the table, the one over which they had conducted her oral, but which now stood back in its original position against the wall and there picked up his kettle, which he busily filled at the tap in the sink by the window, all done between sharp strides. He was back in no time spooning coffee grounds into cups already in place.

'You did yourself proud, young woman,' he said.

Very readily with a pair of nail scissors he cut round the top of a packet of biscuits and made a slit an inch down the side so it was easy for her to lift one out. He now swiftly sat, laid her biscuit and his alongside their saucers and continued, 'It impressed me when I came to reread it as a whole. And Stirling even more. I don't think he expected anything quite as exciting from this place.'

'That's good.'

'He's no fool is Stirling. You may think of him as something of a showman but he's clever and he recognises quality. He saw immediately how much you had read and how well you had used your reading. He sent a written report on your thesis and said how elegantly it was written. You had made the background, both social and literary, wonderfully clear and in such a way that an average student just beginning on the eighteenth century would understand the age. He didn't think the topic was one of the highlights of our literary heritage but you'd made it worth reading about. I'll make sure that a full copy of his report is circulated among the papers the members of the selection board are provided with.'

'His name will be known to them?'

'I don't know about that because I haven't been told who'll be there. There'll be one scientist and probably the professor of

Greek, I expect, and the professor of education at the institute who is thought to be very lively, progressive, all the things your judges will regard as showing he's an untrustworthy, unpredictable lunatic.' He looked at her with a solemn face as he reeled this off. 'And the V-C is said to be sitting with us. This is the first appointment to be made in the English department since they gave me the chair and he wants to see what I'm like in this bit of professional chairmanship.'

'Will he know anything about my topic?'

'I don't suppose so. He'll make out he does. He probably read *She Stoops* at school and will try to trip you with a useless, impertinent question.'

'Such as?'

'The date of *She Stoops* or perhaps Sheridan's *The Rivals*.'

'1773, 1775,' she answered without hesitation.

'Knowing him, he might get hold of some book and drag a name out. For instance, the dates of Addison's *Cato* or Johnson's *Irene*.'

'1713, 1749. I'm good at dates. Within a year or two.'

'So I see,' he agreed, laughing. 'And another thing about him. They tell me he's being buttonholed. The V-C of, well, Lancaster has written privately very strongly recommending one young man to him. He's shown the letter to one or two people, but not to me.'

'Will he?'

'I hope so. Before the interview. But these private letters I'm always suspicious about, as I suppose he is. They may be above board, praising a worthy candidate, but on the other hand the writer may be trying to ease this young fellow out of his way, off his books because he sees no value in him.'

'People do that?'

'They put the university first. That's the way they'll express it.'

'And you can't tell from this man's application?'

'No. It seems perfectly sound. He's four years older than you. He has a First and a Ph.D. on a really acceptable topic: "Pope's Poetry as a Reflection of his Society". Seems perfect. I haven't read it. But what will he be like with his students? How will he fit in with the department? What will he offer the university as a whole?'

'And that's decided by the selection board?'

'Yes.'

'And who has most say there?'

'In this case I do, or at least I hope so.'

'Does it happen otherwise?'

'Yes. Some member becomes thoroughly convinced by a candidate's performance or his testimonials. And he'll argue like mad in spite of not knowing anything much about the subject. If he's the only one it doesn't matter, because the others can vote him down. If he, for whatever reason, so convinces two or three of the others then you are in trouble.'

'Does that ever happen?'

'Not often. But if the V-C is the one who has settled on a wrong choice, well, people will not be keen to get across him, bearing their own careers in mind.'

'Has it happened while you've been here?'

'Once, they say. I was not on the committee. I won't tell you who the candidate was. Except to say that he is a scientist. And, as far as I hear, is doing perfectly well.'

'This sounds very frightening.'

'No. I don't think so. These are rare cases. Usually the university authorities leave heads of departments to make their own choices and thus their own mistakes.'

'Why do they have people from other departments there, then?'

'They may make it clear what the university will expect from the new appointee. That's sometimes useful, especially if there is a suspicion that the department is weak in some way. Or that the head of the department is up to some fancy work, or some nepotic game of his or her own.'

'The fact that I am an old student of yours doesn't come under that heading?'

'It shouldn't. Not if they think I put the university first.'

'And do they?'

The telephone rang. A woman's voice spoke with speed. Conway made short, rapid notes on the writing pad he placed before him. He thanked the caller with his usual politeness.

'That was the V-C's secretary. They've fixed the date of your interview. A fortnight tomorrow. I'm free. The other members are the professors of physics, Greek and education. The V-C, not me, in the chair. I don't know if that's usual. But you can take this from me, I shall fight like the very devil to have you in the job.'

'Thank you. How many are they calling up?'

'She didn't say. They're getting on with it. It's sooner than I expected.'

'Is that a good sign?'

'I don't know. Perhaps it depends on the state of the V-C's diary.'

Both had finished their coffee and they sat in a trance of dumb ignorance of how to proceed.

'Well,' Conway said with a sort of sigh, 'we know where we stand. Another fortnight to fret. That's what university life's like. Now' – he scratched his face – 'what should I advise you to do? I'd write this chapter for Stirling's book.'

'How long should it be?'

'He wants it pretty short, so I'd advise something like 5,000 words. You may think that's hardly worth writing, but it's better than the two or three paragraphs that he had in his mind before. I need to ring him about another matter and I'll do it today, and ask him how many pages he'll allow you. I think he's back in York. As soon as I can wring an answer from him I'll let you know.'

'You think he was serious about the chapter?'

'I do. Stirling's not the sort of man to be carried away by the excitement of the moment. He'd have thought of the invitation while he was reading your thesis and, if I know anything of him, would have mulled it over for two or three days. It surprised me, but it showed how impressed he was by your work. It's a strong point in your favour at the interview. I shall stress it, and Stirling's reputation. As for the rest, they won't question you in detail on your research. General questions such as "Why is this period worth studying?" and of course the V-C may well come up with one of his children's questions: "When did Colley Cibber live?"'

'1671–1757,' she answered immediately.

He laughed. 'You'll do well, I'm sure,' he said. 'But in case something goes amiss, the professor at Warwick rang me about the appointment of a new lecturer on seventeenth- and eighteenth-century literature. I told him about you, but said I hoped to hold you here. They haven't put out an advertisement yet, so keep your eyes peeled. He also said, off the record, he'd like a woman for the job.'

Her face fell.

'Don't you worry,' he said, noticing the expression. 'If I get any further information I'll phone you. A bit nearer the day of the interview I'll tell you what I know, about other candidates for instance, or what other members of the panel think about the candidates. And they'll be coming to me for questions they can put to you. Gregg, the professor of Greek, takes these matters very seriously. Ted Phillips, the physics king here, will think he's on the panel to pick a human being. You'll like him.'

232

'And Professor Morgan, the education man?'

'I've told you that the others'll look on him as a wild card. He's not been at the university much longer than I have, so he'll see himself as on probation.'

'How old is he?'

'Fifty perhaps. I rather like the man. Teaching in schools has altered his view of life. He's said to be writing a big book on modern education and another on the necessity of keeping the grammar school. That isn't popular with everybody.'

'Is he right, though?'

'Like everything in our line, it depends. These comprehensive schools do very well in middle-class districts where the parents support and chase their children and the school; in poorer urban areas the comprehensive schools just become dumping grounds for those deprived, often coloured, children. They need better leadership and money, lots more money. You can see I'm an old-fashioned conservative.'

'There'll be no interest in the seventeenth–eighteenth-century theatre?'

'I shouldn't think so. Phillips will make a point of coming to your subject knowing nothing of it. He might ask me a question or two beforehand if we run across each other. You'll find them all exceptionally polite, but think nothing of that. Of course, one never knows. In your recent viva I expected Stirling to question you more aggressively than he did. My guess is that he had made up his mind, i.e. that you knew a great deal about your subject and he'd therefore question you so that he could learn. If you had done badly on that, he would very quickly have been probing for what you didn't know. That didn't happen, so there was no hole-and-corner questioning, no bullying, merely a conversation between two learned people about the speciality of one of them.'

'It didn't feel like that to me.'

'That's because you don't give yourself enough credit about either what you know or what you do with that knowledge. You will be perfectly all right at this interview. At the viva you really impressed Stirling and me. I thought I knew you, but you seemed a better-informed, more confident student than ever I had realised you were. And I thought highly of you before the viva started.'

'Thank you.'

'I'm not telling you this to keep your spirits up. I am speaking the truth.'

She smiled, vaguely spread her hands, as if she could not understand or bear such praise.

'I must push you out now, Alicia,' he said, 'and return to my chores. I'd sooner talk to you than read these' – he made a pretence of throwing them away – 'effusions. If I hear anything you ought to know, I'll contact you immediately by phone. If I don't tell you what Stirling wants within the next day or two, that's because I haven't been able to get hold of him, and I confess I've found him a tricky customer to contact by phone. If you don't hear from me in the next two days, make a start writing your chapter. When you've finished, if you're not satisfied, you can always try again. If he's not pleased then he can always tell you what he did want. And as soon as the first draft's done I'll read it if you wish me to. Five thousand words is not more than an afternoon's work to read through. And sorting it all out, refining it, reducing it to matters of importance only can do you nothing but good. I think that 5,000 and a good bibliography is all a serious student needs.'

He stood up, came round his desk and stood close to her. He put an arm round her waist and led her to the door. ' "Courage, brother. Do not stumble," ' he said, then he bent and kissed her. His mouth came down awkwardly on the cheek she offered. There was nothing sexual about the embrace; it might have been a kiss from a loving brother, though she had neither a brother nor a sister to be fond of her, but was thinking about something else at that moment. Perhaps he was back to the poorish dissertations, judging them against each other and thinking nothing of her troubles. He had said clearly that he would support her to the hilt and she was certain he meant it. But . . . But . . . He had seemed to have set up the vice-chancellor as an obstacle and she did not know how he would react to his superior's opposition.

Alicia stood for a moment outside Conway's door. She felt still the pressure of his lips on her face and the bristles raking her cheeks. He had not shaved altogether smoothly. That seemed to endear him to her, to make him more of a human being. She imagined him back in his chair, pen in hand, reading glasses low on his nose. He seemed vulnerable, at the mercy of the variable world outside. She wished she could provide him with a cup of coffee and a plateful of a traditional English breakfast. Alicia breathed deeply, appalled at what Professor Conway would think if he came out from his room and found her standing there.

She scuttled away.

XVIII

Alicia found the next fortnight until the interview less stressful than she feared.

She worked away at 'Stirling's chapter'. Conway had telephoned her the day after their meeting and had outlined to her what Stirling had demanded. He had agreed, apparently, that 5,000 words, short as that was, would do, would in fact be admirable if she managed in so brief a space to introduce the subject to a keen student.

Once she understood what was wanted she worked like a dog and felt satisfied with the result. On rereading, she wondered whether she had quite conveyed all the information she considered necessary and whether she had made it interesting enough to be worth including in Stirling's critical history. With a mixture of disconsolate modesty and blatant bravado she posted copies of it to the two professors and anxiously watched the post for replies. She heard, it was to be expected, nothing from either man. They'd be up to their eyes in marking or completing end-of-term administration.

Conway had made it worse for himself by instituting a late short dissertation. 'There's no chance of their getting help, except from a computer, and I've done my best to make sure that the subject matter is such that it cannot be lifted from those essays firms have prepared for the idle student on screen: I could have recognised those easily enough. But there just might be one or two who by conscientious work could arrive near enough to the computer dissertations. So I've given them little time, and on topics the computer brigade wouldn't think it worth tackling. It's bad luck, I know, on the slow workers, but at least that's part of our job, to set them reading, thinking, planning and writing in a comparatively short time.' These were the long essays he was complaining of as being abominably dull last time she had seen him. If it had not been the success he expected, she knew he'd go through them again, making sure that he was not condemning them on the wrong grounds. All this had taken time. He would not have begrudged this loss of working hours since he wanted his students to face the world outside showing a real understanding of the texts they had studied. She could imagine him walking from place to place on the campus, his face creased with thought and his back bent with worry.

The morning of the interview dawned fine, but misty.

She ate a normal breakfast, drank her usual cup of black coffee. She had determined to act sensibly. She had prepared cards of reference, as well as sorting out and reading through those she had used for her Finals at Oxford and her Ph.D. She had no difficulty in polishing her memory on these and was surprised how little her opinions had changed in the meantime. Only on her Ph.D. cards were there differences from those for her first degree. She wondered if, had she studied something different for her doctorate, she would have found she disagreed with what she had written in preparation for her bachelor's examinations. She reminded herself that it was unlikely she would be asked awkward questions on the extent of her knowledge. That would be taken for granted or Conway would vouch for it.

She drove to the university as on an ordinary day. She stopped to buy cobs, butter and boiled ham to eat at lunchtime. As matters stood she had no idea whether she would be called in before or after the midday break. In either case she could retire to her car, to sit out of the way, to reflect on the successes or failures she had had before the morning tormentors or, if she was waiting for an afternoon call, those she anticipated. The car park was unusually empty. She hid her cool-bag and purchases out of the sunshine, which was now bright, and calculated that most of the day her vehicle would stand in the shade. She glanced at her wristwatch. Plenty of time before the beginning of the interview. She barely noticed the door, the terrazzo floors, the two flights of steps up to the English Department office. She pushed her way in, breath short.

All was as ever, people at their desks, working away, toiling and moiling.

Mrs Grainger came from behind a cupboard as Alicia entered. 'Ah, Miss Smallwood. I'm glad you've come. You're all here now. I've just sent Dr Wentworth to the loo. The interviews aren't here today; they are over in the vice-chancellor's office, so you'll be able to take this other young man across.'

236

'Professor Conway thought they'd be in his office.'

'Well, yes, but that was before the vice-chancellor decided he was to preside. And it wouldn't do for him to sit in charge in some bit of a side office, when he can occupy the throne on his own premises. That's something we all learn in time: how silly some men can be, even in institutions of higher learning like this.' She had dropped her voice to a whisper, but now she raised it again. 'You will be the last in. Number four. I don't know if that's good or bad. Do you?'

'I've no idea.'

'No. You don't know where you are with some of these men.' She raised her head, put on a broad smile. 'Ah. Here's Dr Wentworth, back and ready for the fray.' She made the introductions. Alicia shook hands with Wentworth, a pale young man with straw-coloured hair parted low and at length on the right side of his head. His eyes were strikingly green. 'Miss Smallwood will be interviewed immediately after you.' She held up the list again. '(1) Shelton, (2) Smith, (3) Wentworth, (4) Smallwood. Do you know either of the other two?' Both candidates glumly shook their heads. 'You've plenty of time. They'll start precisely at ten, because the vice-chancellor has some other matter of importance to occupy him this afternoon, so they want to get you all out of the way this morning.'

Alicia watched her, face growing redder. Mrs Grainger was adopting this ironical tone to cheer the two young people in their hour of trial.

'Any questions?' She waited. 'No? Miss Smallwood will show you the way.' She opened the door. 'Good luck to you both.'

Wentworth picked up his briefcase from a chair. 'Who was the oracle there, then?' he asked.

'Mrs Grainger. Head clerk to the English department and to the dean of studies, Professor Conway.'

'It wouldn't do to get across her?'

'She's usually helpful. Perhaps she's annoyed this morning because the interview has been moved from her office to the vice-chancellor's.'

They got along at a good pace, but on the way down the second flight of stairs Wentworth slipped on the uncarpeted marble steps, and only stayed upright by dropping his case and holding on to the banister. He pulled himself up, tugged his coat straight, pulled his bag into his chest. He grinned at her, in no way put out. 'That's just like me,' he said. 'I break my bloody neck before I even reach the executioner's block.'

She asked if he was injured. He patted himself all over, claimed he found himself perfect, but on the way out she noticed he didn't let go of the rail. Outside they began to talk again. This apparently was his third application for a job.

'Were you disappointed when you weren't appointed?' she asked. 'This is only my first try.'

'You haven't completed your Ph.D.?'

'Yes. I shall officially get the degree in the next arts graduation ceremony.'

'Were you a student here? For your first degree?'

'No. I was at Oxford. But Professor Conway here was my tutor there.'

'To answer your first question now. Yes, I was disappointed. But you come to see that it's not your lack of knowledge, or even your poor performance at the interview. On the whole the prof knows the person he wants and why, and if he's anything about him he'll get what he wants. If I fail today, and at Warwick, I hope to profit at Lancaster where I am now. The prof has as good as promised me a job.'

'It doesn't seem altogether fair.'

'It isn't. But, as I said, they get what they want. They think their choice is the best for the university. My brother is a university lecturer in science in Scotland; I won't tell you which. He says by far the cleverest man in his department is not a professor, he's stuck at reader. He's a miserable old sod and won't lift a finger to help anyone. He and the prof were appointed at the same level years ago. The prof's quite good, worth having, publishes regularly, sits in judgement on university boards, brings on his students, has sat on two governmental committees. But' – here Wentworth laughed – 'irony has raised its head. This miserable old man is found quoted in all the most important advances in astronomy. His equations have made the universe much clearer. Or so they say. And his name is everlastingly cropping up now.'

'What will happen?'

'They'll give him a chair of sorts. But I bet, or my brother does, that he'll refuse to give an inaugural lecture. Or if he does it will be of the sort that only three people in England can understand. But all the famous astronauts whose names are in the Sunday papers will be there. My brother, who lives for quarrels

238

and rifts and rows, is beside himself. "It's better than the cinema," he says.'

At the bottom of the steps to the vice-chancellor's palatial offices they came across Professor Conway, who seemed to be standing waiting, for them, perhaps. He wished them good morning. 'You're in good time,' he said sociably.

Alicia introduced Dr Wentworth to him.

'Ready for the ordeal?' Conway asked.

'It will depend on its kind,' Wentworth said.

'It won't be too long. The vice-chancellor is due elsewhere this afternoon.'

The trio went up the steps together, Alicia straggling. Through the wide doors a porter, with hair greased flat, wearing a uniform with wide gold braid on collar, cuffs, and down the outside of the trouser-legs, stepped forward. 'Professor Conway,' he said and pointed along the corridor. 'Second on your left.'

'Am I last?'

'No, sir. Professor Gregg has not put in an appearance yet.'

Conway left them smartly without a word.

The two candidates listened to the porter who issued last-minute instructions and seemed disappointed that they had no questions to ask. He then led them pompously, as if at the head of a long, highly dressed procession. He let them into the room where their rivals were waiting. 'It won't be long,' he said. 'Is there anything I can do for any of you?' He stood, disappointedly dumb, when they made it clear by gesture that all was well understood and, as far as possible, satisfactory. 'I'll leave you to it. Once the professor of Greek arrives we can start.' He made a stiff bow towards them and let himself out.

Immediately he was out of the room the men began to talk. Wentworth introduced Alicia to the other two; it was clear to her that they knew one another or at least had met.

'This is the third interview we've shared,' Wentworth explained to her.

'And nobody loves us,' another complained. 'Or so far.'

'It's quite a good-looking place, this. I wouldn't mind working here.'

Another bout of conversation stuttered on. A sharp knock at the door, which the porter opened. He turned to the first candidate. 'They're ready for you now, sir.'

'You've found your professor of Greek?' Wentworth asked.

'We have, sir. This way, sir.'

The door closed behind them as the university clock chimed the hour.

'Dead on time,' the second candidate said. 'That's unusual.' Wentworth, much at his ease, kept them amused with anecdotes about interviews.

'Have we got a good name here for sensible procedures?' Alicia asked him.

'Conway has a good reputation as a critic. He always seems to me to ask the right questions, and then to answer them properly. As to the others, they'll be given questions to pose so they won't feel out of it. Who are the others?'

'The professors of physics, education and Greek.'

'And what are they like?'

'I don't know them at all. Professor Conway was my tutor for part of my time at Oxford and he was very good. He always knew a great deal more than I did, and so could point out errors or omissions.'

'You're old friends, or enemies, then?'

'Yes.'

The second candidate returned after fifty minutes, flushed but cheerful.

'Your turn, sir,' the porter said to Wentworth. 'Just go across the corridor and knock at the door. They'll call you in when they're ready for you.' Wentworth obeyed, waving back to Alicia. 'Collect your belongings, sir,' he said to number two, 'and I'll take you to where we have a cup of coffee and a biscuit or two to keep body and soul together.' He pointed to the chair where the candidate had left his coat and bag. He was then bundled out.

Perhaps ten minutes later, the porter reopened the door, unaccompanied. 'Are you all right, miss?' he asked.

'Yes, thank you.'

'Not nervous, are you?'

'I wouldn't say that. Or not exactly.'

'No. I remember all those years ago when they appointed me. They kept me hanging about all day and I didn't know if I was appointed until a letter arrived two days later. My wife has never forgotten it. She gives me my instructions. "Tell them, as far as it lies in you, what's happening," she said. "These university professors have no idea how you feel." She's sharp. "And be especially kind if there are any ladies there." I said there was you.

240

They'd given me the list yesterday. She's from this university, I told her. I hadn't met you until today, but I saw from the list that you were from Oxford originally.'

'Yes.'

'Did you know Professor Conway there? I suppose that's possible. It's a big scattered place. I don't know half the staff here, though I'm attached to the vice-chancellor's office.'

'No. But thank you very much for coming to talk to me.'

'My wife will give me a thorough grilling when I get home this evening.'

'Thank her, too, for being so kind.'

'Why did you choose to come here?'

'I got on well with Professor Conway and thought I'd like to work with him again.'

'Yes. I don't exactly make him out. He seems quiet, subdued.'

'He can be enthusiastic. I know from his teaching.'

'I don't suppose I should say this to you, miss, but one or two others at my level, so to speak, have hinted that he feels a touch out of place here. Oxford is *the* university and the others are, well' – he sought for his word – 'also-rans. Professor Gregg' – that was the Greek professor – 'once said to me that he didn't think he, Professor Conway, would be here too long. He'd be called back.'

'Yes, that's quite possible.'

'And you're all right?'

'Yes, thank you.'

'I'll be back to show you into their presences. And I'll keep my eyes peeled to lead you all four to the dining room for lunch.'

She thanked him, surprised that he took his duties of care and surveillance so seriously.

When, twenty minutes later, she was called, the interview seemed something of an anticlimax. Wentworth returned, face cheerful, and the porter knocked on the door of the interview room, where the V-C and his colleagues sat together behind a long desk, bench rather, busying themselves with papers. The vice-chancellor welcomed her with a broad smile and pointed out the one free chair, on which he asked her to sit down. She had hardly managed that than he set about reading her curriculum vitae. This did not take long. He nodded to the physicist who said, 'I believe the external examiner insisted that you should be made a Ph.D. with distinction. Were you surprised?'

'Yes. And delighted.'

'He's said to be a man of the highest standards. Had you met him before?'

'Not in person. Only in articles and books.'

He then questioned her, pleasantly, but she thought ignorantly, about what she had learnt from her reading.

The vice-chancellor called on the professor of education, who said smilingly, 'The eighteenth century is not one of the great periods of English drama, I believe. Why did you choose that as your topic?'

She explained that most eras were worth studying if they had produced literature, even if it was not the sort she mainly admired. Then one was able to say why it was not great. This was so with this period, which had great writers of a different sort, such as Pope, Swift, Addison, Johnson. And one must always remember that tastes change and what was despised now could be admired later.

'That does not reflect well on the subject.'

'Why not?'

'If people can change their views so radically. And remember we're not talking about the average person, but the highly regarded critics who've spent their whole life judging poems and plays and so on.'

'Might this not reflect on human beings? And in science brilliant theories are proved wrong, or at least inadequate in their turn.'

'But they discover new facts, which prove the old ideas wrong.'

The two argued for a long time, and once the professor of Physics joined in, to Alicia's delight on her side. The vice-chancellor intervened at this point, saying how interesting all this was, and nodded towards the professor of Greek.

He began after a preliminary coughing bout, 'You were, I believe, at Oxford? Did you find it very different from this provincial university?'

'I was not there except as an undergraduate. I found Beechnall welcoming and pleasant and providing me with all the intellectual pabulum I needed for my research. That was not surprising since my tutor at both places was the same man, Professor Conway.'

'Anything else?'

'I found the library pretty adequate for my work. I had to go to Oxford and London and Dublin from time to time. And this is one of the most beautiful campuses.' She stressed the incorrect Latin plural.

'Did you, do you find the atmosphere here stimulating?'

'Apart from my tutor I did not meet many other people connected with the university. That was probably my own fault. I have a house five miles outside the city and I worked there most of the time. When I needed to use the facilities here, it was in the library. I found the staff there extremely helpful.'

'If you were to be offered a post here, do you think you could add to the "stimulation", I think that was your word, the university offered? And how would you do it?'

'My first priority would be to do my job properly. At Oxford there were people who sent students out of their lectures arguing.'

'Against what they had been told?'

'Rarely. Trying to open the topic up, to see what they could add to it themselves.'

'Is that likely, that a student could add to what his or her lecturer had said, on a subject he or she had studied for years and the student has barely touched?'

'The lecturer had stimulated their thoughts about the piece of verse or prose he was talking about. Their students' conclusions were often raw, even misguided or wrong, but they were trying to think, and in the case of literature, to feel about what they were reading. They were not just serving up the lecturer's ideas, they were searching, trying out their own. They needed further help and correction often, but they were encouraged to look at the text with their own eyes.'

'So you would try to encourage your students to think for themselves?'

'That would be my job. Yes.'

'I try to encourage my students to write in acceptable, correct Latin and Greek. That needs considerable memory and intelligence, don't you think?'

'I'm sure you're right. But it has its limits. That is' – she hesitated – 'more like a difficult crossword than the judgement of a poem, let's say.'

He frowned. 'I've made an enemy,' she thought.

'But they have to read fluently in Greek and discuss the ideas they find there,' she continued, 'to apply the ideas of Plato, say, to their everyday lives.'

'And that will be the purpose of their attending the university?'

'Yes. One of them.'

The professor pulled a lugubrious face. The vice-chancellor

seemed to enjoy this slight passage of arms. Professor Conway rescued her, if that was the word, with a question or two about the theatre, which she answered with easy confidence. He led her on to compare her period with other kinds of dramatic performance. Again she replied without difficulty. For the next ten minutes Conway plied her with questions, which she easily answered; they were old acquaintances from the rehearsal with him for the doctoral viva and the exchanges there. If she missed a chance to shine, Conway immediately supplied her with the opportunity. It was a brilliant performance from both. She even had time, while answering, to look at the other members of the board to see what effect her words had on them. Only the vice-chancellor, she was disappointed to see, showed any animation, now and then clapping his hands together as if in applause. In the end he thanked her and said he thought she had demonstrated her strengths to them adequately indeed. The other members put on non-expressions of pleasure, and the professor of Physics rose to his feet, leaned over the desk and shook her warmly by the hand. As she passed Professor Conway en route for the door he bowed his head and said, 'Well done. Thank you very much.'

'The porter will show you the restroom,' the vice-chancellor called. 'After you have had your lunch, the four of you, we shall announce our decision.'

She slipped out. The first part of the interview had not been to her liking. She had not, she decided, made a fool of herself, but she had perhaps made enemies. During the latter longer part of the ordeal she had shown herself, partly due to Conway's well-placed questions, to great advantage.

The porter hurried along the corridor towards her, glancing down at his watch. 'This way, Miss Smallwood. I suspect a cup of coffee will not come amiss after that little ordeal. I say little, though yours was the longest. I don't know whether that was good or bad. Did they say when they would announce their decision?'

He showed her into a small room where the others sat uncomfortably silent and they poured out coffee from a pot on the table. It was no longer hot, but she wrapped her fingers round the mug, ignoring etiquette, and sipped gratefully. Wentworth, as she expected, was first in with questions. Had it been what she expected? Was it fair? Had she done as well as she expected? She answered with a brief account of the uncomfortable first half

244

and then praised Conway for asking the right questions, which gave her the chance to shine.

'How did he know what questions to put?' one of the others asked.

'He'd read my Ph.D. thesis.'

'Have you got it, then? They call you Miss Smallwood.'

'That's until the congregation when I shall receive the degree.'

'If you've been examined on the bloody thing and they're satisfied, then you've got it.'

His tone of voice seemed to demonstrate his low spirits or disappointment with the place.

The porter returned to lead them in to lunch. As they tramped out on to the campus, he asked Alicia if she had any claims for expenses. She had not. He then told the others that they were to call at his office, where he'd see that they received their dues. 'From then onwards,' he continued, voice more pompous than ever, 'your time is your own until 1.30 p.m. when we shall, all being well, foregather in the room we have just quitted. Some time after that the board will announce their decision.'

'Haven't they made their minds up yet, then?' Wentworth asked.

'If they have, sir, they have not disclosed the decision to me.'

'Is this the usual way, to keep us all hanging about?'

'Of that I am not sure. It is rather unusual, certainly, to hold the appointments committee in the vice-chancellor's office, especially for positions at the lower end of the scale. Potential professors are perhaps treated differently. I am fairly new to my present . . .'

'Eminence,' Wentworth suggested.

The porter's expression did not change by as much as the raising of an eyebrow.

'Did they keep you hanging about before telling you you had the job?' Wentworth pressed his advantage.

'They did, sir. And I was not best pleased.'

The lunch was far from cheering. First a bowl of hot soup (Wentworth declared the heat its only virtue) was followed by a choice of chicken or cold boiled ham and salad, then pears and custard with a large cup of coffee. They were served by a solitary girl who looked, again according to Wentworth, as if she had been sentenced to death within the last two minutes. She spilt nothing, but did not smile, or speak, waiting until all four had finished a course before clearing the table, and then in slow time bringing on the next unappetising tray.

'At least they've washed the dishes,' one of the men commented.

'What is this place?' another of them asked Alicia.

'It's one of the staff dining areas.'

'What a treat for them.'

'The walls are movable. The whole space can be reorganised, made into larger or smaller rooms. In the evenings or at the weekends these can be let out for private celebrations.'

'Hardly the word I'd choose.'

'Was the food at Oxford good?' someone asked her.

'Sometimes. But there were always dissatisfied people, who said they could get better food, and more of it, and at lower prices in the city.'

They returned to the waiting room where they fidgeted, started on conversational topics that did not last. Wentworth, in Alicia's eyes, had more composure than the rest of them. His witticisms, such as they were, raised nervous cackles of laughter. At twenty-five minutes to two someone knocked politely on the door. It was Wentworth who called out the invitation to enter. The professor of Greek came in, gowned, and stood for a moment as if making sure that he had his full audience of four. Satisfied, he unfolded his paper.

'The committee has decided to offer the position to Miss Alicia Smallwood. This was a strong list of candidates and we are sure that you will all secure positions elsewhere. We thank you all for attending. The vice-chancellor and Professor Conway offer their apologies for not announcing to you in person the results, but they have both gone away this afternoon on important university business elsewhere. I'd be glad if Miss Smallwood would walk over to the English department's office to sign one or two documents.' He raised sad eyes. 'Has anyone any queries?' He waited, mouth pouting, but no one answered. 'I thank you on behalf of the university for attending today.' He turned to Alicia. 'If you would be so kind as to call in at the departmental office we'd be grateful.' He looked them over. 'Thank you again.' He swept off through the door.

The three men all turned noisily to Alicia to congratulate her. They each shook her hand and Wentworth, bringing the ceremony to a close, kissed her on both cheeks. The other two looked down in the mouth as they collected their belongings together, but Wentworth appeared cheerful as ever. 'Will try again,' he said,

246

with an air of confidence, as if certain success was not far away.

Alicia's eyes brimmed with tears. She felt sorry for these three, all older than she, in their disappointment at failing to make this first step in their university careers. She shook hands with each and thrust her face forward to be kissed. Wentworth received her gestures with grace, one of the other two was not only awkward but his breath smelt abominably sour. The air of sadness, the disappointment in the room was so heavy that she only slowly took pleasure in her success.

Outside in the corridor, where the men had made last-minute adjustments to their travel arrangements and taken instruction from her as to the quickest way to the main car park, she set off at a fair pace beginning to enjoy the new feeling of triumph. Soon some artistic employee among the building workers would be preparing a small wooden board on which he would then be painting in golden letters 'Room ?, Dr A. C. G. Smallwood', which would be screwed to her office door in preparation for the next academic year. This symbol of her status seemed more important than the work to be done, the payment, the new students to be looked after or helped along.

Inside the English department office all seemed quiet, empty, lethargic until she remembered that it was still the lunch break, and soon they would all return to their rush of work. A single girl sauntered over, took her place behind the enquiries desk and began to move various small objects an inch or two on the surface as if to be quite certain that all was as it should be before the visitor announced her business.

'Yes?' In the end.

'My name is Smallwood.' This rang no bells. 'I was told to come over here, presumably to see Mrs Grainger.'

'What name did you say?'

'Smallwood. Alicia Smallwood.'

The girl consulted some scraps of paper, upsetting a pile she had straightened not a minute before. She was in no hurry and a small frown disfigured her face. She finally picked up a square of notepaper and nodded in satisfaction. 'Smallwood?' she enquired. 'Mrs Grainger wants to see you. Please sit down and I will tell her you're here.'

The name meant nothing to the girl, who walked across the room, pausing to exchange a word with the only other clerk in the room. She reached and rapped on the door of the chief clerk's office, disappeared within on invitation. Alicia wondered what the other girl was reading; she seemed immersed in her dog-eared paperback.

Mrs Grainger emerged and crossed the office with her usual energy. 'Miss Smallwood,' she said. 'Congratulations. Professor Conway said you were by far the best candidate and he's the sort of man who always gets his way. Ah, yes. Would you like a drink?'

'Yes, please. Of water.'

'Tracy. Would you please get a glass of water for Dr Smallwood and bring it along to my desk?' She took Alicia rather fiercely by the elbow and bustled her across the room.

She seated Alicia and returned to her large chair behind the desk, showering Alicia with congratulations. Almost immediately a tap on the door announced the girl's return with her glass of water. She placed it in front of Alicia, on the end of Mrs Grainger's desk. Alicia thanked her peacefully.

'Tracy.' Grainger's voice was strong. 'Let me introduce you to the newest member of the department. Tracy Smith, Dr Alicia Smallwood .' Alicia stood up, shook hands with the girl, who tried to smile. 'Dr Smallwood will join us at the beginning of the autumn term.' The girl nodded and backed out of the place. 'Professor Conway was delighted. He said you did yourself proud. We're all so glad. He apologises profusely that he couldn't find time to speak to you himself, but you know what the vice-chancellor is like. They had a meeting at 2.30 p.m. at Cambridge so that they only had time to snatch a bite of lunch before they set off. They had a big meeting then at three o'clock. I don't know what it's about, but the V-C insisted that Professor Conway accompany him. "I must have an expert there to guide me," he said. Not that he'll do anything silly. Professor Conway gave me a couple of official forms for you to sign, and he'll ring you when he's back and talk to you about what he wants you to do next year. I think he's looking forward to having you in the department. We all are. "We need the ideas of youth," he said, "that will inspire us middle-aged potterers forward."'

Alicia thought that Conway must have had a fair amount of time before he left for Cambridge to make all these speeches to his secretary. Most of it sounded more like Grainger than Conway, but that was Mrs G's role, to put human enthusiasm into the sober expressions of pleasure that were more typical of the donnish professor.

A couple of forms were produced, explained and finally signed. Now she was truly a member of the department. Mrs Grainger drew in her lips and said that if Alicia changed her mind in the next few days these forms would not tie her down absolutely. 'But that's not likely to happen now, is it?' she asked coyly.

'Not as I feel now.'

'Professor Conway will ring you as soon as he gets back.'

'When's that?'

'I've no idea. They're there for two or three days.'

Alicia left the building with further handshakes and congratulations. Once outside in the fresh air, she stopped and looked about her. The sun was shining, but it was still cold. Would summer never appear? The university buildings stood clear and square; the tower boasted its importance. There were few people about even in the lunch break. It looked neat, efficient even officious. The people in charge here knew what they were about; this was a place of some importance; it seemed utilitarian but beautiful. Now she was part of it. Her name would be published in the Year Book; one of the learned.

For a moment she wondered what it would be like to be one of the unsuccessful candidates. They would appear and stare about them, at buildings they could not name or know she could. They'd go back to their friends and report their failure.

'Who's got it, then?' they'd be asked.

'A woman who'd done her Ph.D. there.'

'They'd already decided?'

'I don't know that.'

'Was she any good?'

'She was twice as beautiful as any other of the applicants.' That would be Wentworth's spry answer, cooling his disappointment. She wondered if that was anywhere near the truth.

Walking quickly now, she passed one of the garden staff attempting to start his motor mower. He nodded to her, cheerful in adversity. 'I s'll put my boot into this if it doesn't start soon.'

'Have you turned the petrol on?' she asked, recent success bolstering her impudence.

'Six times.' Sadly he turned to a small tap, which he switched over and back several times, taking satisfaction in the loud click. 'Now see.' He pressed the starter and immediately the machine roared into life. A small shapeless cloud of blue-grey smoke hovered above the machine. 'Well, I'll go to our 'ouse,' the man

249

said. 'You've made it work. You've got the magic eye, miss.' He moved himself and grasped the handles, his arms straight. 'I'd better make a start before it plays me up again.' He set off. 'Thanks, miss. You wouldn't like to walk round wi' me, would you? In case it stops. You never know.'

'No, thank you.'

They parted company. She walked all the more smartly as if she was in some way responsible for the man's return to useful work. It seemed a good omen. By the time she reached the car park she was singing:

'Dear thoughts are in my mind,
And my soul soars enchanted.'

She stood by the side of her car, breathing deeply, her recipe for full fitness. The morning, cool as it was, had grown beautiful.

XIX

Back at home her spirits rose again. She ate a further snack and after she had cleared and cleaned the sink, she walked the length of her garden twice and settled in the kitchen with her newspaper, determined to read it from end to end. Within twenty minutes, almost against her will, she had fallen asleep in the hard wooden chair. She dozed for half an hour, comfortably, so that when she woke she was for the moment uncertain where she was. She stared at the horse brasses by the side of her fireplace as if she had never seen them before. Beyond the window the heavier branches, the small fruits on the apple trees were bouncing in the window, thrilling her. She felt as she did as a child on Christmas Day when she knew unusual things would happen and all of them good.

She took a short walk in the late afternoon and as she made her way down the slope from the front gate on her return, she saw Raynor Wicks standing quite motionless looking over to some huge poplars fifty yards or so away. His head thrown back, arms clasped behind him, he seemed very much in command of himself and all he surveyed.

Alicia waited for him to move, but he did not. She walked down towards him and gently hallooed. He turned, almost guiltily, from his watching.

'Something interesting?' she asked. She pointed in the direction of his vigilance.

'No, the sky. The clouds. We might get some rain. The crows seem excited. And I've a half-day.'

'Oh.' She saw no birds.

He looked her over. 'My, you look the part this afternoon,' he said.

'What part is that?'

'The professional woman.'

She had not changed her clothes since the interview. 'I went for a job this morning.'

251

'Where was that?'

'At the university.'

'And were you successful?'

'Yes.' She lowered her eyes, modestly comical.

'What was it?'

'Lecturer in English.'

'Well done. Congratulations.' He marched smartly up to the low dividing wall and throwing his arms round her kissed her energetically. Having scrubbed her face with his chin, he stood back, but held on still to her shoulders looking up and down in admiration. 'My word, you do the village proud. Did you enjoy the interview?'

'Not at first. Not until Professor Conway began his questions. They suited me and what I know perfectly.'

'Who was on the committee?'

She told him.

'Is the vice-chancellor usually a member of such appointments boards as yours?'

'They say not. I don't know. This is my first attempt to find a job.'

'The only one I know is Gregg, the classics man. He's an old boy of the school and occasionally turns up for concerts or public events. He regards me and my like as unwashed plebs, intellectually speaking.'

'Oh, dear.'

'Nobody likes him.'

She said nothing; he chattered on for a minute or two before apologising that he could not ask her in for a celebratory drink. He was about to drive to the station to pick up his fiancée, who was to spend the next four days with him, returning first thing Monday morning.

'She'll be delighted with your news. I hope that there'll be time for you to come in for a drink, but I never know these days. I have to do as I'm told. Diane decides on these matters nowadays. And that reminds me. We've fixed the day of our wedding. August the fifth.'

'Where?'

'London. St Martin's. I hope you'll be able to come.'

'I'll consult my diary. It's congratulations all round today.'

He consulted his watch, tapped the glass. 'I'd better be off or I'll be in for something else.'

252

'I'd always imagined you'd be a domineering husband.'

He kissed her again over the wall and as he hurried towards his car he bowled a non-existent cricket ball with a gigantic leap into the air. She laughed outright; she had never before seen him so happy, so boyish.

She spent a restless night, for although she fell asleep as soon as her head touched the pillow, she kept waking, dragged into consciousness by anxious, dizzy dreams, set in cellars and attics, where nothing sat straight. Although these nightmares woke her, try as she did on waking she could not give herself any coherent account of what had happened. She remember Wentworth in one, toppling over in the sea and her futile attempts to drag him to safety. In another she and her husband were quarrelling about some decision she had taken. She had no idea what it was, but she felt both guilty and afraid. The queerest aspect was that the husband in this horrid dream was her father. Not pleased, she set about the next day with a headache that left her listless. Burning the toast, she concluded that even the happiest event could bring her no real satisfaction. She wasted the whole day looking for things to do and doing them badly.

The postman called on the third day. He brought no letter from Conway, but one from Professor Stirling praising her chapter for his book. Typically, he made two suggestions for alterations. She thought both sensible and spent her day thinking hard before letter writing, then correcting her changes. She slept on these and was pleased when she read them through next morning, and had them in the first post before she washed her breakfast pots. Yesterday's work lifted her, so that she went about the house singing and was not surprised just as she began to prepare her lunch to receive a phone call from Professor Conway.

He began with congratulations. She had done herself proud at the interview.

'I thought I started badly.'

'Not badly, slowly. And that on the whole is good. You're feeling your way to see what your questioners want, if anything. Once you got into your own subject, you just scintillated. The others seemed dull.'

'Even Wentworth? He seemed lively.'

'So he was, but not in your street.'

'Were the others good?'

'They all were. All would have done praiseworthy research. But we were looking for someone who'd liven the students. There's a feeling about English departments these days that our bright young people can't teach. They'll do well at administration and at their own research, but we, the old brigade, are just coming round to see that inspiring our students, catching their interest is our first job and what we're paid for.'

'And this wasn't so? In your day?'

'So it seemed. Research seemed more important.'

'New ideas, new knowledge must be a necessity?'

'Yes, we need people who can think for themselves and burrow after, find and interpret forgotten or neglected matters. That lights up our subject. But they must be able to catch the imaginations of our young people.'

'If they're clever enough to think up new approaches surely they can, or are more likely to, catch the interest of their students?'

'You'd think so. Some are so fascinated with their own discoveries and interpretations that they forget or ignore all the good ideas of earlier scholars.'

They chattered on for another ten minutes when he said he must prepare for a meeting, which was of no interest to him, but he'd be kept awake by the childish squabbling of two of his colleagues. 'Such is the life of a professor,' he said.

He enquired when she could come to see him so that they could decide the topics on which she'd lecture. 'Tomorrow at ten a.m.? Will that do? Are you sure? Will that give you time to think?'

Conway rang off cheerfully, leaving her quietly pleased.

Almost immediately afterwards her father telephoned to congratulate her on her doctorate and lectureship. 'I can't tell you how delighted we are at home. Your mother's like a dog with two tails. What I was afraid you'd do was to collect all sorts of academic qualifications and not leave yourself time for a steady day-to-day job. It doesn't matter really about the financial side. I can see to that. I earn such ridiculously high sums at the bank with bonuses and consultations that I almost consider myself in the top footballer class. I hope I'm more use to the country than ever they are, but that's prejudice on my part. I don't know anything about soccer. I couldn't play it in my youth, and I'll be blowed if I'll go and stand, or I suppose these days it's sit, in a cold, miserable ground looking at these yobboes kicking a ball around.'

'The market must be good. The clubs must be raking it in, with huge crowds and high television fees, especially in the Premiership, to pay out these ridiculously high wages.'

'Oh, no doubt, no doubt there's money in it. That's the telly, I suppose. That's what annoys me. And if I look at the players' names in the sports pages or the television, there's hardly an English moniker among them.'

'That's a funny word. You hardly hear it today.'

'What? Moniker? It was very up to date in my youth.'

'Are you coming up for the degree ceremony?'

'Ah, well.' The two words gave him away. 'That's really what I was ringing you about. We shall be away on a cruise. On the Mediterranean. Ancient Rome, Greece and Egypt. We'd already fixed ourselves up with this. Your mother was keen. It will improve our minds. Lectures by eminent classical scholars. We're going before they drop them. Now you're on the way to being one. But, d'you know, Ali, your mother was all for cancelling the trip? "It's not every day your daughter is made a Doctor of Philosophy," she said. I said, and I hope I was right, that you wouldn't want us to cancel our holiday.'

'No, that wouldn't be sensible. It will all be very boring.'

'Will you be staying put in the future, in your present house?'

'Yes. It's pretty near ideal.'

'We wondered if the university might want you to live in. As a warden in one of the hostels or halls, or whatever they call 'em.'

'I don't think so. They haven't said as much.'

There was a pause. Was he wondering what to suggest or ask next? 'We're very proud of you, Ali, very proud.'

'Thank you.'

'Is there anything we can do to show you what we feel for you? Does any part of your house need redecorating or altering? Or your garden in any way? Or would *you* like a cruise? Or some jewellery? Your mother and I keep arguing about it. But she's pretty sensible, and says, "Ask the girl herself," and I said you'd answer "there's nothing I want", just as you have.'

'I know what *you* don't know is how glad I am I've pleased you so much. But now you've made it clear this morning, modestly and beautifully. That's all I needed.'

'We're not short of money these days, Ali.' He was obviously embarrassed.

'Good. Spend it on yourselves. I'm sure you've worked hard enough for it.'

'Not really. I've just by luck rather than judgement dropped into one of those jobs that simply coins money for you. Like film stars and footballers in the Premier League. But the good thing is I don't get all the publicity that cripples them.'

'Cripples?'

'Yes. They can't go into the street without journalists worrying the daylights out of them.'

'Don't they like that?'

'They might. I wouldn't.'

'If you were here I'd kiss you to death. You and me.'

'Why, bless you?'

She went away from the phone jumping for joy. Her father had done her well. He hadn't a very high opinion of universities. He had read mathematics, had succeeded well at it, but his teachers had not impressed him. They were clever enough when it came to setting puzzles for examinations, were conscientious, or all but one, at teaching their pupils how to see through the trickeries, solve the complexities, leave nothing enigmatic, elegantly work through problems, but they had not seemed to him anything like human beings. He'd often puzzled himself wondering what sort of husbands and fathers they made, whether they dealt with life's troubles in the same sharp, ingenious way they handled mathematical intricacies. He had doubted it. His friend had put it plainly for him. 'Between them, the whole bloody lot, they couldn't organise a Sunday-school treat for six-year-olds.' Tony Smallwood had thought this judgement hard, even unfair, for he was a just man, but when they encouraged him to stay on at the university to read for a doctorate, he declined and went into banking. He knew that they would write him off as 'a man who works in a bank', a failure, a person of little judgement.

She wondered how he'd enjoy the cruise. His wife had argued him into that. Her pleasure in Alicia's success was shown by the choice. They would listen to the learned scholars discoursing on ancient Greek standards of beauty or Egyptian architecture or Roman law, and both feel she was not being left too far behind by their daughter's rapid ascent into the academic empyrean. She loved her parents; she would not change them for any other. She would receive postcards of the Colosseum and the Parthenon and the Pyramids of Giza all clearly addressed to Dr Alicia Smallwood. No, her mother would not underline the doctor, but she'd hesitate, bless her, before she withdrew her pen.

256

She spent the day happily rushing the vacuum cleaner round the whole house. It was not necessary, but it demonstrated the brightness of the world and her appreciation of it. As she used the cleaner, duster and polish she turned over in her mind the topics she would offer Conway at their meeting next day.

In the morning she was up in good time but spent rather longer than usual in the bath. A slight mist promised, as did the television weather forecaster, a fine summer's day. She had decided on her dress the day before, a frock rather than her student's slacks, or her professional suit. Slightly altering the architecture of her hair, she made up her face temperately, wore summer shoes and almost invisible tights. She stepped outside to test the air before breakfast.

Raynor Wicks emerged from his house, briefcase clutched to his broad chest. 'All right for some,' he called. 'I'm just off to work.'

'I'm going up to the university at ten. To see the professor about my work next year.'

'He'll be delighted to look at you. I thought you were dressed for a garden party at Buckingham Palace.'

'Don't you like . . .?' She waved her hands vaguely in front of her dress.

'Pretty as a picture.' He smiled widely. 'Do you know, Alicia, you look no more than fourteen.'

'Do you think it's unsuitable?'

'If I were your prof and you appeared before me, I couldn't resist any request.' He saw at once that he had made the wrong impression. 'Don't listen to me. I'm only pulling your leg.'

The apology proved ineffectual. She said nothing but straightened disappointment from her face.

He, as embarrassed as she, fiddled with his briefcase, then made up his mind. 'I see I've said the wrong thing,' he said humbly. 'I do apologise.' He raised his hat and made for his garage. 'Every success.'

She retired as quickly indoors and, angrily upstairs, changed into her second professional suit, not the one she had worn for the interview. She was furious with herself, though she knew Conway wouldn't notice what she wore. Here she was, about to take on the further instruction of some of the cleverest young people in the country, put out because her neighbour thought she looked no more than fourteen. She bore no grudge against Wicks; manlike he had said the first thing that came into his head, but against herself for being so easily toppled from equanimity. She stood in front of the bathroom mirror and rearranged her face and hair. This accomplished, she hung away her discarded frock and sat down to calm herself in a chair, which her father had given her on her sixteenth birthday after her marvellous GCSE results had delighted them all. 'There you are. A scholar's chair.' She caressed the polished circular arms. Good old Pa, he wasn't fazed by casual comment.

An hour later she knocked on Professor Conway's door. He was not wearing a tie, but had his reading glasses on the end of his nose. He stood to shake hands at a distance over his desk. 'Drag yourself up a chair,' he invited. 'I must apologise again that I couldn't see you personally after your interview. The V-C and I had to shoot off for Cambridge.'

'Was it interesting?' she asked.

'Yes. In its fashion. We can't make up our minds which pupils to take. If they all get As at A Level, how are we to distinguish one from the other?'

'Are we to set our own entrance exams?'

'I hope not. We've enough paperwork. The department would rise up in revolt. You among them, I suspect.'

She smiled at that.

'Our V-C makes a very lively impression compared with some of the educational notables. And he recognises a strong argument when it's put to him. He's about to chair a committee on university education and that means a further honour. He's on the way up. He'll be a good friend to you. Now, to everyday business. What do you want to lecture about? Surely not a chronological account of the writers and their works.'

'They'd know something.'

'I'm sure they would. Most of the students who come here know very little of the eighteenth century. It's not their fault. Their teachers choose their topics. And Pope does not appear to be popular, either with examiners or schoolmasters. The more academic establishments choose to teach the Romantics and so the heroic couplet comes out badly. It's what Wordsworth dispensed with, "the inane and gaudy phraseology". Mark you, that's better than some of the books some of them have studied for A Levels. I don't know what's happened to schoolteachers. I'd like our students to have some idea what people in the eighteenth century concerned themselves with. So we could start with some of the larger figures. Dryden, three or four lectures. Oh,' he said, laughing, 'I know he died in 1700. But if you spent your first lecture tracing his course from a metaphysical poet to a master of the heroic couplet, I shan't mind. Many of them won't have heard of the metaphysicals. They'll come up again when you make your students read Johnson's essay on Cowley.'

He mentioned the great figures, Dryden, Pope, Addison, Steele, Johnson, Swift, Richardson. She'd have to see how much time she'd need to spend on each. In the second term, he said, she could start on the theatre. That would snatch at the interest of some of the students in all three years. They'd see. 'And it would be unwise for you to go madly outside your special period. It's important to us to get that properly established in the department, but I'd still like you to have another string to your bow and I suggest you might look at Shakespeare's comedies. One lecture a week for as long as you like, and directed to all students, not just the first year. It's usual for one to set and mark one substantial essay a term on one of the eighteenth-century figures and the same on a topic related to a Shakespeare comedy. They'll have to write dissertations for their degrees, so we might as well set them on the right path of righteousness early. It might all seem a lot of work for you, because we shall have at least thirty new students this year. And, oh, I've not finished yet. We'll give you some third-year students, that is one or two, for you to oversee their dissertations for Finals, which will have to be handed in after the Christmas vac. It will depend on their subjects how many will come to you.'

He stopped there, winded, as if he'd just finished a long-distance race. He was smiling, but uncertain of his effect. 'You see what a hard taskmaster I am. Any comments?'

'No. I shall have plenty of reading to do before the end of September.'

'I'd guess you'll need at least three hours' lecturing for each of your big figures, perhaps more. It's up to you. Not more than four or five. That means you'll have introduced them to two poets and one or two prose writers by the end of term. Does it seem too much?'

'No. I take it I can use one lecture period to hand back their essays?'

'Yes. As long as you're covering the ground, it's up to you. You'll soon find out whether or not you're satisfied.'

'And if some don't hand in their essays?'

'With the first years you'll be firm but sympathetic. I'm always surprised how homesick these young people become in their first term. Did it not worry you at Oxford?'

'Yes, but I was fortunate. I could get down to work and that seemed to do the trick. I was occupied.'

'You were lucky.'

He had taken his glasses off and seemed much at his ease as though he had been troubled about this morning's decision. 'I've given you plenty to do,' he said, shirt front flapping open.

'I shall have three months to get ready.'

'But you're unused to giving lectures. They are different from essays. You'll work mainly with the first years, because I want the eighteenth century firmly established in our curriculum.'

'Hasn't it been so before?'

'Your predecessor had been here a long time and was beginning, shall we say, to tire. I'm not saying he deliberately turned them away, but that was what happened. Just one or two clever ones got something out of him since I've been here, but not enough. He would not put himself out. He had been something of a scholar when he was young. Lectures predominate here. At Oxford you could do well if you never turned up for many lectures. You saw your tutor once a week, and he'd keep you in line for your degree if he, and you, were any good.'

'Which do you prefer?'

'It depends on the student, but if the lecture is the principal form of teaching, I try to make sure that what I say is interesting and enlightening, so that the listeners don't go away bored and not looking forward to my next effort.' He sighed, buttoned his shirt front. 'But it's up to you, Alicia. You go away and think about it, and if there are snags, get rid of or round them. I'll be here any time to talk over difficulties. But you'll find yourself thoroughly capable and will make up your own mind.'

He picked up a tie and put it on in front of a small mirror. She watched the swift movements of his fingers. Satisfied, he tugged at the knot. 'Now I'm fit to be seen in public. We'll go down. There'll be two or three members of the department there, I hope, and I'll introduce you to them.'

He did not move away immediately, but stood swaying on the balls of his feet, obviously about to speak again. 'I hope I've made everything clear. It's not really very complicated.'

She nodded, slightly puzzled.

'There's something else I'd like to say to you, Alicia.'

She waited.

'I wanted to get the everyday business out of the way first.'

' "The trivial round, the common task,"' she said, then wished she had kept quiet. He obviously was in some difficulty with what he wished to say.

He stood rubbing his trouser legs. 'Yes, yes. Exactly. But now that's out of the way, at least for the present.'

She waited again.

He began, but hesitantly. 'This is personal.' He almost choked on this and paused again, his lips clamped together. 'I don't know whether it is a suitable time for it. Like a daft old don I saw it as my duty to make it clear to you what would be expected of you. I don't know if this was the right order.' He looked up at her suddenly. 'Do you understand what I'm talking about?'

She shook her head. She guessed he was talking about love, but she did not feel it her place to help him out. If they were a couple of students, she thought, they'd already have their arms round each other.

He began again. 'I've always admired you, even when you were an undergraduate. You seemed to get to the heart of a subject. You worked hard, you had a good memory, you seemed intent on making your conclusions about whatever subject it was clear to me in your essays, and always elegantly. When you suggested that you come over here to Beechnall as one of my postgraduate students I felt flattered. Had I been allowed only one of my Oxford students, you were the one I'd have chosen.'

'Thank you,' she said.

'Now I'm a suspicious person, especially when something touches my own concerns. You were not only clever, but attractive. You were a beautiful young woman. You would think such a thing had no effect on dry-as-dust university teachers. You would have been wrong.'

He raised his head again. 'You may remember, or may not even have known, that I was in trouble at home, with my wife. We had found out that we were incompatible to such an extent that I wondered how we had ever married. We fell in love when we first met, don't get me wrong. That made me more careful this time. I had now convinced myself that you were the woman with whom I would like to spend the rest of my life. By the time you had finished your doctorate I was absolutely convinced. But I did not say anything to you. I hoped you felt the same, but it was my duty to see you through your doctorate. I see now that this was a mere excuse. My cowardice, having failed once, shut my mouth. And this morning I spent my time helping you plan next year's work. Now I can excuse myself no longer, Alicia. I love you.'

She blushed deeply, but still did not speak.

'You say nothing,' he said, 'so I take it that you cannot return my love.' That sounded stilted.

Another awkward hiatus. His hands spread on his desktop and his nails scraped, he did not know what he was doing to the polished top.

She took a step or two, strongly, towards him and laid both her hands on one of his. 'I do love you,' she said.

He lifted his hand from under hers and flung his arms round her. They kissed, rocked, leaned on the desk, which creaked under their weight. When they broke away he stepped back as if to scrutinise her for some new beauty. Satisfied, he came forward and they kissed again.

'I've said it. It's happened.' He gave her time to extract meaning from these two clear, threadbare sentences.

'Yes,' she said. 'Yes.'

'But there is a "but". You know me well enough by now to understand that there's always some qualification.'

'Go on,' she said, half laughing.

'It may make a difference. You may not accept the suggestion I shall make.'

'Let me hear what it is.'

'It is that we shall not announce our official engagement until the end of term, at Christmas. No, don't say anything until you've heard me out.' She pulled a comically wry face. 'This university is a gossipy place. If they don't know the exact details of anything they make it up, embroider what little they do know. If we say immediately that we are to be married, there will be those who will snigger and suggest that I arranged your appointment so that you'd be grateful to me and accept my proposal. It's just my wretched cowardice that makes me tell you this. Nothing could be further from the truth. Your work with me since I first met you has been outstanding. If you had been my worst enemy, my honesty, after I'd read your thesis and after hearing you in the two interviews, would have forced me to appoint you.' He paused, gently massaging his chin. 'This excuse seems feeble enough to me. But I have to put it forward. It also – here's the coward muttering again

'– gives you time to consider the future and to withdraw if you so wish.'

He looked at her again – shyly, was it? Or slyly?

'I am prepared to wait.' She spoke solemnly as a judge.

'And it will allow you to concentrate on your work, will it not?'

'I shall be just as delighted to put my back into my lecturing, whether or not anyone else knows we are engaged. But I see what you mean. Sharp tongues won't be able to mock, "There goes the professor's darling who can do no wrong." And if this makes your position easier I don't mind waiting for six months. Whether I shall be able to wipe the smile off my face each time I see you and think how lucky I am is another matter.'

'I don't come out of this well in my own eyes. This morning I should have proposed marriage first, before we got on to everyday trivia of your teaching. All I can say is that it gave you the chance to see me in another light.'

She laughed.

'I don't find it funny,' he said. 'I might have ruined my chances with you.'

'Do you think so? You couldn't have been very certain, then.'

'I was certain. It was you I thought might be put off.'

'Well, I wasn't.' Her voice changed tone. 'You don't know how happy you've made me.'

'Thank you.' She had never heard two such common words carrying such a surfeit of joy. She thought of the hymn they used to sing at school, 'And, oh, what transport of delight'.

He sidled over and held her hand.

'We'd better go down or the others will be tired of waiting.'

'Right,' he said and dabbed a kiss on the side of her cheek.

'And you'd better take that expression off your face. Or they'll guess.'

He seemed embarrassed as he moved away from her. At the door he stood politely aside to let her pass.

As they walked along the corridor together she was reminded how she staggered along this same stretch, not altered by a shred, after her viva. By coincidence the big man from the maths department she had bumped into on that occasion approached. He was wearing his outdoor clothes and a jaunty brown trilby, which he raised, not without ostentation, to wish them good morning and comment on the marvellous weather outside. Conway grunted in return, but Alicia almost sang her greeting.

'Who's that?' Conway whispered.

'I don't know his name. He's in the maths department.'

'I see him from time to time up here.'

'I cannoned into him once.'

'Oh, did you?' He'd no interest, continuing his steady progress forward.

Down on the ground floor in the Staff Common Room four people waited for them, two women, two men. Conway made his introductions to her. One of the men, she was surprised to learn, was her predecessor, the man who'd lost interest. She had learnt, only this morning, from the professor that the old man – he'd hung about until sixty-five – had not yet cleared his room to make way for her. As Conway went across to the counter for coffee they all declared their pleasure in meeting her, sure she would be happy with them. Conway was a worker, one of the women said, and was full of ideas as he planned the course, unlike Professor Slack – good name, they giggled – who had been head of department two years ago. He'd already made a tremendous difference; the students had been galvanised into action. They'd all dreaded the advent of this man from Oxford, fearful of his superiority, now they were reassured, lifted.

'He taught me at Oxford, when I was a student there.'

'We'll forgive you,' the other, much younger, man said.

Alicia felt relaxed, among friends. She had not attended many departmental social meetings during her postgraduate period and had only met one of the four representatives then.

'Christopher showed me your chapter for Stirling's book,' her predecessor said. 'It was extremely well done. You made me understand what theatre audiences of that time wanted and admired, and you gave evidence for your conclusions.'

'Thank you.'

'You must be the miracle worker,' the young man said, 'who wrote a Ph.D. so good that it forced the monstrous Stirling to insist on giving you a distinction for it.'

'Did you know him?' one of the women asked.

'I'll say,' the man answered, grinning. 'The highest mark he ever gave in my time was beta double minus.'

'But not to you?' the woman mocked.

'No way.'

'Did anyone like him?'

'He was said to be fair. I thought he was barmy.'

'Did you attend his lectures?'

'I did. I'll give him credit. He could catch your interest.'

At that moment Conway arrived with a tray of coffee and chocolate biscuits. That further cheered them. Her fellows, Alicia thought, talked like students, undergraduates, then dismissed the thought as unworthy. They concentrated on making her feel wanted; the meeting was as sunny as the sky outside. Conway said little, sat like a smiling Buddha, content, making no attempt to alter the tenor of their talk. The odd obsequious remark in his direction he received with a deep breath and a nod of the head. He obviously enjoyed every minute, certain he'd done the right thing.

After perhaps thirty-five minutes, when conversation still rattled, still punctuated with laughter, he said, looking at his wristwatch, 'I think Alicia will now need to go. Thank you all for coming. I have relished every minute of this morning's meeting and I'm sure Alicia has. Do you need a lift home, Tom?' to Alicia's predecessor. This was refused; one Elsa had already promised to help him. Alicia stood and moved round the table, formally to shake hands with them all. The gesture clearly surprised them, but they accepted it. The new girl was different.

They moved out of the Common Room in a bunch and broke up with noisy goodbyes.

Alicia and Conway took to his staircase together. On the second flight he grabbed the banister, stopped and fully faced her. 'I think you impressed them.'

'They were very friendly.'

'Yes. They weren't all present, but those who were put themselves out. They're usually a hard-boiled lot.'

He moved off. 'I can't tell you how happy I am,' he said over his shoulder. 'When shall we meet again?'

'Free yourself one evening next week for dinner at my place. Is Tuesday suitable?'

'Monday?' he asked. 'Monday? It's nearer. Please.'

She grabbed his hand and as they reached his corridor began to swing his arm. Like happy schoolchildren they reached his door. No one had seen them.

Inside he pulled her to him and they kissed. They had not a word to say until she announced strongly, 'I've just thought of something. When we're publicly engaged I'll give a private

265

party for you, Raynor Wicks and his surgeon and Clarence Caldwell and his Megan. We, you and I, will know each other better then.'

'Just as you say, dearest.'